Of Man and Animals

Of Man and Animals

Short Stories

Thomas R. Hauff

RESOURCE *Publications* • Eugene, Oregon

OF MAN AND ANIMALS
Short Stories

Resource Publications
An Imprint of Wipf and Stock Publishers
199 W. 8th Ave., Suite 3
Eugene, OR 97401

www.wipfandstock.com

ISBN 13: 978-1-61097-277-2

Manufactured in the U.S.A.

To Kathy—Just for fun . . .

The mind is most free when it is locked in thought

Contents

Preface

I HAD TWO GOALS for these stories which stemmed from two beliefs. First, I believe that sometimes we miss things. We go through life doing what we do, and we miss what is happening around us and what we, ourselves, are doing. I wanted to capture that background truth in these stories. Second, I think a lot of important things happen within our daily routines. I like to describe each minute of our lives as a new "decision making moment." Usually the most interesting and challenging moments occur in commonplace settings. For that reason, these stories are pictures of regular life. I hope they help people think.

If I may, I have some advice: Read these stories for pleasure; Take your time; Use your imagination; Savor the words and thoughts. I know that when I read short stories they are most enjoyable when I don't just plow through them. Read and ponder. Maybe something interesting will find you in these vignettes.

Acknowledgments

I HAVE HAD ONLY a few friends read these stories. Some of them were shocked at what they read; none gave up reading them—even when reading the darker ones. That was encouraging. My biggest fan for my short stories is my wife Kathy. She always desires to read them, and always encourages me to write more—as she encouraged me to get these into a book. In this Qohelet's words fit her well: "*An excellent wife, who can find? For her worth is far above jewels.*"

Butterfly

ABBEY SAT AND LISTENED as Karen talked about the Bible verse. She re-read silently to herself at the same time: *"As obedient children, do not be conformed to the former lusts which were yours in your ignorance."* It seemed pretty clear to her. But Karen was missing it—as usual. She was saying: "... and each person has different former things which they have to deal with. You know what I mean?" Abbey wondered if Karen herself knew what she meant. Sure, everyone had *different* former lusts, but they all came out of the same pool. We all know what the lusts are. Karen was probably making excuses somehow for not wanting to conform herself. Everyone in the group knew she still smoked! And sometimes she swore! Abbey tuned back in to Karen: "... so just because one thing is considered a former lust to you doesn't mean it is for someone else. I mean, it may not be a sin, right? It could just be a cause of failure for that one person. Something they put before God. You know?"

"You know?" "You know?" "YOU KNOW?"!! Abbey was *sick* of that catch phrase at the end of Karen's sentences. No, she didn't *know*! She had *no* idea of what Karen *knows*! She looked over at Sharon and rolled her eyes, silently saying, *"Poor thing still hasn't given herself over to Jesus fully."* Sharon smiled at her and resumed listening attentively to Karen. *"Hmmmm,"* thought Abbey, *"I wonder if Sharon has a few snakes to kill. She acts like she might actually be considering what Karen is saying."*

Karen finished her oratory, and the group fell silent for a moment. Sally cleared her throat, but did not say anything. Abbey took the opportunity to jump in. "I don't *know* exactly what you mean Karen, but I think I agree that we all have our own lusts that we must abandon in order to conform to God's life. For example, my friend Amy doesn't live a Christian life even though she says she's a believer."

Karen nodded and asked, "And what lusts is she conformed to that makes you think she's not living the Christian life?"

Abbey glanced at Sharon thinking, *"Leave it to Karen to need it spelled out for her. Sometimes she can be so dense!"* She said, "You know, all the things that a Christian does."

Karen was unsatisfied. She asked, "Like what?"

Abbey again looked around the room for support. Clearly Karen was missing the point. The point was that Amy was still conformed to her former lusts even though she was supposedly a believer. Karen just could not get that. Abbey said again, "Well, just the usual things Christians do. She doesn't exhibit the fruits of the Spirit." *"How could Karen still not get this?! She was always talking in Bible study, and doesn't even get the simplest point!"*

Karen nodded again and said, "What are the fruits of the Spirit that you don't see?"

Abbey shifted in her chair growing indignant with Karen's ignorance. She couldn't dress her down for it, but it galled her just the same. *"Surely she knows Galatians five, verses twenty-two and three!"* With her lips slightly tight with frustration she spat, "The fruits spelled out in the Scriptures: Love, joy, peace, patience, kindness, goodness, faithfulness, gentleness, and self-control. I've seen her drinking, and the deeds of the flesh include drunkenness and carousing." She clearly had shut down this argument. *"Why are you even asking this? It was funny how Karen just missed so much of the point SO often."*

Still feeling confident with her clarity of thought, Abbey was broadsided when Sharon said to her, "How do you know Amy doesn't have love and joy and those other things?" Abbey swung her head slowly to Sharon as a look of incredulity passed over her features for a split second. *"You've got to be kidding! Our Sunday school teacher's wife asking that!?"*

Abbey was almost dumbfounded! *"How can you explain love?"* She responded with just a tinge of indignation, "Well, I don't see her in church. How does that show faithfulness?" *"That would shut her up!"*

Sharon responded blandly, "Hmmmm, I wonder if that's the only way to show faithfulness."

Abbey was getting angry now. She blurted out, "How can you be faithful at all if you are not among the people to show it?" *"She was going to show these two. They almost seem like they aren't Christians!"*

Sally said softly, "Are we supposed to be faithful to show that we are to other believers?"

Abbey shook her head minutely. That was so convoluted that it didn't even make any sense!

Sally pressed on, "I mean, if we're faithful—we're faithful. It doesn't matter if we are at church showing it off or not, right? My husband works on Sunday and doesn't go to church, but he's still faithful. I mean, he still seems to love, and have joy and stuff."

Abbey pursed her lips. *"That is true, but he's special. If you took that argument, you wouldn't have a church. You'd just have a bunch of believers who got together just among themselves whenever they wanted to! What kind of church would that be?"* Aloud she said, "Well, Craig shows faithfulness other ways. Like being at Bible study the other night and playing on the church basketball team."

As everyone thought about Abbey's response, Karen took the lull in conversation and said to Abbey, "Are you saying that faithfulness is only apparent if a person goes to church and is part of a church group like the basketball team or Bible study or something like that? As long as they are in some church-affiliated group they are ok?"

"Did that need a response?! Of course that's what I mean!" Abbey said back, "It hardly seems Christian if a person just sits at home on Sunday. You tell me what kind of faithfulness that is?"

Sharon chimed in, "What if that person were gifted with a strong desire and ability to pray for others, but hated being in crowds, or was bed-ridden? Wouldn't she be faithful in praying for others, even if she didn't go to church? Or suppose someone went to church every week but didn't participate except to just sit there? Is that faithfulness?" At this there were nods from everyone else!

Abbey looked around her and began to wonder if anyone in this "Women's Bible Study" was even Christian! They seem to be saying that a person could not even go to church and be as faithful as someone like herself who went every week! She looked around and said, "But the Bible says we shouldn't 'forsake our own assembling together,' and that obviously means we have to go to church."

Sally piped up again and said, "I think that verse also says we should 'stimulate one another to love and good deeds' and that we should encourage each other. Like the point of it is that we need to be encouraging and building one another up—you know? It's not really focusing on 'church.' I sort of thought doing that constitutes 'gathering together' because it seems like we can do those things without necessarily being in a *church building*—even the gathering together. I mean, how many people constitute 'gathering together'? Isn't more than one a gathering somehow? And what's the point of gathering together if you don't do the encouraging part? Like if you just sit there and go through the motions but don't really interact with anyone in the rest of your life?"

Abbey looked at her saying nothing. *"She sure talks a lot for someone who just became a believer a couple years ago!"* She said, "Well, I don't know about you all, but Jesus said, "Whosoever loves me keeps my commandments!' and going to church is clearly a commandment."

Sally marshaled her courage and pressed on, "But isn't that what we're saying? That church, like the building and all, isn't necessarily what Jesus was focusing on? Is that the only way to 'gather together'? Is that the only way to be faithful?"

Abbey was now convinced. Sally may not be saved. And if she is, she is really back-slidden. And come to think of it, she misses a lot of church too. She said she wanted to spend time at home after working all week. *"Well,"* thought Abbey, *"She wouldn't have to work all week if she followed God more. They want the house and cars and career and all, and they cut God out to get it!"* She looked at Sally, then Karen. Finally she said, "I don't know about you. But I know God wants us at church. But we're not talking about that right now. We're talking about being conformed to our former lusts. It just seems to me that non-believers don't go to church. And if we don't go either, then we are conformed to our former lusts. Besides that, you go to almost any church and you find the things that make a Christian a "Christian": Music, Bible study, Sunday church service, Youth group, and what not. If you don't do those things, or some of them, how can you call yourself a Christian? You're just a wolf in sheep's clothes!"

Abbey looked around with a set jaw. She knew it was hard to hear, but she felt good about speaking God's will regardless of the consequences. And after all, *"All things worked for good for those that love God and are called according to His purposes."*

Luanne sat quietly throughout the discussion. When the meeting finally closed she walked to her car thinking about her life. She didn't like to go to church. She'd never liked it. She'd gone for years and hated the triviality of it. They talked around the Bible, and around people's lives. Finally, she quit going. She never quit believing.

Luanne sat in her car looking at the church parking lot waiting for Karen. She'd come to this Bible study originally because her neighbor Joan said it was geared to younger women like herself. And after meeting Karen, she thought it would be worthwhile. Most of them were younger. Some seemed in their late thirties. And this Bible study was on her block. It only met at the church once in a while. She didn't attend the church, but Karen had said that didn't matter. She was welcome.

A bird flew over and cast a fleeting shadow over Luanne's eyes. She glanced up and caught a glimpse of robin feathers. Her mind wandered off, exploring the idea of robins. She vaguely recalled something about the birds of the field having from God all they needed to survive. It was funny how people and animals reflect one another so often. She remembered Abbey's phrase, "a wolf in sheep's clothes." It was another similarity between people and animals. She sat and thought. *"Busy as a bee. Angry as a hornet. He's a bull in a china shop. He's a dog. She's a bitch. Make him the goat. Swim like a fish."* "People and animals," she murmured to herself.

As Luanne sat ruminating, Karen came up to the passenger window. Deep in her musings, Luanne didn't notice her until she knocked softly. Luanne turned with a start, and then relaxed at Karen's smiling face. She leaned over and unlocked the door.

Karen got in and said, "Hey Luanne, thanks for waiting. I needed to check in at the office for a moment."

Luanne nodded the explanation away. She didn't mind. It had given her a chance to enjoy the day. She began to start the car, then stopped just as she grasped the key. Turning, she asked Karen, "What did you think of Bible study today?"

Karen looked at her with an impish smile. Luanne knew what was coming and smiled herself in anticipation. Karen said, "Maybe you should tell me what *you* thought."

Luanne mock grimaced at her. Since she had met her, Karen was always making Luanne put her thoughts together into coherent ideas on her own. She said it was because she needed to know for herself what she thought, and by saying things out loud, we are forced to think about them. Luanne was silent a moment, collecting her thoughts. Then she said, "It sounded to me like Abbey didn't think any of us were Christians. She was snapping at each of us." The slightest trace of frustration flashed momentarily across her face.

Karen looked at her closely, pursing her lips. Then she asked, "Do you *really* think that's true?"

Luanne looked out the windshield. A bird had landed on the fence a few yards away. She saw that it was pecking at something in its claw, tearing pieces of it off, one at a time, reducing it bit by bit. She turned back to Karen and said, "I guess I don't really think she believes that. She's always making pronouncements about how Christians ought to be and what they ought to do. It's like she feels she needs to guide everyone into her experiences for them to be valid. I think she goes overboard sometimes."

Karen smiled at her and nodded. It was a sign that she wanted Luanne to continue on her own before giving her opinion. Karen was always expecting her to come up with things on her own. Only when she'd voiced her thoughts would Karen offer her own. Even then Luanne seldom knew how to respond to them. Karen sometimes agreed, sometimes disagreed, but never required Luanne to agree with her. She just seemed to put another point of view forward for consideration. It was not that Karen didn't know what she thought. She seemed to almost always have a good point of view. But she didn't force it on others. She let them hear it, and decide on their own. It was totally opposite of Abbey.

Luanne continued, "I think maybe she likes Christianity to be in a neat little box. You do *these things*, you're a believer. You do *those things*, you're not. She has her purposes and ends that she wants from others. And they are always *her* ways."

Karen asked, "And you? What do you think of that position?"

Luanne answered, "I don't see how that can work. If Christianity were that cut and dried, we'd all do the same things and get along just fine. But we are all unique. And we all do different things. It seems to me the most important point is figuring out how to utilize everyone rather than trying to work them into some set program. I think we ought to get rid of church the way it is. It doesn't even try to identify or utilize people's unique talents. And people like Abbey seem to be limiting God on how he makes and uses people."

Karen looked at her, thinking. Then she said, "That sounds good. Let me ask though, are you saying Christians can do anything? Are there any hard and fast rules of conduct or required behaviors and beliefs?" She said this with a grin as Luanne's face suddenly scrunched up in thought.

That was the problem with Karen, thought Luanne, laughing to herself, she always cut to the chase and made you defend your position. *"Let's see, it makes no sense to say there are no rules at all. That would make everything ok. And clearly not all lifestyles could be called 'Christian.' But what made one Christian a living believer and another a 'wolf in sheep's clothes,' as Abbey would put it?"* "It seems like there are two things that matter: One, there are direct prohibitions in the Bible like 'don't steal' or 'don't sleep around'; and there are direct proscriptions like 'believe in the Lord Jesus.' Then there are those things which we are called to do, but aren't spelled out. Like 'love one another' and 'be joyful.'" Luanne remembered the list that Abbey had quoted as the "fruits of the Spirit": Love, joy, patience, kindness, and goodness. "The fruits of the Spirit that Abbey mentioned all seemed to be attitudes. They could be acted out in a zillion different ways."

Karen nodded and said, "And what about the 'do not forsake gathering together?'"

Luanne looked down at her hands. She'd been taught all her life that she *had* to go to church. She hated church. But she loved Karen, and Joan, and Sally. She loved a lot of believers. She loved getting together with them. Talking about life, about things they were doing, about how God was working in them. She even loved hearing God's Word *at church*. She looked back up at Karen and said with conviction, "I don't think you are forsaking 'gathering together' just because you skip church. There can be other productive ways to gather together. I think Sally had a good point on that. I guess I feel guilty about it when Abbey talks because she seems so sure that you have to go Sunday mornings to be a good believer." She halted and watched the bird pick little pieces from whatever was in its claw. It suddenly stopped and flew off, letting the carcass fall—stripped of almost everything that identified it uniquely. It had been a butterfly. It had one wing missing entirely after the bird was finished and the other was torn in two. It lay on the ground at the base of the fence post and flopped about, no longer having the necessary equipment to fly as it was intended. Luanne watched it lunge about for a moment or two. Then she said, "I feel like Abbey is picking people apart—trying to make them fit her ideal. I know I love God, and I know I'm living in Him. I don't want to conform to her view."

Karen grinned and said, "Then you should keep at it Luanne; go where God leads." And let Abbey keep at it too. Her patterns work for her. And yours works for you. You both are great women, and I'm sure Abbey is deeply appreciated for her services—as are you."

Luanne nodded and started the car. She prayed a quick prayer for Abbey and her other friends as she drove from the lot.

Cat

MARGARET NADINE SKYLER'S EYES knifed open at seven a.m. at the clanging insistence of her old fashioned, round-faced alarm clock. She hated the morning. "If God wanted me to see the morning, He'd have scheduled it later in the day!" she always said. Her pudgy hand groped out from under the covers and slapped down on the alarm, silencing it. She stiffly rose, wrapped a terry cloth robe around herself, and waddled out into the kitchen. She snagged a piece of mushroom from a scrap of last night's pizza as she passed the linoleum-topped kitchen table. Chewing it absently, she loosed the bolts on the door (one had to bolt the door to keep the weirdoes out) and looked down to see her cat, Tracker, waiting to come in for breakfast.

Tracker was a large—some would say fat—three year old, orange tabby. Margaret dubbed him Tracker because when he was young, he would track and catch mice in the back yard. He had pretty much given that up, which was fine with her, since he was getting older and slowing down. Kind of like Margaret. She was almost 35 now. And on cold mornings like this she felt it! It was hard to move her considerable weight when her joints were so cold and stiff, that was for sure. "Ah well," she thought, "no one enjoyed the process of aging." Well, except the physically gifted like that snooty Jean Reynolds. She was God-knows-what age and still ran around the block half-naked in spandex! She was some sort of freak of nature; at least forty and still rather slim and active. Not many were like that, that was for sure! It must be some genetic oddity. "Well," Margaret thought, "she was a 'sports' nut anyway. All that running around. That can't be healthy, obsessing over exercising like that. You need to be more well-rounded, and anyone who runs around the block in the morning is definitely not well-rounded in Margaret Nadine Skyler's book!

Having let Tracker in, Margaret shuffled back through the kitchen. She pulled a nice piece of pizza from the box on the table and wadded half of it into her mouth as she passed the table again. Reaching the pantry, she took a box of dry cat food from the shelf, and returned to the door, cramming the remaining half piece of pizza between her lips. "Stans makes the best pizza," she mused. And if you bought an extra-large, you got a whole bag of cheesy bread with it! Free! She noticed that Tracker's bowl was only half full, and though he never seemed to actually finish his food (he was no "clean-plate clubber!") she filled it over the brim until it spilled out onto the floor. "Damn," she scolded herself, "now I'll have to sweep!" She then went back over to return the box of cat chow to the shelf, appropriating another large piece of Stans' finest on the way.

While Tracker was busily scarfing food, she trundled out to the living room toward the front door. She nonchalantly fisted a few mints from the bowel as she passed the mantle. "It's always polite to have a few sweets out for guests," she'd say. Some people like that Jean Reynolds didn't know that! She'd been to her house a number of times. The Reynolds would have bar-b-cue and invite the whole block! And although there was always a nice selection of food, Margaret noted that there were no "niceties." Things that make a person feel welcome, like mints, or popcorn, or jelly beans. Jean had said she didn't care for mints, but that was not the point! One doesn't just sit around eating mints. They are there as a welcome saying, "Come in! Feel comfortable! Have a mint!" They let a person know they were cared about. Margaret had been to the Reynold's dozens of times and never had one mint! She had received small gifts from them too, and not once was it a nice chocolate or anything of the like! Well, one can't force graciousness on others. She refilled her hand with jelly beans from the table, and went to the door.

It was bright and sunny out, but cold! Margaret hated that. There was Jean on her morning run. Red top today with blue tights. Pretty ostentatious! Jean waved and grinned at her as she passed, her breath pluming out of her mouth. Margaret waved back thinking, "I'm sure glad I don't have a problem with ostentation!" And she lazily thought of her nice conservative brown, tan, and gray wardrobe. No one could accuse her of being self-involved! She dressed demurely at all times.

That damn paper boy! The paper lay at the end of the porch near the steps. Margaret was going to have to tiptoe over the freezing concrete to get it! How hard can it be to toss the paper a few more feet to the mat? Johnny Spellman had been the paper boy for three years now. He never missed Ms. Skyler's house, that was for sure! Though he did on occasion miss the mat. She tipped well at Christmas, and paper boys always wanted more money. She often wondered what fun activities Johnny gave up just to get money. She recalled her own childhood and the fun she had had sitting with her mom in the kitchen baking. They made the best cakes and pies together. She would spend hours with her mom rolling dough, mixing fillings, and all sorts of things. Margaret slipped the last few jelly beans into her mouth still wondering what Johnny missed out on just because he wanted her money. She then lightly (as lightly as her bulk could allow) skipped out to the paper and picked it up (groaning with the exertion). She danced back to the warm carpet inside, breathing heavily, her breath pluming like that Jean Reinhold's, and quickly closed the door. She deftly mouthed a few peanuts from the light stand near the window, and went back to the kitchen.

Margaret loved to read the paper in the morning on weekends. She always got up early, but enjoyed a good long read on Saturday and Sunday. She hated rushing off to work. And she was very conscientious. In at 7:30 (though the office opened at 8:00), and home at 6:00. She didn't mind putting in long hours. The effort had made her manager in four short years, and she enjoyed it too! She moved the pizza box on the table, scooping up the last piece of cheesy bread and popping it into her mouth. All gone and cleared for breakfast! Margaret hated a mess. She knew people who were messy and she could not stand it! They always have a reason for not putting things away or cleaning up. But Margaret had learned from her daddy that "every *thing* has its place and every *place* has its thing." How hard can it be to change that habit? She had been messy once. But daddy had helped her learn to clean up after herself. That's all it takes is a little help from someone who cares. Margaret sighed. Perhaps that was the trouble. People just don't care anymore.

Tracker had gorged on his breakfast and was lying on his side dozing by the door. He was a lovely cat! Pretty cinnamon orange, with orange eyes. He was so soft and cuddly too! Margaret smiled at him as she stood.

She laid the paper out, put out a place setting, and began to make waffles. There is nothing like waffles on Saturday morning! Margaret made a small batch. As she did, she poured Tracker a nice bowel of whole milk. He needed it to settle his nerves. Often after eating he would wheeze and cough as he settled his heft down for a nap. Margaret was sure he was too excited about seeing her in the morning, and probably had some sort of respiratory problem too. The milk helped him to calm down and sleep.

As the first waffle cooked, Margaret nibbled at the jam. Just a few teaspoons to idle the time as she waited. She looked out the window and noticed Brian Gottlieb washing his truck. He sure spent a lot of time doing that! Here it was not much past seven a.m. and he's out washing the truck. People get hung up on things and they can't seem to see they are obsessed. It's not as though the truck was actually dirty per se. He did use it to go "four wheelin'" (as he called it) but most of the time it looked as clean as any other car on the block. Certainly Margaret's car was clean and she didn't wash it more than a couple times a month, if that. In fact, no one she could think of washed their cars as much as Brian Gottlieb. He had a problem with his truck. Margaret spooned a large dollop of jam into her mouth as she contemplated Brian's work. It was really sort of sad that he wasted such time on it. He was a nice looking young man; cute really. But he wasn't married. He didn't even date that much. Margaret doubted any woman would want some guy who obsessed over his truck! That was undoubtedly the problem.

The waffle appeared ready and Margaret dumped it onto her plate. She then filled the waffle-maker again for the next one before she sat down to eat. She quickly buttered the waffle, spooned the jam onto it (raspberry), and poured a little syrup on for extra pizzazz. "The coffee!" she exclaimed to herself. Tracker looked at her and blinked before laying his head back down to wheeze himself back to sleep. She set the coffee maker, and went about preparing her cup hurriedly: A little cream, three tablespoons of sugar, and ready to pour! The Bunn streamed out the coffee in short order and within a few minutes she was licking her lips over the last few forkfuls of her first waffle and reading the paper.

Councilman Dexter was in deep! She laughed to herself. He was notorious for womanizing and had been caught with a young lady in a motel. Margaret did not condone such things herself. She had never had sex as a teenager, or at all for that matter, and felt it was wrong to do so. She was raised right, as a good Christian woman. And respectable, good people didn't sleep around like animals! People were not made to demean one another that way in Margaret Nadine's eyes. Serves that bastard Dexter right if he gets tossed from office! And Margaret almost choked on her bite from waffle number two as she laughed at his duress. "Gotta get more coffee," she thought, and started spooning sugar into her cup.

When the breakfast dishes were cleared, the paper read, and the table wiped down, Margaret settled into her easy chair in the living room. She loved to sit and read on Saturday morning with Tracker. He enjoyed the wide expanse of her lap in which to lie, as well as the occasional scratches behind the ears. He was flopped out on her right now, with his belly up, and his eyes fast closed. Margaret was wading through War and Peace for the second time. She enjoyed reading long, involved books in which the characters were well developed by the author. Count Rostov was her favorite in this classic, and he had just entered the army. Margaret sat nibbling a little popcorn and wolfing down his exploits in the fields of Russia. She glanced out the front window, and noticed Brian had finished his washing and was talking with the neighbor on the corner, Jeff Bonhart.

The Bonharts were very nice people. Well, Margaret thought they were anyway. She had had conversations with Shawna Stewart about them in the past, and had to admit they were sometimes a little selfish. They enjoyed their deck in the back yard, and often sat out in the evening chatting with friends. Sometimes though, they just sat out and listened to music. That was the rub for Shawna and her husband Stacy ("That's a funny name for a man," Margaret giggled. Stacy Stewart! Say that three times fast!). The Bonharts played their classical music too loud sometimes. And Margaret had to agree that it intruded on occasion—though she loved classical music. Some people just expected others to go along with their ideas she supposed. It was a common failing in many people. She could forgive it in the Bonharts. They were full of other good qualities. They sometimes invited her over to sit with them in the evening. And she always had a pleasant time, chatting and snacking on various treats. They would laugh, or sometimes just listen to music and watch the stars. It was nice. Besides, that Shawna Stewart shouldn't complain. The Stewarts owned a restored "street rod" and when Stacy monkeyed with the engine it reverberated through the entire neighborhood! Some people just made more noise than others. And although Margaret would never play her stereo that way, or race her car engine, she had chosen to tolerate the insensitivity of the Bonharts on occasion.

Margaret's musings were interrupted by the sight of Johnny Spellman heading back down the block having finished his paper route. She wrestled herself to her feet, and got to the door, huffing, before he could pass. She leaned out over the cold porch and hollered at him at the top of her lungs, "Hey Johnny Spellman! Try to hit the mat next time, huh?!" Margaret was sure Johnny flashed her a penitent "sorry Ms. Skyler" look before she turned to go in. Brian and Jeff had both snapped their heads in her direction at her bellow that had rung out up and down the street. This partially annoyed Margaret. It was none of their business if she needed to correct the boy!

Brian and Jeff loaded golf clubs into Brian's shiny truck and they tore out to go "hit the pill" as Jeff called playing a round of golf. Margaret didn't go in for such things. She didn't believe in wasting time out of her day. She munched a little more popcorn, and seeing that the morning had disappeared, she ousted Tracker from his sleep and headed for the kitchen to start lunch. Margaret had a hankering for some dogs and beans. She opened two cans and poured them into the saucepan. Before placing them on the stove however, she plucked out two of the little hot dogs that are mixed in with the beans and placed them on a saucer. Tracker paced at her feet expectantly, and as she bent to place the daily treat down for him he squealed a long meow of pleasure. Margaret grinned and stroked him as he began to gobble his snack. She then set her own beans to cooking and looked in the fridge for something to accompany them. "Let's see," she thought, "I have meat in my hot-dogs, so I need something sustaining." She closed the fridge, and opted for a large piece of French bread. Just the ticket!

Having finished lunch Margaret needed a nap. "People just don't take naps as much as they used to," she said to Tracker as they both lay down. Tracker climbed up her side and settled heavily on her stomach in his "sphinx" pose. His eyes seem to say, "I'm lord of all I survey." Margaret scratched him and said, "You are one fat cat!" To this he closed his eyes and purred loudly. She marveled that a cat could get so big. Just the other day she had commented with pride on her tiger sized pet. She smiled softly as she drifted off to sleep.

Margaret awoke as Tracker huffed his way down off her and out of the room. She lay quietly listening, expecting and then hearing the crunch of hard cat food as Tracker began to munch. She lolled over and got up, glancing out the window into the back yard at her over-run gardens. She had had the idea once of growing fresh food, but had only gotten as far as the first year. Truth be told, she had not even harvested all the produce. She had found that weeding and hoeing and what-not was not to her taste. It was Vicky next door who had interested her in the project. She had a very large garden herself. Frankly, it had looked more inviting when Vicky was grubbing around on her hands and knees! Well, you can't accomplish everything in life. You must pick and choose what to fill your time with and there were many other activities Margaret would rather pursue. She dismissed the garden and went into the living room to watch TV. It was near four o'clock by now, and having turned the volume up a little she went in to the kitchen to start dinner. As she passed the table she snagged a few mints.

Tracker was lying on his side by the door wheezing himself back to sleep. Margaret smiled at him, enjoying his color, thinking how happy she was to take care of him—especially with his breathing problems and all. Deep down she suspected he just ate too much, but he was, after all, just a cat and animals couldn't be expected to have self-control like people. She'd watch out for him.

Margaret pulled the ham from the fridge and set the oven. She then prepared it and put it in to cook. She loved a good ham, the kind with the spicy rind. It gave a zesty flavor to dinner that she liked. She then put the cabbage and potatoes into a pot to boil a little later when the meat was near done. Then, she pulled a box of ho-hos out from the cupboard, and began to unwrap them. She knew some folks would say she was nuts, but she liked to arrange even boxed deserts on a plate. She put them down in a star pattern on a plate, nibbling down the extra two (and of course dropping a few pieces into Tracker's bowl). She then went back to watch TV until dinner.

TV was dull. Mostly it was just frivolous pap that wasted one's day. She tolerated it for the two hours it took for the ham to cook and then switched it off with distaste when the timer rang. She prepared the veggies, removed the meat from the oven, cut it into thin strips, and set the whole lot out on the table. She spread her napkin smoothly on her immense lap and enjoyed the fruits of her labor. It was well worth the effort to have a good meal at least once a week, and Margaret always tried on Saturday or Sunday to do just that. The ham was flavorful and tasty, the veggies were just the right consistency, and the dessert was the perfect topper. She sighed with pleasure as she pushed the last piece of ho-ho into her mouth, and sat back to watch Tracker watch her. He always expected something from the table. But he should know that nothing was forthcoming. Margaret knew it was not good to overstuff him. And by now he should know that table scraps were not part of his diet. He ate at set times, with one snack a day. That was set in stone. And no amount of begging would change that. After watching her chew and swallow the last piece of ho-ho, Tracker circled a couple more times and resigned himself to waiting till later.

Margaret cleaned up, and went out to the sofa to sit and watch TV until dinner settled. She relaxed, comfy, occasionally downing a few mints and nuts as she listened. Finally, a few hours later, she headed for bed. On the way she took the box of cat food down from the shelf, and letting Tracker out the back door, she filled his patio bowl to the brim. He meowed thankfully and dove in with gusto. Margaret closed the door, turned the locks, and went off to sleep, leaving Tracker to roam the neighborhood until tomorrow when she would again find him waiting for her.

Squirrel

MEETING. MEETING. MEETING. MEETING. Gotta make the Meeting. Gotta make the Meeting. Gotta make the Meeting. Meeting. Meeting Man. Meeting Man. Fourth and Lane. Fourth and Lane. Fourth and Lane. Fourth Lane. NO! NO! NO! That's not right. Not right! Fourth AND Lane, Lane, Lane,Lane,LaneLaneLane. The alley. The alley. The alley. AND,AND,ANDANDANDANDLANE! Meeting at Fourth AND Lane! At THE alley. They may try to stop me, but I gotta make the meeting. National Security. Make the Meeting.

Bart bends lower in the booth. Why was that woman looking at me? She's looking. Looking at me! "Who are you?! Who are you?! Who are YOU?!" She's looking again. "It's FBI business lady! Just watch it! F-B-I. They know. They make it their business to know!" Looker, looker, she's a looker. Look at me! Stop looking. CIA!

Check the toast. Check the toast. Check it. Bugs. She's looking. CIA bugs. Check the toast. "I know what you did lady. I know the CIA. I know you. F-B-I business is what it's all about. You know it. I know it. THEY know it! I'll eat this, but I know about the bugs. I just want you to know I know." Spooks.

"Hey friend, is there some way I can help you?"

Who's that! Whoisthat?! Another Looker! "I don't need help from the CID. Or the NSA for that matter! I know about the bugs. I know you'd like to get them and follow me around, and know what I'm doing. But the FBI doesn't."

"I don't know what you mean, pal. You just don't look so good."

"Uh-huh. The satellites. They take your thoughts. The CID,CIAFBINSA. You know. I know you know. I know who you are, who you work with, what you do." Spook. He wants the bugs too. I know.

Bart rises to leave. Meeting at Fourth and Lane. Nine o'clock. It's . . . (looking at the cracked watch on his wrist) . . . it's . . . 3:07. Time. Meeting time. Time to meet.

"Sir, you owe $3.00."

A dollar flutters to the table top. "Keep the change. I know they want it." Bart shoves the remaining toast in his coat pocket. "I'll keep track of this."

"Sir, that's not enough money."

Enough. Bart advances on the waitress, "I know what the planes cost. The Satellites. I know. That's dirty money. It's more than enough for them. They want it. They can have it!!" Operative. She may not know. She looks unsure.

Bart whirls on the man rising from his chair. "You can't have it! I'm leaving and you're not taking it!" The man stops. Another is rounding the counter.

"Sir, is there a problem?"

"You know the problem. She's not the problem, but this guy is!" Bart thumbs toward the man by his chair. "CIA. Or NSA. The big cheese." Get out while the gettin's good. Bart moves to the door. Keep your back clear. He turns and leaves. Meeting. This is risky. But the gain. The gain is worth it to keep them at bay.

Bart walks briskly down the street toward the alley. Keep your eyes down. They can't read your mind if you keep 'em down. That guy's look-ing at me. "I could use some cash." Yeah, spook.

"Excuse me?"

"Look, I know you, and what you do. We both know so let's not bullshit, ok? You think you can just follow along, take whatever you want. I'm ok, and it's not gonna hurt the government to supply some revenue. They have the planes and the satellites; they have the doctors and the pills, but those are not coming outa my pocket. All I need is some cash, ok?"

"I don't know what you mean. I don't have any cash for you."

"Look. Go back and report, that I haven't got any cash. Isn't that enough? I have the bugs right here in my pocket. I can decipher them. I can use the data. I need the cash for business. Nothing FBI related."

He's backing away, trying to get by. Spook.

"I don't have any cash for you!" He hurries by.

Bart turns and yells, "I have the bugs! I know where you are!" He turns back to the alley and walks on, clutching his ragged coat against the cold. Meeting. I hope my stuff is still there. Bugged probably.

The alley is dark, and thin. Ahhhh. Safe. They can't see down between the buildings unless they're right above. It's the blind spot effect. Satellites can't see anyway but directly down. Except the infrared ones. They can see into your head through concrete. Bart hugs the wall, staying near the metal trashcans. Interference.

The shopping cart is at the end of the alley. Still there. No spooks. Bart looks at his watch again: Almost time; it's 3:07. He takes the cart, and moves down the alley to the next street. Crosses. Keep to the alleys. I wish the meeting were in the subway. It's safer. The planes can't detect you there. It's the FBI.

"Hey Bart!"

Don't look. Just keep on walking. Bart moves to the opposite side of the alley and continues on with his head down. "I'm not listening. You can't make me listen." Just keep walking.

"Bart! It's John. Want a drink?" John raises the bottle to Bart.

"I don't need that. I have some in my coat right now. I just got them at the diner down the street. They all know about it." Stay cool. He knows I have them. They can try to track me with them. But I've deciphered the code. I know the number of the beast. One!

"Ok Bart. Ok. Just asking. Maybe another time."

Head down, still walking: "Ok. We'll have a drink. Talk about the old days. They can hear some of that. The CIA knows all about it." He was awful close. It may be hit or miss. Checking his watch: It's 3:07! Hurry.

He comes to the end of the alley. A broad street. Check the sky. It looks clear. He removes the cell phone hidden in his duffel. The fools! To have dropped this!

Holding the phone to his ear he says the code word: "Failsafe!" Ahh, 15 minutes of un-monitored time. What one can do with a day free from the spooks.

Bart rolls his cart behind the dumpster. He places the duffel near the front. The bottles are in back. The cardboard goes on top. Still holding the phone to his ear, he walks out across the street. The car squeals to a stop inches from his legs. Bart strides on, head down, phone pressed hard to his ear. "FAILSAFE! FAILSAFE! FAILSAFE!" They cannot touch me now!

"Sonafa bitch! You asshole! What's wrong with you!"

I can get it now. Then they can't track me at all.

Bart enters the alley on the opposite side of the street. The man is leaning against the wall of the building in the shadows. His minion is out on the sidewalk. Spook. He can search, but he doesn't know about the phone. Failsafe.

"What do you want, man?"

"We had a deal." Bart holds out $50 dollars. The minion takes his hand and quickly lowers it, glancing up and down the street.

"What's wrong with you shithead?! You wanna get busted?" He doesn't know about the phone.

"I have the phone. They won't know." He again raises the money. The subordinate hauls him into the dark alley with the man. Then he says, "This asshole says he has some money. We got a deal with him?"

The man smiles.

CIA? FBI? No, he sees the phone. He knows it's no use.

"Yeah, we have a deal." He walks a ways down the alley and moves a bag of trash. He opens a trunk lying under it and pulls a .38 special out. "This is what he requested." He saunters back with the gun. It's a worthless piece of garbage.

Bart holds the $50 dollars up again. But he clutches it tightly. "I need the bullets too."

"For fifty bucks?"—with a crafty grin. You gotta be kidding man. You're getting a deal on this anyway." The gun is old and dirty. It won't fire.

"I know about the whole deal. I know you. You may be an operative, but you're out of touch now!" He taps the phone at his ear.

The man looks at his minion. They smile at one another. The subordinate circles his finger around his temple, giggling. Probably a sign they know. Outa range now cowboy!

The man smiles again. "You gotta come up with more than that pal. I said $50, but this piece is worth at least $80. And shells will be $5 bucks more."

"I know what you're doing!! You can't stall! I know they can't find us! I have a failsafe!"

The little minion slips his hand into his jacket and sidles off to the side. Radio signal. They might have new technology.

"Listen you crazy bastard, $85 bucks or you can kiss my ass!" The man advances a little letting the gun point slightly at Bart.

"Good thing I'm protected!"

The bar slams down on Bart's head from behind. He falls hard dropping the phone. The man and the little minion laugh and turn him on his back. They rifle through his clothes and take the money in his pockets. The man says, "One hundred and two dollars! You squirrely shit. You had enough. Well, this will do." He picks up the phone where it has fallen and looks it over. "Nice—a completely useless broken phone. You're an idiot."

The little guy kicks Bart in the ribs. He rolls to his side groaning and mumbling, "Failsafe, I need that! I have no coverage."

The little guy bends close and listens. "He's saying something about failing!"

The man laughs and says, "I guess he did fail, huh? Why don't ya take him and dump him at the lake? We don't want this crazy shit hanging around."

The little guy kicks Bart again and then drags him down the alley to the car. He dumps him in the trunk. At the lake he finds a dirty area under a series of piers. He looks around, sees nothing. He gets out, unlocks the trunk, bangs his hand in the process, and pulls Bart out. "Stupid asshole." He lets Bart fall to the ground. Kicks him twice. Grabs the superman glasses with the tape in the middle out of the trunk and tosses them on the ground next to the body. "Here's your specks you squirrely-brained bastard." He pushes his boot down on them, relishing the crunch of glass from the one good lens. He gets back in the car and drives off with a grin.

Bart rolls onto his back. His nose is bleeding and blood trickles down his throat choking him. His head flops to the side to see his watch: it's 3:07! I gotta make the meeting! I'm not safe anymore! He took the phone! Bart begins to cry softly as he lies in the dirt.

—

Mary Wallace wrings her hands for the hundredth time. She sits on the couch, leaning forward, worry creasing her pretty face. Bart was gone again. The police are looking for him. But it's been three days, and no word. She frets over a little scar on her finger. A squirrel had bitten her years back. It had been feeding in their yard for a good two years. Then one day, it seemed odd. Out of sorts. It bit her. Her dad had said it was sick and tried to trap it. It ran off. Mary scratches the scar, not thinking about it at all. Poor, poor Bart. Why didn't we put him in the hospital? Schizophrenia.

Dennis sits down next to his wife and puts an arm around her shoulder. "They'll find him hon. They have before. He's sick, but he's not stupid. He's lived a long time on the streets before." They sit quietly. The only sound in the room is the clock as it ticks out the minutes since Bart disappeared. Mary leans her head on her husband's shoulder and weeps softly for her brother.

—

Bart finally stops crying. He's in the open. They can see me! They can see me now! He flails his body over onto his belly and crawls under the overhang of the pier. His body is wracked with heavy breaths at the exertion. Safe. They can't see now. Where am I? What have they done? He was CIA. I hope they don't find Mary.

Hours later, as dawn begins to break, Bart tries to stand. My knee! They implanted something in my knee! He sits back down and leans against a piling. Reaching into his shoe, he pulls the small knife from next to his ankle. I'll have to remove it. There's no other way to escape. He rolls his pants up to reveal the dark bruise on his knee where little guy stomped him. There it is. It's just under the skin. Bart digs the knife into his calf just below the knee and pries a chunk of flesh away. He breathes hard, clenching his teeth. He tosses the meat from the knife and puts it back in his shoe by his ankle. Finally. Now they don't know what I'm doing.

Bart is staggered by the amount of blood pouring from his leg. He unbuckles the belt on his waist, then re-buckles it cinching it tighter. That should stop the blood. Just relax. Hard to breath now. They can't track you without the tracer. He stands gingerly on the painful leg and hobbles about a hundred yards down the shore until he collapses amid a jumble of rocks and dirt. He rolls onto his back and shakes the black spots from his eyes. The cold wind coming from the water chills him, but he can't seem to move anymore. His leg hurts. And bleeds. They must have a new ray. "I'm paralyzed." He closes his eyes.

—

"I'm sorry ma'am. We found him just a little while ago. It looks like he bled to death. We don't know yet if he was attacked or not. He's got some injuries though. He didn't seem to have anything with him, except this." The officer holds out a little cross. On the back is Mary and Dennis' phone number and address. On the front is inscribed, "We love you Bart." "He had it clutched in his hand."

Mary leans into Dennis and sobs bitterly. At twenty-four, Bart seemed to be a baby to her. He was so normal just three years ago. Things change.

Starlings

WOOSTER McDOWEL OPENED THE screen door and carefully made his way to the old rocking chair that sat out on the porch. As usual, his slow progress meant that the screen bumped him as he went by, and as usual, he spilled some of his black coffee on the old porch boards. He hardly noticed anymore. There was a time when he used to try to stop the door from hitting him. And before that, he could get by easily enough without it touching him at all. But those days were long gone. Now that he was past eighty, he moved too slowly to side step the spring that pulled the screen shut. Ah well, that's life.

Wooster turned his back on the chair, bent his legs as far as they would bend nowadays, and reached back with his left hand to find the arm. Once, he had thought he was gonna sit down, and found he had not been close enough to the chair. He spilled a lot of coffee that day! Funny how he always thought of that when he was sitting down now. His daughter had heard about it and given him a good tongue lashing about "now that you're older you've got to be more careful!" and "you could have laid there for hours with a broken hip!" It seemed like her biggest fear was no longer the bogey man he used to clear out of her closets when she was little. Now it was "the broken hip." A tight smile crossed Wooster's face as he envisioned a leg, shrouded in a black cloak, hopping along with that Bela Lugosi music playing in the background!

Finding the arm of the rocker, Wooster settled back and finally plopped the last few inches into the chair. Ahhhhh. He'd been sitting in this chair for sixty years if it was a day. He had to have it rebuilt a couple times. The kids busted it up some when they played on it. That was years ago. They were grown with kids of their own and broken furniture in their houses now.

Wooster's bright and very sky-blue eyes traveled up and down the street as he sipped his cup o' joe. Since his Emma had died, he usually drank his coffee out on the stoop. They used to talk in the morning. They'd sit inside at the table in the kitchen and listen to the radio or TV, commenting on issues. They were very current for septuagenarians. She died of the cancer about four years ago. It was a blessing in Wooster's mind. She'd been sick a long time. He mumbled softly to himself, "I just keep on goin' though." He'd sit out on the stoop and watch the street because it was nice to see people. He could sit inside, but he figured if an old man like him were ever gonna see people, he'd have to go out and do it, "'cause they weren't gonna come to him." And since it was hard to get out a lot, sitting on the stoop was the next best thing.

He'd wave at Don Reynolds as he came out for work. Good man, Don. He'd been at the mill for years till it shut down. That would have broke a lot of men. Some had a hard time changin' once they got settled into a job. But Don took it in stride, got some training, and was now working with computers. Wooster didn't really know much about the field. He did actually have a computer, though. He got email with it. Don showed him how to use it. He set it up too. Wooster pretty much just checked mail. The rest was not of any concern.

Often he'd see the kids on their way to school. Some were brats. He chuckled. He was a brat when he was a kid. But most were good kids—like his own grandkids. "Living large" in the world, as the younger people said.

There was another good reason to sit on the stoop in the morning. It had nothing to do with people. It was for protection! He had to protect his strawberries! Although he was pretty stiff, and it was difficult, he still liked to plant strawberries and flowers in the front garden. Unfortunately, he couldn't just leave 'em to grow. The problem was those starlings. Darn starlings. He couldn't think of any use for that bird. They were actually an import from Europe, he'd heard. He wished they'd have stayed put!

The starlings would fly about in big flocks. They'd hang out on the wires like a gang of dark feathered ne'er-do-wells. They'd be watching the plants growing all over the neighborhood. And when the time came, they'd come and settle on his strawberries just like a bunch of ruffians would take to a single man in a dark alley! They usually worked his berries in the morning. They liked to feed in the morning he figured. Anyway, Wooster put a small scarecrow up, and sat on his porch in the summer to keep an eye on those starlings. Stupid starlings.

While Wooster scanned the street, as though on cue, a small flock of starlings flew in over his house and settled down the block a bit on Mavis's front lawn. "Well and good," thought Wooster, "just keep to her lawn, and leave my strawberries be!"

It was a Saturday morning; about eight or so. Wooster slurped another bit of coffee, and watched as Paul Compton's garage door swung up. Paul had one of those electric garage door openers. Used to be when a garage door swung up, there was someone there to greet 'cause they swung it up by hand. Now it just opened, and maybe someone was there, maybe not. Paul was there. He spied Wooster sitting on the porch and smiled at him, accompanied by a small wave. Wooster smiled back, and held his cup up. Paul nodded and set his tools down. He walked back into the garage and disappeared for a moment. He returned holding a cup. He strolled down his drive, looked both ways, and crossed to Wooster's white picket gate. "Morning Wooster."

"Well good morning to you Paul. Have a cup?"

Paul opened the gate saying, "You know I will." He hefted the cup he had retrieved from his kitchen. It was a gift from Wooster a few Christmases back. Paul said it felt good in his hand and he'd use it when they had coffee. He really did that every time too!

Paul was about forty or so, Wooster thought. He was a nice young man—had a good wife, Loreen, and good kids too. The kids didn't spend much time with Wooster. Most kids had too much energy to spend time with Wooster. He didn't mind. They tired him out just as much as he thought he must bore them! The Comptons had gotten to know Wooster the day they moved in. It was a Saturday, and Wooster had been on the porch watching, as usual, when the moving truck arrived. Their little one, at the time, had wandered over and sat down on Wooster's porch while the adults were busy moving in. Wooster had chatted for a good fifteen minutes with the boy before his mom and dad had noticed he had disappeared. They came a runnin' when they saw him. It gave them all a chance to meet, and they'd been friends ever since. The Comptons had Wooster over for dinner every couple weeks since. They were a nice family. Wooster knew he was an old man, and they were young and had lives. He appreciated their generosity.

Paul came out from the kitchen where he had gotten some coffee for his cup. He pulled the other rocker up a little and plunked down, groaning a little as he did. Wooster looked over at him and said, "So what's on the agenda today? Looks like you were planning some work."

Paul slurped some coffee, then said, "Yeah, that little fir there on the corner of the lot," he pointed by swinging his cup gently at the tree, "I'm taking her out. Loreen doesn't like it." He didn't take the tone that said, "I wish Loreen would let it be." Wooster had heard men moan and groan about their wives' yard wishes before. Paul didn't do that. His wife ran a nursery. She knew plants and landscaping, and Paul knew that she had some plan. He often said she was the brains of the operation and he was the brawn. Wooster knew that Paul had brains too, but just used them in other areas.

"I saw you up late last night" said Paul.

"Yeah, couldn't sleep. You must have been up late too to notice, eh?" replied Wooster. Wooster couldn't sleep too well anymore. His doctor had said when you get older you sleep less. *"Great,"* thought Wooster. *"I've slept crummy all my life. Now I get to sleep even crummier!"*

Paul shrugged, "Naw, I just woke up a little hungry, so I came down for a snack. I saw your light on. Nothing wrong?"

Wooster shook his head, sipped some coffee, then said, "Naw. Nothing special. So how you taking that tree out?"

"I thought I'd first take the branches off, then cut her down to about three feet, then dig the stump out."

Wooster nodded. "Sounds like a plan."

"Yeah. I better get on it too. I want to catch the game at one. You watching?"

Wooster and Paul sometimes watched baseball on Saturday afternoons. Wooster shook his head, "I think I'll pass today if you don't mind. I'm pretty sure I'll need a nap and I don't want to nod off on you." Of course, it would not have been the first time he'd nodded off on Paul. But that was not intentional. He was pretty sure he would need a good hour or so of sleep this afternoon.

Paul nodded and said, "Ok, but if you decide different, just let me know. I'll bring the chips." He grinned at Wooster and drained the last of his coffee. "Ok, I'm on it!" And with that he stood and headed back across the street. Loreen came out into the garage as he crossed to their driveway. She smiled at him, then waved to Wooster and yelled, "Hey Wooster! Good morning!" Wooster raised his cup to her and grinned. She was a nice gal.

It was about 8:45 by the time Paul had assembled his tools. The tree wasn't big, so he was gonna use a bow saw to cut the limbs off and to cut the trunk down to about three feet. Course, size would make no difference to his tool selection. He didn't have much at the house anyway. He began and was about half way through the limbs when Wooster heard Ronnie Waldron coming up the side of the house. Ronnie lived next door. He would come out his back door and crawl under the hedge to get to Wooster's. They often sat in the back and drank lemonade together.

Ronnie was a nice kid, and he was Wooster's speed too. Ronnie was retarded. He had other friends, but most kids (not intending to be mean or anything) just were in a different league than Ronnie. Ronnie was unable to keep up. He didn't speak well. He was uncoordinated. He was slow to think and act. It was like a station wagon at the Indy 500. The cars were all good, but the wagon just didn't fit in well.

Ronnie rounded the corner and flashed a huge smile at Wooster. "Hi Mr. McDowel!" he shouted enthusiastically. He was enthusiastic every time he saw Wooster; like he found a long lost friend anew each day.

Wooster grinned at him and said, "Hey Ronnie! Sit yourself down!" The two fit well at this point in life for one reason. Wooster was a quiet man, and sat a lot on his porch. Ronnie was a quiet kid, who didn't mind sitting on the porch. They were perfect company. "Have a cup?" Wooster prodded with a grin. It was a ritual. Wooster would ask Ronnie if he'd like some coffee, and Ronnie would say, "No. Mom says I can't have coffee."

With a grin to match Wooster's, Ronnie answered, "No, Mom says I can't have coffee 'cause I'm too little." His eyes sparkled, for he knew Wooster was just teasing him.

Wooster nodded and said, "Well, moms know best."

Ronnie came onto the porch and sat down in the rocker left vacant by Paul. He settled back into it, and this left his feet not quite touching the ground. But if he stretched real hard, and pointed his toes, he could make the rocker rock. And he liked that. So the two sat side by side listening to the soft squeak of Ronnie's rocker.

After a bit, Wooster said, "I think I'll get another cup. Would you like some milk, Ronnie?"

Ronnie nodded his head and continued to rock. Wooster ambled past him, got in the door and got back with a cup of coffee and a small glass of milk. He hardly spilled any as the screen bumped him! He handed Ronnie the glass and said, "Now careful not to spill." Ronnie almost always spilled, but Wooster treated him as any other kid. He got the "don't spill" command just like Wooster's kids had when they were little. It didn't mean you wouldn't spill, it just meant, "I love you and don't want you to spill." After all, they were on the porch and heaven knows Wooster had spilled enough milk and coffee out here to fill a bathtub!

When Wooster was seated, and Ronnie had the first coat of milk mustache on his face, Wooster pointed over at Paul and said, "I'm watching Mr. Compton pull that tree out. Mrs. Compton says it doesn't fit there."

That was one thing that tipped you off about Ronnie and his retardation. He didn't respond like you would expect a kid to. Were Wooster to say that to a regular kid, he would probably be regaled with questions like, "Why does Mrs. Compton want the tree gone?" or, "Why doesn't it fit there?" Ronnie didn't ask anything. He just nodded seriously, and stared at Paul. He stopped rocking too. He just sat back, sipped at his milk and watched as Paul worked.

Wooster watched Ronnie for a few minutes. He was a good boy. It hurt Wooster to see Ronnie missing so much. But Ronnie didn't seem to notice very often that he missed things. At least he rarely indicated that he noticed. Now and again he would look . . . wistful (at least that is what Wooster thought) . . . as though he longed for something that he knew he couldn't get. But mostly he just matter-of-factly said things like, "I can't do that because I can't run fast," or, "I'm not strong enough to do that," or, "I'm not smart like that." He knew his limitations, and just worked inside them. It was pretty mature for a kid branded "retarded," thought Wooster.

The two sat and rocked and watched Paul in silence. And actually, though Wooster doubted he could convince most people, it was a pretty good show! Clearly, Paul was not a gardener. He may know how to invest money (he was a stock broker), but it was obvious he did not know about how to take a tree down. His saw seemed completely dull as far as Wooster could ascertain. And often, Paul just didn't position himself correctly to place the optimum force on the blade as he worked. Consequently, he would misfire when trying to stroke the blade along the bark. Or he would bend the saw. It was rather hilarious to watch, and Wooster found himself grinning at the misfortune of his friend. He looked over and saw that Ronnie was looking at him and grinning too. He doubted that Ronnie knew what he was grinning about, but if Wooster was happy, Ronnie was happy.

Wooster winked and said, "This should be good when he gets to digging that stump out eh?"

Ronnie grinned a huge grin and answered, "Yeah."

It was probably ten o'clock by the time the branches were off the tree. Late enough in the morning that Wooster could break out the licorice. Ronnie loved the red licorice. His folks had said to Wooster that it was all right to give it to him too. Ronnie was interesting in that he was very controlled about food. A lot of kids just eat and eat until they are over stuffed. Even the very smart ones would do that sometimes. But Ronnie never did. Wooster could open one of those big ol' tubs of licorice, set it down between them, and know for a fact that Ronnie would not eat more than five pieces. Oh now and then he'd have more. But just as often he'd have less. He just ate till he felt it was enough, and it was never gluttonous. Again, pretty mature for a kid with some mental problems, noted Wooster.

Wooster looked at Ronnie. Ronnie looked back and smiled. Wooster clicked his tongue and said, "You feel like some licorice?"

Ronnie's eyes brightened and he said, "Yeah."

Wooster said, "You know where it is right?" He asked this question every time. Most times Ronnie did know. But now and then he would stare back blankly as though he'd never gotten the tub himself. Wooster just chalked it up to a quirk in his brain that made him forget now and then. This morning Ronnie nodded and said, "I remember." He slid off the rocker and stood there watching Wooster, waiting for the cue.

Wooster would not have minded if Ronnie had scampered off into his house and rummaged around in the kitchen on his own. But Ronnie never did. He would always wait until Wooster gave him the go ahead. He nodded to the boy and said, "Why don't you fetch it for us? Go ahead."

Ronnie smiled and walked to the screen door. He fumbled with it for a second, then disappeared into the house. A minute later he returned carrying the tub of licorice like it was a gold statue from an Egyptian tomb. He treated everything he touched with great care. Wooster thought the boy had probably broken things in the past and after a scolding or two took it upon himself to be diligent with everything he touched. Even plastic tubs.

Ronnie didn't set the tub down. He brought it over to Wooster and stood there waiting for him to take it. Wooster did, and Ronnie turned and crawled back into his rocker. He showed no rush or extraordinary eagerness other than a smile and the fact that his eyes followed Wooster as he opened the tub. Wooster then set it down between them, and pulled a few pieces from it. He handed a couple to Ronnie, and kept one for himself.

Ronnie took them. He folded one over and jammed it into his pocket. The other he began to eat slowly as Wooster did.

The first time Ronnie had gotten licorice from Wooster, he had eaten it down pretty fast. Wooster didn't say anything, knowing that most kids did that. But after Ronnie finished wolfing his pieces down, he watched Wooster eat. Wooster coddled his licorice. He'd suck it a bit to soften it. Then he'd chew a bit. He just savored it as his one vice. He'd had a sweet tooth for red licorice for years.

After that, Ronnie never wolfed his licorice again. Ever. He would eat it like Wooster. At first it was funny. The boy seemed to actually be trying to imitate just what Wooster did. But after a while he just ate it slowly, as though he liked it that way. And why not? It made your five pieces last longer!

The two sat and ate their licorice slowly as Paul began to saw at the trunk of the tree with his dull bow saw. It was comical! The trunk was about seven inches in diameter where Paul was sawing it; about three feet off the ground. A bow saw is just not the right tool for the task though. It kept twisting on him. And the trunk would squeeze down on the blade harder and harder the farther Paul got into the wood, until he had to tug it loose and try sawing in a different place, lining up the cuts so they would meet somewhere in the middle. That, of course, almost never worked just right. Wooster had been there, done that. Even with a chain saw it often didn't work.

Paul was one of those talkers. Some men work silently. They just do their work. Wooster's dad was that way, sort of. He would make noises from time to time. Grunts and sighs, whistles, and quick in-drawn breaths. But he never actually talked much. His thing was his tongue. He'd stick it out when the work got hard. You could tell it was not a good time to interrupt dad when the tongue was out. He'd probably yell at you! Some men need to talk though. They usually talk at whatever they're working on. Asking questions of the project, stating philosophical truths. It could be funny to Wooster. It was like they expected inanimate objects to answer back!

Paul was talking now. Talking to the tree, "C'mon you. Why are you doing this? Why won't you cut through? C'mon! C'mon!"

Wooster was smiling when he said to Ronnie, "Sounds like Mr. Compton is having a few troubles doesn't it? That tree has a mind of its own." Wooster never talked down to Ronnie. He just talked to him like he would anyone else. If the boy understood the subtleties of the conversation, well and good. If he didn't, then maybe he would learn something. Wooster wasn't going to act differently with Ronnie just because he was retarded. Wooster figured Ronnie was like everyone else: He'd understand what he could, and either ask about or ignore the rest. It worked fine for them both. Sometimes Ronnie asked a question, sometimes he just sat.

Ronnie nodded at Wooster and said, "It sure does." Wooster didn't know if Ronnie knew what the troubles were or not. Ronnie didn't ask anything this time.

"You dang tree! C'mon!" Paul snarled it.

Wooster openly giggled. He was not mocking Paul. It was more in sympathy. He'd been in the same type of situation many times in his life. Maddening situations where you wanted something to go a certain way, and it seemed to fight you on every step. It was easy to laugh about when you weren't the one fighting the tree. Still, that was life. Sometimes you were the laugher, sometimes you were the one fighting the tree. Wooster and Ronnie got the good side of the coin this day.

Ronnie said, "What's funny?"

Wooster turned to him and said, "Nothing. I was just thinking." He didn't want the boy to think it was good to laugh at an adult.

Ronnie nodded and said, "I think it's kinda funny when Mr. Compton talks to the tree."

Wooster smiled and said, "Yeah, that is funny, isn't it? They grinned at one another, and Ronnie pulled the bent licorice from his pocket and began on it. Wooster reached down and pulled another piece from the tub. It was good.

Paul was getting more frustrated by the moment. He stepped back from the tree for a minute, leaving the saw hanging in the latest cut he had inflicted on the trunk. He said out loud to himself, "I think I'll pick these branches up." He then began to stack the branches up near the drive so he could later take the whole mess to the dump. It was a good way to step back from his frustrations for a bit. After he had finished picking up the branches, he raked the lawn around the tree, dumping all the twigs and such in his trash can.

"Ok, now I'm ready again," he said to the wind. And with that he began to push the bow saw back and forth again. It tried to twist and bind on him again, but he was getting the hang of it. He found that if he pressed on the top portion of the trunk, it split the cut wider and allowed the saw to move more freely. So there he worked while Wooster and Ronnie watched. His body leaned into his left hand up above the cut he was making in the trunk, and his right hand did the sawing. He got pretty far through this time before he could no longer move the blade. Of course, when he tried to remove the saw from the trunk, he found it took all his strength. But no matter; he got it out.

Paul figured one more cut on the opposite side and he'd have the top of the trunk off. He set to it after a short breather, during which he looked at the ground around the tree. He was thinking it had to be easier to dig the roots out than it was cutting through the trunk with a bow saw!

Ronnie reached down for his last piece of red licorice while asking, "What's Mr. Compton doing standing there like that?"

Wooster said casually, "He's just taking a breath and deciding where to cut next. A man's gotta plan his work out y'know. Like you planning on where to go through the hedge. You can't just dive in anywhere."

Ronnie regarded Wooster for a moment, then said, "Hmmmm."

Paul went back to work on the trunk, and in twenty minutes or so he was rocking the top back and forth trying to break the last vestiges of pulp holding the pieces together. With a powerful shove, the top came away and teetered off onto the lawn. Ronnie jumped off the rocker and clapped his hands, yelling to Paul, "It's off!"

Paul looked across the street at the noise and grinned at the boy, taking small bows as though he were in front of an appreciative opera audience screaming "Bravo!"

Wooster, smiling, watched Ronnie clap his hands. At first he wasn't sure Ronnie was all that excited about watching the cutting of the tree, but apparently he was enjoying the spectacle very much. Wooster shook his head at himself and grinned along with Ronnie. Here he was, eighty plus, and here was Ronnie, ten minus. And there they were cheering for a tree cutting like they were at a World Series game! It tickled Wooster.

Paul sauntered across the street and up onto Wooster's porch. He nabbed himself a piece of licorice, and settled onto the porch next to Ronnie, smiling a wide grin of triumph. It was nice to see his buffoonery with the tree was getting rave reviews somewhere! He winked at Wooster and said to Ronnie, "So you're impressed with my lumberjack expertise, eh Ronnie?"

Ronnie gave him a blank stare.

Paul said, "You know what a lumberjack is, Ronnie?"

Ronnie shook his head.

"It's a man who cuts down trees for a living. Your dad sells furniture for a living, and a lumberjack cuts the trees to get the wood to make the furniture. I'm being a lumberjack this morning." He gave Ronnie a broad grin and tapped his leg.

Ronnie grinned back and said, "You cut that tree pretty good Mr. Compton."

Wooster kicked in, "You sure did Paul!" He winked at his friend. They both had done jobs with the wrong kind of tools in their lives and knew the comical outcomes that could be achieved by amateur homeowners!

Paul said, "Well thanks men. I'm thinking of going into the logging business if the stock market plunges."

Ronnie just nodded as though it was worth considering. Wooster and Paul chuckled at the thought of Paul with a chainsaw. That line from the movie Apocalypse Now ran through Paul's mind: "The horror. The horror!" He barked a laugh.

"Ok men, I need to proceed to the stump," said Paul after snagging one more piece of licorice.

As he headed down the walk Wooster called after him, still grinning, "Give 'em hell boy!" Paul waved a hand without turning.

Ronnie looked at Wooster and said, "My mom says you shouldn't say bad words Mr. McDowel."

Wooster nodded and said, "That's right. I'm sorry Ronnie."

Ronnie looked at him and said, "Ok." He then fixed his attention back on Paul and the formidable stump.

The trunk now was but three feet high. Paul figured he could cut a ring around the base in the ground and chop any roots running out from the tree. Then digging a hole around the tree, he could get to the tap root about a foot underground and chop it off. His main implements for this process were going to be one square head spade, one pointed spade, and a hatchet. He mumbled to himself about having a stone ax out here next. Wooster and Ronnie didn't hear that one.

Loreen came out of the garage just as Paul was beginning to dig the hole around the tree. She glanced across the street and saw Ronnie sitting with Wooster and she shouted, "Hey Ronnie! Are you visiting?" She saw Ronnie sitting with Wooster often.

Ronnie waved back at her and shouted, "Yes! We're having licorice!" He waggled the remaining half of his last piece at her to prove it.

Loreen shouted back, "Great!" Then she turned to Paul and said, "This is coming right along." She'd brought a cup of coffee to him, and she handed it over. Working in a nursery she had done plenty of work with trees. But Paul never expected her to do the work at home. He figured it would be overkill to have to do your job at home and at work too. She always argued that he handled their investments and that was his line of work. But he just put his foot down and said, "Well, you handle a lot with the kids too, so it won't hurt me to do this little bit." She let him, but wished he'd let her just have some employees at her store do the work. After all, she was the boss. Loreen thought that it was Paul's upbringing that made him want to handle the yard work. His dad had always done so, or had his boys do it. And they just expected to do it at their own houses. Even if they were not experts. She let it be after a while.

As Paul drank his coffee he said to her, "I think this will go pretty quick."

Loreen eyed his little hatchet and the spades. She giggled and said, "We'll see."

Paul looked at her with mock indignation in his eyes. He said, "Be gone woman! I can see your doubt!" He slapped her butt and pushed her away.

Ronnie giggled and said, "He smacked her bottom, Mr. McDowel."

Wooster said, "Yep, he sure did. She must have gotten fresh, huh?" He grinned at Ronnie.

Ronnie answered, "My dad does that when I'm really bad. Not very often though. He says I'm a good boy."

Wooster nodded and said, "That you are Ronnie." They both went silent then.

Loreen laughed and took Paul's cup when he finished. She left him to his work and went in to do her chores.

Paul dug the hole down around the tree. He exposed a number of roots and realized he could cut many just by driving the spade through them. Some of the larger ones he had to get down on his knees and cut with the hatchet though. That was difficult at times because he found he could not get a good swing with the little thing. He also saw that he was dulling it quickly every time he smacked it into the dirt trying to cut a root.

He also found that for a little tree, it sure had some good sized roots! He finally ended up using a hand trowel to scoop dirt from around roots. Then he'd whack at them, then dig, then whack. It was tedious! Soon Wooster and Ronnie could hear, "C'mon you stupid root!" and, "Arrrrg!" coming from Paul as he kneeled by the tree.

Ronnie turned to Wooster and said, "It sounds like Mr. Compton is having trouble again."

Wooster wasn't really paying attention just then to the stump. He was watching a small flock of starlings circling down the block. They wouldn't land here with he and Ronnie on the porch. They savaged Mrs. Baker's yard instead. At least it looked that way. They flew over her house and disappeared. Wooster knew she had a nice garden in the back yard. The starlings may not get all they want at once, but they were tenacious. You had to watch them. What they couldn't get one day, they'd come back for on another.

Ronnie slipped from his chair, reached over to Wooster and tugged on his arm. He repeated, "I think Mr. Compton is having trouble again."

Wooster returned from his mental rabbit trail and smiled at Ronnie. Then, hearing another grunt from Paul he said, "It sure does!"

Paul was getting hot, and dirty, and mad. The roots of a tree were nothing like the trunk and branches. They were springy and elastic. They didn't cut so much as chip. They seemed to bounce the blade of the hatchet off rather than split under it. After an hour of grubbing around he had gotten perhaps three quarters the way around the tree. That left a large root on one side, and the tap root itself. He groaned as he got to his feet, his face and upper body covered with dirt. He put his hand on the trunk to lean against it and found that it swayed back a little. Perhaps he could loosen the dirt around the remaining roots by rocking the stump back and forth some. He set his other hand on it and pushed. Then he pulled. The trunk rocked almost not at all.

Wooster watched as Paul tried to push and pull the trunk. He said to Ronnie, "Maybe Mr. Compton is gonna pull the trunk out by hand."

Ronnie looked with wide eyes as though thinking of spider man hefting a truck up or something. He got back into his chair and renewed his surveillance of Mr. Compton's work.

Paul decided that he'd have to get down and cut those last roots some to get the tree out. He sighed and once again kneeled in the dirt. He worked his hands down and started scooping dirt from around the tap root. He probably wasn't going to be able to swing his hatchet at it, but he had a little hand saw too. He could maybe slide that in next to it. As he worked he noticed little white dots coming out with the dirt he was scooping. He was pondering what they were when the first ant bit him. He jerked his hand back and blurted, "Ouch!" It was a second before another bit, and another. Paul jerked back away from the tree and began to slap at his forearms, trying to knock any more ants from his flesh. The white dots were apparently eggs.

Wooster watched Paul bound back away from the tree and he wondered what was up.

Ronnie said, "What's he doing? It looks like he's dancing."

Wooster answered, "I don't know. Maybe he found some bugs."

Ronnie yelled out, "What're you doing Mr. Compton!"

Paul looked up and laughed when he realized how he must look. He shouted back to Ronnie, "Beating off wild ants!"

Wooster laughed and shouted, "You get 'em Paul! You teach 'em!"

Paul gave Wooster a stern look and yelled, "Never you mind, old man!" They both grinned at one another.

Ronnie said, "Mr. Compton said you were old."

Wooster replied, "Yeah, and I am. But he was just funnin' with me. He didn't mean anything by it."

Ronnie nodded and said, "Yeah, you are old I guess." He sat back down and kept on watching.

Having beaten the ants off himself, Paul went into his garage and got a can of Raid. Like all men he applied Raid with the motto, "The more Raid, the more dead bugs!" He enveloped the hole around the tree with a dizzying mist of Raid, undoubtedly drowning most of the ants long before the insecticide could take effect and kill them the way it was intended. He stepped back from the killer haze, coughing and sneezing himself.

Wooster yelled, "Atta boy Paul!"

Paul yelled back, "I think they have one designed for old men too!"

Wooster chuckled for a good few minutes over that. That Paul was a quick one. That's for sure!

When the dust had settled over the killing zone, Paul kneeled back in and started to scoop the rest of the dirt out. He pursed his lips and nodded in satisfaction at the carnage he had reaped on his tormentors. Another line from Shakespeare drifted through his head, "Cry havoc and let slip the dogs of war!" In this case the "Can of war."

With enough room, he sawed away at the tap root until it was almost cut through. Then he worked away on the other main root that was left. He hoped the stump would break off now. He whistled over to Ronnie and Wooster and yelled, "Watch me now men!" Then he put his hands to the trunk to get an idea of how it felt. He pushed and it moved a good deal. He set both hands to it, firmed his shoulders and flung his body hard against the stump. It gave the slightest resistance, and then suddenly snapped back away from him and crashed to the ground. Paul never saw it coming. He hurled after the trunk and tumble to the ground on top of it in a dirty heap.

Ronnie bolted from his rocker and shrieked at the top of his lungs, "All right Mr. Compton!"

Wooster heard him and laughed so hard he almost fell out of his chair. Then he too stood and began to applaud.

When Paul finally sorted himself out, and stood, both Ronnie and Wooster were laughing all out and clapping. Wooster called out between guffaws, "Well done Paul! You showed it!" It wasn't just teasing. He really was glad Paul accomplished his task.

Ronnie clapped hard and kept saying, "You did it Mr. Compton. You did it!" Something had definitely tickled him about the tree-cutting affair.

Paul began to laugh himself, and again took some bows.

Loreen came out of the garage, hearing the noise and started giggling at the sight of Wooster the eighty year old and little Ronnie Waldron standing together clapping and laughing while Paul took bows next to his hole and broken tree. She began to clap along with them as though some monumental task had been achieved. She thought to herself, *"What a bunch of goof balls I live with!"* And she grinned all the more.

Paul chopped the last vestiges of the roots away and pulled the stump over to the pile of branches he had made earlier. He cleaned up his tools and washed up at the utility sink. He then headed over to Wooster's porch. As he once again sat down by the two trouble makers he said, "So I've been a source of enjoyment for you two this morning huh?" He gave them both a mock stern look.

Wooster said, "You're better than TV, Paul. We were mesmerized waiting to see who'd win, right Ronnie?"

Ronnie nodded and said, "You did it Mr. Compton. You cut that tree down."

Paul nodded his head at the boy, mussed his hair and said, "I sure did Ronnie. Couldn't have done it without all your support either."

Ronnie blushed a little and said, "Yeah."

It was near twelve and after they sat for a moment, Ronnie's mom called out the front door, "Ronnie! Lunch time!" Ronnie slid from his chair and said, "I have to go eat lunch now. Bye Mr. McDowel. Bye Mr. Compton." He turned and headed off the porch. He said no more to either man. It was the way Ronnie was. You could get more from him, but it was in little bits. Today he just said, "Bye." Another day he'd say, "I had fun." Now and then he'd even say, "I love you."

Wooster and Paul chorused after him, "Bye Ronnie."

When he was gone, Paul settled into the empty rocker. "He's a good boy," he said. Mostly just saying it out loud.

Wooster nodded and said, "Yeah. He is a good boy."

They looked at one another and smiled. This scene, with variations had been played out time and again, and would be time and again in the future. The two men understood how it was with Ronnie. They knew that what they wouldn't get from him one day, they'd get another day. Both knew that sometimes you just had to be tenacious about the ones you love.

Dog

MARJORIE WILKINS SHOOK HER head and cursed. Then she yelled to her boy Tommy to "get your lazy ass down here to breakfast!" She shook the paper out again and snuffed at the headline once more before turning the page: "Dog beaten by men." It seems some guys had a dog they had found. It was a good dog (so they admitted to the police) and would obey them unerringly. It was friendly, and energetic, and was an all-around good pet. So, since it trusted them implicitly (having been fed and washed for months by them), it didn't fight when they chained it securely and started to beat it to death with baseball bats for the hell of it! Marjorie ticked her tongue with anger and muttered, "They should beat *those bastards* with baseball bats!" She shook the paper again, and growled, "Get your ass down here this minute young man!" at her stupid seven-year-old.

As Tommy careened into the kitchen to quickly take his place, Marjorie made a point of slapping him in the head. "What the hell are you doing?" she snapped as Tommy quietly began to eat his cereal. Marjorie gave a quick lecture on how much effort she had put into pouring the bowl of Froot Loops, emphasizing certain points by wagging her finger at the boy and pounding her fist on the table. Tommy was not exactly sure why mom was mad—it was not even his normal breakfast time—but he accepted the lecture and love-swats in silence, knowing she only disciplined him because she loved him. He knew this because she told him it was that way. Other kids didn't get disciplined because their parents didn't give a damn. Tommy was loved.

Having returned to her paper, Marjorie began to read a few other articles but could not shake the story of the dog. Apparently the Labrador had been a stray that some guy had found wandering near his job. He wanted a dog, and the pup was not too old, so he figured he could still train it. Besides, a lab might make a good hunting dog for him and his buddies. So, he had adopted the animal, and taken it home. The dog was overjoyed. It was being fed, and washed, and petted regularly, and had developed a strong attraction to the man. It had learned to trust him. He told the police the dog would do anything he commanded it. It would come, or sit, or be quiet. It was a good dog.

But then one night the guy had gotten drunk with his buddies and they had turned on the dog. At this point in her meandering thoughts Tommy spilled some milk and needed to be corrected. "You can be so stupid! Why aren't you careful?" Marjorie fired at him. He cleaned it up. Tommy wasn't always like that she thought. He was such a good boy for so long. He'd sleep for hours when she had first brought him home. And he sat with her in his stroller as she gardened without making a peep. Boy, those days were gone! It seemed like Tommy was nothing but trouble now, Marjorie thought.

Anyway, the guys had called the dog one day and it had dutifully come. *"And why not?"* thought Marjorie—*"He trusted that man!"* And they had chained the dog up so it couldn't bite or escape. And they had begun to beat it with bats. Marjorie could not imagine the anguish of that unfortunate animal! Suddenly trapped by the chains, and the one person it expected to take care of it beating it to death! It was criminal! Marjorie could not get the image out of her head. "That poor, poor dog," she muttered. "Put your dishes in the sink!" she squawked, "How many times must I tell you?" Tommy sure was a problem now. She was going to have to teach him.

Marjorie went to the cupboard and took down the spoon. Tommy's color went white as he watched her settle onto her chair. She glared at the boy for a moment before tapping her lap. Tommy needed no more; he slowly slid from his seat, a soft tear welling in his eye, and tread over to his mother. Without help he dropped his pants and underwear, and lay over his mother's knees. She gently wrapped an arm around him and drew him closer to her before she began. The wood spoon sang as it whistled down onto Tommy's bare flesh in a rhythmic pattern. Mom never held back on love thought Tommy as soft sobs sputtered from his lips.

Goldfish

DANCING MOTES IN SOFT, hazy air struck through with prism color, hover above the carpet. Their movement gives life to the hot room. The air seems to swirl in multi-colored vortices, which lead back to the bowl balanced on the flute of dark cherry standing by the window. There he sits, quiet, unobtrusive, stoic, suspended in warm fluid, watching.

Barbara scuffs quietly into the room. She glances at the old clock—10 to 6. Not long to wait now. The window shades are open at present. Not for long, she thinks. She can see the street, framed by sun bleached, blue curtains—their lively pattern of flowers now dim compared to the skein of life against which they lay. Tommy and Billy, the Carney twins, wrestle on their lawn, venting in play what surely lies more darkly in a mature form inside them. She raises her arm and draws the long, dark sweater across her nose. A thin trail of snot marks its passing. She sighs and glances at the clock—8 to 6. Not long to wait now.

Hanging motionless, he watches the dark form slip across the wide, glass expanse.

As she slips across the room Barbara's hands fidget and fiddle with one another, mimicking what the Carney boys are doing across the street. First the left gains supremacy, then the right. One twists away while the other grasps. Constant motion akin to the up, down, in, out of a priest's hands over a dying soul. Only the soul is not dying, and it's not in front, but behind. She laughs softly at this thought when she sees her hands moving in the reflection from the mirror. "And there is no forgiveness from my hands, nor comfort," she whispers. Only tedious motion. Her eyes play over the clock—5 to 6. Not long to wait now.

He angles away as the large white forms flash to and fro above him.

Standing at the window, Barbara can feel the heat coming from the glass. It is near on 100 degrees today. The window is closed, locked, painted shut, and sealed with dust released long ago from the spiral dance that involved it for a moment. At one point, it held a dream of freedom— wild, colorful freedom spinning uncontrolled in the wash of light, weightless and unencumbered; unshackled. But that dream died when it settled down. No longer filled with stripes of color, it sits on the wood sill, quietly, unremarkably, fated. She looks at the sill, "Dusty," she mumbles, and reaches out to trace a finger lightly through the dead dreams. She blankly looks at the clock's reflection in the window—2 to 6. Not long to wait now.

He sinks down; danger looms in the white terror that flashes over him. The water begins to shudder lightly.

Dave's truck pulls into the drive. 1 to 6. The deep rumble of power shakes the world as the engine settles to idle. He listens to the throb for a moment. It matches the pulse lightly tapping his eyelids. The engine shakes the frame softly, keeping it on alert, ready for action. He listens quietly for a few more seconds, then quickly, without warning twists the key, and quiets the shaking.

The water stops shuddering.

Barbara reaches to the shades, shaking, and wearily pulls them to, banishing that world, darkening hers. She scuttles to the far side of the room, away from the bowl, away from the light—just away. Her eyes acknowledge the clock. 6 o'clock—time. The silence is broken by the turn of a key in the lock. The door cracks slightly. The world tries to spill back in, but Dave blocks it, beats it back—envelops the thin line of life with his body as he pushes into the house. She sidles back a hare, head down, eyes looking through lashes at that ever smaller patch of life as the door closes again. Thick grayness fills the room tangibly as Dave sighs out a long, seemingly black breath. He hangs his coat on the hook. She hung that tired, weighed down hook years ago. It is smaller now than it was. The years of weight have rubbed it down, removed its color, and made it invisible.

There are two shapes in the void now. He drifts back to the rear, down to the rock, behind the fronds.

Her "Hi hon!" hangs like a dead animal in a jar of formaldehyde. One moment alive and full of hope, the next, sitting on the bottom, a shadow of lifeless life. Dave turns and glances at her. His eyes penetrate the gray haze emanating from him and pin her to the far wall. She smiles tightly. He advances across the wood floor.

Stay down! They are closer! Behind the fronds, near the rock!

Crack! Her eyes barely open as the first blow lands. She rockets back into the wall. A short grunt of air explodes from her lips at impact. She slides down to the floor thinking muddily, "Stay low, behind the chair maybe, near the chifforobe." She crawls to the right. Sluggish thoughts: "Stay low! Move to the window!"

He settles on the bottom, turned to the approaching shapes, pressed to the far glassy wall.

She settles to the floor by the cherry candle stand. A small trickle of blood wanders down from her left eye, mingling with the snot that runs from her swollen nose. "Crouch low, near the wall." His foot connects hard, pressing the ribs back. Bending, bending, broken. They wander from their place. Needles of bone. Not for stitching however. These are different.

They're right above him! Swim! Escape! But only circular restriction in all directions!

She groans and tries to get out, to flee. She cannot. Her eyes wildly flutter around the room. Nothing but the room in sight. The knife drives into her exposed neck. It cuts between the windpipe and the spine, and finally settles into the crack between the lovely oak boards beneath her. Her arm flails out connecting uselessly with the candle stand; too late. Eyes glaze over. Short, jittery exclamations of the passage of life shake her. A sigh.

The wall slams him from behind! Now blackness rushes at him! No water! Flailing fins. Jittery exclamations of the passage of life. A sigh.

"Damn goldfish!" Dave mutters.

Lemming

Turly Breidablick banged the metal spatula down onto the sizzling grill, swished it under the potatoes and, with flair reserved for the truly talented, flipped the whole mass of hash-browns over. He banged the spatula again, knocking the few clingy pieces of spud from its face, and turned OverMedium's eggs. Glancing up from the grill, as Marty hung another order, he saw AmericanOmelete enter and head for his window seat. As American settled, Turly clanged the little bell and slid OverMedium's breakfast onto the counter for Marty to serve. She took it with a wink, added a pot of coffee in her other hand, and sauntered the whole mess over to OverMedium in his corner by the Coke clock. Turly watched as Marty grinned at OverMedium, plunked the food down, and filled his cup. She then added a little something on his bill (Thanks! And see you again!), tore it from her book, laid it on the table, and turning, slid her pencil behind her ear. On the way back to the counter she dribbled some coffee for ColdCereal, and answered a question from ToastandJuice (like she would actually have anything else!—Turly grinned to himself).

Before she made the counter, AmericanOmelet waggled a finger at her, and without looking to see what he said, Turly cracked three eggs into a metal bowel. When Marty hung up the order, Turly grinned to himself finding it for "Am Om, pots, cof." Imagine that! His eyes twinkled as he swished in the milk and poured the conglomeration onto the hot stove. As it cooked he snagged some cheese, a few chives, and some onions. He quickly grilled the onions and then formed the Omelet into its customary shape.

Ding! Two scrambled eggs, toast (wheat), ham. Funny, HamandEggs hadn't been in for a week now. This order had reminded him of that again. Turly glanced at the Coke clock; 7:28. HamandEggs was always here by 7. But not this last week. Something's up there. Ka'ching; bye Oatmeal. That was a good one. Almost never get Oatmeal these days. Once, to Turly's surprise, he had been asked for bulgur . . . for breakfast! That was odd. We don't have bulgur for breakfast. We don't have bulgur at all. Bulgur doesn't ask for bulgur anymore. Now he has FriedPotatos, low oil. They don't look too good to Turly Breidablick, but then, he's not eating them.

Eight o'clock. Just about usual, most are gone now. BlackCoffee is still nursing his cup from an hour ago. He just reads the paper though. He's not here for anything Turly can supply. Well, there was the once. Rye toast. Just the once though. BlackCoffee pretty much just had the coffee.

AmericanOmelette had taken some time today. Usually he scarfed it down pretty fast. Guess on most Mondays he had to get to work. Though it was hard to be certain. He looked like a rusher. Never took his coat off. Today was different. Long weekend perhaps. He had a good number of cups of coffee. Marty was wearing a rut in the linoleum to his table this morning. Course, he was reading something. Maybe he was working already. Turly squinted his eyes, and turned his lips in for a second thinking. Hard to tell.

He swiveled the order ring around and saw nothing. Taking the chance, Turly slipped into his jacket and stepped out the back door into the alley. He let the little wood block stop the door as it tried to close. The cool of the alley washed over his warm face as he fumbled out a pack of cigs. He pulled one, lit it, and took a long draw, looking up the alley at the few cars passing down on the street. Whew! Cold today! He stamped his feet a couple times and drew another breath of nicotine saturated air. As he leaned back into the brick wall, settling in for a nice smoke, he saw DoubleHash's car pass by the end of the alley. He dropped the cig and stamped it once, re-adjusting his apron. He re-entered the building and made his way to the grill just in time to see DoubleHash bang open the glass door, jostling the "OPEN" sign.

DoubleHash swaggered over to his table and plopped down. He shook his head at Marty and yammered, "Hey honey, I'll have the usual." She nodded and turned to Turly with the order. Like he needed to hear it. Ol' DoubleHash always spoke at the top of his lungs. Seemed to want everyone to know he was there. Once a fellow had looked at him when he bellowed out his order (like he needed to yammer in such a small grill anyway), and DoubleHash had taken a dislike to him. He then pressed him with, "What're you looking at, pal?" and, "You got some kinda problem?" Turly Breidablick thought there was gonna be some trouble that day. But DoubleHash was content to belittle people. Maybe that was the extent of his bravado.

Marty was a good waitress. She had been doing it long enough to get to know the regulars, and she enjoyed people enough to make the once-in-awhile types feel comfortable. It's not that she was just pleasant because she'd get a better tip neither. She was just that sort. Friendly. She'd smile, and chat, and just be a regular person with 'em all. People like that. They like to feel as though they have a friend. Even when they are alone. And Marty was pretty too—at least for a forty-five year old waitress. She was to Turly anyway. Sometimes the night guy would comment on that "piece of nice ass in the morning." Turly couldn't really argue; Marty had a nice ass. But he didn't like Buddy Vashon commenting on it. But it wasn't Turl's way to confront. He'd usually just ignore Buddy. Still, Marty did have a nice ass. The point was Marty was a good waitress. Even to the DoubleHash's of the world with their big mouths and pushy ways. She still smiled at him and kept his coffee poured, and chatted with him. Though sometimes Turly would giggle to himself over what he heard her saying.

Sometimes Marty seemed to just bait ol' DoubleHash for fun. She never was so obvious that he'd catch on, but Turly could tell. He'd known her for years. Like once, DoubleHash had commented on a businessman who'd stopped for a cup of joe. He wasn't a regular; looked like he just needed the joe after a hard night of driving. DoubleHash had been sitting at the counter that morning instead of his usual table. He had winked at Marty and said in a voice loud enough for the stranger to hear, "Some men use their wallets when they're lacking other places." (The guy had paid for the dollar coffee with a fifty.) Marty hadn't missed a beat and replied, "Kinda like some guys using their mouths when their brains are slow." DoubleHash had missed it! Hell, the stranger had missed the whole exchange too, which was probably for the best. But Turly had heard it all and almost dropped his gum when he laughed. He ducked behind the back counter and just guffawed. It wasn't the statement itself, it was that DoubleHash was so full of himself he had nodded in agreement, and winked a wise "you and me think alike baby" wink at Marty! Turly thought he'd bust a rib laughing over that. And it was all the more funny when Marty came 'round the corner and kicked him lightly in mock rebuke for leaving the grill! She whispered a stern, "You get to work Turly Breidablick!" But her eyes said, "What an Ass that DoubleHash is!"

DoubleHash kept his mouth mostly shut today. It was ToastandJuice who was interesting. She had the usual for eating, but not for company. Turly had figured her for a college student. One day he had covered for Marty when she was using the toilet 'cause the other waitress was out. It was a slow day and only the regulars were in. He had filled ToastandJuice's order and was placing it on the table when he saw her open book. It looked like a biology book and had a picture of a lemming on the open page. He had commented on it and she had told him how lemmings run themselves off cliffs sometimes. Imagine that! An animal gets an idea in its head, and that idea defines the world for it. It keeps that idea even when the idea says, "Run off a cliff!" That's pretty strange. Course, Turly supposed animals liked to feel comfortable with their ideas just like people. They keep their impressions of things even when they don't really match with reality. So some lemming thinks the world requires a good cliff jump . . . and off it goes.

Anyway, ToastandJuice came in on Mondays and Fridays and always had the same breakfast with minor variations. She read and ate; usually alone. But this morning she was with a young man. He was wiry, and had dark eyes and hair. Turly thought he was handsome and fitted her very well. He looked like a poet to Turly. Right now they were engaged in a soft but seemingly meaningful conversation. Every now and then she would look around as if trying to see if anyone was watching when they were becoming a bit more insistent. Turly always looked away, acting like he was scraping the grill, or maybe making up a new batch of potatoes.

Maybe the poet was telling ToastandJuice it was over. She didn't seem angry though . . . just vehement. Perhaps ToastandJuice was dumping Poet. But he too seemed not so much hurt, or angry as just animated. He was a hand talker. He'd wave them up or down, tapping out his points in the air as though he were hitting a blackboard. Turly watched as his left eyelid rose and fell whenever he seemed to be making an important point. ToastandJuice would nod or shake her head depending on her response. She was a quiet one. She did bob her head in time to her speech though. Turly could see her bobbing and weaving as though sparring through some onslaught that Poet had just leveled against her. She would also tap her finger on the table at the end of some brilliant point as though saying, "Look, you have to talk with mouth and hands, but I need one small finger to cement my point in stone!" Turly envied ToastandJuice and her Poet. They clearly knew one another well and felt comfortable even arguing. Now and then they'd fall silent, eat a little (Poet had the eggs and sausage. But he was Poet, not EggsandSausage yet). Then they would chat a little. Then grow intense. It was a cycle. Much like life Turly supposed as he covertly watched them while cleaning his grill, and cooking food.

Time passed and the breakfast crowd gave way to the LateMorningers, those from nine to eleven. They were usually retired folk. They had worked and lived and now were happy to stay in bed late and come out for the breakfast special at ten. Sometimes they'd just go right to lunch which Turly liked to cook best of all. That's why he was a morning/day man. Buddy Vashon came on at two in the afternoon with the dinner shift. That was a change in counter people too. Marty left, along with Debbie the college kid and Clancy the washer. In came Brendan (another college kid), Shirleen, and Marty's kid for washing. Turly and Marty were the oldest there. Turly was fifty-two. He was more like the LateMorningers he supposed than the breakfast or lunch crowd. He was beginning to envision retirement from his work, sleeping in past four a.m., and having someone else cook his Monday and Friday breakfast.

LateMorningers were an easy bunch. Well, cranky, but easy if you did your job. They usually had the same things: Prune juice, orange juice, or grapefruit juice; toast or pancakes, or eggs and hash browns. Come to think of it, they pretty much just cut out the good meaty stuff Turly still liked: Ham, sausage, chicken fried steak . . . the *meat* of meat and potatoes! They probably had to. Most of 'em probably had heart problems, and were told to eat right by their doctors. In any event, they were easy to please if you did your job right. If you shorted them on enough potatoes, or didn't get the coffee cup filled, or spilled a little juice, it could be hell. They'd grumble and crab about how service was "in my day" as though they were the only ones to invent good service. Turly would just grin and take it. His pop was like that too. Marty would wrangle right back at the men. They liked it, Turly thought. The women were less open to banter. You pretty much "yes ma'amed" them and let it be.

Turly supposed his pop would be considered a Late-LateMorninger. He didn't really get up though. They gave his food to him through a tube over at Cresten Care Center. After mom had died, he had deteriorated pretty quick. Seemed like just a few months and he was in the Center. It was hard to watch. He went from alive and vital to a lump within the year. And it wasn't like a disease that incapacitates you. It was like he was broken. Like he was withering away from the spirit out. He didn't go out much, even for his walks after mom died. He slept a lot. Turly would go over and try to talk and play checkers and such, but they didn't have the closest of relationships. Still, it's no sight to watch your pop go down like that.

Ding! Sausage and biscuits; one egg. Marty swished it away. Probably the last meat for an hour or so thought Turly.

His pop used to like the meats. He'd have a hearty breakfast on Saturday in the morning. That's where Turly learned to cook so good. Pop would show him all the tricks, like keeping a grill cooler to hold the potatoes in a rush hour, and how to turn the meat just right to get the lines on it. How to arrange the sausages like a star around the eggs. Some cooks just plunked it onto the plate and let 'er go at that. Turly was so practiced at the details that he didn't even notice he did them. Could be fifty people asking for food and their sausages would still come out in stars around the eggs. Astounded Marty the first time she saw it. And she'd seen lots of cooks. The way she commented on it made Turly blush a little.

Turly watched his pop go down until he could no longer go down anymore. He was taken to Cresten in a white ambulance and had been there since. Now he's more a vegetable than his pop anymore. Turly thought his pop would appreciate the way his sausage stars and toast stacks came out. He was a good cook too.

About 8:45 things began to slow and Turly thought he'd take his break before the LateMorningers started to come in. He told Marty he'd be out back, and putting on his jacket, he again pushed out the back into the alley. His first break was nice. It was the first full couple of cigs he'd get after arriving at five a.m. Oh sure, he'd grab one or a half, if it was slow, but mostly he just went without till break. He eased himself down onto the crate he used as a seat in the chilly fall air of the back alley. The rain had wetted the cement, and the smell of the dumpster was just a light fragrance in the air. The cigarette masked it within seconds of ignition. Turly drew a long breath, exhaled, and spat into the small puddle in front of him. He had spent years in this alley. He saw businesses come and go on both sides. He'd seen waitresses, waiters, washers, cooks, and bosses come and go. The alley stayed pretty much the same. Dumpster, graffiti, some garbage, cigarette butts, and Turly. He'd taken his job as cook almost thirty years ago. He didn't go to college. He never seemed to want more than a job and place. He lived in his parents place now. (All paid for thanks to pop and mom.) And he had his job. And not bragging, he was good at it. People came from all over for Turly's food. And the truckers liked to stop too. Yuppies and bums. Everyone liked Turly's food.

As Turly mused about this and that, the door cracked and Marty came out wrapped in her maroon sweater. She clutched it to her body against the chill. Turly offered her a cig, but she was quitting so she declined. "Just came out to chat a bit," she said. They chatted every day back and forth during work. But now and then they would stand or sit in the alley and really talk. Sometimes they didn't talk, but sometimes they did. Turly doubted Marty knew how much he loved her. He had loved her for years. Since before her husband died. He was good man. He always made Turly feel good about who he was. He was a businessman. But he seemed to wear it like a regular guy. It was a drunk driver killed him. Marty and Turly had been through it together as she got on with life after that. They had shared a lot, but never had Turly told Marty how he loved her. They never went out. He was too embarrassed to ask her, being fifty-two while she was just forty-five. And he was nothing to look at like she was. Sometimes, she'd have a day off and bring a date into the grill for some of Turly's cooking. You'd have thought he'd be jealous, loving her and all. But he always made things even better for them. A little more egg or potato. Maybe an extra link of sausage. He did it for Marty. And Marty always introduced him to her dates. She'd say, "And this fine fare is from the hands of my best friend Turly Breidablick," or something like that. He always blushed when she complimented him.

"What's with ToastandJuice?" Turly asked. Marty answered, "I'm not sure, but the guy is cute, isn't he?" She grinned at Turly after she said it because Turly let his mouth fall open in mock horror at her saying such a thing about such a young man. He only held it a second, then started giggling too. Yeah, he was "cute." Marty said they were arguing over some sort of experiment they were doing in a class at the college. Turly couldn't really envision Poet as a biologist like ToastandJuice. He was too, hmmm, troubled looking. He was gonna be Poet to Turly even if he ended up actually being a biologist. Maybe he just missed his calling.

"How 'bout that Stan Karney?" said Marty. Turly looked at her waiting for more. It wasn't her way to talk about customers just for a conversation topic. Sure, she'd talk if they did something of note, but not just to use them as gossip fodder. She continued, "Oh, you wouldn't have noticed being so far in back, but his breath smelled like a brewery today! He tried to pick me up this morning!"

Turly shook his head in disbelief. "He was that drunk?" DoubleHash was a loud mouth, but this was the first time he'd come in drunk. That maybe explains some of his behavior.

Marty nodded and said, "He was drunk or hung over. He wanted me to come with him and massage his head for him." Marty said that with a tone of "can you believe it?!" in her voice. She'd already turned DoubleHash down a dozen times. (You'd have thought Marty would smack him with her feelings about drunks.) He was persistent. Sometimes Turly thought he only came in to try to woo Marty. The order of double hash browns and eggs was just a ruse. Still, he always had it. Turly grinned to himself thinking maybe ol' DoubleHash would ask *him* out if the Marty thing didn't come through.

But Turly's grin faded as he thought about Marty. He looked at her leaning against the wall by him. She looked pretty today. Her maroon sweater looked good with her hair. It was kinda dark and shiny. And there was that nice, uh, shape too. She was very beautiful to Turly. Lately he'd been thinking of screwing himself up and asking her out on a real date. They actually went "out" all the time. To dinner, and a movie sometimes. But it was never as a "couple." It was more like good friends; work friends. There was this good restaurant out on the east side of town he had heard her comment on. Maybe Friday they could go out there together. He was musing about how to broach the subject when Marty tsked her tongue and said, "Well hon" (she called him hon like your mom would), "Well hon," she said, "time to hit the grind." They had chatted and sat for fifteen minutes and it was indeed time to get back at it. Turly nodded to her, stood, and opened the door for her. "Thank you" she said, dipping her head and smiling as she entered the grill again. Turly followed her, retying his apron.

No one new had shown up in the interim (as Turly had expected), and he now had a few minutes or so to wash his hands, scrape the grill again, wipe the cooking area, and get some condiments. About nine the LateMorningers began to appear. Turly knew them by their dress rather than their orders. GolfPants and his buddies came in first usually. Where he got those pants, and how his wife ever let him leave the house with them on was hard to say. Turly was always amazed that there were that many colors of plaid.

A little later the rest came in; mixed in, of course, with once-in-awhile types. There was Bluehair and her friend Hotlips (she always had on the brightest lipstick imaginable, even when it totally conflicted with her clothes). There was Doc and his wife. They came in on Mondays when he was going over to the free clinic. He was actually retired, but still did free exams on Mondays for poor people. It was funny, of all the people who should know better, he'd always order a really big doughnut as an appetizer to his breakfast. Probably told all his patients to watch their diets, but he still had his doughnut every Monday morning! Turly smiled as he watched them sit down.

Mostly the rest of the day went as usual. People came and went, ordered and ate. Turly cooked and cleaned and served the people good food. Marty shmoozed with the regulars and made the once-in-awhilers feel good. The second shift came in at two and took over, and Marty and Turly and the rest went to their respective homes. As Turly sat at his kitchen table watching Oprah and eating hot dogs that afternoon, he wondered how he was going to ask Marty to go out with him so that she'd get it the way it was intended. He usually just said, "Hey, let's go have dinner," and they would go. But this was going to be a different thing. A date. He hadn't dated in years and years. He never found the right woman. And after meeting Marty, he didn't really look. Even though she was married and happy.

It was a hard time for her when her husband died. It was hard for Turly too. He liked Mitch a lot. But way down, his spirit betrayed him and felt a pang of joy at the prospect of Marty being single—available. He was deeply ashamed of that feeling and couldn't look her in the eyes when it came to him. In time he realized it was just his loneliness speaking. But still, he liked Mitch and never wanted him dead. And he especially didn't like the pain in Marty's life. Things had cooled now. Mitch had been dead for years and both of them had learned to live again. Marty with her missing him, and Turly with his guilt at desiring Marty.

Turly finished Oprah. (It was about makeovers this time. He was amazed at how pretty she could make people with just clothes and makeup!) He then read a little and settled into his easy chair for some math. Most people probably thought Turly Breidablick was a good cook and a decent man. And that he was not very smart. After all, he was a grill cook in a diner for twenty-six years. But Turly was not near as dumb people might have thought. He just loved the job he'd taken years ago, and didn't see why he should leave it for something just 'cause he'd make more money. And he didn't need the mental stimulation of another job; he had his math. At night, when most busy business men and professionals were relaxing from a day's work, Turly Breidablick would do math. He loved multi-variable calculus, topography, number theory and many other topics. He would spend hours manipulating numbers and proofs; all self-taught. He had spent a year working on proofs for Fermat's last theorem without success. Even when it had been proven by use of high speed computers, he had still pursued it. If Fermat himself could find a proof that fit into a few pages of his journals without high speed computers, then there was still something to find! And Turly dreamed of finding that elegant proof that would amaze the world. Besides the math also helped him think. And he needed to ponder how to ask Marty out.

Tuesday morning was different from Monday. Less regulars. People just seem to want to start the week off with the comfort of a habit. So Mondays had lots of regulars with regular orders. Get the week off on the right foot perhaps. Tuesday was different. More once-in-awhilers. Writer came in though. She always came in Tuesday through Friday at about eight o'clock. She would take the corner table by the Coke clock (OverMedium's table on Monday) and spread her notebooks out. She would order a muffin and coffee and spend the whole morning writing and watching. Turly thought Writer would probably publish someday if effort were any indicator. She always had lots of stuff with her. And she always showed up. Even on the worst mornings when no one else was out and about. She was there, nibbling at a muffin, drinking coffee and writing.

This particular Tuesday did hold one surprise for Turly. Around seven ToastandJuice and Poet came in. She never came in for breakfast except on Mondays. She'd have lunch sometimes later in the week. But Mondays were dependable. And here it was Tuesday, and she was back! And with Poet again. They took a table off to the side too; not ToastandJuice's regular table this time. They ordered two Omelets, no potatoes, juice and coffee. Turly grinned when he saw the order. Poet was having an impact on ToastandJuice! Turly again envied ToastandJuice and Poet. He wondered how they met, what they had said. He needed something to break the ice with Marty and ask her out. Something that would signal more than another dinner. It was going to take some thought. It would be easiest to just say what he felt. How he loved her, and wanted to go out with her. But for all Turly's intelligence with numbers and food, he was not able to express himself with people that way. This was going to take some effort.

That effort never produced something all week long. Opportunities arose. Breaks alone in the alley, early morning preparations (Turly and Marty were the only ones who came in at 5. The others came at 6). They even talked about the very restaurant Turly was picturing them at. But he never could get the right words together in his head before they moved on to something else. Friday morning came with ChickenFriedSteak, Teaandtoast, and SausageSandwich, but Turly ended his shift with a mournful, "See you Monday!" and no date. Marty was going to a garage sale this weekend with her daughter Sylvie to look for dinner ware. Sylvie had a new apartment and needed to get something to eat with. She also was in school and had little money. Therefore, they went to garage sales a lot! Turly spent the weekend solving multi variable equations and watching football. He was a Vikings fan and since they were better the last few years he actually got to see them play some. Usually the big broadcast stations only had the best teams on. He'd have traded the football and the equations for a date with Marty.

The fall went by as it usually does: Cold and rainy. It was dark when Turly and Marty showed up in the morning and usually gray when they left as well. The regulars continued to come as they always did. HamandEggs came back after a month. Marty told Turly he'd been on a cruise. That would explain the deep tan in his face. He never missed a beat when he came back. Like clockwork he came in after about a month being absent and on the ticket in Marty's scrawl were the words Hm&Egg, cof. Turly smiled to himself. He wondered if HamandEggs had had ham and eggs while he was on the cruise. Were they as good as Turly's? He caught Turly's eye and nodded to him when Marty brought them to the table as though proposing a toast to the best ham and eggs money could buy. Turly had grinned back at him and given his head a quick nod of acknowledgement. He quickly dipped his chin and concentrated on his grill, hiding the blush of pride that swept him. Regulars are regulars for a reason he thought, smiling.

ToastandJuice and Poet continued to keep company at breakfast (Turly had taken to calling them DoubleOmelettes now and then, though they tried many different things on the menu when they were together). They came in more often and sat mostly at the side by the wall. They laughed and talked, and Turly thought better and better for them until one Thursday. It was late, near on to quitting time for Turly when Poet came in with another girl. They sat at ToastandJuice and Poet's table and ordered burgers and onion rings. Turly watched as they chatted, noted how Poet's hands sometimes trailed over to touch the girl's. It seemed pretty intimate at times. Still, it could be they were just close friends, maybe even relatives. ToastandJuice and Poet continued to meet in the mornings and they seemed happy.

Then one day Poet and the girl were having lunch (late again) and in walked ToastandJuice. She didn't often come in late like this, but it had happened in Turly's experience. Apparently it had not occurred to Poet. Had the diner been just a little less crowded it may have never come to anything. ToastandJuice came in as though she was very late for something. Her head was down, and she was grasping an armload of binders in one arm and trying to read a handful of papers as she walked. She rushed in without glancing around the room, ordered, and had seated herself to wait for the burger hardly taking her eyes off the papers she clutched. It was ordered "take-away" so she was just sitting until it was done and bagged. She retrieved her order, had turned and even started walking out through the crowd, when she was jostled a little too hard by a waiting customer. The binders she was holding were jarred loose and tumbled to the ground causing her to tear her eyes away from the papers. As she looked up, her eyes unfortunately passed directly over the dumbstruck face of Poet and the girl he sat with.

ToastandJuice stopped dead in her tracks and for Turly time came to a standstill as he watched what was unfolding before him. The rest of the diner hardly paid heed. (Even Marty was swamped with orders and didn't seem to see what was happening.) A man stooped to pick up the binders for ToastandJuice, but when he had retrieved them, she no longer stood where she had dropped them. Instead, she was standing next to Poet's table. For a second, Turly thought nothing was going to come of it. Surly Poet wouldn't bring a contender to the same diner! It must be a friend, or relative. But the next moment proved Turly wrong. The chatter and usual sounds of a busy diner were cut with the words, "I thought you loved me?" uttered with such despair, and at such a volume that they cracked her voice as ToastandJuice pronounced them. She took a ragged breath, and followed with, "I thought she was over," clearly referring to the girl sitting with Poet.

Poet's face, from the angle Turly saw it, was ashen. He was caught at something that could not be explained away to ToastandJuice. And needed no explanation for the many bystanders. His head shook slightly and he glanced furtively around the room, but in the end he said nothing. And it wouldn't have mattered anyway, for ToastandJuice had wheeled around, taken her binders, and bolted for the door. That was the last time Turly had seen ToastandJuice. It had been weeks now and she had not come back. Memories maybe. Funny how one gets a picture of what reality is, and follows that reality even if it leads off an emotional cliff. She had believed Poet and thrown her heart into his abyss, only to have it smash on the reality of a short affair.

Turly thought ToastandJuice was gone for good. Then one Monday the ringer at the door chimed and when Turly glanced up from his grill, there stood ToastandJuice eyeing the room. Evidently she didn't see anything foreboding for she headed back to her table (not theirs by the wall), and when Marty put up the order, there in her scrawl was Toast, juic. Turly nodded to himself, thinking back to the book he'd seen her reading so long ago. Some lemmings survive the fall. He put an extra slice of toast on the pile. Along with Marty's "nice to see you again" he saw a smile cross ToastandJuice's lips as she opened her books and began to eat.

Turly watched her for a while; the diner was fairly empty at the moment. Then he realized something while watching her and Marty chat a little. ToastandJuice had not disappeared forever. She had not lost her life as a lemming who throws itself from a cliff. She had taken up her life again, and seemed genuinely happy again. At least she smiled and seemed herself with Marty. She had jumped, been broken, and recovered. She had taken the chance, trusted the odds and leapt into the dark. And she had not won, but she had not lost all either.

Turly mused over it for the few minutes Marty and ToastandJuice chatted. When Marty came back to the counter, Turly scraped his grill one last time, arranged his apron, and said "Martha, will you go out on a real date with me?"

Sheep

TERRY BAINS LOOKED OUT his bedroom window, tip-toeing to see over the shrub in the rear yard that partially hid Dolly. The Bain's property butted up against the Coldridge farm along the back yard, and from Terry's upstairs window you could see all the animals easily. That is, you could see them if they didn't crowd the fence, looking for the tallish grass that only got cut when the weed eater came out of the garage and coughed to life. That only happened when Terry's dad told Terry to do it. He never volunteered for that job.

Terry stood as tall as his 5'7" frame allowed. He could just see Dolly's rear haunches as she wandered near the fence. His right hand trailed to his neck and absently scratched at a pimple. He had too many pimples, and each and every one seemed inflamed all the time. (Though in truth, he only had a few on his teenage face.)

Dolly looked bad. He could see large areas of pink skin showing where her coat should be. Terry had no idea if her name was really Dolly or not. He had seen an article about cloning a sheep named Dolly years ago and had just sort of transferred the name to the largest female across the fence. Over the last year or so he had been watching his sheep (he even thought of her as *his* sheep) every day. Just sort of taking in her lifestyle. God knew he had none of his own to take up the time. His face wore a very dark look as he strained to see her. He squinted his narrow set eyes and tried to sort out just what exactly had been done to her three nights ago—the last time he'd seen her out in the field.

Dolly's haunch was torn up pretty bad. He could see tuffs of wool hanging from her, and large swatches of yellow stain on her bare flesh.

That must be disinfectant sprayed on by the vet, he thought. She limped badly in back, and it looked like red wheals ran the length of her rear leg. She shied from the other sheep who wandered around, keeping her injured side to the fence line, away from physical contact. Still, today she wandered out to the farthest reaches of the Coldridge property, and that had to signify something good. At least that's what Terry figured.

After watching her a few minutes Terry's calves grew tired of keeping him on his toes, and he settled down onto his feet. Dolly, who had now turned, slid from view, all except her docile face, which stoically stared over the field, her teeth grinding away at the grass. From this distance Terry could not really see her eyes, but he imagined a look of pain as she limped from place to place, grazing silently in the soft drizzle that dampened the air.

Terry surveyed the field, counting five sheep, one goat and a short black llama he dubbed Picard. (He seemed to be in charge most of the time, pushing all the sheep around.) After noting the usual number of animals, he sunk down into his desk chair and idly opened his math book. Geometry. Lines, shapes . . . and angles. He looked at the set of problems he had finished in class earlier, and casually read the next chapter. All the while he replayed what had happened to Dolly.

The dogs had come after midnight three nights ago. Picard was good about protecting the sheep, but there must have been a lot of dogs, because they got to Dolly pretty good. He had heard what he thought was screaming coming from the field, and had bolted awake the way you do when something is terribly wrong. There is no transition period from unconsciousness, to light slumber, to resting quietly, to wakefulness. Instead, his eyes had crashed open and all his senses had arisen within seconds. He rolled from his bed and stared out his window but could see nothing in the dark. The entire time though, he had heard snarling and that screaming; is someone being attacked!? He had then seen a light in the Coldridge's barn, and heard a gunshot. Then, everything had grown quiet again. No police came. No more noise erupted. He had stared across the field at the distant, dim light, seeing the Coldridge's moving about at the pens. Then they had turned the light off again, and that was it. Terry watched the darkness a while more, but nothing else happened, and shuttering with cold he had returned to bed and quickly fallen asleep.

The next day upon returning from school his mom had told him what had happened. Some pack of dogs had jumped the fence round the front of the Coldridge place and savaged the sheep. Well, had really only savaged Dolly. Mom didn't call her Dolly because she didn't know Terry had named the animal. She just said some sheep was hurt. Terry had not seen Dolly until today when he had come home, and straining on tip toes he had caught a glimpse of her wandering out in the field again.

That had been a crummy day. Jered Stark and his friends had come upon Terry at lunch and decided to have some fun with him. Jered was a senior with the brains of a sixth-grader. At least, that was the estimate Terry had of him. He thought Stark was border line retarded, though he knew that that really could not be the case. After all, Stark was smart enough to take normal classes, play sports, and actually do pretty well in band. In fact, and he hated to admit this, most people would consider Stark a pretty decent kid. Well, most people hadn't been punched in the face by him. Although, for the most part (and this was probably another sign of his intelligence) Jered hit Terry in the ribs and back. Nothing ever showed outwardly, unless he took his shirt off. Then the bruising could be pretty . . . psychedelic. Terry lifted his shirt and looked at the black and yellow flaring of color on his ribcage. It was better now.

He wasn't actually hit in the cafeteria by Jared. Jared just happened to "trip" next to him and dump food in Terry's lap by accident. After a profuse apology, and lots of covert snickering, Terry had been left alone to wipe hot sloppy joe sauce from his groin while Corine Traylor at once tried to help and not actually touch him in any way. Corine was nice, and she, Shiela Marten and Laura Long all ate with Terry and his friends. Terry had laughed as he swiped the goo from his crotch. He both wanted to move away from them and clean up alone and also stay with them and talk the whole scene into the past. Ron, Jerry, and the girls had not taken off, but sort of stood around silently sympathizing with Terry's plight. Finally, he had left to go to the bathroom and try some water on the mess. He limped away, trying to keep his flesh from the hot stain on his pants, looking stoically at the ground as he passed through the crowd.

Later, as Terry finished his few remaining Geometry problems in last period (he always finished homework in class), he had watched the soccer team load up their bus. They had an away game, but not too far so they could leave during last period. He closed his book with a few minutes to spare and reflected on the day. His pants were starting to dry a little. His groin would need a good looking over when he was in the privacy of his own room. There was no way he was going to ask to go home at lunch with the excuse, "My crotch was burned." He would see if there was any real burning at home when he could do it alone.

When the bell rang, Terry gathered his gear and headed out. He didn't really need to take any books home. He was smart, and usually finished all his work at school. However, as most smart kids will tell you, part of getting things done at school is being prepared. So he lugged a few tomes home in his pack: Geometry, biology, history. He would read the chapters tonight, and be ready for any homework handed out tomorrow. To Terry it wasn't brains he was gifted with . . . it was the ability to apply real work in the most productive manner. That and perseverance. That always helped get through those sax scales.

As Terry sauntered along the street, absently picking at a pimple, he eyeballed the weeds poking through the sidewalk. This was a mistake. Jered and his pack came up on him before he even knew it. He raised his eyes to glance at a bird, and there before him stood an ugly reminder of his scorched crotch: Jered Stark. Jered giggled and slapped Terry's pack to the ground as he yelled out, "Hey zit boy!" This elicited growls of laughter from the lesser lights that circled him. Terry tried to shy off and get his books quickly, but as he bent to retrieve geometry a foot kicked the book away. Simultaneously, a hard crack was laid across his lower back, knocking him down. "How're the balls?" barked Jered as he attempted to kick Terry in the area of his question. Terry curled tightly and warded the boot off just as he took another toe in the rear thigh. At the same time, someone bent and planted a solid blow to his ribs, crushing the wind from his chest. Fortunately, just when the savaging was about to get serious, a car rounded the corner and instead of a serious beating two sets of hands (belonging to Stark's minions) indelicately lifted him to his feet and shoved his book bag into his arms. Terry grimaced with the pain in his thigh and ribs, but took the items and watched as the pack retreated slowly from him, all the while eyeballing the intruding car and Terry himself. He also spared a glance at the car that had slowed and pulled to the curb. It was Corine. She waved Terry to the window and offered a ride. Terry gladly took it, gingerly settling onto the seat. It was when he had gotten home that he had heard about Dolly from mom.

As Terry remembered how he had felt being beaten by Jered and his buddies, he turned his thoughts to Dolly. It was amazing that the animal had survived and was out munching grass. Clearly the injuries she had received were not trivial. She was usually out in the field every day. Every single day. Without miss. Then, after the attack, she was in her stall for three days. Terry wondered what she must have been thinking and feeling as she lay in the hay, her sides torn up. Did she eat? Could she eat? How did she feel being alone through the day as the animals went out on their daily treks to the grassy field?

As Terry had watched her today, barring the clear evidence of a serious thrashing, she seemed to be exactly the same. She munched grass, wandered around—basically followed her group. Terry envied her. She seemed to throw the near death savaging off as though it were just another happening. And she was just a stupid sheep! He could never imagine himself, a fully rational human being, having the ability to just go on after such an experience. Terry's eyes trailed over to the clock. He had been musing for near on to forty-five minutes. He shook his head and cracked his history book. Chapter 4 before dinner he muttered as he fell into his nightly routine.

Corine sat in her room before supper with her flute music on the stand in front of her. She had played all the scales, and the music, and had hardly missed a note. However, it was not what she considered a good practice session. She couldn't help but think of Terry. They had never dated even once. They had known each other from grade school on, and she had watched her friend become the hunted by boys like Stark and his pals. It didn't make any sense to her either. She liked Jered! She sat near him in band, and shared other classes with him too. He was never, ever mean to her. But when he got with his friends, for some reason, he liked to pick on weaker kids. And Terry was a prime mark.

The thing that really amazed her was the way Terry went on. She had seen this same pattern before, beatings, humiliations and the like. One time, she recalled, Terry had been lifting weights in the gym on the mezzanine. The girls had gym class on the court below, while another class (mostly guys) had Weight Lifting on the mezzanine. Terry had taken the class thinking he could get bigger and then would be left alone. (She wondered how he got the nerve to join a class he knew was populated with jocks in the first place!) However, what happened was Terry had been squatting with very little weight (though it was an improvement for him), and Brian Stossel (one of Jered's friends) had jerked his shorts down! Most of the girls had looked up when the boys burst into laughter, and had spotted Terry in his jock strap. He naturally could not replace the weight quickly, so he was viewed for more than a few seconds. The remarkable thing was that the next day, he was back lifting weights (though this time with draw-string sweats). But the point was, he always returned. He always went back to his routine, his life, his pursuits. She shook her head at the music in front of her and said aloud, "I wouldn't have done that."

Shark

Dr. Marie Stavin angled across the parking tower's fourth floor garage toward her 1996 red BMW. She always seemed to get out late from her pediatrics practice. Although, she thought, that was not all bad. She missed rush hour, for instance. And looking out the open sides of the structure, she took in the city lights, bright and pretty in the cool fall air. It had always been her way to take life in the moment. That was why she was such a good children's doctor. She could focus on the person (and children were people too!) in front of her at the moment. They (and their parents) appreciated the sense of intimacy she projected. There was no feeling of hurry, no push to get the next patient in the door. When a patient looked at her deep brown eyes, they were met with an open, caring look in return. And that was different than the haggard, blank stare so many doctors responded with.

Marie's heels clicked on the pavement and echoed around the structure as she made her way to her car. It was the one perk she had gotten as soon as she could after opening her practice three years back. And although it was pricey, she loved the car. It was one of the big seven hundred series that she'd seen in England. Well, big for England that is. It handled well, and looked like the kind of car a Doctor should be driving. She convinced herself that it projected the air of competence her clients subconsciously expected. Whether that was true or not was not that important. She justified her owning (and paying for) the car that way.

Upon reaching the car, Marie clicked the remote and with the flash of lights and the snap of the lock she smoothly opened the driver's side door. Simultaneously, she tried to single out the ignition key and sweep the errant strand of black hair from her left eye. But she completed neither action. With the door still open and her hand still fumbling for the hair (why don't those clips stay put!) she was crushed forward against the car. The breath was torn from her lungs and her purses' contents clattered in all directions at her feet. Her knees cracked against the open door frame next to the seat, and her hands flailed against the car keeping her somewhat erect after the first blow. As she began to wheeze out a bewildered moan, white light suddenly speared her eyes as something again banged against her shoulder, bashing her face into the door just above the nose, and causing her to slump sideways to the ground. Marie's eyes slid across her surroundings dully as she fell, glimpsing a black shape cutting through the light. Her mouth tried to form the word "no" and one hand lazily attempted to ward off the predator as he/she/it approached once more. With one final spasm of clarity, Marie wondered where the predator had come from. Then she died as the .44 slug ripped directly through her face.

That night Kboy sold a red BMW by the lake to Craft, who, in turn, after chopping and refitting as necessary, sold it to Wheels, who scored $1600.00 dollars from a skank, drug dealer on the west side. Kboy then boosted a Chevy Gran Torino on 32nd and Lewis. He settled into the vinyl seat with $478.00 dollars in his pocket, and drifted off into the hot night heading south.

The paper noted that a doctor was murdered the night before by an unknown assailant.

As Marie Stavin died, Julia Jenson circled her lips into a tight "O" and blasted the breath from her eight year old lungs. The flames directly under the torrent of air snapped over, trembled for a split second, and vanished. Julia circled her head to the left and assaulted the candles there next. They too could not withstand her excited siege, and quickly fell under her breath. Finally, shifting right, Julia emptied her lungs on the few remaining sticks of burning wax. Some, the farthest from her, quavered, trying to somehow retain the right amount of heat, air, and fuel to remain lit. But in the end, Julia's little lungs prevailed and all the candles lay dormant, spewing little curly wisps of white smoke above a vanilla cake topped with blue icing and red letters which read, "Happy Birthday J!!" And the "J" was big and bright like Julia's smile.

Julia giggled and clapped her hands, beaming at dad and mom and little Lauren, who could do nothing but sit in her chair and flail her arms and legs around with a happy grin on her face. Julia giggled at that too, watching as Lauren's eyes now and again focused on her surroundings. She was only six months old, so she had never been to a birthday party before, but Julia was convinced she was having fun. Mom winked at Julia and handed her the large stainless cake knife they used to cut pastries at the Jenson house. Usually dad cut the cake for the family. He was an expert he'd said (though he always seemed to wink at mom when he made such pronouncements). However, this night Julia herself was going to cut her birthday cake.

The knife was big for her delicate hands. The handle was ivory, probably from some wild, rogue elephant, Julia had thought. The steel was bright under the lights and glinted around the room as she slowly drew the formidable weapon back and forth over the cake, deciding just what approach was needed to properly cut such a large piece of pastry. She finally settled on the first slice between the "H" and the "a." She then halved that piece, and gingerly wiggled them onto the little paper plates mom had laid next to her other hand. (They were yellow with balloons flying away from a little girl as she ran through a field.) Then, in a flash of inspiration, Julia deftly sliced a box of cake encircling the big "J!" She bit her lip pensively, and using her other hand (you could use your other hand to touch a piece of cake you yourself were going to eat), she wheedled the piece out of the body of the cake and onto another plate. At this point she triumphantly raised her eyes to her parents and grinned! They grinned back, and dad handed her a red plastic fork, ceremoniously laying it across his forearm as a knight would proffer a blade to his queen. Julia nodded her head, as any proper courtesan would, and took the fork, by the hilt as it were, and planted it into her big birthday cake "J." At this signal the whole family clapped and began to eat desert. Mom and dad commented on what a lovely and intelligent pair of girls they'd been blessed with. Julia savored the sweet taste of store bought birthday cake, and Lauren contented herself with spreading icing over her hair and cheeks, occasionally touching a bit to her tongue in the process.

Later that night, as Loree and Jason Jenson lay in bed, Jason tsk, tsk, tsked his tongue quietly reading of the death of a doctor up north. He finished the story, and turned his light off, thinking idly how large the ocean of people was and how lucky he was to live in a secluded inlet of that ocean. He drifted off to sleep, secure in the belief that because sharks attack only rarely, one need not fear the ocean.

Three nights later a Chevy Gran Torino grumbled into town and choked to a stop in the E-Z Rest Hotel's parking lot.

The sun was brilliant. Julia Jenson, Levi Cohen, and Sharri Peterson laughed and skipped along the hot sidewalk downtown toward Carrin's grocery. The girls had not been to Julia's birthday party last night, but today they were all going to have dinner at the Jenson's after playing. Dad was making hamburgers on the grill in back, and the Cohens and Petersons were coming over along with their daughters. The three were steadfast friends, and had been together at each other's birthday parties since they could remember. They all went to the same church, and same school, and liked to play the same things. They were like sisters in each other's eyes.

Levi was dark haired, and dark eyed. Julia thought she was by far the prettiest among them. She also thought her name, Levi, was exotic. Not like Julianne. In fact, even Sharri's name was more interesting than hers, because Sharri was short for Sharrina. That always made her envision a Jungle empress. And with her dark skin and flashing black eyes, she was exotic also. Julia was just plain when she looked at her two friends, but she didn't dwell on that. They loved one another and had so much fun together. Of course, Levi thought that Julianne Loreena Jenson had the prettiest name, and Sherri thought Julia's blonde, curly hair and bright blue eyes were the prettiest. It seemed like each one wanted the other's qualities. And were they to actually possess them, they would probably think the other's again were the most attractive!

In any event, the three were enjoying the hot day in their tank tops and shorts, skipping and giggling up the street to Carrin's for some candy. None of them ever noticed the slim (gaunt is a better word) young man leaning against the building by the alley across the street. He made no sounds, drew no attention to himself. He stood in a darkish pool of shadow cast by the overhang of the building across the alley from him. His black, stringy hair lay limp around his face, almost touching his shoulders. His eyes peered at the girls from a lowered head, looking through long, black lashes as the little ones danced along before his eyes, inviting him to play with them, maybe even kiss them. Kboy felt a slow stirring in his pants as he watched the little girls, and slipped back a little farther into the dark of the alley. He liked the blonde one.

Mr. Carrin was behind the counter as the girls swept into his shop. He knew them all by name, and greeted them accordingly: "Hello Miss Julia, Miss Levi, Miss Sharri." He was very formal every time he spoke with them. They each said "hello" back, and headed for the candy. After picking what they wanted, they plunked their money down on the counter, and waited for Mr. Carrin to give them their change. He sometimes talked about the weather or his knees when he was making change. Levi said he wouldn't say much until he got your money, and then would make you stand and listen to his chatter knowing you wouldn't leave without your change. Sharri had said she didn't mind, because he was always nice to them, and her grandfather was sort of the same way. Julia felt no commitment to either theory; she just tuned him out when he got boring.

Having gotten what they were after, the three ran out, almost knocking Mrs. Roland over in the process (which drew a barrage of, "What's wrong with kids these days!?" and, "Didn't your parents teach you manners!?"). The three yelled their apologies, and scuttled off down the sidewalk, leaving Mrs. Roland to turn her guns on Mr. Carrin. Maybe he would parry her attack with a treatise on the ills of arthritis of the knees.

All through the afternoon, the girls chattered and gossiped about school, and friends, and church, and adults. They wandered all over town: To the park and to the store (for more candy), and over to the mini-mall by the theater, and to Levi's and Sharri's houses. They were more motion than rest the entire day. And all that walking seemed to tire them not in the least. And all the while they were shadowed by a tall, thin, (gaunt really) black, stringy-haired man; though none of them ever noticed.

As evening approached, the three finally headed home to Julia's. It was almost four o'clock, and dinner was supposed to be at five. As they trudged up the walk (well, maybe they were just a teeny bit tired), they noted Levi's and Sharri's folk's cars parked in front. As they walked along the hedge around the right side of the house, they could hear their parents laughing and talking. They looked at one another, and hunkered down just at the corner of the house, planning their attack. At the count of three they leapt from their cover and screamed their greetings at the top of their lungs. After the shock retreated, Loree Jenson waggled her finger at her daughter and said, "You know better than to frighten people,

Julianne Loreena Jenson!" Julia giggled and nodded, noting her mom's twinkling eyes as she reprimanded her daughter's outburst. Of course Levi's and Sharri's moms chimed in, but in the end the girls knew their parents were only acting out a parental duty to quiet all children. They were not really in trouble. In fact, within minutes of the reprimands, they were all laughing and eating dad's grilled burgers with abandon.

None of them saw the dark eyes through the hedge in back as they watched the girls—and Julia in particular.

That night, Julia finally settled down in the cool of her darkened room and thought of the day she'd had. It was soooo fun! Her friends were fun, her parents were fun, and she was especially fun! She sighed and drifted off to sleep with the sound of the TV softly coming from the other room where her parents watched the news.

Kboy watched as the last light snapped off in the girl's house. He had noted with glee the open window of her room as mom and dad had snuggled her into bed. She was wearing a night shirt, for the air was cool now that the sun had set. She could not have been more than ten he figured. She had pretty blonde hair, and a happy smile. He could not wait to taste her lips; they were full, and red, and pretty. He lit another cigarette and settled into the front seat of his car. He had brought it up near the house about an hour ago, and the curb by the window was now littered with butts as he wiled away the time. Sometimes he would look through the pornography he had with him. Sometimes he would masturbate, and think of the girl. Mostly he just sat and smoked, biding his time until he could get her and they could go play together. Kboy was going to play this slow, not wanting to make any mistakes. Bad enough being in jail for boosting cars. He did not want to go to the pen for snatching some fun! He drew a long drag of hot smoke into his lungs, and flicked the butt from the window. Exhaling, he scrunched down and closed his eyes, trying to get a few hours' sleep while the parents dozed off.

About two a.m. Kboy's eyes slitted, then opened. He yawned, looked at his watch, and grinned to himself like a hungry barracuda preparing to strike. He glanced at the house, saw no lights or movement (what a jerk-wad town!), and pulled the lock up on his door.

As Kboy slipped from his car, he dropped his knife. He swore and quietly clicked the door shut before squatting down to retrieve it from the gutter. He reached for the hilt, and just as his hand touched it, his face was crushed into the side of the car. He groaned and dropped forward onto his knees, his hands resting against the cool metal of the car. He tried to grab the knife, but this time he felt a deep, tearing pain in his chest, and looking down, he saw a glint of metal protrude from his shirt on the right side. It looked like a piece of rebar! Kboy slumped to the side and onto his back sending waves of shocking pain through his body. He tried to scream, but had no breath in his torn lungs. His eyes quested for who or what had attacked him. He saw nothing at first, then realized he could see nothing but blackness. Slowly, sight returned though, and he made out a form standing over him, and directly in front of his eyes was a large black cylinder from which the .44 slug drove directly into his face.

Jason Jenson tsk, tsk, tsked his tongue as he re-read the story in the paper about the killing last night down the block. The man had been a stranger in town, and a known car thief. The police thought he might have been looking to steal a car to replace the Gran Torino he was found next to. It had been stolen, the paper said. Apparently, predator had become the prey.

Salmon

IT WAS FLAT AND dusty and straight.

The flat was flat like poured cement. It wasn't the rolling flat which is called flat but really is not. The flat was the flat of fields tilled until any bump or hollow is gone. Flat from the wind taking the soil year in and year out and moving it to fill in the holes and pare down the rises. The flat was flat like a person gets when every last remnant of newness is worn off the world leaving just the familiar.

The dust wasn't just the kind that sits on the ground and is stirred by tires or feet either. There was also the dust that hangs in the air, and clings to the flesh. The kind of dust that is whirled in dust devils giving the impression of a tornado until it touches you and you realize it is nothing but dust and wind cloaked in a tornado's guise. It is the kind of whirling dust that on the outside gives the impression of depth and inscrutability but in the end is just plain dirt.

And it was straight. Straight like a closed, unimaginative mind. It went straight out and straight in. No deviation at all. No up, no down, no left, no right. It started, and went straight, and came to an end. That was all there was to it. It was long. One could say that. But that isn't much of an attribute when long meant no more than lots and lots of the same, over and over and over again until you felt like you'd been on it forever.

It was flat and dusty and straight. And it was hot. But hot wasn't part of it. It was just how it was today. Hot like a furnace. Hot and sticky.

Corlen twitched his head as he scraped along flicking sweat from his eyelashes where it threatened to flood his eye with a salty twinge. His eyes were already red from being awash in hot, sticky sweat which he had not twitched away soon enough. He didn't look up. He didn't look to the right, or to the left. He didn't watch his feet plod along the dust, his boots stamping little puffs of dry dirt into micro clouds around his laces. He looked ahead, and down, so that his eyes rested on the ground a few feet in front of his body, which was slogging along the straight line toward life. At least he hoped it was toward life.

Corlen couldn't hear anything but the whisper of the wind and sigh of grass as it waved in the surrounding fields. He could no longer hear the echo of his folks in his head either. He was totally alone now. He was alone, and hot, and dusty, and sticky.

It was called a driveway. But for Corlen there was hardly ever driving. It was more a walkway in his mind. Sure, he'd driven it, but more often than not he'd walked it. He walked from one end to the other, out to the highway and back. Sometimes to get the mail. Sometimes to walk with Brittany, his dog. Sometimes he just walked it out to the end, the far off end, to see the highway and dream his dream. At times he felt like he had probably worn most of the bumps out of it. Though that was not true. It was flat, and straight ever since he could remember.

The highway was his dream. Or part of it anyway. HIGHWAY. The term itself held power for Corlen. It was different from a *low* way or *regular* way; different from a *boring* way or *average* way. It was the HIGHWAY. The only way out of his dead end eighteen year old life on a farm he didn't care about. Corlen had brothers to care about the farm. His dad could be proud of them. They tilled, and harvested, and planted, and sold. They did everything he asked with eagerness. It was their life. The highway was not a HIGHway for them. It was merely a roadway—a way from one farm, or auction, or sale, or visit, to another. It was not freedom, but passage. It was a short drive from life to an appointment and back again to life. For Corlen it was life itself. Or the promise of life.

A cloud of gnats buzzed across Corlen's path and spattered his downturned eyes with wings and his ears with noise. He hardly noticed them as he casually flapped one hand across his face and brushed them aside. The gesture could include all around him. Brush aside the dust, heat, grass, crops—life up to this point. Brush aside the interminable hours of harvesting and bucking hay. The years of numbing reminders about work, and responsibility, and making a way. Brush aside with a flick of the hand all the dead dreams and lost opportunities, the lectures on wasted time and laziness. Scatter them like the gnats and wade through to the highway. The way above, and out.

Corlen's case banged against his leg now and then. He was reassured by the feeling. Every now and then he'd hear a low rumble and glance off to the left and out. He could see maybe a glint of metal and he'd imagine the wind racing over a steel cab, the miles pouring by. He'd nod imperceptibly to himself and quicken his pace then for a little bit, eagerness overwhelming his muscles.

One of those would be his ticket. One of the fast moving steel monsters that ate up the highway and spat out miles. It wouldn't be the one he'd just seen—too far away. But it would be the next, or maybe the next. There were plenty and he'd catch a ride from one. They were long-haul truckers. They were freedom to Corlen. His eyes quested over the distance for another bit of freedom. After a while he returned to looking ahead and down, contemplating.

As he walked Corlen's right hand twitched in familiar patterns: Arpeggios, scales, chords, rest strokes, free strokes—all the hours of practice passed through his hand as it idly hung at his side. At the same time he recalled again his father's chides, "What are you gonna be? A musician? Do you know how many make it as musicians?" He never actually stopped Corlen, but he never actually helped either. He allowed guitar lessons 'cause mom wanted some music training. He went to the recitals, and permitted practice. He even bought a cheap guitar. But always there were the comments: "You need to find something that will make a living. You can't live off music." Always the underlying belief, "You can't make it—don't try."

Corlen shook a bit more sweat from his eyes and spat some dust. Like the previous wave of his hand it too said I'm spitting out this past— all of it.

Finally reaching the highway, Corlen stopped at the center of the drive on the edge of the blacktop. The heat radiated from the asphalt in waves making the air shiver and twist. Corlen watched the twisting, turning air for a moment thinking of the possibilities of life before him. No more straight, flat, dusty paths for his life.

He glanced up the road, to the east. Nothing in view right now, so he began to walk. The other way, to the west, to his new life. It was hotter on the asphalt next to the burning highway. He didn't care. Again his hand began to unconsciously pluck and push at invisible strings as it swung at his side. A grin stole over his face as he thought about how hard he'd worked. How many hours he'd spent late into the night working through music. He knew he was ready and a feeling of joy spread through his body starting at his moving fingers and ending at his sweat soaked hair. He almost yelled with the feeling of life flooding through him, the feeling of being that came from his music. He knew without doubt that he was going to be a hit—somewhere, soon.

Far off he heard a sound behind him. He stopped and turned, his eyes questing for the truck he hoped would pick him up. As it came over the small rise about three miles distant, he set his guitar case down and put out his thumb. He grinned thinking of his posture. Standing there in the heat, his thumb out to the highway. The universal symbol for looking to ride! His folks would disapprove. They thought to keep him on the farm a few more years by withholding a car. They never would have believed he'd hitch! But he didn't care, he just wanted to move. To make it happen. To live. And besides, he didn't have that far to go. Just a few hundred miles to the Roadhouse.

The distance was actually more than Corlen realized. The Roadhouse was almost 600 miles distant. Still, its reputation had spread even to the remote farm life of Corlen and his musician friends. It was common knowledge that agents and recording execs would come there to find new talent. Jimmy Cragen was discovered there! He was not a huge act yet, but he was on his way. And secretly Corlen thought he could play better than Jimmy. He'd heard him in concert, watched his hands. He knew he could play every song. He could play them better too. If Jimmy could be discovered, so could Corlen.

The truck was growing nearer now. Corlen could see the heat swirling around the engine as it plowed through the heavy air. He could just begin to hear the coming roar and imagined the driver down shifting as he spotted Corlen by the road. As the truck got even closer, Corlen picked his guitar up again and prepared to trot to where it would stop. He thought of how he'd say "hi!" and how the driver'd answer "where you going kid?" To the Roadhouse. To freedom. To life. The truck was no more than a 100 yards away now and surely the driver could see him. Corlen stepped tentatively away from the lane allowing room for the big rig to pull over. He raised his thumb a little higher and put a smile on his face.

The smile faded with the wind as it died. The truck had screamed past leaving Corlen standing in a swirl of dust and heat. He had turned at the last minute to avoid the shower of small granules of sand kicked up by the huge tires. His last image was of a man's face as it peered at him from the passenger side window of the cab. The face was wearing sunglasses and a ball cap and Corlen could have sworn its owner was shaking his head at him! Within a few seconds the last hint of sound had disappeared, the last remnant of blown dust had settled, and Corlen was again standing on the deserted highway watching the heat rise from the asphalt in twisting eddies. He sighed deeply, watched a hawk hover over the field across the way, and then began to walk again. This time his eyes did not smile, his fingers hardly played. He set his gaze ahead and down, like the driveway, and dropped into himself.

It seemed like a long while later that Corlen looked up again. He spotted a hawk sitting on a fence post next to the highway. It was looking at him as he trudged up the side of the road. He wondered if it was sizing him up. Probably too large for prey he thought, laughing a little. He had really expected to be picked up quickly when he hit the highway and walking so far without a ride had at first depressed him—made him wonder if his folks had been right. He wasn't ready to move on. But after walking awhile he realized that one truck does not a life destroy. There are always rides, always cars, always trucks. He wandered on in a somewhat better mood. He did wish he'd brought some water however. He had expected to be picked up within minutes (probably a foolish expectation, now that he examined it) and had really not thought he'd need any water. Now in the scorching sun he wished he'd been more practical—something his dad said he completely lacked. (Why else would he think he could make a living from playing the guitar?!)

As Corlen walked and thought, he again heard the distant sound of a truck passing along. He turned again and a ways down the road was another truck cruising toward him. He stepped to the lane and once more hooked his thumb out. He didn't put his guitar down this time. He wasn't taking a ride for granted. However, as the truck neared he heard the driver begin to downshift, and as he stepped back the truck rolled by him to a stop some fifty feet beyond where he stood. He ran to the cab and leaped up onto the foot step. He pulled the door open and was greeted by a smiling man and a small terrier of some kind. It was brown and gray, and seemed somewhat offended at being forced to relinquish its seat. As Corlen stepped up however, the driver picked the dog up and deposited it behind him in the cab. He asked "Where you headed, kid?"

Corlen grinned as his ruminations came true when he said, "To the Roadhouse."

The man grinned back, eyed the guitar for a second, and nodded understanding. He had picked up many young men headed to the Roadhouse. He knew which one. He said, "Put your guitar behind you there." And then Cobalt jumped into Corlen's lap reasserting himself. The man quickly asked if Corlen minded the dog. Corlen shook his head and scratched Cobalt along the back. At which point, after a quick sniffing, the little dog lay down and promptly set itself to napping. Mack Dreyton smiled at the dog and said, "He's good company, but not much for conversation on a long-haul." Corlen laughed and settled into the seat to watch his life unfold before him.

As it turned out, Mack had been driving this road for years. And he did indeed know the Roadhouse well. He and Corlen chatted about the weather some, about Cobalt, and animals, and about Corlen's music. Corlen especially loved to talk about it. Mack even had him pull the guitar out and play some. It was quiet without the little amp, but the guitar was acoustic so it was not imperceptible. Corlen ripped out some blues, jazz, and some rock and roll. His fingers felt great considering they had not played for a few long hours and he'd been walking in the sun. All the walking makes a person's fingers grow thick and stiff. All that blood rushing to the hand as it swings at the end of the arm, Corlen supposed.

Mack was appreciative of Corlen's talent and made him feel good. He hardly knew the man but liked him a good bit from just the few hours of driving. Mack had four boys and a girl at home. One of the boys wanted to play sax in the Marine Corp band. Mack was very proud of all of them, and especially of the one headed for the service. It was a far cry from Corlen's dad, who discouraged his music whenever opportunity arose. He pretty much discouraged everything that didn't mesh well with his own interests. As Corlen listened he found himself wishing he had had a father like Mack. Not that his own dad didn't care. He probably did. But caring with no action seemed the same as not caring in Corlen's mind.

It was near to five o'clock when they passed a small diner. Mack said he ate there all the time and wanted to stop for a bite. Corlen agreed. When they parked and it was time to get out Corlen hesitated unsure of what to do. He did not want to presuppose that Mack was going to give him a further ride, though they were clearly going the same way. Mack saw him reach back for his guitar and cleared the matter up saying, "You can probably just leave that if we're going on."

Corlen smiled at him and said, "Thanks, I wasn't sure if you wanted me along any farther."

Mack laughed, answering, "Heck kid, I love the company. You're doing me a favor as much as I am you." At that he slammed his door and came around to check the lock on Corlen's after he had jumped down. He said he never left his truck unlocked when Cobalt was along. Corlen noted that Mack had cracked his window before he closed the door. Cobalt was in the driver's seat and looked like a very ugly little troll driving a big truck. It was probably the red bandana around his neck that gave the impression of a little person. Mack saw Corlen looking at him and said, "He's pretty funny when I put his little cowboy hat on!" They both laughed at the thought of Cobalt driving an eighteen wheeler in his cowboy hat and bandana.

Dinner was a pair of hamburgers. They were good, though Mack said there was another place where he'd had the best food ever. The cook was named Turly, and he had a reputation for great food, especially his potatoes. But dinner was nonetheless good. Corlen finished eating first and excused himself to go to the restroom. As he stood over the sink, he leaned on the porcelain and stared at himself in the small mirror. He was so grateful for the ride he'd gotten. And Mack was a good man. He'd met truckers before who he wouldn't have ridden with had they been the last ride in the world. But Mack had made him feel like he mattered; like his life was not a foolish pursuit of wasted time. Funny how some people make you feel good about yourself.

Before Corlen returned he stopped at the cash register and paid their bills. It was the least he could do for the generosity he'd been shown. One thing mom had drilled into him was appreciation of a kindness, and he definitely appreciated Mack. He then walked back to the table and plunked himself down with a smile. Mack was perusing the local paper they'd found on the seat and drinking his coffee. Corlen watched him a minute, and then asked, "Why did you help me out?" He knew Mack had said he liked to talk while he drove, but he seemed too caring at times for just that.

Mack looked up at him and smiled. He said nothing for a second and then fired back "Why not?" Corlen didn't take the answer as a brush off, but as a real question to which Mack expected an answer. Corlen twisted his lip in thought for a moment, then said, "Well, I could be a weirdo. I could have had a gun and attacked you. And even if I were a normal guy, you probably won't see me again once we part ways."

Mack assessed his answer and said, "True, very true." But I didn't pick you up for your benefit. I picked you up for my benefit. When I was a kid, probably your age or so, I was out on my own. My dad and mom had thrown me out of the house. It wasn't their fault and I don't blame them. At least not anymore. (This last he said chuckling a little, which made Corlen feel a little more at ease. When Mack had started talking he had sensed a gravity about his casual words. As though something important were being shared in the guise of a little personal history.)

"Anyways," continued Mack, "I was living sort of hand to mouth on the road. I would hitch rides when I wanted to go somewhere, and just settle into part time jobs and a cheap hostel or something for as long as I liked. Then I'd move on. I enjoyed seeing things. I guess that's why I like trucking, 'cause I enjoy seeing places and moving around some. Course, my wife has taken a lot of that outa me. Now I like being with her and my kids.

Well, one day I was hitching a ride and got picked up by a couple guys in a pickup. They said get on in back and I did thinking nothing of it. Long story short, they kicked the living snot outa me and took my wallet. I was hurt pretty bad and they'd left me out in a field a few miles from the road. So I had to walk and crawl back to the road all busted up, and with no money. I was sitting by the highway not even thumbing when a guy stopped and picked me up. He not only gave me a ride, but he took me to a clinic and then a shelter for some new clothes and food and stuff. I told him I'd be around for a while and I wanted his name and address 'cause I was going to pay him for his help. He just smiled and said something that stuck hard with me: "You can pay me by giving back to someone else what you got."

I'd been raised a Christian by my folks and pretty much discounted most of what they taught me. I guess I was too silly at the time to think about it and had it too good. But after a good pounding and having everything taken away, I suddenly saw lots of things in a new light. I knew this guy was a Christian too 'cause he had a bible on the seat when he picked me up. He never mentioned it once the whole time. I found out later he was a music minister at a church. I never went and heard him lead or anything. But I remembered what he said. I owe him something. And I owe myself something."

At this point Mack looked Corlen right in the eye and grinned. Corlen smiled back, unsure of what to say. But Mack continued, "I picked you up 'cause I want to do right by a man I met one time. He totally changed my life, and didn't even ask my last name. I'm passing on what he gave me."

Corlen swallowed in a tight throat. It was not the story itself that had struck him. He'd been raised Christian too. Been to church all his life. He'd heard lots of stories about people and kindnesses and whatnot. It was the directness, the intimacy of what Mack had said that held him. He did not see Mack as some acquaintance sharing a story. He was giving Corlen truth, personal truth. Truth drawn up from inside where most people aren't allowed to see. He was opening himself for Corlen to see. And he hardly knew the man. It was something he'd sensed from the moment they began to talk. Mack was a man of integrity and honesty. He had an agenda and it was for good. Not good for himself alone either, but for good, period.

Corlen nodded tightly as Mack smiled at him. He still didn't know what to say. Mack saved him again though and said, "Well, better pay our bills and get on the road, eh?"

Corlen grinned, and said, "I covered it. Least I could do for your help." He expected to have to argue over it with Mack. But Mack just grinned at him and said, "Well thanks Corlen, that was good of you." Corlen lowered his head at the praise and fidgeted a little in his seat. He felt like it was so little for all that Mack had done. And not just the ride. The ride seemed the smallest of things at this point. Mack had made him feel like a man, a good man. Like a person who could be someone, and was worth listening to. He didn't know exactly how he'd done it, but Mack had given Corlen confidence and pride and a good feeling about himself and others. The check was a small recompense for such a gift.

They headed out to the truck. As they approached they saw Cobalt up in the driver's seat straining to look out the window. His size prohibited much of a view when he abandoned his place on the dashboard. However, he knew Mack was coming and wanted to get down when the door opened, so a few seconds of sight was all he needed.

When Mack opened his door Cobalt barked and jumped about. Mack didn't pull him down though. Instead he patted his leg and said,

"C'mon studly! C'mon down!" Cobalt's tail looked like it would wag off, as he eyed the precipice before him. After a few hesitant moves, he flew down the path he always took: To the floorboard, out the door to the first step, down to the running board, and onto the ground. Why he hesitated only he knew, because he'd gotten out alone thousands of times. Mack laughed and said to Corlen, "He thinks if he acts a little skittery I'll pick him up and carry him down. The little con artist! I'm on to him though. He gets down just fine without me."

Corlen noted with a grin, however, that the minute little Cobalt's feet hit the ground Mack picked him up and hugged him before letting him wander around and stretch his legs. The two men got up into the truck and sat with the doors open while they watched Cobalt pick the right place to relieve himself. Then he scampered around a little enjoying himself. Mack explained that the little dog was trained pretty well and didn't run off. He just stretched his legs for a bit and came back. And sure enough after ten minutes Cobalt was whining to come back up into the cab. Mack laughed at him and after a few unrequited plaintive barks Cobalt proved that he could easily get back into the truck too. He just preferred to be lazy and be picked up.

The day disappeared into night as the two drove toward Corlen's destination. They talked for a good deal of the time. But the last hour they just drove along in the dark. Corlen could not believe how lucky he'd been to get such a lift. He remembered the awful feeling he'd had when the first truck had passed him by without even slowing. How he had been angry about not getting the ride he so desperately wanted. He looked back now and found he desperately did not want that ride at all. And he hardly wanted this one to end. He felt like a bird stuck at the point of flight. He was so confident and comfortable around Mack that he felt he could do anything—fly like an eagle. But when he thought of actually leaving the cab and this new friendship, he found he didn't want to! Of course he had to; there was no way to stay in a stranger's cab (though he did not really consider Mack a stranger anymore). It was strange. He supposed he would have to just deal with it when it arrived. But for now he was content to ride and contemplate.

Coming around a long, smooth corner, Mack said, "The Roadhouse is on the left just up here a bit." And sure enough it was. It had a large, red, neon sign that declared "Roadhouse" on the front, and the parking lot was packed with cars and trucks. Mack didn't stop as they went by.

They had talked a bit about it and He had recommended an inexpensive Motel just up the road about a quarter mile. It too was on the outskirts of the little town. He said the rates were good, and the rooms were clean. And Corlen agreed he wanted to get a shower and a good sleep before he approached the manager for some stage time.

When Mack had stopped the truck Corlen was at a loss. Mack saw his indecision in his eyes and said, "Now I'll be passing along here pretty consistently for the next few months. I have a permanent run for a while. I may just stop in and hear you play if you don't make it big too quickly and leave."

Corlen grinned and shook his hand, saying, "Sounds like a deal!" He pulled his guitar out and stepped out onto the running board. He turned and patted Cobalt once more and said, "Thank you—for everything."

Mack grinned at him and said, "You can thank me by passing it on Corlen." And with that they parted ways. Corlen stood in the parking lot under the lamp for a few minutes watching the truck disappear from view. When it had been gone for a while he sighed, turned, and headed for the office of the Motel.

Apparently other musicians had stayed at the motel—The Lazy Night. And some had left an unfavorable impression, because the first words from the old clerk's mouth after "Number twenty-five on the end" were "and we don't truck no loud music late nights!" This was said while he eyed Corlen's guitar suspiciously like it not only may hold a guitar (which would surly give out loud music) but might also be a bomb or old time tommy-gun.

Corlen almost burst out laughing at the old guy staring at him. He was sort of a caricature of a desk clerk. He was one of those desk clerks from a Perry Mason episode, or from a cheap Who-done-it. Corlen supposed even those characters were based on some shred of fact; and here it was looking him in the face and saying, "We don't truck no music late nights!" Corlen grinned and replied soberly, "no sir."

The clerk must have taken the grin in the wrong way because he frowned and said, "Well, see that it don't happen! Or else I'll have you outa here!" And with the "outa here" he hooked his bony hand over his head with such a jerk that Corlen thought he'd tear his arm off, or accidentally poke himself in the eye! Corlen pursed his lips trying to stem the laughter that threatened to erupt from his mouth. He could just envision the old guy with his bony arm laying on the counter and a thumb stuck in his eye-hole! He'd look at Corlen and squall, "No music boy! You hear me! My Arm!!"

As Corlen got out the door he almost exploded with laughter. The skinny old clerk watched him proceed toward his room. Every time Corlen snuck a peek back to see if the old guy was still watching he'd laugh harder. All he could see in his head was the old guy holding his right arm in his left hand, shaking it at Corlen and yelling at the top of his lungs, "NO MUSIC, BOY! NOMUSICBOY!!"

The old clerk, ticking his teeth and muttering about the indolence of youth, just watched the young man recede. Musicians. Hmmmmph.

The room was what Corlen expected. One small single bed, a tiny bathroom, an old color TV, and a small cooking area (Corlen had requested a room with a kitchen). He was actually surprised at how clean and pleasant the room was, for from the outside he wondered if Mack had remembered this place very well. It had appeared somewhat run-down with peeling paint in places and a rather shabby "Lazy Night" sign in front.

He remembered the trips his folks used to take him on when he was little. They stayed in nice little motels too. Much like this one. Except there would be two big beds: One for mom and dad and one for the boys (which could get very crowded at times!). The only difference was that they would arrive frazzled from an eight hour car trip filled with threats of violence for being "too loud" or "not looking out the window at the scenery" or "complaining about being hungry," etc. Dad liked to drive a lot, and didn't like distractions from worn-out children kept cooped up in a car for five hours at a time. Corlen remembered the relaxing trip with Mack and how different it was compared to the tense hours spent with his folks crammed in a car with his brothers.

Corlen put his guitar down and unhooked the satchel attached to its case. It was small, but he thought it held enough. His mom had made it for him after he described what it was he wanted. It was large enough to hold some clothes and traveling gear, provided you went light. Corlen didn't have much, so he pretty much always went light. Of course this was the first time he really "went" too. He had not needed to carry clothes with him in the past. He'd used the satchel when he went to a friend's house sometimes, but never for traveling. Now he was seeing just how little it held! However, he took his clothes out, and hung them in the little crevice by the bathroom.

He then sat on the bed and played a little guitar, relaxing himself. His fingers were a smidgen stiff, but he loosened them with scales and a few songs. As he played his mind wandered to how it would be when he had a limo to haul him around, and concert tours, and CDs and an entourage. Life would be great! And all he'd do is play music all the time.

After relaxing for a while Corlen took a shower and turned on the TV. The room supposedly had cable (the sign said they all did), but "cable" seemed to mean basic cable: Local stations only. He surfed around for a bit and landed on a PBS show about bears. They were lunging around in a river hooking salmon with their claws and devouring them. The salmon, on their part, were attempting to make it upstream to spawn. They'd maneuver through small obstacles, then larger ones, then attempt to go through the bears if they could. But it seemed a desperate struggle.

The bears apparently knew the salmon were coming because they'd turn out en masse to greet them at the appointed time of year. The fish would fly through the air, leaping up the small waterfalls, trying to get to where they were born so they could make the next generation go through the same trials every year! Corlen rooted for the bears. And they were doing a good deal of salmon eating by the looks of it. But the salmon didn't stop. Even when they were hurt they would still head toward their goal. More often than not, once hooked, they were in no shape to move on and they would circle about miserably until some bear ate them, or maybe one of the circling birds. Corlen watched wondering why the salmon didn't just settle for a different pool in which to spawn. Why did they have to keep trying for that one pool? He supposed it was something peculiar to salmon. They couldn't take "NO" for an answer.

After watching for a bit, Corlen turned out the lights and turned on his travel radio. He lay in the bed, arms behind his head, rehearsing what he would say the next day to the Roadhouse manager. If he could just get a chance to play he could prove he was worth a gig. He'd bring his guitar and go early. Probably less people around early in the morning, and he might be able to corner the manager.

The next morning was cold and crisp and sunny. Corlen awoke early and grabbed a shower before heading out. He put his guitar away, gathered his favorite picks in his pockets and stepped out into the morning air. He was nervous, and hoped the quarter mile walk would calm him some. As he headed to the Roadhouse, he again thought about how to go about convincing the manager to let him play. It struck him that he had counted on a house band to back him since Jerry, Brian and Tim had not shared his vision of music in the big leagues. They shared his dad's vision of farming in the big leagues. Consequently they had not come along on his journey to stardom. There was no convincing them now, and he was stuck with his plan of auditioning alone. He could make his instrument sing well enough alone that he did not worry much about the audition. It was the ongoing performances that really needed a band to go right. Still, he knew this would turn out well, he was feeling more and more confident as he approached his destination.

The parking lot was more crowded than he had expected. There were a lot of big trucks and not a few pickups filling the spots. He'd blanked out the fact that the Roadhouse was not just a music place, it was a diner. It had a business to do consisting of more than producing music stars. And the sign on the front door pointed out that it did its business "24 hours a day!" Corlen pushed the door open and shattered his vision of the Roadhouse.

He had expected something out of a movie: Saw dust floor, maybe truckers and bikers holding a tense truce while guzzling beer. The kind of gritty bar that a place named "Roadhouse" should be. Instead it was sort of a cross between a Denny's and a bar. It had nice floors, and comfy booths as well as tables. The stage was pretty good sized, and there was a small dance floor in front of it. The waitresses wore the usual polyester one piece dresses (in red), and you could smell the breakfasts being cooked back in the kitchen. He thought the place was going to Rock! And now he wondered how anyone made it here!

Still, he knew the reputation the Roadhouse had, and Mack seemed to know it too. He walked up to the counter and a young woman said, "Hi, one today?" Corlen nodded and said "Yes, and is the manager here now?"

Terri (so her name tag said) smiled and said, "The morning manager is here. Do you want to talk to him?" She eyed Corlen's guitar case doubtfully as she asked and her tone made Corlen think it may not be of use. However, he said, "Yeah, I would if he has time." Terri nodded and said she'd send him over when he came out of his office, provided Corlen could wait. He said that would be fine and followed her to a table by a window. She left him a menu and he scanned the choices. A few minutes later another woman (Donna) came by with a pot of coffee and asked if Corlen was having. He definitely was, he said, and she smiled and agreed, "I need my jolt every morning too!" They nodded in unison, and she left, returning a few minutes later to see if Corlen was ready to order. He had eggs and bacon.

About half way through breakfast, the manager came up to the table. His name-tag said "Mr. Johanson." Corlen quickly swallowed the mouth-full of toast he'd just bitten off, and tried to stand, knocking the table enough to spill some coffee out of his cup. The manager waved him to sit back down, noticing the guitar sitting by the table. He sat down across from Corlen and smiled as he said, "What can I do for you sir?" Although, it seemed apparent to Mr. Johanson that he already knew somewhat what he could do for Corlen.

Corlen went entirely blank. He could not remember all the catch phrases he'd been rehearsing. He could hardly remember his name when he introduced himself! He stuttered out, "H-h-hi. I'm Corlen Grimes." Corlen's mind screamed at him the minute he said it: Corlen Grimes! What the hell kind of name is Grimes!? That's no star's name! Why didn't I change that!? Mr. Johanson didn't seem fazed in the least. He nodded and said, "I take it you play guitar Mr. Grimes?"

Corlen nodded back and said, "I was hoping to play here. I wondered if I might audition for you." "*You're an idiot! That was smooth… real smooth!*"

Mr. Johanson answered politely, "Well Mr. Grimes, I really have no say in who plays here at night. I'm the day manager. You need to speak with Red Kaiser; his nick-name is Kodiak Red Kaiser. He comes in around four. I could leave a note telling him to expect you if you wish?" Mr. Johanson didn't seem too interested in Corlen and his music. He had probably seen his fair share of musicians.

Corlen said that would be great, and standing up (without incident this time) he offered his hand to Mr. Johanson before he left. He hoped to at least make a good impression so the note left on his behalf would be a positive one. Mr. Johanson shook his hand brusquely and left. Corlen slumped back into his seat and stared at his cooling breakfast. That had been a disaster. It had lasted perhaps three minutes, and he had all but made himself seem like a brain-dead yokel. Corlen Grimes! He breathed a heavy sigh.

Corlen paid his bill and left. He lugged his guitar back to his room and set his watch alarm to ring at 3:30. He pulled the guitar from its case and absently played around while he brooded over his morning fiasco.

The note would probably say, "New yokel in town wants to see you Red. Brush off!" Corlen sighed and concentrated on some songs.

As four o'clock rolled closer, Corlen again picked up his guitar. He was in high spirits after playing for a good long while. He realized again that he was a great guitarist. And he felt confident that he would do well with Kodiak Red. He grabbed his guitar and set off down to the Roadhouse once again. This time he was going to make it happen!

Entering the front door he was greeted again by a young lady, but this time her name-tag read "Diane." He asked if Mr. Kaiser was in, and mentioned he'd talked with Mr. Johanson earlier. He told her it was about a music job, and she went off to inquire about an appointment. A few minutes later she came back and directed him to Mr. Kaiser's office in the rear of the building by the kitchen. Corlen's stomach growled as he passed between the grills, smelling the burgers and other entrees. He was hungry but too anxious to eat!

Mr. Kaiser was a little, sort of fat man with a shock of red hair. (Corlen figured that was why they named him "Red" perhaps.) Corlen stood in the doorway as Mr. Kaiser turned in his desk chair. He waved Corlen in to a seat across from him and said, "Corlen Grimes is it? Sten Johanson left me a note about you. He said you were asking about an audition?" He seemed sort of gruff to Corlen—very "stick-to-business."

Corlen swallowed and nodding, said, "Yes sir, I wondered if I might play some for you and perhaps get some stage time."

Kaiser chewed his lower lip and shot back, "Sure, let me hear something." He seemed ready to listen and equally as ready to dismiss Corlen. It was more distracting than Corlen thought it would be.

Corlen took his guitar out and started to play a little. He ran some difficult licks, and showed off his range. The whole time Red sat, seemingly non-plussed about anything Corlen was doing.

When Corlen finished, he'd barely looked up when Kaiser spit at him, "So do you have any experience at all?"

Corlen answered, "I've played at church and at school. And I've played at the fair some." He could not believe how lame he sounded. Couldn't Mr. Kaiser just listen to his playing?

Mr. Kaiser shook his head a little and said, "I have a pretty full bill of musicians right now. And they all have more experience. I really can't use someone right now. And besides, it's just you, right? There's no band?"

"No sir, just me. I was thinking the house would have a band for me to play with" answered Corlen.

Mr. Kaiser "harummphed" as though disgusted. He then said, "Well, I'll tell you what. I just can't use you right now. Maybe farther down the road if you come on back. I have a full list of acts for the next month right now, and could pencil you in for the month after that. Maybe. We'll see. But I have nothing right now for you."

Corlen's eyes glazed slightly. Mr. Kaiser seemed impatient to get him out of his office. He had slapped him down and tossed him aside. Corlen stood and put his guitar away. He shook Mr. Kaiser's hand (which seemed like an imposition on the man), and left. Mr. Kaiser hardly paid the boy a minutes notice when he turned back to his desk.

Corlen stepped out the front door of the Roadhouse and sat on one of the long benches stationed there. It was still sunny, and warm now after a full day of sun. Things were not going right at all. He only had a few weeks of money, and here he had no chance to even play and earn more for at least a month! And Mr. Kaiser acted like he didn't even know music at all, like he didn't care either. Corlen shook his head as all his dad's warnings flooded his brain, "How are you going to make a living playing music? You need a real job that will pay the bills. Only a few can make it" (meaning you're not one of them).

After a few minute of watching people come and go, Corlen got up and headed back to his room. He intended to come back that night and listen to some of the bands. He'd be back every night until next month if possible. Of course that all depended on how he'd work out his finances.

In the early evening, Corlen wandered into town. He needed to pick up some food at the store. As he bagged his groceries he noticed a board on the wall of the store which read "Ads." He walked over to it and began to scan down the little note cards and scraps of paper advertising odd jobs, cars, rooms, and other paraphernalia. His spirits brightened somewhat as the possibilities of work and a place to stay opened before him. He needed three things basically: A room, food, and a job to pay for them. Preferably all in walking distance because he had no car.

As he read down the notices he came to one for the store he was standing in right now. "Help wanted—stocker." He looked around at the small store and wondered how that position had not been filled already. The work couldn't be that involved (there just weren't that many shelves!).

He took the ad from the wall and walked over to the cashier who'd just rung him up. He smiled and said, "Ma'am, is this job still open?"

She looked up from her furious nail filing (maybe that's why they needed a stocker, the checkers only checked), and said, "What's that, hon? The shelf stocker?"

Corlen nodded.

"Yeah, I think it is. You need to talk to Mrs. Cannager though. Over there. The white door." She pointed with her nail file to a white door across the little store. It stood a few inches ajar and a light showed in the room.

Corlen thanked her and headed for the door. He set his groceries down by its side and knocked. A woman's voice came from inside, "Come in!"

Corlen entered and found an older woman sitting at a little desk doing something with a pile of papers. She peered at him with old looking cat-eye glasses and said, "Yes, may I help you?"

Corlen put his hand out and said, "Hello. I'm Corlen Grimes." The woman reached over the desk and shook it lightly, then she motioned to a little chair by the wall. Corlen continued as he sat, "I noticed you had a card advertising a stocking job?" He tried to read her face for the rejection he was becoming accustomed to. To his surprise she smiled and said, "Yes, yes. That job is still open. Been open a long time. Are you new around here? It seems like so many young folks move, or want more pay, or don't like the hours, and all sorts of other excuses why they can't work. We just couldn't fill it! No one was interested."

Corlen softly breathed a sigh of relief. Finally! Something goes right! He said, "Well I'm just in town yesterday. And as long as I can live off the pay, I'm interested."

Mrs. Cannager sat back in her chair and went on, "I guess it depends on how you live whether you can live on the pay. It starts at $6.35. If you do well, you may get a raise. Course, you'll have to fill out an application. I need to know some details." She handed him a sheet of paper taken from the bottom drawer of her desk. It was not very complex. Schooling, job history, place of residence.

"Hmmm," thought Corlen. Place of residence could be a stickler. He thought he'd broach the subject right off and take the consequences. "As I said, I'm just new here yesterday. I don't have a place of residence yet. I'm staying at the Lazy Night motel right now until I find something I can afford."

Mrs. Cannager looked at him as though appraising the young man. She then said, "I may be able to help there too. I have a room near the back that I rented out to the last stock boy. If I hire you, would you be interested in that too? I could take it out of your pay. It has a small stove and such, and a bed, but not much else."

Corlen was feeling better and better. He'd swum around another obstacle and found a way to move forward. He nodded and said that would be great, provided she hired him.

Mrs. Cannager said "ok" and told him to fill out the application. Corlen secretly thought that she'd be willing to take anyone by the sound of it. It was her good luck to get him, he thought. Of course, it may not turn out so good if he quit in a month. But that would be a month of good, hard work she got too. So he didn't mention his musical ambitions. She told him to come back later that day and she'd have an answer for him. So Corlen left with his groceries and walked back to his room.

Eight months later Corlen lay on his bed in the back of the store, having just finished his shift. He was propped up against his pile of pillows and had a bowl of Raman balanced on his stomach. As he ate, he casually flipped through the meager selection of channels on his used black and white TV. Channel four: News, Channel six: Wood working show, Channel seven: News again, Channel eight: News again (lots of local news for such a boring place, he thought), Channel ten: Re-run of the stubborn salmon documentary (PBS ran their documentaries a lot). He gulped down the remainder of Raman, walked over, and flicked the TV off. He had practicing to do. And big Kodiak Red Kaiser said that next month he might have an opening.

Rabbit

JENNIFER STILMAN AND MARY Cortage were polar opposites. On the outside, their differences were obvious: Jennifer had light blonde hair; Mary had blazing red. Jennifer's eyes were light blue; Mary's were dark brown. Jennifer was a petite 5'3" and 106 pounds; Mary was a voluptuous 5'8" and 137 pounds. The one outward fact that was true of both was that they were attractive. But most would describe Jenny as a wholesome next-door neighbor type, whereas Mary would be described as a Bombshell.

On the inside the differences were just as pronounced. And yet, they stemmed from similar skills: Both had a knack for looking into people. They could size others up and know them with very little contact. Both were well educated, having graduated from good colleges. Both were strong willed and desired new challenges. The difference was this: Jennifer was open and friendly. She could make people feel good about themselves. Mary was open and friendly too, and could make people feel what she wanted.

The one thing they shared entirely was their dislike of one-another.

One down, twenty to go. Jen was so bored with this job! Typing, filing, editing, appointments. She wanted to move up. She wanted to be office manager. The job was open, and there was no reason she couldn't fill it. It wasn't as though she lacked experience. She had been with this company for four years! She had proven herself, worked her way up. She was ready to take the responsibility. All she did now, for the most part anyway, was edit copy. And she was sick of it! She sighed and started on the next blurb to be edited. Sick as she was, she was going to do a great job. Even if it meant being bored for another four years!

Mary arranged the pictures again. She was tired of arranging pictures. She had done it for eight months and was ready to quit. She stood in her cubicle and looked around. No heads. Everyone was working away. Drudgery! And all these drones. They bought into the program and walked through life like automatons. Morons.

Mary was not an automaton. She glanced at the pictures on her screen. Who cares!? Whatever she did would be ok. It's not like any of them could do it any better than she. Except Jen. Jen was always getting "Office worker of the week" or "Office worker of the month." She was always praised by that stupid Mr. Hancock. Until he died that is. Mary snickered to herself. Poor baby had an accident. Poor little boy's gun went boom boom in his face! She giggled. What a wussie! She had screwed him for a few weeks. Until he got boring. Then she had dumped him like a sack of shit. After she showed him the pictures she'd taken of them that is.

Little wussie Hancock had cried and whined: "I have kids! I thought you loved me!" She smiled at it. What a crybaby he'd been. It's not like she'd asked much. Just quit and recommend her for his job when he left. The asshole had quit all right. Quit life. He'd left a typical crybaby note about loving his wife, and making mistakes, and being ashamed. He hadn't mentioned her (he was so stupid!). And more importantly, he hadn't recommended her either. So she had mailed the pictures to the grieving widow. They had not shown her face, so she had taken no chances. Only his big, fat, naked ass and a woman in a cat suit! It was pretty funny watching the poor widow at the funeral. And when she'd gone up to her and given her condolences! At this Mary openly laughed in her cubicle! "I'm so sorry Mrs. Wussie. He was much beloved." Mary sat down and covered her mouth to hide her guffaws.

Jen finished blurb number two and pushed back from her desk. She got up and walked down the aisle to the water cooler for a drink. As she passed Mary's cubicle she noticed the woman giggling about something. She hurried by hoping not to be spotted. Mary was a horrible woman. She couldn't stand her. She had disliked her from the day she'd come to work. Jen was a likable and easy going woman. But Mary had crawled up under her skin like a tick from the moment she'd met her. She was all smiles and openness on the outside, but her words were condescending and rude. And she was always hinting about others. Things like, "I saw Maria with a man the other day at lunch" (implying it wasn't her husband), or, "Mr. Hancock seems to like you Jen" (said in a way that really meant "He'd bone you good if you let him, you frigid bitch!) Jen did her level best to ignore her.

Mary caught a glimpse of Jen's back as she passed, but made no move to speak to her. She hated that bitch. Jen was one of those "Do it for the team!" sorts. She made Mary sick. And unfortunately Jen was probably next in line for wussie Hancock's job. Especially since she was always fawning over the owner when he came by. She would always coddle him with "yes sir" and "no sir." Staying late and sometimes showing up early. Like her job was so important and she was so much better than everyone else. Bitch. She'd get hers one day.

Mary sat back and thought about the office. Jen, Stacy, Maria, Scott, and Ronald. She didn't have to worry about Scott. He'd been led by his prick and fallen into the same troubles as wussie Hancock. He'd do whatever she said. Or that pretty little wife of his would get a manila envelope just like Hancock's did. And he knew she'd do it, so he was keeping his pie hole shut.

Ronald was a little more trouble. He was probably a fag. Or so stupid that he wouldn't know what to do with a woman. He'd totally ignored Mary every time she'd come on to him. Still, it hardly mattered. He was lousy at his job and everyone knew it. He'd be lucky to have it once she ran the place. He was fat and lazy and that was a bad combination in Mary's book. He wasn't even pleasant to look at!

Maria and Stacy were good workers, but they had no drive. The only one that really was a problem was Jen. Mary sat thinking about it when her train of thought was broken, "Hi Ms. Cortage. Here's your mail." It was Barry the mail kid. Mary snapped her head around and a small scowl passed her features before a smile covered it. She took the mail and said, "Thank you Barry." He nodded and answered, "You're welcome, ma'am." All the "yes ma'ams" and "no ma'ams" made Mary laugh. Like he was going to get any promotion from her! What a joke! He returned to his cart to push it on down the line. She slid her chair over to the entrance of the cubicle to eye his ass as he moved on. He was an idiot. But he was eighteen and had a nice ass. Maybe she could use him a little. Break him in someday. She laughed to herself—it was a dirty sound.

Jen settled herself into her chair. She thought she heard Mary passing some words with Barry. She wished Barry wouldn't even talk to Mary. She could hear something in Mary's voice that she was sure Barry couldn't hear. He was a great young man, and had a lot of future ahead of him. She hoped he could steer clear of Mary long enough for herself to be promoted. Then Mary wouldn't be a problem for anyone. The first opportunity she had she was going to fire Mary. And it wouldn't be tough to find an excuse. Mary was always late for work, or late back from lunch, or missing some meeting. She had no idea why Mr. Hancock had put up with her so long. Well, no use thinking on it. Thinking on Mary just made her mad, and she preferred being happy, so she set back to work and put Mary out of her mind.

A few moments later Barry was standing before Jen. "Hi Barry," she said in a cheery voice. She liked Barry. He worked hard and was always helpful.

"Hi back Jen," he answered just as cheerily. Barry loved working with Jen. He'd volunteer for extra work just to be around her. She was good looking and not that much older than him. He didn't know if she felt the same way. But there was really nothing to it, because he knew she was happily married. Still, it was nice to chat with her. "Here's your mail; not much today," he said as he handed her a small stack.

She took it and smiled, saying, "Thanks." She was always courteous with him. He was a great kid. He was going to start college next fall and become an accountant. Along with mail room work, he'd occasionally hang out with Mr. Randle when he did the books each month, gaining some on-the-job experience. He was a go-getter and would make a good accountant for someone one day.

Jen was re-working some text on her screen later when she felt her hair rise on the back of her neck. She unfocused her eyes from the words on her monitor and settled them on the reflection of a red business suit behind her. She turned, putting on the best smile she could while her stomach churned. Mary. She had no idea how long she'd been standing there doing who knows what instead of working.

"Hello Hon," Mary breathed. Her smile was sultry. She seemed to always be oozing sex. Even when she talked with other women. Jen shook off the instant desire to shiver and said, "What can I do for you Mary?" She tried to be pleasant but knew that her voice betrayed her disgust.

"Oh, there's nothing you can do for me," Mary answered, "but I have some papers for you. Just helping you get ahead, you know." She handed Jen a file with some work she'd finished. Jen was temporarily in charge while they settled on a permanent office manager, so she had to approve everyone's work.

Uh-huh, just helping me get ahead, Jen thought. She took the envelope and set it down on her desk. "Thank you," she said, and turned to go back to work. She put Mary entirely out of her mind and tried to concentrate on her monitor. However, she noticed that Mary had not left. Sighing to herself, Jen turned back around and asked, "Is there something else?"

Mary smiled and said, "I just wanted to remind you that I'm leaving a little early today. Doctor's appointment you recall."

Jen nodded and said, "Yes, I do recall. As I said, that will be fine." Mary always played this little game. First with Mr. Hancock, and now with Jen. They both knew Jen had approved her leaving this morning. She didn't need to remind her again. Jen had said she could go when she needed to. Jen continued, "Well, if that's it, I really need to get back to this project." She smiled a "please leave and thanks for your time" smile at Mary and turned again to her computer. Thankfully this time she heard Mary wander out of her cubicle and back toward her own. She shook her head and ground her teeth silently. Mary's work was good. She was smart, and pretty, and had everything going for her. Why she had to act like that was a puzzle to Jen.

Mary smiled to herself as she walked to her car. She'd left not long after talking to that Stilman bitch. She was so stupid. Mary had had some time to think on the problem of how to get Jen out of the way. She would set her up. And the first move had taken place right under her nose. Mary tossed her keys into the air and confidently caught them. She had about two free hours to get home and get online. After that Jen would change the computer password she was using and had carelessly allowed Mary to see.

Mary's car turned into her driveway in time for Mary to see her two-year-old stumble across the lawn and fall in a heap. She hopped from the car and walked over to him with a grin. Reaching down she picked him up and said, "How's my little man today?" Then she plopped a big kiss on his head. He squealed and grinned back, hugging her. At that point Connie the sitter walked over from the porch where she'd been watching him and said, "You're home early. Are you well?"

Mary smiled and said, "Just an early day. I have some business to do on my computer for a bit. I'll need you to stay for a little longer if that's all right?"

Connie smiled and said, "Sure, I planned on being here anyway." And with that she took the boy from Mary's arms and they all walked toward the front door. Mary said she'd be inside for a while, and Connie and Todd went back to playing on the front lawn. Todd did most of the playing while Connie watched.

Once inside Mary went right to her bedroom and turned on her computer. She'd gone into the company system a number of times using her own passwords. However, she had done it merely to get a feeling for what the system was like. She had no real use in doing so. Well, there was the work she was to accomplish. But that was not a use to her so much. The only one that handled the money transactions was the office manager. And though he was a wussie, Hancock had never given his password away. But Jen was silly enough to have let hers go already! Mary laughed to herself as she waited for the machine to boot up. When it did, she connected to the office machine and entered her own password. Once in she could find out if Jen was still online. If she was, Mary would have to wait.

She scanned through the list of users online. Jen's name was not lit. "Hmmmm. I wonder if I'm not the only one wasting time today," she mumbled to herself. But she knew that Jen only went online when it was required. And no payroll work had to be done today, so chances were she wouldn't be on. Mary logged out, and then quickly logged back in using the stolen password. It worked! She had worried that Jen had changed it when she had gotten off earlier. But as usual, she was a creature of habit. She and Hancock both only changed at the end of the day.

Mary quickly entered the Payments section. She went back to the second of the month and entered a $4000.00 check made out to Stylus One. What the hell that meant was meaningless. She just thought it was a cool sounding name. Then she transferred the check to a discretionary fund under the name of JS. She coded the JS account with a password: Robert. That was Jen's husband's name. Then she buried the JS account in a series of meaningless files as though it were supposed to be hidden. The files were located on Jen's portion of the network work area. She knew that the books would not be balanced out until the end of the month. When they were, the Stylus One check would be automatically flagged before payment because it was a new customer (supposedly) and not permitted automated payment until the proper channels were set up. She finished by trying to open Jen's private calendar. No such luck though; she used a different password. So she settled for attaching a note to one of the buried files reminding Jen to "repay the borrowed 4." Mary hoped that would look like Jen had taken the money as a secret loan with the intent of paying it back before it was missed. It was a subtle first move. It may not even cost Jen her job, but the lying she would appear to be doing by denying it may.

Mary exited the system and turned her computer off. She lit a cigarette and lay down on her bed. She smiled up at the ceiling thinking of Jen's squirming when Mr. Randle came in to question her about Stylus One and a certain $4000.00. At the very least she was going to get that promotion over Jen. At the best she would get Jen fired for theft. Either way, Jen was going to be gone.

Jen finished saving her new password and cleaned her desk. She hated showing up the next day and having a mess from the previous one. She preferred to mess things up anew each day. As she straightened she called out "good-nights" to the various other employees as they left. It was a pretty good group. Ronald was a little slow at his job, but he got his work done and it was ok. She'd have to help him improve over the next few months or he may not make it.

The only real problem in her mind was Mary. She knew that the others didn't care for her either. They would talk about it with her. At least they used to until she was put in charge. Now she was a little more boss-like and you don't complain about your co-workers to the boss. Just to one another. Jen smiled at that. Funny how the rules develop. Still, she knew of the discontent and felt the same way. The problem was that Mary did great work. She could be a valuable asset if she could learn to function with others. But she seemed so—self-involved. Jen wavered back and forth between desiring to fire her the minute she was promoted, and wishing to work with her and correct her many strange quirks. "That's just the loving mom talking, Jen," she mumbled to herself. Some people could not be fixed!

When everyone was gone, she turned the lights off, and left. She set the alarm, locked the door, and trudged to her car; her head still danced around what to do with Mary. It was heavy on her mind today because of the phone call earlier. Mr. Lannery had called to inform her that "just between them" she was probably going to get the promotion to office manager. They had looked at a few other candidates from outside, but he was partial to her. And he was the final decision. It was not that the others were not good. They were. But she had worked hard and been loyal, and he respected that in an employee. He all but said he'd be in Friday to promote her officially. Jen was thrilled, but not long after she had had to talk with Mary and once again wondered how she could keep her. Although it must be admitted she was often on time now that Mr. Hancock was gone and Jen was in charge. But she didn't like the dissension she sowed among the employees. It was a problem.

Pulling up to the house, Jen reprimanded herself for taking work home with her. She needed to be sure she did not let work spill over and interfere with her home life. So before she went in, she prayed that she would not dwell on the problem. Then drawing a deep breath she tried to clear her mind of it. As she got out of her car she realized that it was sort of like telling someone, "Don't think of number thirteen!" Then they can't not think of it! She set her attention on fixing dinner and pushed it as far back as she could.

Bob would be home in an hour or so. She first went to their bedroom and shrugged out of the blazer she was wearing. It was one of her favorites because it fit so well. Sometimes it was murder getting something that fit just right. So when she found something, she kept it as long as possible. She hung it up carefully and picked a piece of stray lint from the back.

As she returned from the closet, she looked at herself in the mirror with the assessing eye only a woman can bring to their figure. She liked how she looked and smiled at herself. She usually did not change clothes before Bob got home. She knew he liked to see her dressed in skirts and heels, so she waited until he was home and they'd eaten before she put on her nice comfy jeans. She considered it a concession on the part of their marriage. It was no problem to wear her nicer clothes an hour longer. And sometimes it even drew a romantic reaction! She smiled to herself, wondering if that would happen tonight! She thought she might make it happen. Bob liked it when she was a little aggressive too.

She walked into the kitchen and poured a glass of water. Taking sips from it while she worked, she prepared a light dinner of pasta and chicken. They ate a lot of pasta and chicken. They were saving for a little bigger house, and maybe some land. With both their jobs going well, they were sure they'd get them in the not so distant future. Especially with this new promotion and money it would add.

About an hour later Bob came home. He kissed her and tried to move on, but she held him close for a moment or two. He giggled as she snuggled his neck, and finally he cracked under the tickling and pushed her away with a broad grin. "What's in you tonight?" he asked enthusiastically.

Jen was suddenly filled with the repressed emotions of being told she was going to be promoted. She had, to this point, really just put the excitement away and focused on the job ahead of her. But thinking about it now (now that Bob asked) she bubbled up with the prospects of a new job. She gushed out her news (properly muted with the appropriate cautions that she was informally told about the promotion). Bob gushed back with pride and assurance that the formality of giving her the job was only a step away. She thought so too, and they chatted over all the new possibilities during dinner. It was nice. And Mary hardly came up at all. In fact, by the end of dinner, Jen felt like Mary was not such a big problem, and she could perhaps encourage her to become a team player after all.

The next day Jen arrived a half hour early, as usual. She opened things up and turned on all the necessary equipment. She then settled herself to begin work. She arranged her files as to priority, and began wading through them. She could not wait to dump some of this on someone else and take on a few more challenging jobs.

Around quarter of nine everyone else arrived, except Mary. She never crossed the doors before nine sharp. That was when work started and that was when she arrived. She could then charge the company for taking her coat off and getting coffee. It always burned Jen up, but she had a new lease on Mary after the confident and positive talk she'd had last night with Bob. She was going to set herself to get along better with Mary.

Mary strolled through the door at 8:59:47 (she looked at her watch and smiled). She was never late for work since Jen had been in charge. And after Thursday she may not have Jen to worry about at all. Then she could go back to coming in when she wanted. She went straight for the coffee machine and poured herself a cup. Occasionally she even left some money for the coffee fund. But not this morning. Todd had had a bad night and she hadn't gotten a cup at home before Connie had come to watch him. So she was in no mood to be generous. Let the company pay for a lousy cup of coffee! It was the least they could do.

Mary then shrugged out of her coat and hung it up. She straightened her prim attire for the day in the mirror on her desk. She had decided to wear a little more conservative clothes this week. Just in case the boss came around and she wanted to work him. Couldn't hurt to project the buttoned down business woman thing for one week. She even had one of those stupid ivory pins with the woman's head in profile on her blouse. Her ex-husband's mom used to own it. Mary didn't care for it when she took it, but she wanted to spite the old hag in some way. Her ex was just like his mom. Loud-mouthed and annoying. They had been over to dinner one night and mom had been hassling her about not seeing Todd enough. Mary didn't want to expose her son to that hag any more often than she had to, so she constantly was being lectured by her about not bringing Todd over enough or inviting her over to dinner enough. Just on an impulse Mary had pinched the pin. She had then invited mom out to a dress-up dinner a few days later. And told her to wear her Sunday best. Of course mom always included that god-awful pin. But when she went to look for it, it was gone! Mary laughed over that for weeks.

She smiled again as she looked at the ugly pin on her chest. She was dead sure that someone like Maria would find it "beautiful." Well, no accounting for taste. But the pin did serve its purpose for her now. Maybe she would break it and send it back to mom after she was promoted!

Around mid-morning Jen had to run over to a client's for a meeting. Mary watched her leave, and then wandered over to the mail room. It was not a large affair. Not like in a huge company. But they received enough mail and work that they did need someone to manage it and sort it out. Barry was the boy for the job. He put in about four or five hours a day doing mail and other odd jobs that came up. Right now he was sorting through parcels and envelops, and generally straightening things up. He also brought supplies to people when they needed them.

While Barry's back was turned, Mary eased into the doorway and undid the top two buttons of her blouse revealing the top of her lacy bra. She then cleared her throat. Barry turned, smiled, and said, "Hello Ms. Cortage. Can I do something for you?"

Mary thought he was such a rube. But damn if his ass wasn't great! She answered, "Yes Barry, I need some red-markers."

Barry turned and squatted down to open a lower cabinet. He rummaged around in back and produced a variety of red markers for her selection. As he stood he said, "Here we go. I have some for transparencies, some for plain paper, some for dry erase boards, and some pens. What would you like?"

Mary answered with a wink, "I'll take the one for transparencies." And she put out her hand to take the pen.

As Barry handed it over, Mary let it fall from her fingers, feigning clumsiness. Before Barry could retrieve it, she squatted down and leaned over by his feet to pick it up. This gave him a good view down her blouse at her breasts. She could not help but grin at what he must be thinking. But she kept her eyes down so he would have ample opportunity to check her out.

After retrieving the pen, she stopped to inspect a nail closely still squatting in front of Barry with her eyes down. She pretended to fiddle with a chip for a good minute or so before she looked up suddenly and said, "I thought I broke a nail!" She was quick enough to just catch Barry's eyes moving away from her open blouse. And had she not seen the movement, she would have confirmed her belief of his inspection by the slight redness in his cheeks. He was eighteen but seemed to have the sexual experience of a fifteen year old in Mary's eyes. Of course, when she was fifteen she'd had the sexual experience of an eighteen year old! In any event, the ploy had worked and she now knew he could perhaps be manipulated.

She put out her hand and said, "Help me up Barry, these shoes are murder on the balance."

Barry took her arm daintily, trying not to get too close. She made sure she brushed him with her breasts on the way up to her feet. And she almost burst out laughing when he drew his arm in as though it had been burned. He had such a guilty look on his face at touching her breasts with his forearm! Mary could not wait to teach this virgin some tricks that would make his whole body red with embarrassment!

Mary smiled and said, "Thank you honey" patting his arm in appreciation. And with that she turned and left, letting Barry have a good look at her ass in the tight, dark blue skirt she wore. She deftly buttoned her blouse again on the way out. When she finally was seated at her desk she giggled at the teasing she had given the young man. She'd have him sooner or later. And then she'd discard him.

A little while later, having completed some work, Mary walked up to Stacy's desk and inquired about when Jen would be back. She explained that she needed to get some things from Jen and had some things to give her too. Stacy (as dumb as a doorknob) said she had put the required file on Jen's desk that morning (which Mary had seen her do) and it was still sitting there if Mary wanted it.

Having covered her tracks, Mary proceeded to Jen's cubicle. She surveyed its contents, looking for something useful. She landed on paper. Again, it was a small thing, but it would do. She took two reams from her printer stand, and covering them with the file, she quickly walked back to her own cubicle, squeezing by Barry on the way. She then mentioned to Scott that she had left something in her car. She threw her purse over her shoulder, took the reams of paper with her, and once outside checked Jen's car. It was not locked. She quickly popped the trunk and put the paper under the golf clubs that were in the trunk. She loosely closed the trunk and returned to the office. Now that she knew Jen's car was open she would make a bigger play. Thank god for the company car Jen was driving right now!

Mary knew Barry was pushing his cart around, so the mail (and supply) room was empty. She quietly slipped in and dumped a bunch of supplies into her bag. She then went to her cubicle and sat down to work a few minutes. After a short while she told Scott again that she had forgotten something else in her car. And again she went out to Jen's. She dumped the supplies in the trunk, and locked it. Then she hurried back to her cubicle and worked the rest of the morning on her projects. She felt great! No one wanted even a petty thief as an office manager. This was working out terrifically.

About twelve o'clock Mary heard Barry say, "see ya!," to Maria. She had actually been so engrossed in her work that she had lost track of the time. Barry's "see ya" had been loud enough to catch her ear, and she had equated it with lunch time. She pushed back from her desk, slipped into her coat and walked out for an hour away from work. As she got into her car she saw Barry fiddling with his pack. She waved at him as she passed out of the parking lot and flashed him a sensual smile and wink. He nodded his head at her as she passed. She would definitely have that boy!

Barry approached the door to his folk's house at about 1:00 p.m. As he passed the flower bed near the porch he noticed the sea pinks had been nibbled almost flat. Those rabbits! He know his mom loved those plants. And those rabbits apparently did too. The rabbits were wild and lived in the forest just over the hill. They were always in the housing development eating from people's gardens and what not. He was going to stop that one way or the other.

As Barry came in his mom rounded the corner from the day room dressed in red tights and a sports bra. She greeted her son with a sweaty kiss on the cheek and said, "I made some tuna for lunch if you want some. I'm off for a shower."

Barry's mom and dad were in good shape for being mid-forties. His friends had commented on what a babe his mom was. He'd always loved to work out too and it showed in his hard body. He supposed that was why Ms. Cortage was always flirting with him. He was not interested though. He preferred Ms. Stilman, even as a friend to Ms. Cortage. She was kind of strange sometimes.

Barry called after his mom as she walked away, "Did you see what that rabbit did to your plants?"

She turned before entering his folk's bedroom and said, "Yeah. Ruined my sea pinks!"

Barry said, "I'm going to stop that." He put on a mock insane look and grunted, "Nobody messes with my momma!"

Amanda grinned at her son and said, "Just don't kill them, you loon." And she disappeared into her bedroom.

Barry figured he'd just trap them and see what the humane society said he could do with them. He knew he could get a trap from animal control if he called. He'd take care of this situation.

Dad was backing the rabbits on the issue. He figured if they ate the plants there would be less yard work to do. He always winked at Barry when he made this argument to mom. She didn't buy it, and usually told him to zip it! His back-up position was that Barry should handle it. It would teach him something, or help him mature, or something like that. Basically it was a way for dad to pawn the job off on Barry.

Dad pretty much hated yard work. Barry figured it was probably because dad had no green thumb whatsoever and he invariably killed any plant he touched. Dad said he believed the plants were out to get him.

Barry, on the other hand, had inherited mom's green thumb and enjoyed working in the yard. Consequently, when he'd grown big enough, his chores had always included yard work. It was fine with Barry. He didn't mind the work. At least no more than any other teen minds working at home. And now that Barry was getting to be an adult, he felt more obligations to work around the house. After all, his folks were letting him live there rent free during college.

The next day, Wednesday, Mary came early to work. She was the first in the door, except Jen of course, and her lap dog Barry. Mary waved a "hi" to Jen and settled into her cubicle. (She didn't say anything to Barry. He was in his store room.) The look on Jen's face when Mary walked through the doors at 8:37 was absolutely comical! But Mary paid it no heed. She played around for a few minutes, and then grabbed up the folder she'd laid out the day before. Mary then walked down to Jen's space and laid it down on her desk. Jen was at the coffee maker at the time. As Mary entered Jen's cubicle she called over to the other side of the room, "I'm leaving some work on your desk Jen." And she gave a little wave as Jen looked up at her with a half poured cup of coffee.

As Mary laid the folder down, she bent and opened the second drawer on Jen's desk. She tossed the golf ball she'd stolen from Stacy's desk into the back and shut the drawer in one smooth move. The ball was signed by Nancy Lopez. Stacy had picked it up at a golf tournament she'd watched. She had been so excited to get the golfer to sign the damn thing. Mary thought it was one of the stupidest things she'd ever heard of. Who'd want a golf ball, no matter who signed it? The only good that came from that stupid ball was the use she was putting it to now. Jen had commented on how neat it was a number of times. Now it was going to look like she'd taken it.

Mary returned to her desk and went to work. Jen returned to hers and perused the file Mary had brought her. It was good work, as usual. She didn't like Mary around her desk when she wasn't right there. She just did not trust her. And although just the night before she had dedicated herself to getting to know and appreciate Mary, she could not shake her mistrust of the woman easily. Still, everything looked in order, so she began to work and quickly put it out of her mind.

The others came in shortly thereafter, and the room filled with chatter. People talking about what they did or didn't do last night. Jen heard snippets of Scott expounding on his "Facial" at the basketball game last night. It was funny to listen to him as he imitated Marv Albert saying, "Facial!" It was even funnier when you saw all 5'10" of Scott! It was difficult to imagine him giving anyone a "facial" in any manner. He was not in the best athletic shape as well as not being all that tall. But he was a great story teller. And by the middle of his tale you believed he was Michael Jordan reincarnated in a short, white guy's body! Jen smiled to herself when he came to the climax of his story and again yelled out, "Facial!!" in his Marv voice. He was a hit because everyone else laughed as well. Except Mary. She never bothered to listen to Scott's stories. She treated him rather shabbily mostly. But Scott strangely never argued with her. It was as though she had some way of controlling him.

By nine o'clock everyone was seated and working. Phones were ringing, and computer keyboards were clacking away. Jen needed to head over to a meeting again today. She stopped by Stacy's desk on the way out and said, "I'm leaving for a while. I'm having my calls transferred to you while I'm out, ok? Just handle whatever comes up."

Stacy smiled and said "Sure Jen."

Just as Jen turned to leave, she looked up at the shelf behind Stacy and noticed her golf ball was missing. She commented, "Did you take the ball home?"

Stacy looked at her blankly and said, "Excuse me?"

Jen pointed behind Stacy's head and said, "Nancy's golf ball. I see it's not there anymore. I just wondered if you finally took it home to the mantelpiece or something?"

Stacy stood and looked at the shelf. She turned a moment later and said, "No, I haven't touched it in weeks." She reached up to move the other memorabilia on the shelf, thinking it was just moved behind something else. But it was not there at all. Stacy's eyes played around her cubicle as she shook her head. She looked back at Jen and said, "I think it was stolen!"

Jen replied, "Are you sure? You didn't move it and then forget where it went?"

Stacy shook her head again and said, "I know I haven't touched it. Have you seen anyone in my cubicle lately? I know it was there last week because I dusted it."

Jen thought for a moment. Very rarely did clients actually come to the office. They usually dealt with people at their offices, or over the web. She shook her head and said, "I don't recall anyone being near your things. The only people who've been in the office are the usuals. Great thought Jen. I hope we don't have a thief among us. Jen's thoughts immediately turned to Mary, though she had no scrap of evidence to point that way. In fact, Mary had commented about how silly she thought the golf ball was!

Jen said, "I'll ask everyone when I get back. You just try to think if maybe you moved it and forgot, ok Stacy?"

Stacy nodded and sat back down. She said, "I sure hope I don't lose that ball. I liked having it."

Jen was more angry that someone may have stolen it. But right now she had to get to a meeting. So she was forced to put it off. She'd deal with it when she got back.

Mary had heard the whole thing. She giggled to herself thinking how it was going to look when they found that ball in Jen's desk. After Jen left, Mary made a point of walking by Stacy's cubicle. As she pretended to pass she glanced in at Stacy and said, "Did you finally take that silly ball home Stace?" She just wanted to get Stacy talking on the subject.

Stacy looked up and said in a rather peeved voice (she knew Mary didn't care about the ball one way or the other), "No, I didn't take it home. It's missing."

Mary put a quizzical look on her face. "What do you mean missing? Did someone steal it?" It was all she could do to not laugh at the look on Stacy's face.

Stacy didn't answer for a second. Then she said, "I don't know what happened."

Mary turned to leave, then said, "Well, I hope you find it." It was a little lame sounding, but the intent wasn't as important to her as the words being said. She wanted to be able to go on record as being on Stacy's side.

Near lunch, Mary waited for Maria to leave. When she and most everyone else was gone, she quickly took some small items from Maria's desk. Nothing big: A pen she liked, and a supposedly lucky penny she kept. She put the pen on Jen's filing cabinet where it could be seen by someone walking past her cubicle. She placed the penny in the middle drawer of Jen's desk, near the back of the organizing tray. It was wrapped so it would be identifiable if found. She hoped someone would notice the pen (preferably Maria herself). But if no one did before about one p.m., she'd give Maria a little nudge. Jen wasn't going to be back at least until two or three, so that would leave plenty of time for a village uprising. (Mary pictured her coworkers as the stupid mob that chased Frankenstein. All pitchforks and clubs; basically a bunch of low-brow goobers!)

Mary left for lunch after her chore in Jen's cubicle. She felt great and wanted to celebrate somehow. All her plans were working out just right. And the coup d' grace would come when Randle did the books on Friday. That was going to be great!

When everyone had returned and gotten back to work, Mary prepared herself for a little rabble-rousing. She smiled to herself at that word: Rabble-rousing. What an appropriate moniker. They were the rabble and she was going to rouse them all right. And when they were aroused, they would turn their dislike to Jen.

The first opportunity came when she heard a discussion between Stacy and Maria.

Maria asked, "Stacy, was Barry here over lunch while we were out?" Barry always was here from noon to one. Usually everyone didn't leave for lunch at the same time, but if that happened, Barry was to keep an eye on things. Since most people dealt with the firm by email, Internet and phone, it wasn't a problem leaving him around alone.

Stacy looked up from her work and answered, "Yeah, he was here. I saw him leave after we got back."

Next Maria said, "Was anyone else around?"

"No. No one I saw." said Stacy. "Why do you ask?"

Maria bit her lip softly and said, "I can't seem to find my pen. You know, my favorite one I always use?"

At this point Mary sidled up next to Maria as she pretended to walk down the aisle. She stopped and said, "Excuse me Maria, do you mean the burgundy one, with the gold accents?" The gold was Maria's name printed on it. The pen was a gift.

Maria looked back over her shoulder at Mary, noticing she was be-hind her in the aisle. She said, "Yes, that's the one. Have you seen it?"

Mary shook her head as though she was not quite sure. "Hmmmm. It seems like I have, but I'm not sure where." She chewed her lip as though concentrating on a difficult conundrum. Then she said, "I think I saw it in Jen's cubicle!"

Maria hesitated a second and then said, "Jen's cubicle? Are you sure? I wouldn't have taken it down there."

Mary shook her head and said, "Well, maybe I'm mistaken. You could check if you want." And with that she continued on over to Scott's desk and began to talk about something work related she'd been saving for just this moment. As she positioned herself in Scott's cubicle, she kept one eye on the aisle to see what Maria would do. And sure enough, a few moments later she saw Maria casually walk down past Jen's cubicle opening. She watched to see if Maria would locate the pen. Maria ducked into Jen's cubicle. After a minute or two, she exited with a pensive look on her face, returning to Stacy's cubicle. Mary was sure she'd found the pen, so she broke off with Scott and returned to her cubicle to gloat.

As she passed Stacy's cubicle again, she heard Stacy recounting how her precious golf ball was missing too. Mary almost skipped with delight knowing the two morons were comparing notes on what may have been taken. And now that Maria had the pen, perhaps some gossip was beginning to spread about Jen and sticky hands. She paid no heed to the look Maria shot her as she passed.

Jen returned later that day. Quite late, really. Well past when she was supposed to. It frustrated Mary because there was no time for much chit-chat before everyone started leaving. She did notice a few passed words between Stacy, Maria and Jen, but it didn't seem to amount to much. Damn. Mary hated it when her plans didn't come to fruition on schedule. Still, she couldn't hurry things. They had to unfold naturally. And they would. She was sure of it.

Coming in Thursday, Mary was excited to see what would happen. She sat in her cubicle just wasting time (she'd done most of her assigned work anyway; well, for the most part). She did try to do some work, but kept finding herself listening to the conversations around her. The problem was, she could not hear them very well sitting at her desk. And she couldn't keep walking around pretending to be on errands. The office wasn't that big and there was no reason to be walking around so much.

Mary did hear one thing that she thought would develop nicely. Maria had come down to Stacy's cubicle (which was closer to Mary), and the two of them had talked quietly for a short while. Mary couldn't hear most of it, but a few phrases came through clearly: "She's going to have to figure it out. I think we should just allow an inspection of work areas." That was Maria talking. Stacy didn't argue (at least not that Mary could hear), so Mary thought she probably agreed. People were pretty close here and didn't worry much about workers' rights and all. They all seemed to think they were on one team; both management and employees!

Although it was not much, Mary thought she could use the snippet of conversation. She allowed some time to pass. Maria went off to get coffee and then went back to work. Then Mary sidled into Stacy's cubicle and said, "You know Stace" (as though they were friends!) "I was thinking about your missing ball. Any worries about other employee's honesty could be cleared up by just inspecting each cubicle. I don't think we'd find anything, but it would set everyone's minds at ease. The only person I'd suspect is Barry. We don't know him that well. Not like we know one another. What do you think?" Mary thought she'd make it look like she had absolutely no suspicion concerning Jen. Then when they found the stuff in her cubicle, she would act greatly surprised and ashamed of her!

Stacy looked at Mary and her first thought was, get out of my cubicle. She didn't ever recall Mary being too concerned over anyone else in the office. But she said, "I think that's a good idea Mary. Although I must say I know Barry pretty well, and I trust him as much as anyone." She then seemed to almost dismiss Mary and went back to work!

Mary was somewhat puzzled by Stacy's actions. She thought she'd be more enthusiastic about the idea. Still, she was agreeable. Just not excitedly so, as Mary would have thought she would be. After all, it was her stupid ball they were trying to get back!

In any event, nothing more came of the whole conversation that day. Things just seemed to simmer. Jen talked with Stacy and Maria a few times. But no one seemed to fight over anything. The only hint that things were happening was at the end of the day. Before everyone left, Jen made an announcement: "I want everyone to get together tomorrow morning around eleven. Mr. Randle will have finished the books by then, and I want to speak with all of you." That was it. She said no more except "goodnight." And that didn't seem strained in any way. Things were moving ahead, but it was difficult to decipher how.

Friday morning came and Mary could not wait to see the upshot of her week's work. She had lingered late last night at work on the pretense of doing some overtime on an account. She actually had done a little more stealing and planting. She had taken some things from Scott and placed them in Jen's cubicle. She noticed as she was in there that the pen she'd put on the filing cabinet was gone. Someone had found something out. It couldn't have been Jen because she made no protestations of innocence that Mary had heard. Mary found new places to put Scott's knickknacks in Jen's cubicle. Almost every drawer, whichever was opened, held a stolen article now. She could not wait to see this!

When Mary entered the office, everyone was there. They all seemed to be working. Mr. Randle arrived not long after nine and he and Barry went to work on the accounts. Barry always got to help with that because Mr. Randle liked him. Mary thought it was probably a way for Barry to get out of his real work. All he did with Mr. Randle was watch really.

By eleven they were finished and Mr. Randle left. Everyone else gathered over by the large conference table, Barry included. (Though he was just a mail boy.) Mary thought this might be because she had mentioned to Stacy her suspicions of the boy. She hoped that didn't get back to him. She still wanted to screw him after this was all over. But, she would get to be office manager, and that would apply some pressure to him whether he wanted to succumb to her or not.

Jen stood and began the meeting. "I want to thank you all for the hard work and loyalty you've shown after the loss of Mr. Hancock. I really appreciate all the support you've shown me taking over for him temporarily."

Mary just looked at her as though she really cared. It was a struggle! Get on with it!

Jen continued, "However, something of a problem has come up. It seems some personal articles have come up missing from people's cubicles. Stacy's golf ball for one; some things from the storeroom; and some things from Maria's desk." Jen looked around at everyone for a moment before she continued. Mary put her most innocent face on. Jen went on, "I know that we all trust one another, and that we will undoubtedly find that somehow someone outside the office had gotten to these things. However, a number of you proposed we check cubicles. I would not agree to this unless all of you assented. In addition, I want you to know that my reason for checking cubicles is not to find someone guilty of theft, but to perhaps allow others to suggest places to look that may have been overlooked in haste."

Mary concealed the rolling of her eyes at that statement. The bitch was on a hunt and probably couldn't wait to find the stolen articles. She'd get hers.

"In order to be sure we don't offend anyone, and to make sure the company has representation, I've asked Mr. Lannery to join us. He should be here any minute. Until he arrives, does anyone want to comment on this idea?"

Everyone basically said the same thing. They all agreed that checking cubicles wouldn't hurt anything and they didn't mind. Mr. Lannery showed up during this discussion and apologized for being late. He said he had an errand. When everyone had had a say, they all went down to the first cubicle in line by the door: Mary's.

Mary tagged along at the rear thinking about Jen's face when they found the things in her cubicle. She knew that Jen hadn't found any of them because she hadn't reacted to them. Meanwhile, Mary was going to have to wait while they went through every nook and cranny of each person's cubicle finding nothing because Jen's was the last in line. At least that would provide some drama in an otherwise boring procedure.

Mr. Lannery and Jen were the only two to enter the cubicle while the others stood watching. Jen asked if Mary was missing anything. Mary said she didn't think so, though she hadn't really looked lately. Inwardly she kicked herself for not thinking to plant one of her own items in Jen's cubicle. That would have been the smartest thing to do. Damn!

Mr. Lannery opened the top drawer of Mary's filing cabinet. Mary was looking out the window. A moment later she head Stacy say, "That's my ball," and Mary felt the looks of those around her. Her head snapped around to see Mr. Lannery holding Stacy's golf ball! He was looking at it, and then he turned his gaze to Mary.

For a moment Mary was speechless. She looked at each face and then at the ball and said lamely, "I don't know how that got there!" Just then Jen pulled a number of items from Mary's desk drawers: none of which belonged to Mary. In fact, everything she'd taken was turning up in her cubicle! Mary pushed into her workspace and said, "I didn't put these here! I don't know how they got here!"

Jen assembled all the stolen articles on Mary's desk and said to everyone else, "I would appreciate everyone taking their things back. Let me know if anything is still missing. Mary, I'd like to see your car if you don't mind."

Mary looked at her. Why did she want to see her car? She nodded her head and followed Mr. Lannery and Jen out front. Upon opening the trunk she saw ream after ream of paper from the supply room! More than she had taken to put in Jen's trunk! She turned to protest the fact that the paper was there, but met stoic and hard faces looking at her. And over their shoulders Mary saw Barry watching from the window.

Mr. Lannery signaled to Barry, who came out and began to unload the paper onto a dolly. He took it all back inside, followed by Mary, Jen, and Mr. Lannery.

Over in Mr. Lannery's seldom used office, the three sat down. Mr. Lannery took a breath and then said, "Mary, it appears you've been stealing. Do you have an explanation for how these things got into your desk and trunk?"

Mary just sat. She could think of nothing.

Mr. Lannery continued, "Although I find it unsavory that you would steal knickknacks from your co-workers, there is a more important issue I wish to discuss. He turned the computer screen to Mary so she could see a line of figures. In the line he pointed out a check made out to Stylus One. He then switched screens and indicated the payment of the check was to Mary's checkbook account! How on earth could that be!?

Mr. Lannery said, "We found this error in the books this morning. Well, actually Barry found it while working with Mr. Randle. It was not well covered Mary. Can you explain this?"

Mary was completely in shock. She sat quietly for a long moment. Then she turned her eyes to Jen and said, "You bitch! You set me up didn't you? You stole those things and put them in my desk! You fixed the books!"

Jen watched her and shook her head slightly. Mr. Lannery said firmly, "That's enough Mary. The transaction was recorded as coming from your own desk. And I found this in your top drawer along with the other items." He held up a piece of note paper with Jen's access code on it. But it was an access code different from that which Mary used! How could that happen!? Mr. Lannery went on, "Mary, I could have you arrested for this. But instead I'm terminating you. Clean out your desk, and leave the premises. You will not receive any recommendation from this firm."

And with that Jen ushered Mary out the door. Mary stood for a moment. Everyone was watching her with cool stares. She walked stolidly down to her cubicle with Jen in tow, watching her every move. Mary had little in her cubicle that was her own. That was partly why she had not thought to include something of her own in the stolen property. But that would not have mattered anyway. It all ended up back in her desk!

Barry came up with a box to hold what she had. As she took it from him, she saw a glint in his eyes.

Upon loading all her things up, Jen, Mary, and for some reason Barry walked to the front door. Barry even carried the box. At the door only Mary and Barry exited to the parking lot. Mary coldly opened her trunk for the box. And after placing it inside, Barry stopped by her open door window. He leaned close and said, "No one messes with my friends, bitch."

Monsters

Jayme Creider stumbled out of her bedroom at 5:30 a.m. trying to keep her eyes slitted, so that only the tiniest crack of the world would show through. She hated the morning. She reached out her right hand, and groped about for the rail to guide her along the dark passageway. Her slippers swished along the carpet as she moved slowly down the hall. Her hand felt the familiar bumps and bruises of the rail as she proceeded. Two steps: Mark banged his head. It was really his teeth because there was a little half-moon shape dug into the wood. A half step: The cat jumped up and clawed the rail. Four little troughs dug along the top. Two more steps: Baseball bat swung by some unknown stranger (so the boys said), leaving a big dent. Two more steps: The turn for the stairs. Five steps (watch the cat, she sleeps on the left side of step three or four). Landing: Rubber cat ball on the right; kick it to the side. Eight steps: Living room.

Jayme's eyes were opening a little by now. This was both because she was waking up, and because she was in a mine field. She wove her way through the mess heading for the kitchen. Gaining her objective, she again closed her eyes a little more as she flicked the light on over the sink. The little light, not the full kitchen lights. She hated that retina burn from the overheads first thing in the morning. Following the sting of the little light, she snapped on the Bunn. Her brain was whining: Coffee! Now!

Life was beginning to flow into Jayme's brain and body. She hugged her robe around her, pulled a coffee cup from the cabinet, and turned to grab the pot. As she did she came face to face with the vampire! Well, his face to her knees. He looked up and growled grimly, "Rrrrrrrrr!!" His pudgy hands menaced her with a rubber knife and a red squirt gun. Funny, she thought, I never knew they used squirt guns. Knowing of only one defense from such a beast, she suddenly bolted forward swinging both arms around the small demon and kissed his neck, exhaling all her air and making a terrible brrrrrrrppppppp sound against his warm skin. He shrieked with agony and collapsed in her arms in a gale of giggles. He was finished. Even his plastic teeth fell from his mouth and clattered to the floor. He had drooled himself.

Feeling confident that the danger was passed, she laid the miserable creature on the floor on his belly and put her left foot on his back. Then she squiggled her toes in triumph at her flawless victory. It was her undoing. For at that moment the vampire's cohort—it seemed to be a Jedi knight with nerf gun and a football helmet—attacked her from the other kitchen entrance. The nerf arrows blistered her bottom and back, driving her from her victory stance. She danced left, turning and advancing on her next foe. But he proved too quick. At once he scampered off into the living room to plot a new attack. When she turned she discovered with horror that the vampire had not been extinguished after all. It had risen and disappeared. One thought burned in Jayme's mind: God help Chris.

Fearing for her husband's life, Jayme poured herself a cup of coffee and sat down at the table. She had set out breakfast cereal for everyone last night, so she could sit and sip her coffee while the monsters slew Chris. It was a treat for her.

A moment later all Jayme's worst fears were realized as she heard from upstairs a terrible scream followed by some thunderous thuds and crashes. They were on him. May he rest in peace. Shrill laughter and garbled phrases filled the house from the upstairs master bedroom:

"Oh yeah!?" Chris yelled.

"I got you! You're dead!" It was gloating from the vampire, thought Jayme.

"I got you!"

"nu-uh!!"

The Jedi had evidently turned on the vampire in the fracas. It was a bitter struggle. She smiled as Chris rounded the corner with a nerf arrow in his hand. He had survived. She tapped the cup of coffee she'd poured for him sitting next to her at the table. He leaned over and kissed her as he passed to take a seat. He seemed none the worse for wear considering the brutal attack.

A moment later the vampire and Jedi returned sans weapons. Jayme said to them sternly, "You two sit down and pick a cereal." They complied grinning. She watched as they shrewdly gauged the quantity of sugar in each. In the end it was Count Chocula for the vampire and Captain Crunch with Crunch berries for the Jedi. She poured the milk for them giving each a kiss on the head when she finished. It was a tense truce.

She then poured herself a bowel of Grapenuts. The chewing woke her up. The vampire eyed the woman as she ate. He knew her ways. He pondered his next attack as he munched on chocolate eyeballs with blood. Little did she know that he had secreted a bomb into his p.j.'s under his cape. It would be her downfall yet. He looked over at the Jedi. He too would taste the wrath of the vampire. Right after breakfast. And after he cleaned his room and made the bed. He knew the Jedi was armed however. It would not be easy. He too had secreted a most deadly weapon on his person: It was a cap gun, and a handful of brappers. The attack would need to be stealthy and well-planned. It would probably be when the Jedi came from his bath. He would be naked and defenseless. Unless they bathed together. That would foil the plan.

The Jedi was plotting his own reprisal for the treachery of the morning. The vampire had turned on him during the fray with the man-demon and revenge would have to be exacted. Sure, one could interpret the slash of his light saber across the vampires back as a traitorous act if one wished. But the true facts were that the vampire was going to turn on him. He knew that. Striking first was an act of courageous insight. In any event, the Jedi was planning a heinous act of reprisal which had not been witnessed since the dawn of . . . dawn. He was also going to steal some Count Chocula. It was the best revenge. He eyed the vampire as he ate, smug in the belief that his cereal was safe. But the Jedi knew that the vampire would need to go to the bathroom soon. He bided his time. Watching. Waiting.

Chris finished his breakfast quickly and said he was going upstairs to dress for work. It was his first mistake. His second was turning his back on the devils at the table. They eyed one another, then hurriedly gulped the remainder of their food. They threw caution to the wind and prepared to strike, unleashing the evil inside them, reigning death upon all who crossed their paths! But first they asked permission to leave the table. They had to finish their milk first and carry their bowls to the sink. It was small price to pay for the carnage to come.

Jayme thanked the fiends and mussed their hair before they ran off after Chris. She smiled thinking how much she loved them. As she mused, the Jedi returned and grabbed a handful of Count Chocula brandishing the cap gun. Triumph! He then sped off upstairs with the vampire. Jayme had seen that look before on the young Jedi's face. Monsters were afoot, and trouble was in the air. She picked up her bowl and put it and the others in the dishwasher.

Wasp

FIVE YEAR OLD KATIE Marie Stengle sat in her bedroom by the night
stand with her back pressed to the wall. Her body rocked imperceptibly back and forth across the bumpy surface of the wall so she could
feel the little bumps dragging over her spine. She was not consciously
thinking of the little bumps, but she continued to move back and forth
using them as a yogi might use a chant to attain focus. Her knees were
drawn up to her chest, and her arms were wrapped around them tightly,
squeezing her flesh and intensifying the throb of her heart at many
points of contact. It was her heart that Katie was trying to feel.

Until last week Katie had not even thought about her heart. She
knew she had one, and she liked the sound of her folk's hearts when she
laid her head on their chests. It was nice to curl up with one of them, lay
her head down, and listen to stories. Dr. Seuss's were her favorites. She
would hear the sound of her mom's or dad's voice as it alternately grew
loud or quiet with the movement of the story. She would hear it both
with her ears, and with her head, as it traveled through their bodies,
and resonated from their skin to hers. At the same time, underneath the
sound of the story would be the soft breathing which (especially when
dad read) would lift her little body slightly as his chest moved up and
down. And always keeping time would be the thump, thump, thump of
their hearts, beating along. Katie had always associated that sound with
a warm, cozy feeling. You never heard someone's heart unless you were
close, and quiet, and happy.

Now, sitting in her room, Katie's mind quested back over her life remembering her own heart. The time she had raced down the grassy hill, stumbling over some object and, still laughing, tumbled into a heap of little girl and soft grass. She used to giggle and laugh at the memory, but now she thought about it closely and was frightened by the elements she'd forgotten or ignored in the joy of the moment. She now remembered her ragged breath, the way she panted as though there was not enough air to fill her greedy lungs. That had seemed like a good thing at the time. She now recalled the feelings of almost dizzy pleasure as her body heaved while dragging in the good air and blowing the bad away. She remembered the way her skin tingled as the grass whispered along it, moved by the wind, raising the hairs of her arms. She remembered the way her back wriggled and twisted to move off the little stick that poked her. And finally, now with dread, she remembered her heart. It had seemed nice at the time too. The blood was almost audible in her ears. The steady, rhythmic pounding of her heart filled every pore of her body. She could remember almost feeling like her body was alternately growing and shrinking as her heart pounded from the exertions, like a cartoon character who blows up with air, and then shrinks back down when it is exhaled.

Katie remembered the time she and dad had gone to the fair. They had gone on the zipper together. She recalled her dad, kneeling down, and looking her in the face. He had said they could go on the ride, but that it might be scary. She didn't have to go if she didn't want to, if she got scared at the last minute. She had nodded her head and grinned back at him. She wanted to be scared! She wanted to scream and spin, and twist about, out of control! And she had; they both had. And when it was over, and she had stepped out of the little car they had been strapped into, she now remembered her heart pounding. There had been no exertion that time, only the exhilaration of the ride. But her heart was beating as though she'd run for miles, as though she had twisted and rolled and spun about by her own power. Katie shuddered slightly and a little tickle spasmed the back of her throat, making her think she might cry.

Up to this point in her short life Katie Stengle had not thought much about her heart. As she examined these and many other episodes, she realized she had enjoyed it though, reveled in the feeling of her heart pounding in her chest, delighted in the feeling of utter exhaustion that accompanied its powerful exertions. After last night, she wondered if she had terribly misread all those feelings.

John Stengle sat with his wife, Theresa, and his daughter Katie chatting over dinner the night before. The topic that night was gross to Katie: Parasitic wasps. They would lay their eggs in other insects and attack them from the inside when they grew up. Why her mom watched those nature shows was beyond Katie—they could be so, so—yucky! Still, Katie loved to listen to her parents talk. They did not exclude her, even when the topic was beyond her comprehension. They often favored her with loving looks and questions about matters which concerned her. Sometimes they yelled at her for not eating, but even then she did not feel like they were yelling. Though they were! Somehow they seemed to make even discipline seem acceptable— seem—loving. She knew they loved her dearly.

As they ate, dad had commented on a strange feeling in his chest. Katie paid it no mind, though her mom seemed concerned. In fact, Katie had begun to wrestle with her peas, attempting to eat them with her fork (like her parents did) instead of a spoon. As she struggled to order the little spheres on the tines, she suddenly started when her dad moaned loudly and slipped from his chair. Her mom rushed around the table and flashed her a look she had never seen before. Katie's eyes widened as she froze in her chair, panic flowing from her mom's eyes to hers in a split second. Tears welled up in Katie's eyes, though she did not really understand what was happening. She only knew mom was scared. She sat stolidly, as mom raced to the phone and called someone. What seemed like hours later, firemen came in a van and took dad away. All the while they waited, mom kept trying not to cry. She alternately held Katie, and dad's hand, speaking quietly to him as he lay asleep on the floor.

When the firemen had driven off, mom had bundled Katie up, gotten them into the car, and raced to the hospital. She said she didn't know what was wrong with dad, but the doctors would figure it out and he'd be all right. Katie sat numbly, having no idea what to do. (Thinking back on it, she could not recall her heart beating. She had been scared, but it was not like the scared of the fair ride. It was a cold, restrictive scared, which seemed to shut her body down and still her mind.)

It was at the hospital, sitting in the blue plastic chairs, that she had first heard the phrase that consumed her now as she hunkered against the wall of her bedroom. A doctor in a long blue coat and white tennis shoes had come up to mom and asked to speak with her. She stood, and turning to Katie, said, "Wait here a minute hon, I need to talk to the doctor about daddy." She then walked across the room with him and began a quiet, but seemingly intense conversation. Katie couldn't hear much of it, and what she did hear she didn't really understand. But one phrase was said a couple times, and stuck in her mind: Heart attack. Dad had a heart attack.

Sitting in her bedroom, scrunched down against the wall, feeling its little bumps drag over her spine, Katie rolled the phrase over again in her mouth—heart attack. What does that mean? Her eyes darted back and forth, looking at her dolls, their smiling faces staring out at the world. How can a heart attack? She shivered and felt the thump, thump, thump of her own heart. What if her's attacked? How could you fight that? Dad had fallen over and now was in the hospital. If he could not fight his heart, how could she? How could it even attack like that?

The questions buzzed through her mind, but she had not had the opportunity to ask her mom. Shortly after the conversation with the doctor, her friend Jenny's mom had come and taken Katie home, saying mom would come later. Mom had come later, but it was far too late, and Katie had fallen asleep. The next day, today, had arrived, and mom had gone to the hospital very early. Jenny's mom was staying around to watch Katie. Jenny's mom was nice, but Katie could not ask her the questions she was forming. She needed her mom to tell her what to do. Her body shivered, and once again she thought of her heart.

Would it kill her? Would dad's heart kill him? As she pondered her heart she realized again she had always found its beating to be a comfort. It raced when she was excited, or scared sometimes. It quietly thudded when she was resting. She never thought of it as something that would rise up and attack her.

Theresa sat next to her husband as he lay in the bed. The nurse had said he was sleeping, so she had entered the room as quietly as possible. The doctors had performed whatever voodoo doctors perform on heart attack victims and had left John alone.

Theresa watched his chest rise and fall, and listened to the faint beeps of the monitor that declared his heart was beating normally. She watched the little screen that showed a line with its jagged breaks indicating each rhythmic beat. She felt the cool skin of his hand as it lay in hers. And she again realized how much she loved her husband. His face was still, but in her mind she could see his grin as he swung Katie around in the back yard. Then she saw his eyes as they looked into hers before he kissed her. Her lips moved the tiniest fraction as she pictured them pressed to his, their arms around one another, his love flowing into her and pressing on her as his body did at night when they lay together. She flicked her head to toss the hair from her lowered face, and quickly dried the tear forming at the corner of her eye. As she did, she wryly giggled about how John would chastise her for crying at sappy commercials on TV.

Jenny's mom knocked softly at the door of Katie's room. Katie lifted her head as Mrs. Caples entered and crossed over to her. Donna kneeled down next to Katie and took her hand in her own. She ran a few fingers through the girl's hair and said with a soft smile, "Your mom said we could go down to the hospital to see your dad this morning. I thought we might go now."

Katie let her breath out. She had been holding it since hearing Mrs. Caples knuckles gently rap on her door. She had wanted to squirm away from Jenny's mom the minute she entered the room. Not because she didn't like her. She loved her almost as much as her own family! It's just that she was sure there was something bad coming. Adults always let the kids know last. Sometimes you found out on your own. Sometimes they sat you down and finally told you why they had been acting strangely for days. Katie had been sure that Mrs. Caples had come in to say, "I'm sorry honey; your mom's heart attacked her last night too. She's also in the hospital now." Katie breathed a quiet sigh of relief that these words had not come from Jenny's mom. She nodded at Mrs. Caples, and after rising, accepted a hug which both reassured her and unsettled her again. In the brief contact between them she felt Mrs. Caples love for her, and for a fraction of a second she also felt/heard the soft beat of her heart, evoking a shiver of fear. Could someone's heart attack someone else?

The two wrestled into their coats and headed out. On the drive down to the hospital Katie asked Mrs. Caples if her heart could attack her. Mrs. Caples looked at her for second, as though she did not comprehend the question. This was a bit frustrating for it made complete sense: Dad's heart attacked him, so, could Katie's heart attack her? Donna said no, that couldn't happen, but she didn't seem convincing. Why not? She gave no reasons why not. Katie settled back into stillness and silently urged the car to greater speed. Mom would know.

When they reached the hospital, and had exited the elevator, mom was waiting on a bench down the white (and funny smelling) hall. She was not at all like she was the day before. She smiled at Mrs. Caples and thanked her for her help, hugging her briefly before she kneeled down and gathered Katie into her arms. She held her close, and whispered, "Hi honey" in her ear. And for a few minutes Katie forgot her fear and again felt the deep comfort of her mother's soft hair, and warm arms, and the indistinct continuity of her beating heart. Katie gripped her mom fiercely and drove her face into the cruck of her neck, pressing her body to her and lifting one leg to her hip as she used to when she was very little and wanted to be picked up. (She was a big girl now and rarely wanted to be picked up, especially in front of others like Mrs. Caples. But she did not care at the present moment; she needed her mom desperately.)

Her mom laughed quietly and pulled her up onto her lap as she sat back onto the bench. Theresa looked at her daughter closely, and realized the fear that was sitting on her spirit. The fear that had sat on her own spirit until John had awakened, and confirmed what the doctors had said about his being in good shape. His eyes had opened and a small grin had crossed his lips. Theresa had leaned over him and kissed his forehead hard. He had bitten her chin! And one hand had lifted from the bed to tickle her breast softly through her sweater. That small act of indecency had made Theresa laugh out loud, releasing the fear and worry that she had held at bay through the night. John would need some care, but the future looked bright they had said. His little naughty touch shared his belief that they were still together, still having fun, still alive.

Looking at her daughter, Theresa realized how deeply Katie needed that same intimacy right now. She needed something to say, "We are alive," "We are still together." Theresa reached under her daughters coat and tickled her ribs while pressing her lips to Katie's neck blowing air through her mouth and tickling her throat. Katie screamed at the sudden shock of sensations, trying at once to grip her mother, and escape her fingers and lips at the same time. The two wrestled for a few seconds before mom relented and again held her daughter close, smelling her hair, hearing her heavy breath. She let Katie calm down for a minute, then looked her in the eye. Still some worry, but less. She said, "Daddy is ok, and wants to see you."

Katie's eyes widened for a second as she assessed the truth of her mom's words. She paused for a split second, then nodded, and slipped onto her feet.

Entering the room, Katie felt at once happiness, and a twinge of fear. She knew that sometimes "ok" was not really ok. Mom said dad was ok, but sometimes "ok" meant "I'm not telling you everything." When Katie saw her dad's face, she knew mom had been true. Her dad held his arms to her and she rushed to him, hardly noticing the wires hooked to his body. They held one another for a little bit, while mom just stood and watched. She had a tear on her cheek, Katie noticed, but she knew mom sometimes cried at weird times—even during TV commercials!

Katie blurted out to her dad her fear of her heart attacking her, and both of her parents, for a quick second, had the same look that Mrs. Caples had had in the car. It said, "What do you mean your heart attacking you?" Katie sucked in her breath wondering if she had misjudged her reading of her folk's apparent good moods just as she had misread the good feelings about her heart in the past. However, her dad's eyes suddenly revealed he got it. He looked at her for a second (sometimes he did not answer her questions for a good deal longer, as though he needed to think about them quite a while). Then, he said, "Listen Kate, you've misunderstood. My heart did not attack me, it was attacked by something called a blockage. It slows the blood flow through my veins and caused pain in my chest. But the doctors are taking care of it. My heart, and yours, are part of us, and don't ever attack us or anyone else. Get it?" Katie watched intently for signs of partial truth in her dad as he spoke. She saw none. She knew he wouldn't lie to her ever, but sometimes he didn't tell her everything either. In this case his face was open, and at that moment she gave all her fear to him. Their eyes locked for a long moment as she emptied herself unconsciously of the terror she had harbored.

Theresa watched as her daughter drew from her dad what she had drawn from her husband a while ago. She also saw the strength flowing from Katie to John, and hoped the same had happened when they had shared earlier. She stepped closer and laid a hand on Katie's shoulder, kissing her lightly on the head. The three of them laughed and talked and forgot how fragile the human heart can be.

Elephant

RICHARD HUDDLED IN UPON himself in a fitful sleep. He was at times awake, at times asleep, and often in that in-between state where dreams mix with conscious thought to produce a horrible world where flights of fantasy are reality and reality is twisted into nightmare.

The drizzle in the pre-dawn chilled to the bone. The thin cloak wrapped around Richard's body and clutched in his numb fingers gave little protection from the cold. He tossed and turned, knocking into his camp-mates as his body tried to generate heat by shivering and twitching. The ground was almost mud at this point in the campaign. And laying down meant accepting being wet, cold and dirty on most nights. It was almost better to take duty during the night. At least one could stamp his feet and rub his hands. And only the soles of the feet would lie in the mud. Then in the day one could sleep near the cook fires and if it was at all warm use one's cloak as a bed instead of a top covering.

Richard fought for the last few minutes of sleep—even when a large droplet of rain runnelled down his forehead and into his nostril. He shook his head spasmodically, blowing a hard breath at the same time to drive the water out. He tried to ignore it, but with that his eyes popped open. They immediately closed to slits while his pupils adjusted to the faint light. He caught a glimpse of clouds, broken at places to reveal only the few strongest stars that could still be seen as dawn approached. He saw the very early beginnings of sunlight, really just the hint of pink, silhouetting the hills in the far distance. Another drop of rain slapped him in the eye and he quickly blinked, fuzzing his vision for a bit.

He regained his sight and looked around himself, trying not to stir much. There, a foot or so away, was William's back. And there was Robert's. His cohorts were stirring slightly, fighting as Richard had to regain their sleep. But as Richard had found, one cannot fight the body's clock. It was almost assembly, and the body knew it. In a few minutes the horn would sound and the Captain would scream at them to "Fall in and be counted, you dogs!" As Richard awaited the assault on his ears, Robert rolled and faced him almost nose to nose in the early light.

"Awake?" Robert asked in a hoarse whisper.

"Yeah," answered Richard in his own raspy voice.

They both had probably been sick half the time they were on campaign. Only William, of the trio, seemed impervious to any disease which assailed the army. And there were many. One week you would be heaving your food in great clouts of vomit. The next you would be shitting the day away. Perhaps the next you would be hot with fever, or near to breaking bones with the shaking of a hard chill. Some who could take the war could not fight the disease. They would go to bed thinking, "If only I can sleep and be warm for one solid night I will be well come dawn." But dawn would come and instead of vigor and returned health (or at least the cessation of ills) they would be found soaked in rain, staring at the stars or early morning sun, stiff from death, and without further cares.

And someone would have to pick up the bodies. Richard hated that detail. Rounding up the dead from the night before. They were dead, but without fighting chance. They submitted, were forced to submit really, to an enemy which made no mistakes, feared no weapon, and only stopped after severe damage proved unable to kill.

Some would win the battle with disease only to lose the war. For they would go into battle the next day, man against man, and be so weakened that they really were only in a position to die standing instead of laying down. It was no way to die in either case. At least in Richard's mind. And in both cases, whether death in the night by the warlord of disease, or death on the field as an effect of his weakening, Richard or someone else would still round up the dead. It made no difference to Richard why the eyes were cold and fixed. He didn't care if the struggle was against man or disease. He only saw the twisted flesh, the rictus on the lips, the vomit, the frozen fear. It was there one way or the other. The idea of an easy death seemed foreign to Richard after his year of service to the Captain.

Robert broke Richard's darkening thoughts, saying, "I wonder what we'll be up to today?"

Richard's head rocked minutely with recognition of the words, and a short expulsion of breath expressed his disdain for anything that was proposed. He didn't have to say anything else. Robert nodded his agreement. No matter what they were going to be "up to," it would certainly be no good. It was going to be presented rationally, as though it made perfect sense. And it could be proved beyond a shadow of a doubt that it would be "no good" only for the enemy. (Although one must say, the officers never—EVER—were asked to prove the logic of their orders. That could get the questioner killed faster than the plan being presented!)

Whatever was presented for them to get "up to," it would certainly be presented as "no good" for the enemy, but manifestly advantageous to the men carrying out the plan. Even were they ordered to stick arrows fletch first up their arses, walk up to the wall, and fart them out at high velocity, they would be shown (were it ever explained) that this is definitely the best way to take a castle. Yea now, listen! Not only would such an attack be most fruitful, it was a wonder that all the great and legendary generals of history had somehow missed such a most fruitful strategy. The Arrow and Arse Strategy (as it would come to be called) would prove so successful that it would be taught at the best military schools in the world. Yea, even kings themselves would wish to learn and execute such an attack.

Richard just shook his head minutely thinking of the many "prestigious" missions he'd been assigned while they waited for the one tried and true method of battering down a defended castle: The Trebuchet. He decided he could wait indefinitely to find out what they were going to be "up to" this new day.

Last week the Captain had declared that they had waited long enough. (He was an inherently impatient man as far as Richard could tell.) He strode out and said to the men, "The time has come!" as though he had planned on his men lounging in the freezing rain and wind for three months, and only then was ready to spring his ingenious plan. At assembly he had ordered five men to come to his tent for a secret planning session. Lord pity the men who were chosen. Richard watched their faces as they marched to the Captain's tent after formation. They carried the look of men who thought they were to be knighted or at least given some special honor by their liege. Richard had long ago accepted that such honors were few and far between. And in most cases they were never given.

The five had disappeared into the tent for about an hour. Richard had forgotten about them in all honesty. He didn't care what duty others were assigned. He just wanted to do his own and return to the fire to try to drive the incessant chill from his bones. He and William had been standing by a fire, warming their hands, when they saw the five exit the tent. Gone was the look of honor and glory from their eyes. It was replaced by stark fear.

Richard had wondered often since then why they had been chosen. It was no surprise that they were not *regular* military. All the worst jobs went to the conscripted "rabble" as they were called by the full-timers. But these men were not experienced even in comparison to many of the conscripted. To the contrary, they had been conscripted just a month ago from the surrounding villages. They were not large men, perhaps it was their slight builds which singled them out, for the chore they were assigned, in hindsight, was probably best accomplished by men of smaller build.

The Captain had decided that since they could not bull through the walls they would tunnel under them. The castle seemed to have an unending supply of arrows however, and bowmen quite capable of using them with deadly accuracy. It was with peril that anyone came closer than about 200 yards from the walls. Closer than that, and an arrow was likely to be sent your way. Often even at the longest ranges, luck would direct it to a hit. And God forbid you were closer than 100 yards. At that range you were signing your own death warrant. Therefore, tunneling was not going to be an easy option.

The Captain decided that they would have to do it in the secrecy of night, and with a small force. The men would sneak close in the night and begin to dig. They would not be expected to dig all the way, but only enough to conceal themselves the following day. Then they would lay low, in their own tunnel, during the day, and the next night dig again. This procedure would continue until they had dug a tunnel completely under the wall. Each night a few more men would be sent to dig, and they too would hide in the newly lengthened tunnel the following night. After a week of digging the Captain was sure the wall would be spanned.

Then the force would enter the castle by cover of night and take it. And to the "men" (i.e. the *officers*) would go the spoils.

The only problem was the Captain's enormous ego. And the moat. He assumed that all men were his inferior and therefore had no idea of how to wage war as successfully as he himself could. This castle had no moat on the outside of the wall, so it was poorly designed. However, the owner was not a fool, but on the contrary seemed an insane genius. He built his castle on the edge of a small lake, and with a moat on the inside of the wall. There was a spring inside the four walls, unbeknownst to those besieging the castle. He over-stocked the front and side walls with arrows, millions by the looks of it, and had archers of the best quality. He knew he could defend against a frontal attack. He also had strange holes in the walls twenty or so feet above the ground. Their use became apparent when the wall was successfully breached.

The men had done their work, day after day. Richard assumed they had overcome their fear as the days wore on and the plan seemed to progress. Neither he, Robert, nor William had been sent to digging duty during the week. They were luckily not attached to the small force that quietly crept to the wall and into the tunnel on the final night either. Thanks be to God that they were not! When the men had dug far enough up toward the surface, they suddenly learned of the inner moat by the crashing down on their heads of tons of water! It flooded the tunnel and killed many just by collapsing the sides into wet, choking mud. Those that were near the rear, or just against the outside wall of the castle itself (and therefore not drowned) learned the secret of the holes in the walls. As they backed away from the torrent coming out of the tunnel they received from the holes above a shower of stones and rubble. It cascaded down on them, crushing heads and breaking limbs, pushing bodies into the muck that flowed from the engulfed tunnel. Within minutes only a few were left running across the field to be shot at from the dark towers. A few made it. It was difficult to see, being night. The next day the unlucky were seen spiked to the field by long-bow arrows.

No one went out to retrieve the bodies. The crows came and picked at them; they were still doing so for that matter. Richard shook his head just thinking about it.

A moment later William pushed his head out of his cloak and rustled around to grin at his two friends. "Hey men!" he said without a trace of the raspyness the other two possessed. As was noted, William never succumbed to any disease. He said it was because he was a true and virtuous man.

To Richard that very well could have been the truth too. William never missed his prayers at night. He always saw the vicar before battle, and sometimes, he even gave away his spoil (if he found any) to the poor people who constantly seemed to be about the outskirts of the camp. Robert and Richard, though not deep in debauchery, had partaken of some of the young and willing women to be found in the villages they'd passed, but William was chaste as a newborn. He said he would wait for his one true love or die with a clear and honorable conscience. Although Richard and Robert teased him (partly because he was the youngest of the three), they deeply respected him too. He was wise beyond his years, and fierce in a fight, yet with compassion. Richard had seen William fall a man, and after the battle was over, help that same man if he still lived. William was destined for something great in Richard's eyes. Provided he lived out the year.

They had been three months on siege duty with nothing to do but be showered with arrows and exposed to the elements. As the three lay in the morning quiet before assembly, they each had one thought in common: I hope I live to sleep again. All three had been conscripted about the same time a year ago. The Captain had been sent to take down a rogue landowner who had declared himself king of all the surrounding parts and had ceased tax payments to the true King. The great, high, lord, king of England did not stand for such foolery. So he sent the Captain off to take the rascal down hard. Since most of the army had been sent to Scotland for war, this small bit of dirty work was to be handled by an army (or rabble) assembled from the indigenous (and supposedly very nationalistic) population.

Richard, Robert and William loved England. In that sense they were nationalistic. They loved it as any person loves the place they live. But none of them had the slightest interest in anything in a district 100 miles away, let alone an interest in warring with the Scots over some distant crag. They loved their fields, their homes, their friends and family. They loved their villages and the world they inhabited daily. They did not care about politics and empire. It was with very little enthusiasm that they entered the service of the Captain as his small force passed through and invited them to join them. Invited them at the point of a spear, that is. "God save the King, we'd love to defend his honor." Or so they said.

The first few months had been hard and dangerous. None of the boys knew a thing about war. Yet they were given swords and pikes and other paraphernalia and told to fight. Each little village they came to in the kinglet's territory was viewed by the Captain as a major city to be ransacked and subjugated. The villagers probably didn't care who was king just as Richard and his friends didn't care. But they also were not going to let a rag-tag group of pseudo-soldiers gut and raze their land! So every village was a fight. And since the army was not well-equipped (though they were promised the needed equipment by the time they reached the castle) the battles were often quite even and hard fought. Most turned into huge bloody brawls with little coordinating structure.

The three lads had come together within a few weeks of their respective conscriptions. Richard had been first to be drafted since his village was the first (of their villages) encountered on the way to the kinglet's territory. He joined perhaps 100 trained soldiers and 500 semi-trained "volunteers." He was lined up with the other lads of the village and told that a great service needed to be performed for the king. There was treason in the land—blah, blah, blah. The upshot was that he kissed his weeping mother and sisters good-bye, and joined the army. It was the only option at the time.

There was a young man in his village who felt conscription was not appropriate. He was actually working with the local monk, learning how to read, and pray and what not. He was destined for a spiritual life for all intents and purposes. He was pretty well educated by the monk and felt he might be able to convince the Captain (or his sergeant really) that he was not a fighting man, but rather a man of God.

The sergeant was not impressed. He cuffed the young man to the ground and told him to get in with the others. His book learning and holy gobbledygook was of little interest to the King and his needs. Well, the boy ran instead. Walked actually. He said he would have none of this murderous business, and just turned and walked away thinking the sergeant must relent. He seriously misjudged the situation. The sergeant took a spear from a soldier and coming up behind the lad, thrust it through him until it poked out his sternum. The lad fell face down, squirming around, trying to extract the spear. He died with his face in the dirt.

Richard recalled the look on the face of the sergeant when he glanced around at the people standing about. He looked like a feral animal. He pointed and said, "Anyone else care to ignore their duty to the King?" Richard marched out with the army the next day. None of them cared to ignore their duty.

A few days later the same sorts of scenes were played out in William's and Robert's village. Some other lad tried to hide in a root cellar. He was found and beaten. When his mother would not let go of him, she was forcefully taken away. Richard saw her the next day when the army left. She had a great, black bruise on her face where she herself had been beaten. She probably tried to ignore her duty to the King too.

The three did little more than act as pack animals much of the time that first month. All the new men got pack duty for a while. They were issued weapons, but not taught how to wield them properly. They did watch the more experienced men practice some and that helped. And most swung the swords and things around when they had a spare moment. But for the most part, they just carried things for a long while. It was not until they passed into the kinglet's territory that they were truly introduced to the art of war. And of course, their real tutelage was under the duress of actual battle.

Why Richard, Robert and William became friends was hard to say. They knew each other's villages, so that was less of a barrier. They were all about the same age. Robert and William already knew one another having grown up together in the same village. Mostly it was because they were assigned duties together. They would go out and retrieve food from the surrounding farms. They would dig holes. They would tend animals. They just grew into the habit of being around one another in leisure as well as work times. They soon were sleeping near one another, and ultimately became fast friends.

Having ruminated long enough that morning, Richard shook his head, scattering drops from his wet hair, and stood up. He was uncomfortable, as usual, after a fitful and wet night. Robert groaned as he too stood and shivered his body to wakefulness in the predawn. William hopped up as though he hadn't a care in the world. He looked as though he had never been ill in his life, and had slept on a feather mattress in a warm room. Stupid William.

The three stamped their feet and tried to shake off most of the muck they'd acquire during the night. Even the hay they'd laid down to cover the mud was wet and dirty at this point. Everything was wet and dirty thought Richard.

A moment later the barking of the sergeant, predictable as a cock crowing, filled their ears. "Get up you dogs! Get in line! Hurry it up or you'll be carrying shit for the rest of your lives!" The same sorts of threats were present every morning. The three men hurried over to the assembly field and got in line. They were pretty good at lining up by now, having done it for a year, every morning and night. They were actually pretty good at a lot of things. You had to say this: They weren't the most trained army. But the sergeant did expect them to try. And he made them do things right. After a year of such command they actually were an army of sorts, though they still had less than optimum gear for the job.

This assembly in the morning and evening was not just a requirement for discipline. It served a purpose for the officers too. They could count the men and determine if any had gone missing in the night. And it was not uncommon for some of the newer recruits to take it into their heads that they could escape their "duty to God and Country" by hightailing it out in the cover of darkness. None had ever made a clean break. Hoskins and his small band made certain of that.

Hoskins was a full-timer with lots of time under his belt. He had apparently served with the Captain for years and years on many campaigns. For a regular soldier, he was afforded special graces at times that others were not. He received kegs of beer on occasion. He even dined with the Captain now and again. Richard had heard it was because Hoskins had saved the Captain's life once when they were young. The Captain had never forgotten his debt to the man, and kept him as his personal bodyguard and errand boy.

One of Hoskins' recurring errands was to hunt deserters. He and his six men were a ferocious team of thugs and brutes. And they could just about back up any swagger they exhibited. Richard had no desire to interfere or even interact with any of them. He had never seen them lose a fight, and never seen them give any quarter. They were cunning too. You could perhaps beat some thugs because they were stupid as a sack of rocks. Hoskins and his crew were not such types. They had been refined in battle, schooled in tactics, and hardened by the elements. As far as Richard could tell, they were impervious to pain and extended no mercy. He was glad they were fighting with him and not against him. Although he had no doubt they held him and all the conscripts in contempt, and would just as soon kill them as the enemy.

In any event, the morning and evening assembly's gave opportunity to count the men. Few disappeared if they had seen Hoskins and his band retrieve a deserter in the past. They were under orders to bring them back dead or alive. He seemed to prefer dead. And if they were alive, Richard wondered if they would prefer to be dead. Most were beaten quite badly. And if they were in any semblance of health after dealing with Hoskins, they faced a lashing for desertion the next day. It was not a pleasant punishment, but it certainly instilled a respect for loyalty among the men.

Richard stood stoically recalling the conversation with Robert this morning in the mud. What would they be "up to" today? He was tired of the whole operation. And the Captain was so very impatient for a conclusion. He was dangerously impatient at this point. Richard worried that the tunnel was just the first of a series of operations bent on wresting the castle from the enemy before the siege engine arrived. As though the Captain would garner more praise and honor from his King if he took the castle under the most difficult of circumstances.

Perhaps the Captain was just as homesick as the rest of them. Perhaps that was why he was so willing to sacrifice men to achieve a goal that could not be achieved without the proper tool. Richard didn't really care if the Captain was homesick or not. He just wanted to be alive when the time came to go home. It would do him very little good to quench his homesickness by having his body carried back and put in the ground in the back field. He'd much rather sleep in mud for another year than risk sleeping the sleep of the dead for the rest of eternity. Of course, William would point out that we do not just sleep at death. We go to face our Maker, and then live forever. Richard believed that in his mind. His heart was less convinced. If he was going to meet his Maker, he wanted to do it a long time from now.

The sergeant was waiting for his underlings to finish the count for the day. No one had run away and no one had died during the night. One small victory. He then called out a few special orders. None applied to Richard and his friends. Assembly broke and everyone headed for breakfast. One of the main differences between this army and a group of rag-tag rabble was the food. The Captain served in the real army and knew that to keep the men fighting they had to be fed. There was not a great deal of food, but what there was, was found and utilized. So every day in the morning, at noon (or after duty) and at night, the men were given a meal. Usually it was the same things over and over. Bread, broth, meat now and then, porridge. Things like that. It was not always tasty, but at least you did not starve. And the men were allowed to catch and cook what they wished on their leisure time. This morning there were small hard biscuits and a thin gravy. It may have been just the fat in which the biscuits were cooked. Each man received two. No more.

Having stood in line (there were always lines), the three got their food and moved off to find a place to sit and eat. There was no rush in the camp to finish quickly. There was not that much to do for the most part. They waited outside the castle. Beyond that there was nothing else. The castle expected no support from anyone. The whole territory surrounding the kinglet was in the King's hands. Therefore, they did not have to patrol the surrounding territory looking for some enemy who may sneak up on them. It would really be just a matter of starving the castle out—if the Captain and King had patience for such a move. Unfortunately, they would have to keep the army there until the castle gave in. And that cost money and time. And the King didn't want to waste such money and time. He wanted to make a point and crush the rebellion as hard and fast as possible. And a year on campaign was already far too long in the Captain's eyes.

They found a log a good distance away from the group and sat down. William stood leaning against a tree because he always had too much energy. Richard couldn't imagine how William could still be so energetic after a year of this. He was a different animal somehow. Even on the less than optimum amount of food, he still had more energy than anyone Richard knew. They scarfed their biscuits quickly and set their cups aside for the moment.

Robert said, "Do you think the tunnel taught Cubit a lesson? Maybe we will just sit and wait it out now."

Cubit was the name the men called the Captain. Just as Longshanks had gotten his nick-name from the long shins on his body, Cubit had gotten his because of the long length of his forearms. Cubit didn't know he was called Cubit by the men. It was more derogatory than descriptive.

William said, "I doubt Cubit learns much these days. He seems obsessed with finishing this campaign. On our broken bodies if need be."

Richard nodded and added, "I'm just hoping to get rear guard duty."

They all chuckled. Rear guard duty was the euphemism they used for spending time in the company of a young lady. There was no real rear to guard in this fight. No one was coming up behind them. And everyone knew it. They also all knew that if they were going to attack (which would be suicide) they would commit everyone.

"I don't see why we don't just make our own siege engine," said William. He said this a lot. He rarely listened to the reasons why though. Sometimes Richard thought he did it just to get people talking.

Robert answered dutifully, "I told you already. We don't have any carpenters. We don't have any plans. We don't have the tools." He counted off on his fingers as he made the points. He had done this before. It never sunk in.

William answered back, "I know those things. But we could at least try. Cubit and the full-timers have seen one. They know how they are built. And we could get lots of tools from the people here about. They would probably give them to us happily if it meant we would leave that much sooner!"

Richard countered, "And what about the trees?" It was obvious that there were no huge trees around to cut into the swing arm. And the size and thickness of the walls of the castle were going to require a very large trebuchet.

William sucked his lip. He had no answer for that. He never did. He had once proposed they lash a few largish trees together. But he had no idea of the forces required to hurl 250 pound stones 500 feet in the air.

Richard then added, "And we still have no stones. We would have to get them from somewhere." It was less of an argument because you could fill the sling with irregular smaller stones which could be dug up right around here. Richard had heard tales of Saracens even putting heads into the slings and hurling them at the enemy. He shivered thinking of a head hitting him.

William didn't respond. He was smart enough to know they had to wait. It was his desire to get into the action that prompted his argument. He was not blood thirsty. He didn't enjoy fighting. But he hated sitting even worse. He just wanted to be as active as possible. He probably was more interested in the building of the machine rather than the use of it. He probably didn't care if it worked or not. He just wanted an excuse to labor at something intensely.

Robert brought the discussion back to his original question saying, "So do you think we will get to sit and wait now?"

Richard thought a moment. Cubit was impatient. But truthfully, the debacle in the tunnel was pretty overwhelming. At least it was to Richard. Now that he thought about it, he wondered if it was to Cubit and the full-timers. He had heard some of them recounting tales of previous battles they were in. They'd seen a lot of things that Richard didn't want to ever see.

One fellow had watched as his buddies had received hundreds of gallons of scalding oil on their heads from a castle wall. The Captain that time (a different one apparently from Cubit) had had them build a ram to batter the gate down. It was an older castle with no covering towers out front. Therefore the ram could be rolled straight up to the gate and smashed into it. He said his friends were at the front of the ram, and after they hit the gate, the men on the walls had poured hot oil on them and the ram. That burned them horribly right off. But on top of that, they'd then shot burning arrows into the mess and set them alight. He'd watched his friends burn to death. The castle defenders didn't waste arrows shooting burning men. They let them burn.

You'd have thought that was enough. The men were burning and screaming and running around. The smart ones saw the water in the moat under the bridge the ram was sitting on and dove in to try to quench the flames. They didn't realize the moat was only a few feet deep and the owner of the castle had put spikes in the bottom pointing up. When the men hit the surface they were impaled through their eyes and faces and necks. Some didn't die right off. They were skewered like beef on a stick with their legs pointing up, on fire, and their faces under the surface of the water. They burned on one end and drowned on the other. The whole time kicking and wriggling around like a fish on a hook.

Richard shook the thought from his mind. He didn't want to fool around with attack in any way. He just wanted to wait for the trebuchet. He was no coward, but he was not in a hurry to die either. And this kinglet didn't appear to have overlooked any possible way of attack. Richard didn't want to end up burned, drowned or any other nasty way of becoming dead. He said, "I don't know if it made an impression on Cubit or not. I hope so."

Robert mumbled his agreement. He was a relatively quiet man. Richard had actually seen him when they left his village. He left quite a large family. His mother, father and a number of other children. His dad was a blacksmith, and Robert knew a good deal about the art. He could, in all truth, be quite useful at times fixing things and making articles of war. However, he mostly knew about making things used in a little farming community. He had not cried when he left. But his family had shed many tears. Especially his father. Richard thought he must have had a very special bond with the man. Although in the year since then Robert rarely talked about home. It was as though he put it out of his mind. Like to mention it was to soil it with the enterprise they were currently embarked upon.

Robert thought often of his family but didn't talk about his thoughts. He missed them terribly. Especially his fiancée. No one knew that he was to be married. The wedding was just months away when he was taken into the army. Marienne was so crushed that she did not even see him off. She wept and wept the night before he left. He could not console her no matter how often he told her he'd be careful, and he'd come back. It was all Robert could do to keep his own tears in check. He did not cry often. But his heart broke at leaving his soon-to-be wife. They had had great plans for a house and children. He would be a blacksmith and she would care for the family. It all seemed so distant now.

The three sat for a while just watching the drizzle that was beginning to fall. They were somewhat sheltered under the tree by which they sat. They were supposed to have tents to sleep in. They made lean-tos of sorts. But the wind would get strong and tear them apart. Camp was just not comfortable. And the tents would probably not stand much better than the lean-tos. Although Cubit's tent seemed to stay put pretty well. Not that he spent much time there. He often stayed in a little house he'd commandeered just the far side of the field. He was always warm and comfy.

They sat a little longer, then packed their cups away and prepared for their duty assignments. They knew what they'd get to begin with. Everyone got one of a couple different things: Go and get water, firewood, supplies or take care of the animals. After those things were done, they drilled for a while usually, and then practiced with weapons for a spell. The days were usually the same. They were not surprised to learn they were assigned to firewood gathering. At least they would be in the trees and out of the heavy rain when it came.

When they picked up their hatchets and axes for work, William again put in a plug for building their own trebuchet, "We have these tools. We cut trees all the time. I don't see why we can't just make something ourselves." It was almost as standard as the chores they were assigned. Richard and Robert winked at one another with grins. Rather than be annoyed, they appreciated the tenacity of their younger friend. He may be irritating at times, but that same quality of never giving up made him a good ally in a battle.

One time they had been in a dense, dark forest, fighting. It was tough going and the enemy knew the land well. They were constantly being surprised by small gangs of men, and soon everyone was separated into little groups all throughout the area, each fighting their way toward the village. Of course Richard, Robert and William had stayed close and ended up together. They had worked their way down a small gully and were just coming up the other side when some attacker had hurled a large rock down from a tree above them on the slope they were climbing. It had glanced off William's head and cracked down on his shoulder with incredible force, smashing him back and rolling him down the hill. Richard knew for certain he was dead.

A moment later four men appeared in front of them, swords drawn and ready to finish them off. Robert and Richard turned and fled down the hill, past William's prone and lifeless body and up the other side of the gully. They hoped to at least face their adversaries from higher ground since they were outnumbered two to one. The enemy saw what they were about and scrambled after them hoping to catch them in the gully bottom and finish them. They had not planned well enough, having not stationed someone behind the threesome to cut off their retreat. Richard thought they had probably believed the steep hillside would be deterrent enough. And it turned out they were partially right. Richard and Robert could only get a few steps up the other side when they were forced to turn and defend themselves from attack.

The one thing the enemy didn't account for was the strength and tenacity of William. He had had his collar bone broken, but he only feigned death. After the four attackers had run by in their headlong rush to pin William's friends against the steep gully hill, he had risen behind them with his ax ready for blood. He waded into the rear most attacker and took his head off with one brutal stroke. Before the body even fell he was upon the next in line, who happened to turn and see the headless corpse falling over. His view was obscured by the ax splitting his face open from eyes to chin. At that point the last two realized they were besieged from the rear and they tried to escape along the gully bottom. But Richard and Robert were quick to take advantage of their sudden fear and slew them handily.

When all was quiet, except for the heavy panting from the exertions, they grinned at William and slapped him hard on the back. (This made his eyes sparkle and his head swim with pain from his broken collar bone.) They were just so happy to have had him behind them, especially since they had thought him dead. Robert drolled in his usual low-key way, "Nice work Will, good of you to help out." It made them all laugh with the sort of laughter that flushes out the sure knowledge that they would all be dead were it not for the amazing stamina and tenacity of young William Cowler. On Will's part, he just wanted to wrap up his arm and get back to work. It was all Richard and Robert could do to convince him to sit a while and recuperate. His youth was going to get him killed!

Robert hefted his ax from the pile of firewood tools and slapped William on the back saying, "Ok Will. You finally convinced me. We'll build the siege engine today in our spare time after lunch." He winked at Richard as he passed heading out to the forest to start cutting firewood. Richard clomped after him grinning and laughing at the look on Will's face. He had brightened for a split second before he realized Robert was teasing him again. Then his countenance had fallen into the angry look a friend gives another friend who will not take him seriously. Finally he had followed the two older men out into the forest muttering to himself about "not taking a person seriously" and "don't think I couldn't do it if I had the right tools." Richard and Robert guffawed with laughter, catching the protestations of their young friend.

Firewood duty was really not too bad in the men's eyes. The camp was fairly relaxed and the men had the freedom to do their work through the day. They only had to be at appointed places now and again each day. As long as they accomplished their tasks, they were in no danger of being disciplined.

And it was not like the three would not have had such duty were they home with their respective families. One needed to collect firewood regardless of your employment. So whether it was here or at home, they would need to be out doing the chore one way or the other. Besides, you could almost imagine being in a forest near home when you were away from camp and with your friends, alone in the woods. The only drawback was that they had no cart to haul their wood. They had to strap what they cut to their backs and carry it back to the camp on foot. So they could not go so far as to make it impossible to carry the load back in a reasonable amount of time. But there were many out on this duty, so they did not have to have too much. A couple loads apiece would be good work.

It was not uncommon for the three to go farther than others. They were young, and did not mind a little walking. They wandered out into the wet forest away from the camp and the castle. Now and then a bird would chirp at their passing. They moved quietly through the underbrush, beneath the spread of oaks and elm trees. If they had been camped near a forest of good tall firs or pines they might have actually been able to make a siege engine as William desired. But they only had deciduous trees in the vicinity. They awaited an engine being brought by reinforcements from another battle somewhere. It was all sketchy to Richard just why they were waiting so long. Regardless, they did not have the right stock here to build one. The trees were bare, for it was already fall. The nights were getting colder and wetter, and they were hoping relief would come and end this campaign before the first hard frost hit. And they prayed nightly that snow would not fall. It may be unlikely, but they took no chances. God heard that request on a regular basis.

After walking in silence, grinning now and then remembering Will's indignance at being made fun of, Robert pointed to a downed tree. They tried to take fallen trees if possible. No need to cut one down if there was one already down and dead. They surrounded the fallen lord, and began to cut it up. For a good hour they worked in breathy silence. Only the thunk, thunk of axes hitting wood was heard. Now and then one would cough or sneeze, but they usually followed their system. They cut the wood up as quickly as possible and prepared it for carrying. If the tree was large, like this one happened to be, they would prepare as much as they could for a few days' work. The chances were good that they would get firewood duty every day. The young always did get the heavier chores. And there was also almost no chance of someone else from camp finding the wood. The others usually did not come so far. So if they had a few days ready, the next day they could just hang out in the woods until it was time to haul the prepared firewood back to camp.

So, having cut up the wood and prepared it for hauling, they would then just lounge around until they'd used up their time. Then they would haul their loads back, and get their next duty. This way they could hunt for something at lunch if they wished, or just sit and talk. Some men would waste time cutting. Stopping often to chit-chat, or just leaning on their axes. They would wile the time away, having to continually get back to chopping and carrying. Robert, Richard and William preferred to work hard and finish the task. And then take the rest of the time for themselves.

After working hard and getting it all done, the three sat down under a tree. They lit a small fire and put their feet up to it to help dry out their wet boots. It was quite nice really to just sit and enjoy the forest, knowing they had nothing required of them for at least four hours. The rain was beginning to fall more heavily as they sat, making it all the nicer to be under a tree. Though there were no leaves on it and some rain did get through, it was still better to be out on their own than in camp where any passing officer could recruit them to some chore.

They were sitting and chatting quietly about nothing in particular—the weather, the mud, ways to hunt, anything but the campaign—when William said, "Do you know what I heard the other day?"

Richard and Robert looked at him, waiting for him to continue. William always seemed to have some interesting bit of information he'd gleaned from someone. It was probably his open and naïve looking face that prompted people to talk around him. The full-timers would tell him stories sometimes, even though they had little use or time for most of the conscripted rabble (as they called them).

William continued, "I was sitting by the fire the other day, just warming myself and listening to some full-timers talk. They were talking about wars they'd fought and ways of battle and what not. And one of them said he'd heard of some people, hmmm, I can't remember their names, but some people using huge animals for war. They were called elephants. And they are like gigantic cows, but they are gray, have a huge nose and ears, and stand fifteen feet tall. He said they crash them into the enemy and sometimes just the sight of them would win the battle because the enemy would run in terror." William looked at his friends with a look that said both "It's amazing" and also asked, "Could that be true?"

Richard nodded thinking of it. He said, "I would surely not want to be crushed by a gigantic cow. Did you know the one talking?"

William said, "Yeah, it was Shelton."

Robert nodded as though he were about to speak, but as was more usual, he said nothing yet. He shifted a little and looked at Richard to continue.

Richard went on, "Well, Shelton, of all the full-timers, does seem like a pretty honest fellow. He taught me how to thrust and parry with the pike when he saw me blundering around with it one day. Course, he said it was just so his own back would be protected and not because he gave a rat's ass about some part time soldier."

They all chuckled quietly at that. Shelton was all blustery in that way. But truly he was a good man. It was not that the full-timers hated the conscripts. Most were typical soldiers and typical men. It was just that they didn't like the idea that some conscripted farmer could pick up their job like they picked up a hay bail. They felt that the conscripts needed to learn that war was an intricate art and not a hobby. Many appreciated the extra manpower, as long as you understood who was experienced and who was not. If you acted like you knew more than a full-timer, they'd make you pay for it. If you treated them like they knew their business, many would take pity and help you learn. Shelton was that type. He'd be tough, but he'd be helpful if you gave him his due.

Richard, Robert, and William never had a problem giving the full-timers their due. It was probably because they were young and were still taking some orders at home when they were drafted. Some of the older men had a hard time taking orders and being quiet. It made sense to Richard too. He wouldn't want to be drafted and then forced to take orders if he had a family and farm at home which he was used to running. And not all the men conscripted were single. They just took the men they wanted, who were fit and able. It was hard on a good many of them. It was hard on all of them in one way or another, come to think of it.

"Shelton is pretty reliable I think," said Richard.

Robert nodded again and this time said, "Yeah, I trust him."

William nodded agreement too. "I do too. He said these elephants were amazing beasts. And the keepers would ride them into battle like huge war-horses. They would crush whatever was in their way. It sounded a lot like what a trebuchet will do. Crush anything in its way."

They had never actually seen a trebuchet. Never even heard the word before. "Tre-bu-shay" was how it was said. They had been told they were waiting for a siege engine or trebuchet by the Captain. It was being hauled in along with stones to fling. It was supposed to tear a castle apart. William imagined a huge monster of a machine hurling 1000 pound boulders incessantly at the castle until it was smashed to dust. He wanted to see that.

Robert clucked his tongue twice. They all sat perfectly still, knowing that was a sign to them. Richard and William looked at him and he flicked his eyes over to his left. They followed without turning their heads as best they could. A ways away, maybe fifty feet, partly hidden by a tree, was the rear haunch of a deer. The animal had wandered toward them without hearing them due to the rain and the fact that they were talking quietly. Its head was clearly down and it was munching grass.

The three looked at the deer, then at their bows set neatly down ten or so feet away. They had no chance of getting to them without the deer hearing them, so they resigned themselves to just watching the animal. It was a good sized buck, and would have given a good deal of meat. It moved around the tree, coming closer to them. Suddenly, its head shot bolt upright and it peered across the short distance to the three figures sitting and watching. For a second nothing moved, then it turned and bounded away, tail raised in warning. It was a pretty animal in Robert's eyes. Would have been a shame to kill it, though he would have regardless. A person has to eat when the opportunity arises.

William idly pulled his knife from his belt. He was working on throwing it. And he was getting pretty good at it. He could imbed it deeply into a tree trunk at thirty feet with accuracy. He hardly ever missed these days. A full-timer had shown him how to hold the weapon by the blade and let it slip from his hand. It should only turn once in the air before it strikes the intended target. William had been hurling it improperly, and once he had the right technique he quickly grew proficient. He was working on moving targets now, and would hang a bag from a tree and try to hit it while it swung back and forth. He also would try for rabbits if given the chance. That was his intention now.

He got up and walked out into the woods leaving his friends by the fire. They looked at one another and smiled. They knew that William would try to get enough for all three of them. They decided to let him hunt alone for a bit. Robert had also set a trap earlier in the week. He checked it almost every day and would again today before they headed home. Richard had provided two pheasants last week for them, so he was letting the others hunt and provide this week. If they failed, they would not starve for there was always the food at the kitchens. It was not that tasty, but it was filling. They would probably get biscuits again at lunch today since they had had them for breakfast.

Robert turned to Richard and said, "So you never said what you really think. Is the Captain gearing up for something?"

Richard shook his head. "I hope not, but I think he is. What's frustrating is that I also heard that the trebuchet is going to be here at the end of the week. I heard the sergeant say it to some of the men that it won't be long now. I'd hate to die in a scheme just as the real answer to our troubles is rolling up the front gate."

Robert nodded in agreement. "What'll you do when we're done?" It was an often asked question. But it was never unwanted. They liked to dream about returning to normal life.

Richard answered, "You know, I think the first thing, when I get back that is, is to have a great big feast of all the good food I know. Not that we're going hungry, but I want it to taste like food too!"

They both laughed, knowing exactly what he meant. Eating wasn't enough. They wanted that flavor that said someone who cared for you made the food. They wanted the companionship of their families. They wanted to sit at a warm table and laugh and drink and eat without being wet and tired and, at the extreme, wondering if they'd catch an arrow in the back.

Richard continued, "And I was thinking that maybe we might live near one another. You know, you and me and Will? I know we're from different villages, but they're not that far apart. Split the difference and we're practically neighbors."

Robert again nodded and smiled. They'd talked about living near one another before. It would be nice to continue their friendship beyond what it was here. Realistically he didn't know if they would. Part of him loved his friends and owed them much and wanted to stay close forever. But part of him wanted to shut the door on this awful chapter of his life and move on. Sometimes he just wanted to marry Marienne, settle down and completely forget fighting.

A whoop sailed to them through the rain from off in the woods. Not long after William returned carrying two rabbits in his hand. He held them up, grinning in triumph. Both Richard and Robert stood and slapped him on the back congratulating him on his successful hunt. It had only been about an hour too. William regaled them with his prowess with the knife; how he had caught one on the run and one while it hunkered, trying to hide. He could get excited slopping pigs! Taking two rabbits with his knife put him into complete exhilaration! And why not?

William was young and still took great pleasure in even the most mundane tasks. He just had a natural verve for life and could find interest in anything. His friends appreciated his attitude.

They decided to cook the rabbits right then and avoid the envious looks of their campmates. Even though they could go and get rabbits as easily as William, many of the men preferred just to eat what was given. Richard, Robert, and William never enjoyed that. Besides, the time spent hunting was more time with each other and they enjoyed the company. They had become surrogate family in the absence of the real thing. And all three were young enough to need that.

The rabbits were not big, but they looked tasty. Richard skinned and prepared them while Robert set about putting up some sticks for them to hang from. William, as hunter extraordinaire, reclined at the fire and let his friends prepare what he'd provided. He absolutely beamed when they were finally set over the flame and the smell was wafting up. It made him feel good to do a good job. And looking at the approval in his friend's eyes, it made him feel good to give them something. He knew they teased him out of love and not disrespect. And he knew that they had watched out for him. Though he was but three or four years younger, he felt like they were more like elder brothers than equals. They seemed to know many things he didn't, and both had good steady minds which he respected. He sometimes chastised himself for his rashness and foolishness. It would have surprised William to know just how much Richard and Robert held him in respect. He was much smarter than he himself knew.

The three finished their lunch and quick-timed it back to camp with their loads. They dumped their wood and wandered over to the kitchens for whatever the cook had prepared. The rabbits, along with the lunch, would be more than enough for them to feel full. Richard was right. It was biscuits again.

After lunch they had drills. Each man brought his sword, ax or whatever he was good at, and they all gathered out in the field (away from the castle) and practiced. They usually did not use their weapons, but instead used wood copies. That way they could accidentally whack one another without much damage. William was very good with his ax. So good in fact that the full-timers would sometimes let him practice with them if they needed another man. He was big and strong and what he lacked in finesse he often made up for in ferocity. Even at practice he did not like to lose.

Sometimes they would just stand and work on moves. The sergeant would walk around and correct form or engage someone now and again. Slash, parry, thrust, turn, cut. They would go over it and go over it. It seemed repetitious at first, until that first time in battle when a practiced move suddenly worked so fast you forgot that it was a set pattern. Then you thanked God and the sergeant for making you do it a million times.

Today they were hacking away at dummies when the sergeant yelled out a list of names. Richard's, Robert's, and William's were all included. There were perhaps twenty in total. The three lowered their weapons and looked at one another with that sinking feeling that they had just been chosen for a singularly unwanted honor. They assembled to the sergeant who led them off a short distance to a tent with no sides. They could all crowd under the top and stand out of the rain as he told them about their "honor."

Richard's worst instincts were confirmed. The Captain was gearing up for more attempts to subdue the kinglet by means other than waiting for the siege engine. Like the last time, this attempt was to involve stealth under the cover of darkness. At least they wouldn't be walking out into a shower of arrows, thought Richard. He glanced over to his friends and saw Robert just shaking his head imperceptibly.

The sergeant had laid out a map of their situation. There was the castle, set at the end of a large field. About two-thirds the way down to the other end of the field, was their encampment; it was about 240 yards away. The Castle's rear wall sat against a small lake, but not right at shore height. There was actually a fairly sheer cliff leading from the water's edge up to the castle wall. In the center of the rear wall, at the base, was a small opening where the overflow from the inside mote spilled out and made a waterfall down the 130 feet or so to the lake surface. It was this opening that was apparently going to be the focus of attack now.

Richard listened as the sergeant laid out the plan. A small force, those presently listening to him, was going to climb the face of rock from the lake to the outlet in the wall. Usually, when a castle has a stream or spring which empties through the wall, the opening is barred so no attacker can get in that way. This castle may not have those bars since the water comes out over a 130 foot cliff bordering on a lake. Any craft which approached the wall could be burned in the water, and even if it made the cliff, the men would still have to climb up to the opening, maybe even through the waterfall. And that is precisely what the Captain was ordering them to do. Of course, they didn't have a boat to row over to the wall. They had to swim there, hauling anything they were going to take on small rafts they could build and tow.

Richard was soon shaking his head along with Robert. How in hell the Captain came up with this was beyond him. Although the idea could work, theoretically, Richard did not believe it was going to. The swim in the cold lake alone was going to be a taxing ordeal. And then to have to climb the rock face with some gear would be almost impossible. And God help them if they were somehow spotted. They'd be pinned to the rock with who knows what hurdling down on them from the castle above.

While Richard waded through his dark thoughts of their chances, he glanced over and saw William had scrunched up his face and seemed to be concentrating on how best to get up onto that wall! He even spoke up and asked, "Is that cliff actually smooth or does it have cracks and things to hold onto?"

Most of the silent men around him just looked at him as though he had a third eyeball in the middle of his forehead! What the hell was he saying! Was he buying into this? The sergeant replied, "Good question man, and that will be your first assignment. You swim out there today and inspect that face. See if we can get up it."

Nice one William, thought Richard. Now you've stuck your foot in it! The plan was simple—yep, a nice simple way to get killed. Of course, now that William was in it, that meant Robert and Richard were too. Richard had thought about feigning illness, but that was out of the question now. He was stuck.

When the short briefing was over they had their work to do. William was to swim over to the face and look at it. Still shaking their heads, Richard and Robert volunteered to accompany him in case he needed help. The others were to start making small rafts to float their equipment along with them. There was to be no moon two nights from today, and on that dark night they would attempt their entry.

The three went over to the kitchen to get some grease. They didn't want to be in the cold water without covering their skin with a thick matte of lard for added insulation. It may or may not help, but William said he'd heard it was done. They got a big bucket from the cooks, and headed off to the woods and down to the lake.

Unfortunately, the nature of the task required that they have light to view the rock. They would rather have swum over in darkness to avoid any chance of detection. But if they did that, they could not see the rocks to survey them. And if they lit a torch at the cliffs base, they may be spotted. They would have to find out if the face could be climbed in the dark, by feel, only by going over in the day and looking up. They couldn't climb up at night as a sort of dry run because they would not be able to get down again in the night. Anyone who ever climbed a rock face knows that going down is almost impossible compared to coming up. That's because going up you can feel your way with your fingers, but coming down you only have your feet to guide you. And they are far too insensitive to climb and feel along at night.

So, whether they liked it or not, the three were off to swim out in the daylight to inspect a rock face that none of them (although William seemed somewhat excited) wished to ascend two nights hence. They didn't talk much on the way. Well, William chattered for a bit, but the silence of his cohorts quieted him. They, evidently, were not in the mood to discuss their options.

It was only when they reached the water's edge, that Robert said out of the blue, "Why did you ask that William?" He had a grin on his face which at first seemed contrary to the question in Richard's mind. "What the hell were you thinking son?" His inflection made clear that he'd come to terms with the situation, and was now making the best of it by returning to the banter common amongst the three. His voice took the tone of teasing a little boy over some silly action he'd taken.

Richard chimed in, "Did you think you were gonna get a big crown upon completion of this mission or something?" He put on a mock puzzled look as though he really needed to be informed of the intricacies of William's thought processes.

William began to stutter through his explanation, but Robert and Richard kept cutting him off with silly questions about this and that. After a bit, a serious William finally figured out they were again teasing him, and fell silent in disgust. This made Richard and Robert laugh all the more. Probably to shed nerves at what they were about to do as much as to hassle their younger friend.

There was no putting it off any longer. They shed their clothes and scooped out handfuls of grease from the bucket they'd gotten. They slathered the goo all over their bodies as thickly as possible and took one last look down the shore to their intended target. It looked quiet on the castle. No movement anyway. Of course, one never knew what was behind those slits in the walls. They would swim along the shore close to the brush as much as possible in order to stay hidden. That way, if they were spotted, they could at least hunker by the shoreline from the arrows.

The water was cold. But not freezing cold as Richard had feared it would be. He didn't know if the grease was helping or not, and wished he'd felt the water before he rubbed the grease on to see what the water felt like to the naked skin. At least he could have tested the theory of grease as an insulator. "Ah well," he mumbled, "one can't remember everything when one is about to die." It was funny the thoughts that went through your mind when you were in a stressful situation.

William took the lead and swam more quickly than the other two would have liked toward the cliff. They decided that it was probably in God's hands as to whether they died or not, so they swam after him, relinquishing some of their bushy cover for speed in the water. They decided to go into the lake about 200 yards away from the castle since about half that distance was flat field out from the castle side walls. At the half-way point, when the shore did not provide any cover because they had reached the field, they swam as hard as they could without splashing around. It was with heaving and relieved breaths that they reached the castle rear-wall and a sense of some protection again. Although in fact they were perhaps much less protected because above them were the same sort of openings as were on the other walls of the castle.

As Richard looked up, he thought of the men last week being crushed and killed by rocks and debris cascading down on them from those holes. He shivered in the water thinking of broken arms and the inability to swim; sinking down into the depths until you could no longer hold your breath and succumbed to the frigid death that forced itself down your burning throat.

As he looked up though, he noticed something else. The cliff was not sheer at all. He joined his companions closer to the waterfall and said, "This does look climbable doesn't it?" He spoke a little louder realizing that the water cascading down from above would mask their voices.

William didn't answer, but reached for a hand-hold and tugged his body up out of the water. Richard watched as he climbed up six feet or so from the lake, bouncing on the holds he'd taken to see if the rock was stable or not. He watched a bit, and then in sudden alarm realized that

Robert was no where to be seen. He quickly turned 360 degrees in the water searching for his friend. He hadn't heard anything that sounded dangerous. As he contemplated what to do, Robert's head suddenly emerged from the water in front of him. Richard realized he'd been holding his breath and released it in a grateful rush at seeing his friend. He said, "Where were you? We're looking at the wall, not the water!"

Robert beckoned him to follow saying, "Look at this," and he ducked down under the surface again. Richard dove after him and followed him toward what should be the cliff face. When they came up they saw that the cliff was untouched behind the waterfall. The water fell a good five or six feet in front of the cliff. If they could climb behind the waterfall, they would be under cover most of the way. The only drawback would be that at the top they would have to traverse an overhang directly in the torrent of water, or move to the side and climb up the last bit in the open at the castle wall's base. As they looked about, suddenly William's head bobbed up near them. He swam closer and said, "We can climb this wall men. At least I know we three can. I'm concerned about some of the others. Not all are as fit as we are."

Robert nodded and added, "I was thinking the same thing. I feel better about the whole thing knowing we would be climbing under cover of the waterfall. Perhaps we could take the most fit with us, maybe two or three of the rest, and convince the others to just tow the rafts." As it turned out the rest needed very little convincing. Having not seen the cliff, they still believed they were probably in for an arrow through the top of the skull, regardless of what the three scouts reported.

They swam back in dusk, having gone out late in the day. When they returned they reported to the sergeant who called the others together for a briefing on what they'd found. They suggested their idea of just five or six climbing the wall, and were pleased to find that there were no objections at all. The only thorny matter was picking the last three. Robert and Richard had hoped that doing the scout might somehow exempt them and William from the real climb, but the sergeant's logic was that they already knew the face now, so they must be part of the climbing team. Robert shook his head in grim fashion having already guessed that would happen.

The sergeant also asked for William's, Richard's, and Robert's input as to who they thought would be good to accompany them up the cliff. William was secretly honored to be asked his opinion by his superior.

He didn't realize that even the full-timers had recognized his intelligence and good common sense. Richard and Robert were not surprised to be asked. They figured they had a right to choose who they'd die with.

Looking at the men assigned to this task, they had little choice. All twenty were conscripted soldiers (what did that say about Cubit's confidence in his plan?) and most were still farmers at heart and not soldiers. All three had ideas, but Robert was the best judge of men among them. Everyone was sent off to dinner and the three remained a short while to discuss their thoughts. William suggested a couple of men who were certainly fit enough for the climb. Richard nodded his agreement and added a couple others who might do well. They had chosen based solely on physical build, thinking that the men must be strong and able to physically accomplish the task. That was true acceded Robert, but he reminded them that physical ability must be accompanied by mental strength. In those terms, at least two of the other's suggestions clearly were not suited to the task. One tended to be a quitter, and the other a complainer. Neither trait was wanted in a life and death situation like they were facing. Best leave them in the water where they can swim off or drown on their own without taking their compatriots.

Robert then suggested two slightly older men. They were not as strong physically perhaps, but Robert said he knew their temperaments, and knew they wouldn't give in under duress. And it was not like they were weak either. They were strong men, and able. Richard and William agreed and they reported back to the sergeant their desire to take Neville and Eric, limiting the climbing group to five total. The sergeant OK'd their plan and sent them off to eat while he informed the other two. They half expected an argument of some sort from the sergeant, assuming he'd have his own opinion, but he seemed agreeable to whatever they thought. Maybe, thought Richard, he figured obviously dead men should have a right to at least plan their own demise.

After dinner Richard, Robert, William, and the thoroughly unhappy Eric and Neville sat around a small fire talking about their plans.

Eric said, "How the hell did sergeant Woodling decide on me anyway?" He looked at William when he said it as though Will had some close contact with the sergeant. Eric didn't know that in fact, Robert had suggested him and Neville for the chore. And clearly the sergeant hadn't told them that the three had chosen their own companions. Richard said a silent thank you to the sergeant for that. All they needed were two cohorts angry about their selection to the team.

William began to speak, but Richard broke in quickly fearing he would say bluntly that Robert had selected them, "It doesn't matter how the sergeant decided. You were chosen and that's all there is to it. The matter before us is what do we bring with us?"

Neville chewed at some jerky, spitting now and then into the flame causing it to hiss for a moment. He sighed and said, "Well, we don't know for certain that there aren't any bars across that outlet. Seems to me we have to bring at least some weapons and some cutting tools."

Robert broke his usual silence and said, "Then we need to think of what sort of tools. If we bring some saws for a wood barrier, which it is unlikely to be wood I might add, but if it were, and we bring saws, we could cut it pretty quick I would think. Now if it's iron bars, which I think more likely, we have two options. We can bring something to cut the iron, which I doubt we could do, or we must bring chisels to chip the stone away around the bars. Cutting them out in essence."

Richard added, "Yeah, I doubt it would be wood. That would rot too easily. If they think they have need of a barrier, then knowing this kinglet, it will be an iron one."

William jumped in saying, "We could easily carry up some chisels and hammers. I would bet, by the looks of the castle, that the bars are old and the rock weakened by the flow of water too."

William was right about that. The castle was older. You could tell by looking at the rock in the walls. They would have to hope that the king-let didn't spend too much time thinking about the small outlet on the lake side of the castle. Perhaps he was over confident on that one little point in his defenses. Unfortunately, the rest of his defenses showed no over confidence, just good planning. Richard 'tsked' his tongue thinking about it.

Eric ruminated, "I wish I wasn't going." Richard hardly knew the man as Robert seemed to. He wondered if he was such a good choice af-ter all. But Robert was good with men and said he'd be ok. Eric went on, "You know, if we're bringing hammers to chisel out the bars, we could use them to help the climb too." Richard pondered what he was saying. Eric continued, "We could bring some nails and see if we could drive them into the cliff as we go, sort of as an insurance against falling. We could hook some ropes to them and tie them around ourselves. Then if someone falls, they are caught by the nail in the rock. If we can get them in good and deep."

Richard discarded his worry over Eric. He may complain somewhat, but he was thinking too. That was a great idea. The cliff behind the waterfall had one drawback: It was slick. Not completely slick, but slick enough to be dangerous. They couldn't risk splashing noisily into the water below if they fell. The fall might kill them, but if it didn't, the sound would bring those who quickly would. Richard envisioned the rocks smashing his already stunned body as it floundered around in the lake after a fall from the cliff. The pins would keep them safe from falling and making noise. He said, "That's a good idea Eric. Where'd you come up with that?"

Eric half smiled at him and said, "Dumb farmer surprised you, eh?" He didn't actually answer the question.

Richard grinned and said, "I think they've entrusted this jaunt to a whole bunch of dumb farmers!" Everyone laughed the nervous laughs of people realizing they were in a tough spot with only themselves to get out of it.

Two days later there was no laughing as the group, plus a few support personnel, stood next to the lake in the cold, dark of a moonless night. Richard, Robert, William, Eric, and Neville stood nearest the water next to one tiny raft to which were lashed five short swords, the climbing implements and their tools. They were going to swim over first and begin to climb. Then a few men at a time would come over. This way they would avoid a large group of men in the water at one time lessening their chance of being detected. The men would just have to endure the water, or they could climb up on the face of the wall for a spell. No matter how you sliced it, they were in for a very cold wait while the other five climbed above them. And they thought the climbers would have it bad.

Richard glanced at the others up the bank and again wondered why they were even there. The five were to get in and open the gate. They could pull their own gear over the cliff. The rest were just more chance of being heard in Richard's thinking. But Cubit demanded twenty, so twenty walked into the forest.

The water actually felt a little warmer at night. It was probably because the air was freezing cold. The men didn't use grease this time either. They knew that it would just cause problems climbing and besides, they wanted to wear some clothes. It was tougher swimming though.

The weight of their clothes made it harder to float and move. So instead of actually swimming, they mostly strode chest deep as quietly as possible along the shoreline, towing the raft behind them. It went relatively well. No one splashed or fell. Of course, the five didn't think they would cause any problems. They worried more about the others; those who were less interested in even getting in the water.

Reaching the base of the cliff under the castle, they ducked through the waterfall, and pulled the raft close. William scrambled up onto the face. He had been chosen to climb first, for he was the youngest and most agile. Additionally, he volunteered for the job. Whether they liked it or not, Richard and Robert were stuck with the fact that William saw an adventure and challenge in everything. To hell with the danger, he just wanted to get to work.

Neville handed William the bag of long nails they'd brought and he hooked it to his belt. He then slipped a short sword into the scabbard on his back. The hammer went into a loop in his belt on his right side. He felt around above him for handholds, and finding some, he began to climb before the others even left the water.

It was tricky business, climbing. He could not step blindly with his legs and feel for holds very well with his feet. He had to know where to place his boots or he would be groping around in the dark. He had to locate holds with his hands that would serve not only for his fingers, but also for his feet as he moved up the wall.

When William was about fifteen feet up, he stopped and retrieved a nail from his bag. He turned it blindly in the dark so the point was toward his little finger and held it. He then felt for a small crack to drive the nail in. It was difficult to locate something in the almost complete darkness, but he knew from his scout there were many small cracks all along the wall. If all else failed, they had each brought small candles to light.

That was another of Eric's ideas. He was full of interesting thoughts when it came to planning the infiltration. He had brought along a bag of extremely thick pitch, and another of some tiny shelf like pieces of wood, no bigger than half a hand. These two bags hung from Richard's belt as he ascended the wall behind William. As Richard climbed, he would occasionally light a small candle (which was surprisingly easy considering the water falling just five or six feet away) and using the pitch and little boards he would affix it to the rock face. Those that followed had a sort of lit trail to follow as they climbed.

The whole process, William putting in nails, Richard marking the way, tying the ropes around each man, worked smoothly and without many hitches. All but William were somewhat astounded at the ease in which things were working. The procedure made Richard uneasy because his experience in this campaign so far was that nothing worked easily unless it was about to take a turn for the worse! It was with a great deal of trepidation that he settled in behind William at the top of the cliff next to the water outlet.

When the water falling behind William was within about four feet (roughly thirty feet from the top of the cliff), he had moved out to the left of the falling water and continued there. Mist coming from the falling water filled the air more fully once they were out from under the waterfall, so the last thirty feet of cliff face held no candles, for Richard could not get any to light and stay lit. This was probably for the best because out in the open the little flicker of light would be surprisingly bright, and could be seen from the battlements above.

There was hardly a need for quiet at the top either. The water pouring from the exit hole in the wall was under a lot of pressure and made a good deal of noise as it surged from under the castle wall and out over the cliff. Therefore, William had pounded five nails in around the opening for each man to tie into once they'd reached the top. He and Richard waited as the others arrived, for they could not begin knocking out the stone holding the iron bars until they could drop it without hitting one of their own.

As Robert waited patiently in the dark, hanging on a rope, deafened by the sound of water, he wondered if the other fifteen men they'd left behind had the sense to stay out from under the waterfall until they were sure the opening had been breached. They had been briefed that there would probably be rocks falling from above while the advance five opened the waterway, but Robert wondered if anyone was listening at that point. They may have been thinking of how to get out of this mission altogether. He'd hate to accidentally kill one of his own with a falling stone.

When all five were up at the top, they realized the plan to get in was probably going to work. The opening from which water poured was about five feet square. The water level was about 3 feet from the top of the opening. Through this opening they could see into the open space of the castle. The moat seemed to be about fifteen feet wide, and they could also now see how it was kept full. There was a spring bubbling up in the center of the square which emptied into a large basin, which in turn emptied into the moat, keeping it full. The amount of water filling the moat was equal to that which flowed from the opening before them. Thus the moat stayed full, and was much like a contained river. It was a great setup for a castle, thought Richard.

There were four vertical iron bars blocking the opening. The water obviously flowed through, but no-one could crawl through. Looking at their position, hanging in space, Richard doubted the kinglet really ever believed he could be attacked from this point anyway. It did seem preposterous that someone would attempt to climb 130 feet of cliff, and gain access to the outlet hole.

However, as they looked at the hole, they realized that they could, in fact, gain access. The rock showed severe signs of wear. It had been worn down by the greatest force of wear known: Water. The bars were rusted too. Looking at them, Richard thought a good large team of horses could probably pull them from their moorings if they were surrounded by dry ground.

After surveying the courtyard through the outlet, William signaled to Neville. Neville swung closer to the opening, found footing, and settled his weight into the rope holding him. (At this point, unknown to his cohorts, Neville said a very sincere prayer to God for the strength of the rope holding him. He did not relish plunging 130 feet to the water below.) He next pulled a two foot iron rod from his back pack. He touched the tip of it to the stone about a foot under water and to the left side of the opening, and retrieving his hammer, he struck a blow to the other end of the rod. The reaction almost made him lose his balance and fall! The rock was indeed quite worn, and when he struck the rod, it immediately pried a foot long chunk of stone from the wall, which almost hit him as it flew out and fell.

At first the others had wondered why Neville had not attacked one of the bars itself. But on seeing what happened, they realized they would not have to remove the bars at all. They could probably chop enough stone out to one side to get through. Once the stone on the outer wall was removed, the water pressure itself would sluice the inner fill out. Walls of these kinds of castles had two stone outer edges anywhere from one foot to many feet apart. Then between them was just fill of some sort: Dirt, rocks, even timbers sometimes. This was an old castle. The outer and inner stone faces were just two feet apart, and the inner fill was mostly dirt. Once the rock on the outside surface was chipped away, the dirt inside was washed out by the passing water.

There was another advantage to this that they had not previously thought of—at least none of them but Neville. Once they had opened a hole to crawl through, they would have to wade against the pressure of the water pouring out the hole. They had thought they could perhaps use nails again to hold them from falling as they struggled against the water. But now, they could slip in next to the bars and then lean back against them. The bars would serve as a safety net in effect. If they slipped and were washed back, they would crash into the bars. It was better than falling.

Seeing how easily the first rock had dislodged, Neville set to work. He quickly opened the hole he'd started, and soon water was pouring out next to the original opening, driving dirt and fill with it. Within an hour, they had opened enough to get through. And the whole time, their efforts had been almost entirely muffled by the roar of the water itself. Richard had actually been hoping they wouldn't be able to get through. He didn't want to get into the enemy's castle! He preferred waiting for the trebuchet. Now he realized there was nothing for it but to climb into the very lair of the kinglet himself. His heart sunk a bit as he watched William prepare to crawl through the opening.

William struggled against the current of water, but managed to slide over against the bars. The water flowing out then actually held him in place, pressed against the inner side of the bars. From this position, leaning back against the bars, he could reach forward and tap a nail into the mortar that held the stone together on the inner side of the wall. It was here that he actually needed to be careful. For now he was visible to anyone walking the inner court, and could conceivably be heard as he tapped the nail in. But again (unfortunately in Richard's eyes) luck held and William got the nail set without detection. He looped a rope around it and within a few more minutes was standing on the moat floor (for it was only about five feet deep) pressed against the inner wall of the castle. The rope he tied to the nail was washed out to his companions on the outer side, and using it, they too managed to crawl through. It was not much later that they all were standing in the moat, in the dark, looking at the inside of the castle they had been staring at for months from the field outside!

They were all silent as they pondered the next move. Eric's head shook imperceptibly as he muttered to himself quietly, "How the hell did I end up here?" He was a bit predictable.

Things had gone so well to this point that Richard felt pretty optimistic about their chances. They had two assignments to complete and they were done. (As done as a man can be standing in the middle of the enemy's stronghold!) They had to get the other fifteen men up to the entry hole and into the castle with some degree of stealth, and they had to somehow seize and unlock the gate mechanism. Then one flaming arrow out over the wall and the rest of the force would attack as the gate opened. Hopefully this would all take the defenders by surprise.

The five men looked about for another few minutes, just standing and assessing the situation. No one and nothing moved. There seemed to be animal pens at the far side of the inner courtyard, and even the animals didn't stir. They had decided to just cut directly across the courtyard since it was dark. When they were convinced everything was in order, Neville took a step toward the inner edge of the moat. He just about completed his second step when the arrow tore through his neck. It was so dark that the others didn't even know where it had come from. Neville heaved back, thrashing around in the water, trying to pull the arrow from his throat. He didn't succeed before the flow of water tugged him out the hole they had just crawled through. He was not able to scream as he fell to the lake below. He had missed the bars and plunged through the hole.

As Richard watched the scene, almost frozen in fear, he could not help but think Neville was going to raise the roof with all that floundering around. It struck him a moment later that the roof was raised already, and they were in deep trouble. It was while he was still thinking this that a voice rang out in the dark, "Stay still! If you move you die like the other!" No one moved. At least, at that point no one moved. In the first seconds of Neville's death William had plunged into the water and gotten back to the bars. He had looped the safety rope around his waist, and following Neville's body had let himself be dragged out the opening. He fell a good thirty-five feet before being jerked up short and slammed into the cliff. The jolt left him limp for a few minutes which probably saved his life. For after Neville was shot, and the defenders realized the spillway was breached, they had gathered above the hole and started to chuck rocks down into the lake. William, just by luck lay limply against the cliff, hanging by the rope. The rocks plummeted down around him, but none actually hit him. When he did regain a clear head, he could just hear screams coming from below as the rest of the men realized they were being pelted with stones. He pressed himself to the cliff and prayed he would not be hit and dislodged. All he could do was watch as the men were killed below him. And who knows what befell his friends inside. He did not think they had followed him.

Robert, Richard, and Eric stood in the moat, with hands raised, backs pressed against the wall. They watched as a number of torches flared to life and approached from many directions. Soon, fifteen feet away on the dry ground of the courtyard, there stood a small group of men with torches and bows. And to no surprise, none of them looked pleased. They ordered the three to walk over and get out of the moat. They did. Almost immediately, upon exiting the water, each received a solid blow to the face or stomach. Richard fell, his head swimming from the punch. And soon a number of boots began to work them over. Richard's last memory was of Eric's voice muttering, "How did I get picked for this." Then blackness set in.

William waited until the shower of rocks ended. He could hear nothing from below or above. Especially because the water still roared in front of him. Had he not fallen to a point behind the waterfall, he would probably have been shot or hit by the men above. As it was, he hung in more or less one piece, in the dark, alone and unhurt. Mostly unhurt. He winced as he moved his left leg. He was going to have to look at it when he got back—if he got back. The ropes they had used to climb were still on the cliff, hooked to the nails. Thank God for Eric's idea of the nails. William decided it was quiet enough to attempt escape. He began to fish about for the next line. He moved his body back and forth along the cliff face, swinging from the rope tied to the nail in the outlet hole itself. When he found the next rope, he transferred to it. And descended to the next rope. And on he went until, with great relief, he slid into the black water at the base of the cliff. He was totally exhausted and wondered if he could even swim the 100 yards to cover without drowning.

But again luck was with him. He noticed a small raft of those they had pulled over to the cliff still bobbing around not far away. He pushed off toward it trying to be as quiet as possible. He was sure they were still watching the dark water, listening for sounds of life. It was after but one or two strokes that he found the first body. A young man, about the same age as William, with a crushed head floating face up. William jerked back at the touch, but then steeled himself and pushed the body aside. He made for the raft, encountering another body and some smaller chunks of wood on the way. It was grisly to think what else he was swimming in. It was good to have the dark to hide it.

If you could call it luck, William had good luck. He reached the raft, and kicked all the way to the cover of the brush at the shore without incident. He didn't feel lucky, having seen his friend killed, lost his other companions to capture, and been battered falling from the castle. But as he hauled himself up on the shore, he realized he was very much alive and he could not bar the feral grin that crossed his lips. Life was something you rejoiced in, even when it seemingly cost the lives of your friends. He felt a pang of guilt at the thought of his friends. But pushed it away for the present. He was alive.

Richard stirred and let his eyes slit. A thin beam of sunlight crossed the stone wall across from him and highlighted a dank, smelly cell. He lay on a cold, rock floor. As his mind swam to consciousness, his eyes drifted around him. There against the wall was Eric by the looks of it. His face was puffy as though he'd been kicked squarely in the cheek. And there was Robert, laying just a ways to the left. His face was turned away, and he didn't move.

Richard looked down as feeling filled his body. He saw the black spider which had tickled his hand and drawn his gaze. It crawled slowly across his knuckles, stopping for a moment, before moving on. The involuntary twitch of Richard's hand made it skitter away into the darker portions of the cell. Richard let his head lay back and he stared at the ceiling. The light came from above. There was a square door in the ceiling, and the sliver of light showed from a slit cut in wood. Apparently they had been tossed into this room from that door. No wonder it was cold and wet, they were underground in a dungeon.

Richard shook his head, testing his wits. He quickly stopped when a sick feeling of nausea swept his body. His head must look worse than Eric's! He felt like a sledge had pounded him. He slowly inched his way to a sitting position, noting the pain in his left wrist. His hand was not bent right. It looked like he had broken the wrist, or more accurately, had it broken. He scraped over to Robert and rolled his friends face toward him. His eyes moistened at the sight. Robert looked at him with the cold gaze Richard had seen a hundred times while collecting bodies.

He was dead—and he'd died hard if the countenance on his face was any indication. Richard noticed his legs then. They were broken. Badly. It looked like Robert had bled to death from the fractures in his knees. His left foot was turned in the wrong direction. He was clearly beaten and dropped into the cell while unconscious. He must have landed wrongly to break his legs so badly.

Richard sat for a second looking at his friend. He didn't think under the circumstances that he could be affected any more than he had, but without warning he suddenly began to weep softly. He pushed Robert's eyelids down, and placed his hands across his chest. He then just sort of slumped down and wept quietly. He didn't cry just for Robert, but for the whole situation of his life this past year. He was sick of being a soldier in a fight that wasn't his. He was sick and tired of being ordered away from his farm, his family, his friends. He was tired of living in fear of death. He was now facing death at the hands of people he didn't even care about. He had no quarrel with these people. At least not until now. He wept for a long while. And hardly noticed when Eric slipped down beside him and put an arm over his shoulder.

William walked into camp alone, shivering with cold and barely able to stand. It happened to be Shelton who found him laying by a fire. He had heard that all the men had been killed in the night raid. He looked at the boy and could hardly believe his eyes. He picked him up and rushed him over to the sergeant's tent. They called the physician, and the cook and they began to treat his wounds. The cook brought soup, the doctor brought herbs and poultices and what not. In all truth, the boy was not hurt too badly, but he looked entirely exhausted.

It was the next day before William could sit up alone and debrief the sergeant on what happened. He related the climb, and the ease with which they broke in. He then told about Neville and falling out the hole and hanging by the rope as the men below were bombed with rocks. The last bit, walking back to camp was a bit sketchy. You could see that William had been running on empty at that point and most of the walk was a blur to him. Shelton was impressed he made it back alive. He was a good kid for a conscript.

It was that very afternoon that the trebuchet arrived. It was in pieces, but could be assembled easily. William sat by the fire and watched as the men put the massive piece of equipment together. He had been put on no duty until he recovered his strength. He watched, alternately marveling at the huge machine, and feeling depressed at the fact that it came a day after his friends were killed. Killed for no good reason in William's mind. They should never have attempted that attack. He now saw how stupid it was, especially as he realized the power of the machine being assembled before him. Why they didn't wait, as Richard had said, was incomprehensible.

He thought of the elephants Shelton had talked about as they attached the sling on the huge swing arm of the catapult. He imagined them trampling down the enemy with their big noses swinging back and forth. He hoped this machine would crush the enemy as completely. Though he knew his friends were not alive to see the destruction of their killers.

Eric and Richard settled near the wall of their cell. It was at least two days, as far as they could tell, and they had not been fed. They had not even been questioned. Of course, what was there to answer to. They had attacked, been caught, and now were probably going to be executed.

Near the end of the third day, the door in the ceiling opened and a bundle was dropped down into the cell. Richard wondered if he would receive an arrow in the back from the door above when he walked over to retrieve the parcel. It was some cloth wrapped around a crusty piece of bread (with some mold on it) and two dead rats. He convulsively dropped the bundle when he saw the rats and stepped back. Eric looked at the rats from where he sat and just shook his head. Richard liked Eric more and more each day. He was like Robert in many ways. He said little, but was intelligent and witty when he did speak. Eric sat for a little longer in silence, then said, "Well, if there is any way to survive and return home, it will be spoiled if we starve ourselves."

Richard had no argument for that. They had already eaten a few of the more palatable bugs in their dungeon. Rat was probably a step up from those. He leaned down and picked up the bread, breaking it into two pieces as he did so. He tossed one to Eric. As he was about to bend for a rat, the door above opened again. He was hit on the back by a skin of some kind. It turned out it was full of water. He breathed a sigh of relief, both at not getting an arrow in the back and at not having to drink rat blood to quench his thirst. Richard retrieved the skin and the rats, and sat back down next to Eric. Eric's ankle was turned so he was not getting up much if possible.

The two sat for a moment, picking mold from their bread. Then they munched it down in silence, washing the flavor from their mouths with small swallows of rather murky water from the skin. "With the spring right there in the courtyard" mumbled Eric, "no wonder the water tastes so good." His face held just the hint of a smile.

Richard looked at him, then realized Eric was joking for the water tasted brackish as though it had sat in a cistern for a long while. A little chuckle escaped Richard's throat, and Eric smiled a little more fully with him. They nodded in silent agreement at their terrible predicament and the fate that undoubtedly awaited them. It was surprising they received food at all.

There were two other problems that neither of them wanted to address. One was that of Robert. Their captors had not removed Robert's body. Richard had moved it to the wall away from where they sat. But it was not pleasant being in the cell with it. They had tried to cover it with Robert's clothes. But bugs still were finding a way onto it. It was rather gruesome to have to watch, especially for Richard. But again, there was no choice in the matter.

The other problem, though not as important yet, was there was no place to relieve oneself. They had not had much need since being caught. But then, they had a lot of time to think of such things since they were just sitting. They both wondered how long they were going to be in the cell.

It was amazing the speed with which the crew had set up the trebuchet. It came in already constructed pieces along with huge balls of rock to hurl. It was practically another army that brought the whole thing. They just set it up and pieced it together. They worked all day and night for two days and now it was almost complete. William watched with growing eagerness as he envisioned the rocks hurtling down on the castle, crushing the men who killed his friends. He wished he could help somehow, but still was pretty banged up. At least he was going to be able to enter the castle when it fell. He hoped the kinglet didn't surrender. William wasn't feeling forgiving at the present.

It was the third day of sitting in the near dark when the door in the ceiling opened and a ladder came down. A face appeared in the opening and said, "Give us the body." Eric and Richard squinted in the bright light shining in. They looked at one another, then walked over the Robert's body. One of them would have to heave him over their shoulder and climb up. Richard bent to do it. Eric was a bit lame, and Richard was Robert's friend. He hoisted the cold flesh onto his shoulder, grimacing at the dead feel of his friend's once vital shell. Eric steadied him, and then

Richard slowly climbed the ladder until hands pulled Robert from his shoulder. He received a boot in the back which knocked him down into the cell again. The ladder was pulled up, and the door closed. No more words passed between the captors and the captives.

Eric and Richard sat again. There was not much to do. No way to escape. They had only to wait until they were either starved, or killed. It was perhaps a few hours after Robert's body was taken that they both jumped at the sudden crash. The floor shook and dust sprinkled down on them choking their breathing. Richard covered his face as best he could with his cloak, and when things seemed quiet again he whispered, "I wonder if the siege engine has arrived."

Eric looked back and said dryly, "I was thinking all along I would not be on the receiving end when it began to fire."

Richard nodded. He had heard a lot of stories about how they would crush the castle. How the men inside would quaver in fear not knowing if they would be smashed by a huge stone. Or perhaps the walls would fall upon them and crush them that way. Richard had never envisioned himself inside at the time. He had not really thought of what it would be like to be *in* the castle. He heard the stories, but had not put himself in the shoes of the men being attacked. Now his outlook changed. It changed concerning his present abode too. He was grateful for the stone walls all around. Provided the ceiling didn't crash in on them or a projectile slam through the door and roll about the room breaking them into pieces. At least he was not in the open with the chance of being hit directly. Both men hunkered down near a corner, trying to feel somewhat protected from whatever may come.

After the first ball had been sent at the castle, William was actually excited again. He saw it fly over the wall and heard a great thump. He pictured it rolling about, maybe hitting the man who shot Neville. He didn't smile, but he nodded his head thinking of the justice in that. The arrow had caught Neville without any warning. Just as well the man be hit by a stone with no warning either. William couldn't wait to see one or two balls lay into that wall. Having seen it up close, he didn't think it would last too long under the heavy pounding it would take. The balls were perfectly circular, and weighed between 250 and 300 pounds apiece. He watched as the men rolled them into the sling and reset the throwing arm. It was a massive thing, and now he realized why they could not have built one on their own. The balls would fly a good 200 yards in the air before striking home and when they did, he imagined they would pummel anything in their way to dust. He waited eagerly for the wall to start taking impacts.

His countenance fell however, when he saw what the kinglet did next. Above the crenellations on the wall were sheets of wood that covered the archers from arrows falling down onto their positions. These ran across the whole top of the wall. As William watched, he saw some men tying another man down, spread eagle on top of these sheets of wood just above the gate. Any arrows or balls that hit them would hit the man too. William didn't need to see a face, he knew it was one of his companions. They weren't all dead. And the kinglet was using them as human shields. William didn't realize that the man being strapped down was Robert, and in light of the situation, he was already dead for all intents and purposes.

William didn't know what to expect next. He thought they would have to cease their attack. But watching the crews of men he realized they were not about to do that. The Captain, Cubit, did not care if he killed his own. He was going to have that castle one way or the other. William strode over to Shelton as quickly as his stiff body would allow. He shouted at the veteran, taking his arm, "What are we doing? They've staked a man out in the way. We can't crush our own men!"

Shelton looked at the boy. There was anguish in William's eyes. Shelton had been in his place before. What could he say? Men died, and there was no way around it. He knocked William's hand from his arm, which had the desired effect of reminding William who he was shouting at. Shelton then gritted, "Look boy, they're dead anyway. We may not hit them, but if we do, they'll die easier than if we leave 'em to the enemy!" He turned and went back to his work.

William felt like one of the huge ballistae had hit him in the chest. It suddenly came clear in his mind that Richard, Robert, and the others were not going to make it home. He had somehow kept that idea out of his heart since escaping. He knew it in his head, but he had not faced it inside. Now Shelton's words had brought home the truth. His last view of his friends was when he'd run and escaped capture. He wished he'd been killed with them, instead of abandoning them like a coward.

A second boom crashed above Richard and Eric. This one brought more dust from the ceiling and sounded much closer. Richard wondered if the cell they were in was in the center of the castle's courtyard!

He huddled down farther next to Eric who seemed remarkably calm considering they may be squashed at any moment. He was wondering why Eric was so relaxed when the door above flew open and the ladder dropped down again. An angry voice screamed down, "Get up here now pigs! Get up now or we kill you where you are!"

Richard and Eric climbed up the ladder. The last portion they were hauled roughly by their clothes. Four very angry men with swords menaced them as the door was shut again. One said, "I say we cut their guts out now and then stake em!"

Another countered, "No, we want 'em to scream good and loud when they're up topside."

Richard and Eric looked at one another with dread. It occurred to Richard that Eric was so calm before because he knew things could be much worse. Now they were. It was with a little relief that Richard saw some agitation in Eric now. At least it signified that perhaps there was nothing worse than whatever was coming up! Richard wondered again at the strange thoughts that pass through a man's mind when he is facing death. He was actually a little comforted by his friend's fear.

The men pushed the two captives ahead and poked them in the back with spears to herd them along. They were driven up some stairs onto the battlements. From this vantage point they could see the huge machine standing out in the field in front of the castle. It was terrifying. Richard now understood what the full-timers had been talking about; the fear that could be inspired by such a machine of war. It was no wonder that the men around him were angry. They were afraid for their lives.

Richard looked around. He had no idea what was going on. How could it help to bring them up here. He thought they were going to kill them and toss them over the wall for his companions to see. Maybe hoping that would stop their attack. When they pushed him up some wood steps onto the wood covering above he realized their fate. There about half way across the wall was Robert's body, spread out on the roof. Their captors thought to stop the catapult by using the men as human shields. Would the Captain chance crushing his own men? Eric and Richard had little doubt they were expendable. They were certain the last shot from the trebuchet had been after Robert had been staked out. The camp would not have known he was dead at the time. They did not care.

Richard was tied down on one side of Robert's body and Eric on the other. Spread eagle, facing the field. They would be able to watch the missiles coming in on them. They were dead center over the main gate, which would be a natural target on which to fire. Both men felt short of breath and totally out of their element. When they had been taken into this army they had expected to fight man to man with swords and what not. But to be staked out and fired upon by a massive instrument of death, crushed by a huge boulder, was overwhelming. Even Eric, who almost regularly had one short, dry-witted quip to offer, was completely silent and terrified. Richard longed to hear him say, "How the hell did I get here?" But even that usual complaint was frightened from Eric's lips. After tying both men down, the others returned to the battlements. Richard could hear them yell across the field, "Fire away pigs! Crush your own men like worms!" Then ragged laughing of men who knew they lived on borrowed time.

The challenge didn't go unanswered. Richard's eyes widened as he saw the huge swing arm release and snap a stone at the castle. It looked so little way across the field. But as it approached in a long arc, it grew, and grew, and grew, and Richard could not help but scream as it approached. It seemed dead on to his face, but fear made him perceive it that way. In reality it landed just short of the wall. They had hurled two stones over the wall, and then had backed the machine off a little to try to land them directly on the gate. They had misjudged and the stone fell but a few feet from the gate in the road leading in. Richard didn't see it hit from his position, but he heard a huge thud. He looked over at Eric who looked back in wild-eyed terror. Richard had screamed involuntarily when he believed the huge ball was going to hit him; Eric had just fallen completely silent. He looked at Richard, his eyes revealing that he was close to unconscious with fear. "It may be a better state than my own!" thought Richard.

It was agony waiting for the next projectile. It took time to reload the machine. During that time the two men ferociously tugged and jerked at their bonds. They would have chewed their legs off to escape. Were they free, Richard was not in the least bothered at jumping from the top of the wall to the field far below. He didn't care if he got an arrow in the back as he ran or crawled away. He did not want to be crushed under a missile from the monster in front of him!

They were still snugly tied when they heard a distant voice scream out, "Pull!" They watched, almost in slow motion, as the machine again whipped a huge ball of rock at them. This time it seemed they were dead.

Richard watched the ball silently now as it came on through its long, graceful arc. It seemed to come faster and faster once it reached apex, and though he wanted to, Richard could not turn his head. He watched as it came down, at the last almost too fast to follow. It hit Robert's corpse. "God bless that ball!" was the only thought that passed through Richard's mind as he felt the boards under him begin to collapse.

The ball had gone right through Robert's body; Richard had seen it with his own eyes! In a split second Richard saw that Robert's legs and arms were still there, but his torso was gone. The wood frame under them collapsed when the ball crashed through, and the boards on which Richard was tied fell into the castle. It was thirty feet to the ground. Richard thanked God until he hit the ground and was knocked unconscious. The ball had embedded in the earth next to where his head lay. Debris covered both the ball and Richard.

Eric opened his eyes and shivered. Robert's legs were there, but the rest of him and Richard were gone. How his portion of the structure had remained standing he did not know. And he cursed Cubit, their "Captain," again as he watched the men across the field reload the machine. He actually had little to fear from the trebuchet any longer though. The last shot had provided enough information to the sergeant and his men. They could home in on the exact spot now: The center of the gate itself. Eric closed his eyes. He did not care anymore. He gave up, gave in, quit. He was no longer a soldier in this damned campaign. He vowed he was just a farmer again. From this moment on.

William cringed as the ball crashed down on his friends. He could not watch at the last second, and turned away. He heard a great cheer from those around him, as though they did not see that the ball had torn a man in half! He bent over and vomited. He felt more like killing the sergeant in charge than the kinglet at this point.

The next hours were spent hurling ballistae at the gate. It fell methodically. A hole here, a hole there, a crack grew, joined with another, a wall fell. When the chore was almost complete a white flag flew from the battlements. The men prepared to enter the castle. The flag meant nothing to William at this point. As soon as the servant from the castle had been shown to the Captain, and the surrender agreed upon, the men were sent to secure the castle.

Ordinarily when the fighting was over, the army entered an enemy's camp in a certain order: The full-timers marched in first. They deserved some loot and if there were any trouble they could fight too. Then the Captain and his officers came in. Then the conscripts came last. They got very little.

William shoved his way up next to Shelton in the ranks of the full-timers as the men mustered to march into the castle. He did not care what consequences he might face. When one full-timer tried to turn him with an arm on the shoulder, William almost took his hand off. He turned and glared with such animosity that the battle hardened veteran stepped a pace back. He'd seen that look and knew better than to press the issue. Some men were better left be, even farmers. Shelton just nodded to William as he stood next to him. The boy had some due coming after the last few days.

As they approached the castle, William kept his eyes on the figure still tied out on the remaining panels above the battlements. He hoped one of his friends yet lived. But as they got close he saw that a number of arrows had been shot up through the wood. It was Eric who was dead, sprawled out before them. William's heart dropped. He now knew for certain that at least Neville, Eric and one of his close friends was dead. It was a revelation when he realized that he had once again held the belief that his friends were not dead. He had acknowledged with his mind, when he'd first escaped, that they were dead, only to find when he saw one staked out that in his heart he believed they were alive. Then, after seeing one torn apart by the crushing stone of the trebuchet, and another shot through with arrows, he realized that he had secretly held the belief again that maybe one of his friends survived the ordeal. He realized that until seeing the body of the last man, he would hold that belief. But he had seen him crash out of sight when the stone hit the castle.

Entering the gate, William realized why the castle had surrendered. The balls which were shot over the wall had bounced around on the stone courtyard, crushing whatever they hit. And the rocks which flew from the wall as it was battered down also took a toll on the bystanders. And there, right inside the gate was a pile of debris that could only be that of the fallen covering which his friend was tied to. It was a jumble of wood, and stone from the broken wall. William slipped out of line as he came to the pile and just stood staring at it. The men had split up and were roaming about the castle, inspecting rooms and taking prizes. He didn't want any prizes. He wanted his friends.

His eyes scanned the mess. Lots of rock mixed in with the wood. The fall alone would probably kill a man. He knelt, then sat back on his legs. The noise of the men around him made it difficult to hear, but there was a systematic tapping sound coming from somewhere. William cocked his head to try to pinpoint the sound. He got up and scrambled closer to the pile of debris. A boot! He pulled some stones and wood away. Legs! William tore at the pile, throwing broken wood and dirt aside. William yelled to a passing man. He walked right on with hardly a glance carrying a silver candlestick.

Richard felt the slight tremble as a stone came off his buried leg. He shook the cobwebs from his head and groaned. He felt a piece of rock under his fingers, and he began to tap it against whatever was laying close. He seemed to be still tied to the timbers, but also somewhat buried. His legs hurt and though he found he could move them, he was pretty sure the left was broken. He continued to tap the stone, hoping someone would hear. Though he probably would be killed when found.

William found the hand. It was tapping with a rock. His eyes filled with tears as he felt it. Warm and vital! He realized that the sheets of wood to which his friend was tied were intact and had covered him. They undoubtedly saved him from the falling rocks. William cleared the rubble, reached under the planks and turned them over as one turns a sheet of wood. There, still tied down, was Richard! William shouted with joy. He turned Richard's face to him and bent close. "Are you alive? Are you injured?"

Richard shook his head again, he felt like he had been given a terrible blow on the head, but he managed a smile and whispered, "I'll be better when I'm not tied down."

William took his intent and quickly cut his bonds. He could not believe Richard had survived the fall and whatever else was done to him. He slipped an arm under Richard's shoulders and legs and picked him up bodily. He carried him off to the side, and laid him on a long bench situated near the wall. He then ran to the spring in the middle of the courtyard and drew a ladle of water. He carried it back, sat down and placed Richard's head on his lap, propping him up slightly while he placed the ladle to his lips.

Richard sipped the water. It was pure and clean. It helped loosen his tongue and he rasped, "Robert's dead, Will." William nodded and said quietly, "I know." The two men sat, watching the scene before them.

Now and then William would give Richard some more water. And after a while Richard fell asleep. He dreamt of elephants and dead men. He didn't hear when the sergeant announced that all conscripts were hereby released from service to their Lord the King.

Mouse

S HE SAT IN THE tunnel. It was a small tunnel, a cardboard tunnel. The far end was almost buried in wood shavings, and their smell permeated the entire cage. It was the smell of cut cedar, the smell of woodland undergrowth, comforting. She stared out the other end at the light that flooded her world. Minnie was light brown and very small. Her black eyes darted back and forth as she munched the tiny sunflower seed in her paws. She could just see the gleam of the wheel as she watched the world outside her tube. The noise went on—beep, beep, beep.

Rachel sat quietly by the bedside. The whole room still made her nervous, but she came every day. Once, it seemed like years ago, lots of others had come. Not just Mr. and Mrs. Jenkins and Todd and Karie, but others as well. They would stand, or sit, look out the window, or watch Signe. Some would bring presents, some would read to her. Rachel liked to do that. She brought all her favorite books, and read them to Signe. Sometimes she just talked to her. She could talk for hours! She had always been the talker. It's not that Signe would not talk at all, but she talked a lot less! "Even less now," mused Rachel.

Rachel watched the organ pump. She didn't know what to call it. It had a name. Just like everything in the room had a name, but she didn't know what it was. Mr. Jenkins once cried while watching the organ (it pumped up and down, and seemed to make Signe do the same thing). Rachel had stood in the corner. She didn't know what to say or do. She hugged her books close to her chest, and lowered her head, just peeking through her lashes as his back shook. You could hardly hear it! Once, her little brother had hurt his hand playing with a screwdriver. She remembered him screaming and crying. The sound blanketed their house and yard, and mom had come running from the kitchen with wide eyes. Dad had come around from trimming the hedge at a run too! In fact, now that she thought about it, she had come running too to see what was happening! And when they all had reached Josh, she remembered dad kneeling down on one knee and holding Josh's arms, looking into his face with a look of fear and concern. And mom had come up behind him and wrapped her arms around his chest, leaning over him, and trying to understand what he was saying as he cried.

No one came when Mr. Jenkins cried. He lowered his head, and she could hear soft moans coming from him. And she saw his body shake. And then after a while he just got up and kissed Signe's hand, and left. He didn't even see her as he opened the door. No one had hugged him close and said it was ok. And no one made him better. Not one person had come to peer into his face, to see what had been broken or scraped. But Rachel knew there wasn't anything anyway. It was looking at the organ that had done it. And looking doesn't hurt you. He never cried again. At least not that Rachel saw.

Mrs. Jenkins was often there when Rachel came in. She would smile and ask how school was. Then she often left them alone. She didn't cry anymore either. She cried more than Mr. Jenkins, at first anyway, but it wasn't the organ that caused it. Sometimes the tubes did that. Rachel didn't like the tubes either. They went in and out like clear plastic snakes that eternally slither along. You never saw the end or the beginning. Well, the end maybe. They always ended in something she didn't understand. Some bag, or machine, or sometimes they broke out into more tubes all ending in more machines or bags.

Minnie scurried out into the light. Rachel saw her paw up another piece of the mouse chow she had poured when she arrived. The little green pellets were her favorites. She thought Minnie had eaten them all, but now she emerged from the bowl of food with another. A piece of buried treasure. Rachel giggled with the thought of Minnie with a tiny eye patch and a little teeny parrot on her shoulder. "Avast y'maties, here be mouse chow!" Signe shuddered and some liquid dripped from her parted lips.

Rachel took Signe's hand and squeezed it a little. She was warm, just like they would be after riding down to the lake and lying in the warm sand. They would bury their legs and hands and let the sun beat down on them for hours before splashing into the water and banishing the sand to the bottom. Signe always had warm hands. Especially when they had been in that sand! Rachel's were not that way. She looked at their hands joined on the bed spread. (That icky tube was just a little ways away!) She looked at their hands more closely. Rachel's was thicker now. Although she was the skinny one. But Signe was the skinny one now! She was bony. She never moved, except when she coughed. (That tube in her mouth probably made her do that!)

Minnie was Signe's special friend—*her* mouse. The Jenkins had given her to Signe last year for her birthday. And Rachel had promised to watch out for Minnie the last time they had talked. The last time Signe had ever talked, that day on the pavement. Signe hadn't cried like Josh did. She just laid there with blood dripping from her nose and mouth. Just a few moments before they had taken the vow. Signe would watch out for trembler (Rachel's hamster, who always seemed afraid of everything), and Rachel would watch out for Minnie—if they ever got lost or something that is. Then they had walked into the street. Then all the noise. And Rachel was fine; she told everyone she was fine; but Signe needed help. Bad. She recalled crying and staring at that line of blood coming from Signe's nose. It was really red. She had gathered her books too. And since then, every day, she would come to feed Minnie and talk to Signe; 'cause her mom said Signe could hear.

No one else came anymore. But Rachel understood that. They knew Signe like Rachel knew lots of kids. Her parents told her she didn't have to go everyday either. But they were kinda like the other kids. They knew Signe, but they didn't really know her; not like Rachel did. When you were like Rachel and Signe you didn't *not* come. I mean, would Jordan not come to see Eric? Pulease! Or Carmen and Lydia? They would come to each other. Rachel came every day. Minnie needed to eat, and she couldn't get to Signe's lap anymore without Rachel's help. It's funny how people forget other people when they are not around. But it's not like they didn't remember them. Rachel would talk about Signe at school and everyone remembered her. But it made sense too. You can't be like Signe was to Rachel with everyone! You had to be that with only one person; maybe two (those Marion boys with Tom Shepard for instance).

Johnny Townsend didn't have someone. Rachel would see him sitting alone at lunch. No one would visit him. Signe hadn't moved in months, but she still was not alone. Poor Johnny Townsend was. He ran around the play field. He talked in class (and Mrs. Kerrington would yell at him). He answered questions. He was smart too. But he didn't have anyone. Rachel wondered if Mr. Jenkins had anyone. No one had come when he cried.

Signe's chest heaved and her head flinched to the side. Rachel watched her spasm lightly for a few minutes then settle down to nothing again. She released her hand and walked over to Minnie. Reaching into the cage she drew her out and began to stroke the fur on her back. She had made a vow, she had to care for Minnie now, 'cause Signe had gotten lost.

And Signe couldn't notice the tear delicately coursing down her best friend's cheek.

Mole

SWEAT TRICKLED DOWN FIVE year old Joshua Jordan's face in the wavering heat of mid-August. He did not look up when the crow drifted across the fence and into the neighbor's yard. He did not shift when his mom drew the sliding glass door aside and reached out to dump a glass of water on the small ficus by the back porch. When Sally lumbered past, tail wagging, on her way to her house in the side yard, he did not favor her with even a short glance. His eyes burrowed into the dark, amorphous shape that rested on the grass fifteen feet in front of him. The tension lay across his young brow like a broken electric line lays in a wet tree. Short jolts of high energy crossed and criss-crossed his eyes as he scanned the dark shape in front of him. It had moved.

Two days ago it had not been there. Joshua had been sure of that. He and Billy Tyler had played over the whole back yard, staining green into their knees, dirt into their palms, and generally grubbying each other up to their heart's desire. No mound in sight. Then, yesterday, as he was opening the door in the morning to let Sally in, he'd seen it. It was still early, no one else was up. He had opened the door, and Sally had waddled in, and begun to munch on her dog chow. (Which wasn't all that bad considering how hard and dry it was, thought Joshua.) He had run his hand over Sally's back as she passed, and when he looked up, he saw it. A shadow lay upon it, and at first he didn't think it was anything at all. But being curious, he walked out into the yard and investigated. It was dark, like dirt, with a hole in the middle. It was wet as though newly disturbed. And as Josh watched, it seemed to wriggle in the middle, just below its skin. Cold sweat broke out on his forehead, and he edged back toward the house. He felt his foot hit the back patio, and risking it all he turned his back on the breathing, dirty organism and bolted into the house, driving the door home with all his strength. Sally lifted her head for a moment, then returned to her morning meal. He pressed to the side of the door, using the vertical blinds to partially conceal his body from the invader in the rear yard.

Joshua was still surveilling the threat when his mom flicked on the kitchen light and said warmly, "Good morning young man." She did not know of the threat to her son's life yet. Not a moment later Josh's dad rounded the corner, suit on, tapping his watch muttering about the time. He grinned at Josh, and began to pour two bowls of Froot Loops. Dad and Josh always had Froot Loops together on Wednesday morning. It was a ritual Josh was going to miss if that thing ever got at him! Josh caught his dad's eyes, and crooked a finger at him, silently asking him to come over. Dad, obviously seeing the situation correctly came over and knelt down. That was good, thought Josh, better to stay hidden at first. Josh pointed out at the evil blob on the lawn and hissed into his dad's ear, "What's that?" His dad squinted into the deep dark of the shady lawn. When his eyes came to rest on the blob of living dirt, he stood and began to open the door. Joshua quickly stayed his hand and whispered "It's alive! I saw it move!"

Josh's dad was a brave man, and after a slight nod, he stepped out into the yard and advanced on the entity . . . unarmed! Josh watched, admiring the way his father went to his death with his head raised. However, to Josh's surprise, when his dad reached the evil intruder, he was not . . . "blobbed" on the spot. Instead he was allowed to inspect the thing, and then, straightening up, to return to the house. Josh breathed a heavy sigh of relief as dad came back in and announced, "We have a mole!" Josh wisely locked the door as dad sat down.

A mole. Hmmm, what do I know about a mole, thought Josh. They are blind, slimy creatures of the dark. They live underground, and never come out. So what was this one doing? Josh was pretty sure the mole was dark because mom said the thing on her arm used to be a mole, and she said it was dark. And she had had it removed! (That's why she now just had that scar.) She said moles can kill you if they start to grow. So it's best to watch them. Dad and mom were just talking about the day and their plans. They clearly were hiding their concern over the killer mole in the yard. They did that sometimes to protect him, he knew. Like when grandpa died last year. They said he could go to the funeral, but he didn't have to look in the box if he didn't think he wanted to. It might be scary. He didn't look 'cause mom and dad are usually right about scary stuff.

Josh went to the table and began to eat Froot Loops. A mole. In the yard. He had not realized moles could get into people *or* be outside. Since you must watch a mole to see if it grows, Josh decided to watch the mole. It had, after all, grown big enough to poke out of the ground! And he was sure it actually moved when he had looked at it! A mole. A black killer mole!

He had thought of the black killer mole—and that was how he always named it in his head now—all that day. He had watched it on and off through the day, but had not seen anything untoward. It must be crafty, and having caught it move on the first day, it probably did not want to be caught growing again. Josh decided it would take an intensive effort to watch the black killer mole. And come to think of it, he was not sure exactly what watching in and of itself would accomplish. But he knew that a mole would kill you in your sleep if not watched (he was positive mom had definitely said that), so he had to watch it.

He had settled into the lawn fifteen feet from the black killer mole after breakfast today. It was now almost noon and the heat was bearing down on him. Josh had not seen anything yet, and that must be good (he was sure nothing happened when he was reading comics either). The black killer mole could not grow! He decided however, that he needed to creep closer, to see if it was breathing. He wiped his face with his arm, and began the slow, life and death crawl toward the black killer mole. Each time his hand pressed into the warm grass he could smell the tang of broken blades. He could hear the whiz of bugs as they retreated before him, jumping up and flying off in fear. Perhaps the black killer mole would do the same? He did not think so. Mom came out and went around the side of the house to hose her plants. She was oblivious to the danger!

When Josh was within a few feet of the black killer mole, he stopped and again resumed his inspection. To his utter dismay, he saw something which tore the breath from his five year old lungs! The surface of the black killer mole was moving! It undulated, probably digesting some poor cat or something that strayed too near! Josh's breath stopped as he watched. Bits of dirt would now and again fly from the hole. He was reduced to panic and in terror he sped away to his room. THE BLACK KILLER MOLE WAS GROWING!

That night Josh came to his dad with his research well organized. He laid the facts out clearly so his dad could follow. First, he was playing with Billy. Then, they didn't see it. Second, It was breathing on its own. Fourth, moles are killers. It was plain as day! Dad listened intently, clearly impressed with Joshua's grasp of the mortal situation. He was a good dad. It was time for Star Trek, and then perhaps the situation could be handled. Josh walked over to the TV and left his father to contemplate the black killer mole situation. After Star Trek, and his snack, Josh was pretty tired, so he had no problem falling asleep. Besides, Dad could probably deal with the black killer mole. He seemed to understand the problem pretty well when Josh had explained it to him.

The next day Dad had gone out to get mole poison and he had poured it down the blob's mouth. Josh had watched from his window, fearing Dad would be taken before the poison took effect. However, he seemed to be on the offensive pretty well. He had driven a shovel into it, and then pressed the blob flat so it appeared to be just a dirt area waiting for grass to overgrow it. Dad then came in, and he heard him say to mom, "That will do the trick." Joshua grinned at their victory over the black killer mole.

Three weeks later Josh saw the remnants of the black killer mole for the first time. Dad and he had found it while playing catch in the back. It had clearly shrunk when killed for it now resembled a small mouse. It was nothing like the giant black blob Josh remembered that boiled and surged over the back yard! It seemed quite helpless now. Josh knew dad would be able to kill it. But he was doubly impressed by the poison that had turned the black killer mole into such a pitiful remnant of its former self.

Dad seemed to handle most things pretty well thought Josh. He hoped he could do that someday. For now, though, he would watch for more black killer moles.

Cockroach

Winter

THE STREETS WERE WET with rain. The evening was dark with the thick clouds that blanketed the sky.

Reggie Walters sped down 32nd Street catching lights in green or yellow and occasionally red. He needed to get home, and fast! Sharie was due home in about twenty minutes, and not only was he supposed to have been home two hours ago, but he was supposed to have made dinner as well. Course, what Reggie had been doing was much more enjoyable than making dinner.

Reggie's mind wandered back over the last hour or so with Sophie. She was twenty-five. They had met at his work, and hit it off so well. She was taller than his wife, had long brown hair, and lovely deep brown-gold eyes. She was thin too—shapely and thin; and for the past eight months they had been lovers. It was incredible! They had shared in ways he had never even thought of with Sharie. Sharie was nice, he told himself, but that was it. Just nice. She had no passion, no excitement. She was pretty too; he'd seen men look at her. But a canvass without paint is like every other. You only commented on the ones that were painted. And it was amazing the emotions a painted canvass could elicit, thought Reg as he barreled through the last light before his street. Sharie was a pretty, intensely white canvass that is amazing for its potential, and equally dull for its lack of anything else.

The car rocketed into the drive with fifteen minutes left till Sharie got home. Reggie bolted from the door, jumped back in for the bottle, and then ran into the house in seconds, tossing his coat onto the bed and crashing into the kitchen. As his shadow crossed the floor a large brown roach suddenly skittered like lightening from under the table toward the sideboard under the sink. It was so fast that Reggie almost missed it, but only almost. He veered toward the retreating intruder and slammed his foot down with a *crack!*—yelling at the same time, "Dirty Roach!!"

Reggie hated roaches! They always snuck around when you were out of the room. They were ugly, and diseased, and sneaky! They were insect vermin, who deserved to be squashed into pulp! But the problem was they were cunning—for a bug that is. They would scuttle around in the dark; you'd even hear them sometimes. Mostly though, you'd just sense their presence. And the minute the light came on, the minute you went to inspect—nothing. They would scamper back into their holes and disappear. Reggie hated them!

Well, in any event, this one had done the disappearing trick again, and Reggie had other things on his mind. He yanked open the cupboard and shuffled through the cans on the middle shelf: Mushrooms, tomato sauce, tomato paste, tomatoes (lots of tomato stuff!), black olives—ah hah! Baked beans! He slammed the can into the opener and buzzed off the top. Then he dumped the slop into a bowel and punched in three minutes on the microwave. Was that a roach?? He thought he heard a scuttling somewhere . . . never mind.

Next Reggie yanked some eggs from the fridge and cracked them into another bowel. He mixed them roughly with a fork and set them by the stove. Then, he pulled the big skillet from the drawer and lit the flame under it. Seven minutes till Sharie!

Reggie could not just dump eggs and beans on the table and say, "Voila!" He had to do something that said, "I've been thinking of you, baby." So he pulled the bottle he'd brought home from the paper bag, and drove the cork screw into the top. "Perfect!" he laughed to himself as he flipped the cork out of the bottle. Sharie loves red wine. This would be the perfect icing to an otherwise crappy entree! Reggie giggled to himself, and set the wine aside to breathe. He set the table, and just began cooking the eggs when he heard a key turn in the lock at the front door. "Is that you baby? I'm just getting things hot," he yelled from the kitchen as he quietly placed the silverware around the plates, finishing the table settings.

Sharie went to the bedroom, dropped her things, and then came down the hall to the kitchen. She smiled and hugged Reggie as he faced the stove, nuzzling his neck in back.

The roach sat quietly in the dark. It had been out on the flat, retrieving large morsels of food. It ran its legs over its body, cleaning away any debris that may have caught in its shell. Both eyes flicked about, and the antenna criss-crossed in front of it experiencing the black hole to which it had retreated. It had not been caught by the shadow that suddenly had displaced the bright light. Now, in the darkness, it could sense the movement of something out on the flat. It waited.

Reggie sensed the love emanating from his wife. He put Sophie into the back of his mind and waited for the evening to pass.

Sharie surveyed the food that was about ready. It never ceased to amaze her that Reggie could spend an hour making something as basic as eggs and beans! Even when you count running out for wine (which he probably picked up on the way home) the whole meal couldn't take her more than twenty minutes max. Sometimes she had an unsettling feeling over the issue—but that was silly, she told herself. What could poor cooking indicate? She smiled to herself and poured a glass of wine.

Spring

It was cold this year. It was wet too. Sharie Walters was sick with some bug Tammy had brought to work. "Tammy, what a ditz!" thought Sharie. It always seemed like Tammy was, hmmmm, how best to say it—*infecting* all her coworkers. She would bring something to the picnic—something with food poisoning for instance, and soon everyone would be barfing. She would come to work with a cold, and soon everyone would be sneezing. She was always—sharing the joy. Sharie giggled to herself. She liked Tammy as everyone else did; that was infectious too, she thought. But Tammy always seemed to be on the cutting edge of calamity!

In any event, Sharie had picked up some gift of Tammy's and was on her way home early. She felt fine at breakfast, but after a good morning sneeze from Tammy, she steadily had progressed to the point of giving in and going home—at only one o'clock! Sharie shook her head, and was at least grateful for the quiet time she'd have. Reggie worked till five as she usually did, and wouldn't be home till five-thirty. That meant a bath and a nap were free for the taking!

As Sharie turned onto Creston Drive, she pursed her lips at the red sedan in front of the house. "Dang! Why today?" she thought. It wasn't unusual for a car to park in front of their house on Wednesday, since the Weldons had their Bible study that night. People would fill the whole block before Sharie got home and sometimes she had to park around the corner herself! (Unfortunately, the TWO-CAR garage was more of a storage bin than a garage, and Reggie's car was on one side of the driveway, and his boat was on the other. Consequently, Sharie got the street in front of the house.) But today was Monday, and the street was empty and funny— Reggie's car was in the drive right now. (She inwardly sighed, and a fleeting feeling of—something wrong—rippled through her.) And that stupid car was in Sharie's spot and now she was going to have to walk that much farther to get her nap! She slammed the door hard getting out!

Reggie hurdled from the bed, kicking the dresser on the way! A car door had slammed, very, very close! Sophie was sending him a quizzical look as he parted the blinds in their bedroom for a quick glance. SHARIE WAS WALKING TOWARD THE HOUSE! Reggie skittered to the bed and tumbled Sophie unceremoniously out of the covers. She knew from his expression and the hissed command to "get dressed" exactly what was coming. She scrambled into her clothes and bolted for the back door, half dressed, still carrying a number of garments. When Sharie's key sounded in the lock, Sophie's feet were propelling her down the back steps and across the yard to the alley. As the front door cracked, the rear door passed the same distance from open on the way to closed. Sharie heard a click in the kitchen, as she entered, and called out, "Reggie, you home?" As she shut the door behind her, sniffling (that's odd, there was a passing hint of some scent in the air), she caught what she thought was the shadow of her husband going from the kitchen to the bedroom. However, when she walked down the hall and into the bedroom, Reggie was lying face down on the bed, apparently just waking.

He rolled as she entered, and coughed, "Hi hon."

Sophie sat in her car, brushing her clothes into some semblance of order in case any debris got on them. She smoothed her hair and straightened her make-up. The first thing she had done was pull her car down the block and turn the corner. She sat in a shadow under a tree. Her eyes quested to the mirrors occasionally, and up the road. Nothing was approaching. She waited.

Sharie sniffled and said, "Are you sick baby?"

Reggie nodded and wheezed (in his best sick voice), "You too?"

She nodded back and dropped her stuff by the dresser (it seemed out of place, pushed aside somehow).

Reggie opened the bed covers for her, and patted the sheet, motioning "come on in with me."

Instead, Sharie pointed to the bathroom and said, "Bath first."

Reggie nodded with a half-smile and hid a sigh of relief. When he was alone he straightened out the dresser, replaced the mirror Sharie had failed to notice had been moved, and slipped out of the satin boxers he had donned, replacing them with gray sweat pants. He settled into his side of the bed, and waited patiently for his wife to return—and fall asleep.

As Sharie settled into the warm water, she tried to shake the feeling of something in the house. She hadn't actually seen anything, or anyone, but something seemed—strange. Probably just the cold. She closed her eyes, and slid back into the water.

Summer

It was HOT! After the horrible winter and spring she had endured, Sharie was thrilled with getting to don shorts and a tank top every day at home. She looked about the bed she had planted, pleased with the growth of the bright colored flowers over the last few months. Her favorites were the Sea Pinks. The long tendrils, emanating from the green blob of succulent foliage, that ended with a round small bouquet of pretty pink flowers the size of your thumb nail. They looked like sea anemones with brightly colored antenna. The slight breeze drifted over them and they seemed to wave at her in unison. She giggled, and continued to weed, shaking off for a moment the dark feeling she had been carrying for the last few weeks.

She and Reggie had originally planned to go to the beach together on her vacation this year. But inexplicably, something had "come up" at work for Reg again. Sharie ticked her tongue against her teeth as she worked, realizing again she was immersed in the darkness. Things had been "coming up" a lot it seemed in the last few months. Well, that wasn't fair. Having thought about it, the last year seems to have been mis-planned over and over, resulting in Reggie being gone for a few days, or his being home when she was gone.

Sharie stopped her weeding a moment, and sat quietly. She squeezed her eyes shut, knowing what was there in the dark, but until this very moment, denying its existence. It was a black secret she held away from her own self, or at least had tried to hold away for a long time. But in the sunny garden, on her knees, with the Sea Pinks waving at her, she suddenly broke like a piece of fresh ice dropped into hot water. Her eyelids tightened a little more (if that was possible), but still the single drop pried its way from the corner of her eye and sluggishly trickled down her cheek. The only sound she heard for a brief moment was the sighing of the wind, and then her shoulders began to shake, and a deep, wrenching sob escaped her lips. She drew her hands to her stomach (had someone kicked her?! It felt like God himself had kicked her in the gut!). She ground the dirt on her gloves into her pretty white and blue tank top— the one with the little flowers that everyone commented on: "*That is just sooooo pretty.*" She held her spinning gut as she began to sob, deeply yet quietly, alone in the yard. The sun highlighted her soft auburn hair, and twinkled on her glistening thighs, wetted from the torrent of tears that now poured from her red, swollen eyes.

She knew without doubt that Reggie was having an affair. She had sensed the presence of something wrong for a long time. She had seen his eyes flicker across the room as they talked, as though scanning for evidence, as though looking for a hiding place. She had seen remnants of . . . of . . . an intruder; of some vermin who had infested her life and diseased her family. She could never support such an accusation. She never caught them in the act. But she knew, completely, unconsciously first, and now consciously. She spent a long while grieving in the sunny yard, with the Sea Pinks.

Reggie sat in his office wasting time. He knew he should be working, but Sophie waited in about an hour, and he just was not in the mood. His mind wandered around, finally settling on the problem of the roach. Damn roach! He never caught it scuttling about, but always there were the glimpses, the shadows, the noises. He knew without doubt that it was living in the baseboard of the north wall of the kitchen. He didn't want to spray the whole house for one roach, but was it just one? You'd think he'd see more if there was a colony of the little vermin! He idled away a good portion of the hour contemplating the end of the roach.

Sophie looked herself over in the mirror. She tsked her tongue a couple times, nodded with a smile and tugged lightly on the extremely short, black skirt she was wearing. The small, clingy shirt could tuck into the waistband, but it was so short it always crept out and revealed her navel. She didn't mind though, her belly was one of her sexiest assets. She knew this even without the many times men had told her so. She liked the way her legs lengthened with the heels she had chosen too.

She was a full three inches taller with them, and clearly her time on the treadmill had paid off as well. She took one last long look and then went to the living room and sat down to wait for her Reggie.

Her Reggie. Sophie smiled as she thought about the way he looked at her, touched her, talked with her. He was a good time, and good sex. But lately she was growing bored with him. He always seemed to need to rush off. He would make an excuse, but she knew why he really left. It was her. His wife. He had to keep us "under the radar" as he always put it. It's not that she wouldn't sneak around. She had done it before with other men, and even mildly enjoyed the dangerous feelings it evoked. But she wanted to be more important than his wife. "He should make excuses to her and come to see me!" she muttered. It was getting old. Perhaps it was time to break it off and find someone else. After all, men are a dime a dozen when you looked like Sophie. And she had seen some of the other men at the office glancing her way as she worked. There were morsels everywhere. Sophie smiled to herself, then feeling a tickle, quickly headed for the bathroom. She was sure she may have a yeast infection or something. The itching was driving her nuts. Tomorrow the clinic, she promised herself.

Reggie relaxed in his car for a moment before heading into the house. He loved the feeling of complete control when all his plans went correctly. He had spent a good two hours with Sophie this afternoon. Then, he had stopped by the Savings-King and gotten something for that damn roach. Something the clerk had recommended. It was supposed to entice the roach to eat, and then kill it from the inside. He had even picked up some flowers from one of those street vendors for Sharie. Sitting in the car, watching the sun setting, he felt just great!

Sharie was at the stove when Reggie came in. She was oddly dressed he thought to himself—wearing her tank top (which was full of dirt stains) and shorts. And her hair was sort of mussed up too. Reggie came up behind her and slipped his hands onto her waist. He kissed her head and said, "Hi sweetie."

She smiled back at him and said, "How was your day?"

He grinned back at her thinking of Sophie in the shower with him earlier and said, "It was ok. Just had some cleaning to do." He admired himself when he played with her so artfully.

She nodded and said, "Get washed up, because dinner is almost ready."

He headed for the bathroom almost giggling over her use of the word "wash."

When Reggie returned Sharie was seated and their plates served. He sighed quietly to himself knowing that this was a prelude for something. She almost never had dinner set and ready to eat. At the very least they would serve their own plates, and usually they just ate by the TV and watched the news drone on. He sat across from his wife, relishing the few hours he spent with Sophie even more because he had a feeling things might not be so enjoyable here tonight. It was probably that stupid paint again. She had a burr up her ass over that spare bedroom and there was no way to get it out of her mind. He was going to have to paint it. That was without question. But he was putting it off as long as possible. Unfortunately, every now and then Sharie would dredge it back up to "current" status, and he would have to wriggle out of it again for as long as possible. She should paint her own damn bedroom if she's so hot on the subject!

Sharie looked at him as he sat, smiled blandly, and began to eat. He too dug into the food with gusto. (After all, he thought, good sex makes a man hungry!) He laughed a little evoking a questioning look from Sharie. He blew it off as just a passing thought about a joke he had heard at work. She prodded, "Tell me," with a grin. He recounted some old joke he'd heard (and probably told her once before) and they both chuckled for a bit between bites of mashed potatoes, pork chops, and green beans. (Another reason he thought the bedroom was coming up for show again—all these foods were his favorites.)

The time whiled away, and nothing happened. Reggie learned that his wife was sort of dirty from working in the garden. She had lost track of time and had to prepare dinner without a shower. Reg was carefully watching his words, hoping in no way to hint at the plight of the bedroom. He finally finished desert, and scuttled to the couch to read the paper while Sharie cleaned up. It was kinda nice when she had a day off from work. She could act like a real wife and do some chores around the house. He cracked the sports section wondering if he could ever get dinner made for him every night of the week. Probably not, he thought. And if he did, it would probably be by a wife who was dirty from gardening!

Sharie came into the living room and flipped on the TV. She sat in the loveseat, and while still looking at the screen, offhandedly said, "Honey, there's something I wanted to do."

Reggie sighed as covertly as he could, realizing the time had come to marshal his excuses as to why he should put off the bedroom project. He then said lightly, "What's that babe?"

She totally surprised him. It was not about the room and paint at all! Instead she said, "I think there is a roach in the house, and I want to kill him. Is it ok to have someone remove him?"

He smiled, extremely pleased at not having to defend himself again, and gushed, "Sure babe, call whoever you want. I had gotten something at the store today, but if you think it requires a professional, we can do that." It was such a relief to not have to argue about the painting that he would consider the roach chemicals a write off!

Sharie smiled and said, "Great, I'll get right on it tomorrow. I think it may take a pro."

The two wasted another night watching TV. They then went to bed around ten. The next day Sharie called the police bright and early to collect Reggie's stiff, lifeless body. The men came and collected it into a black bag and removed it from the bathroom where he had died retching up the poison. Sharie watched as they drove away idly thinking how hard it is to remove pests on your own.

The roach sat in the crack by the baseboard and waited for the dark.

Winter

Llama

Brian Geesler. Hero. Human llama. He sat on the cold, rigid surface, his handsome, chiseled visage stoic against the driving wind and rain. The fat, icy drops pelted the skin of his hard set face. His grim features were tight to the pounding as he surveyed his dismal surroundings. Winter had set in during his expedition and he was now confronted with the choice of giving in to the elements or enduring the pounding he would take over the rest of his quest. His head swiveled minutely under his parka hood as he took in the wintry surroundings. Nothing but menacing rock in every direction. He looked up the way to his goal. It was a difficult and arduous path he was to take. He scoped out the mission ahead and began to fiddle with his gear, preparing the tools necessary for the next assault.

It had been three days on his journey. He began in the sun, but the weather had turned to rain the second day. Now it was cold, and intermixed with the drops of rain were slushy flakes of snow. Occasionally at night, as he huddled in his sleeping bag, he would feel ice crystals tingle his face as the temperature dropped. He woke this morning to a damp, icy world. It did not look like the trip would be a quick one.

He had begun with two fellow trekkers. They had planned this undertaking for almost six months together. Shiela had been the first to suggest it, for she was the most experienced. They had met at the YMCA. He had been playing basketball and she was rock climbing on the artificial wall. As he had wandered by, his head down, bouncing his ball and listening to KISS on his headset, he had accidentally run into her. She was geared and ready to ascend the rock wall, but her turn had not yet arrived. From that casual meeting they had moved to coffee, then lunch. Then she had introduced him to climbing, and he had taught her basketball.

It was at the Y's climbing wall that they had met Tom. They had seen him around before, but neither had known him. While sitting and chatting, listening to music, he had struck up a conversation about the band on the radio. It turned out he was a metal head too, and they had gotten to know one another over the last year or so. Then, six months ago, Shiela had suggested the plan. They had all agreed. They had all prepared for the odyssey. But now Brian was alone. The others had dropped away, citing the cold and hardship as their reason. Brian was angry. But he was proud and stubborn and would not be deterred by the weakness of his friends. Their abandonment made the effort much more difficult though. He was on his own. He had expected to endure with their support. Now he had only his inner fire and the desire for the goal. It was beginning to tell on his mind and body.

As Brian surveyed the line before him, he settled on the best approach. He reached down and tightened the laces on his boots. They were good boots that took the severe weather and kept him firmly in place when needed. His socks were wool and warm—though he had a constant battle with the cold. His pants were mere jeans. But he wore long johns under them, which helped. His parka was North Face. It was bright yellow and buttoned up against the elements. He made sure his gloves were pulled tight to his fingers.

Having resigned himself to his route, he settled back to finish his cup of coffee. He lifted the plastic cup up to his lips and drained the last remnant of liquid. "MMMMM . . . The best Arabica beans," he whispered to himself. A tight smile creased his cold face as he swallowed. It would be a long time before he drank it again with his friends and family. He stowed his thermos and made final preparation to begin his move. Brian Geesler, Hero. One of the youngest to attempt such a feat.

At that moment a sharp blow and horrendous cry battered into his revelry. He felt it again and again as time after time something slammed into his leg and lower back. His head jerked up fearing the worst. His eyes were at first blinded by the bright light reflecting from the glass wall in front of him! He wondered if this was the end of line!

Mom knocked him again with her tennis shoe and yelled, "Brian, I brought you some lunch. Now eat your soup."

The boy beside her added, "Yeah dude, and the ticket booth is finally open! Get moving, huh!"

Brian snapped out of his day-dream, pulled his ear buds out, got up off the sidewalk, picked up his pack, and scuttled forward for his chance at the concert tickets.

Ferret

T IM BROUGHT THE ANIMAL home in the car. He had gotten the cage, its cover, food, and a book at the pet store. The lady said ferrets were very nice, smart, and full of energy. Last week he and Molly had seen them, and she had fallen in love with them. They were cute. You had to admit that. Molly had especially liked the very dark brown one. He had black eyes, and a few patches of white on his feet. Tim had put his foot down. No ferrets. However, he knew after two minutes he was going to get her one for her birthday.

So, this afternoon he'd gotten off work a little early, stopped by the pet shop, and picked up the ferret. He'd phoned the day after they were there and reserved the exact one Molly had swooned over. The lady at the store said they had named the animal Captain Jack. He had a habit of keeping one eye closed now and then. It looked like he had only one eye. Tim wasn't going to mention the name unless Molly asked. The animal would be named whatever she wanted as far as he was concerned.

As for Captain Jack, he seemed rather quiet in his cage. The lady said that the cover served to calm him a little. Ferrets get in trouble when they see too much. Curiosity gets the better of them and they begin to cause trouble. Right now the animal seemed to be causing no problems.

When he got home, Tim put the cage on the kitchen table. He brought the cake in and put it on the table too. Then he opened up the boxes of candles and placed them in a square on one side of the cake. The square of candles was about three inches on a side. Molly was forty-two this year. He put the card he'd gotten next to the cake and stepped back to look at the effect. When Molly rounded the corner she'd see the kitchen

195

table with the cake in the middle, the cage to one side, and the card on the other. Perfect. It was small, but nice. Tim pulled a few plates from the cupboard and placed them and a cutting knife near the cake also. Then he covered the plates with little napkins that read, "Happy Birthday!"

Picking up the phone, he dialed Craig's number. Susan answered on the second ring, "Hello?"

"Hey Susan, this is Tim."

"Oh, hey Tim. What's up?"

"I just wondered when you guys are gonna get here. Molly should be home in about forty-five minutes."

"I'm not sure yet Tim. Craig isn't. . . ." Tim could hear something going on in the background. Then "Here he is now."

Next Craig said, "Hey man! Just got home. I thought I'd grab a quick shower and then we'd come right over. K?"

Susan and Craig lived just a few doors down. Tim answered, "Hey Tim. Yeah, that sounds great. You know we're having cake too, right? We're gonna spoil your dinner!"

Craig laughed, "Yeah well. I'm always ready for cake, both for dessert and as an appetizer."

Tim laughed along, "I hear that. K. C'ya in a bit then."

"All right. Bye." And he hung up. Which turned out to be perfect timing because Josh and Stephanie rang the doorbell just as Tim set the phone back on its cradle. He hustled over to the door, threw the bolt and lock and opened it to Darby Felder smiling up at him. Before he could invite them in, Darby opened her arms wide and said, "Hi Tim!"

Tim scooped her up and said, "Hi back Darby! And Hi to you guys too!" He nodded to the Felders and stepped back from the door, motioning them in with his head. "How are the Felders today?"

Darby said, "Fine."

Steph laughed and said, "Tired." Tim knew that Darby could be a handful sometimes. She was three and turning into a wild woman!

Josh slapped Tim on the back and said, "I'm great. And hungry for cake!" he grinned as he headed for the kitchen.

Tim yelled after him, "Don't touch it Felder! Have some coffee for now!"

Josh tossed, "yeah, yeah, yeah" over his shoulder as he continued on toward the kitchen. They all ended up in the family room seated and talking.

About twenty-five minutes later the Raines arrived. Craig looked like he was hot out of the shower. Susan was her usual smiling self. Laid back. They came in and settled down with the others after ooing and ahhing over the pretty cake.

Tim said, "I think Molly should be home pretty soon. And as though his words made it so, they heard a car door slam in the drive. A moment later Molly's key turned the lock.

"Hey Tim! Are the Felders here?" She closed the door and walked around the corner to the kitchen to put her lunch things down. As she came into view, everyone yelled, "Happy Birthday!"

Molly grinned and stopped in her tracks. She looked at everyone and said, after a brief silence, "Tim Grayton, you better have cleaned this house before inviting guests over!" She waggled her finger at her husband while she said it. Everyone burst out laughing.

Darby ran up to Molly with her arms wide open and squealed, "Happy Birthday Molly!" Molly picked her up and said very politely, "Why thank you Darby! Would you like some cake?"

Darby nodded her head vigorously and looked over at the lovely white icing on the cake. In pink letters "Happy Birthday" was spelled out, and at that moment Tim was trying to light the tight square of candles.

When he had succeeded lighting the candles, the flame that arose from them was disturbingly high. He beckoned to Molly to hurry up and blow the thing out before she died of smoke inhalation! Molly gave him an annoyed look and said, "Ok, ok. Darby, help me blow.

She bent over to blow the candles out and gave it her best shot. But they re-lit! Everyone immediately looked at Tim with expressions that said, "You used trick candles didn't you!?" But Tim just shrugged his shoulders and said, "I didn't, I didn't! They weren't supposed to be anyway. They just keep re-lighting because of the heat from all those candles!" He grinned at Molly as he said it.

Molly elbowed him in the ribs and with help from a few of the others they got the candles extinguished. Tim giggled at his wife. She was a few years older than he and he rubbed it in on birthdays. Molly ignored him and chose instead to talk with Susan and Steph.

Josh had the cake knife in hand and was badgering Molly, interrupting her with "C'mon birthday girl, cut the cake already and stop jabbering." Josh could act like Darby when it came to sweets. The only reason he wasn't five hundred pounds was because he played a lot of basketball.

Molly set Darby down, took the knife and went over to the cake. As she was looking at it, suddenly there was a chirping sort of sound from the . . . whatever it was on the back of the table. Molly looked at Tim with a questioning look. Tim said, "You'll just have to pull the cover off." Molly put the knife down and did just that. Looking back at her was the very ferret she'd pointed out to Tim the other day! The one he said "no way" to! Molly grinned and hugged Tim saying, "The ferret! I love it! Thank you hon!"

The others looked at the animal with surprise. Molly had mentioned it to both couples, explaining how cute they were, but also saying Tim had said no to having one. Josh punched Tim's shoulder and said, "Wussy!"

Tim laughed and replied, "Just because I know how to scheme and you don't doesn't mean I'm a wussy. You're just not bright enough to see the intricacies of my plan, boy." Craig nodded and said, "Yep, that Tim; He's a regular double-naught spy." This sent images of Jethro Bodeen into all their minds and they cracked up. They were all more than old enough to remember the TV show "The Beverly Hillbillies." Jethro was a doofus hillbilly who wanted to be a "double-naught spy" just like 007, James Bond. He didn't quite cut the mustard.

Molly, however, cut the cake just fine and they were soon seated again, except for Darby, chatting and eating cake. When the second pot of coffee finished brewing, Tim jumped up and refilled everyone's cups. He'd gotten some blend of coffee that Molly liked. It was a little to . . . something for Tim. He liked his coffee black and plain. This had a flavor of nut, or something in it. He drank it, but didn't really care for it.

When Molly had finished a piece of cake, she went over to the cage and looked at her new pet. She said to everyone, but mostly Tim, "His right eye is closed again. I wonder if there is a problem with it."

Steph walked over and looked. "Yeah, it is closed," she said. "I don't see anything that indicates a problem though. I mean, it's not swollen, or watering or anything."

Molly nodded. It wasn't doing anything like that.

Tim added, "Remember the lady at the store said it was just something that particular ferret always did. There was nothing wrong with the eye."

Molly answered, "Yeah, that's right. She did say that. I forgot. He's so pretty I wasn't really listening when she was talking to us. Did they name him?"

Tim said, "Yeah, they named him. I thought you could call him whatever you want though." He turned to the men and said, "You guys want more cake? If you do, just grab it." And with that he got himself another piece.

Molly asked as he cut the corner piece with the pink rose of icing, "What did they name it at the pet shop?"

Tim licked his fingers, then said, "Captain Jack. The eye made them think of a pirate." He bit a forkful of cake.

Susan had been listening. She was always that way. She'd sit most of the time and just relax, listening to the conversation around her. She participated mostly with nods and laughs, or whatever was appropriate. She only spoke after taking some time to think about things. At this point she said, "I like that name. Captain Jack. It seems to fit."

Steph nodded and said, "I do too. It's good—fitting."

Molly agreed saying, "Same here. I think he'll be Captain Jack. Besides, he probably already knows that name." She bent closer to the cage and said to the ferret, who was just then rooting around in his little house, "How 'bout it boy? Captain Jack?" She seemed to expect an answer from the little beast. He continued to root around, oblivious to her question.

Darby came up then and said, "What is that?" She pointed to the cage.

Molly looked at her, still bending down, "That's a ferret. Tim gave it to me for my birthday."

Darby said, "Can I see it?" She looked at her mom for affirmation as she asked, then back at Molly.

Steph nodded, and Molly said, "Sure, let me pull him out. Just remember to be quiet and careful. They can get scared."

Darby nodded her head solemnly as though by not saying "ok" out loud she was reinforcing the ban on noise, which would scare the animal.

Molly opened the cage top and reached down to get the ferret. Just as at the store last week, the animal showed no fear and came out of its house to see what the commotion was. He allowed himself to be picked up at once, and seemed to enjoy the feeling of Molly's hands on his body.

Molly bent down and held the animal out for Darby to see. She said, "You can pet him. Just be nice and gentle with him. He'll sniff you, but just let him—He won't bite."

Darby tentatively put her hand out to run one finger along Captain Jack's head. He raised his head to smell her and she pulled back thinking he was raising his mouth to bite. Steph leaned down and said, "Watch me hon. He's ok." And she put her hand out and let the ferret smell her. Then she proceeded to scratch its little head.

Darby then tried to imitate what her mom had done, and within a few minutes she was holding the animal in her little hands. She couldn't support it too well however, so Captain Jack was squirming around for purchase. After watching things progress until it looked like Darby was having trouble, Steph took the animal from Darby and said, Why don't I hold him for you and you scratch him behind the ears?"

Darby began to pout a bit, but seeing that mom wasn't actually taking the animal away, she settled for just putting one of her little hands on her mom's, and petting Captain jack with the other.

Susan watched for a bit, wishing she had a daughter of her own. She turned and interrupted Josh, Craig and Tim, saying, "You know hon, we could have a girl and a ferret too." She grinned at Craig, knowing she was applying just a little pressure. They had talked about kids often. Craig was not sure he wanted any, but Susan's biological clock was ticking away and she was growing more desirous of starting a family. Seeing little Darby usually allowed her an opportunity to broach the subject with Craig again.

Craig looked at her, and feigned ignorance of what she'd said, "Huh? What's that?" he pushed a big piece of cake into his mouth and grinned at her through it.

Susan just rolled her eyes and kicked him, saying, "Yeah right. Like you didn't hear me."

Tim and Josh looked at one another, then at Craig. Then they laughed. Tim and Molly didn't have these conversations anymore because they had both determined they didn't want to have children. Josh and Steph already had Darby. So when it came to needling about becoming parents, Craig was all alone. He looked back at them and pursed his lips, saying with a glance, "Yeah, yeah, yuck it up boys. But I really have to deal with this!" They just laughed all the more.

Craig put Susan off for the moment with "yes, we could also have a BMW and a mansion. Though that's not going to happen right away either is it?"

Susan let it be for the moment. She'd made a point again. This sparring was going to continue until a decision was made. Craig loved kids. He was just not sure he was ready to have one. However, Susan was pretty sure she was ready. And it wouldn't be long until Craig figured out he was too. At least in her mind.

Having petted the ferret enough, Darby ran off and began to play somewhere else in the house. She had free run of the whole place when she came over. But usually she played in the work-out room. It had weights to pick up, and a big open area where she could lay around and play with any toys they might have brought. It was near enough to hear her and far enough to allow the adults to talk in peace.

Steph handed Captain Jack to Molly and both of them joined the others. Captain Jack sniffed and looked all around, but seemed content at the moment to curl up in Molly's lap and view the world from that vantage point. He must have desired comfort rather than exploration right now. After about half an hour of petting and just holding him, Molly put him back in his cage. He immediately went to his house, curled up and fell asleep.

After another hour or so of talking, Craig finally rose and said, "Well, we better get going hon."

Susan looked at her watch and said, "Yeah. I think we've wiped out enough of Molly's cake." She smiled at the men when she said it.

Steph got up then and said, "We're off too."

Josh, of course, jumped in and said, "We know *you're* off, but *I'm* not off!" He grinned at his wife. She just rolled her eyes and stuck her tongue out at him. Goof-ball!

They all gathered their coats and things. Molly sent some cake home with each family. After they had all left, she and Tim sat down at the table and looked at the ferret. It was almost seven and he was beginning to stir. They could see him rustling around a bit in his house. Molly said, "I sure love this gift." She looked at Tim and put a hand on his.

Tim smiled and said, "I knew you would. I'm glad." He loved to get things for Molly. She was appreciative, and it made him feel good to see her happy.

After cleaning up the messy dishes, they watched some TV for a bit. About nine or so Molly said, "I think I'm going to bed." She would often go to bed about nine and read for a while before she fell asleep.

Tim nodded and said, "I want to check email and do a little work before I come to bed. I'm not that tired." Usually Tim didn't get to bed until one a.m. or so. He enjoyed working on his computer at night when it was quiet. He liked to play video games too, and would do so for a little while each night. Molly hated them, so she was glad to just go to bed and leave him to it.

Molly kissed Tim and left him booting up his computer in the study. She had her own computer in the kitchen that handles all the things she cared about: her recipes, email, and letter writing. Beyond that, she didn't care about computers at all. Tim, however, loved to work at his, and sometimes would spend all night doing whatever he did. Molly didn't really understand the fascination. But then, Tim didn't really understand her interest in gardening either. To each their own.

After Molly had gone, and Tim's computer was up and running, he settled into his game. He turned off all the lights in his study. Last night he had quit at the entrance to a marketing firm. Tim didn't just play games or check email. Tim loved to hack. And he was extraordinarily good at it. He was no longer just "Tim" when he was hacking, he used the alias "Slayer." He had destroyed countless databases and systems over the years. He had entered any number of forbidden sites, cutting through security protocols like a hot knife through butter. He could out-smart most systems in his sleep.

Last night he had broken the encryption codes for a security system of a marketing firm: "Conexshuns." It appeared to be some hip market-ing company that specialized in cutting edge advertising. "They need some introduction to cutting edge uses of the net, I think," mumbled Tim as he entered their system. He had gotten out last night fairly early, having scanned their files in short order. He spent the rest of the night tweaking an exceedingly nasty virus he had built, specializing it for this company in particular. However, once it did its work on their files, it would mutate and explore all their contacts in the sales folder.

Tim found what he wanted and entered the virus. It was quite small really. He didn't set it to work. He preferred to always let the receivers of his gifts set them in motion. Consequently, he placed the virus in the email application of one of the lower rung execs. The young lady would open her mail program, and without knowing it, begin to destroy the firm's files from the inside. It would take less than an hour to leave their entire network blank. Then, the virus would mail a trigger off to all the recipients of an email it had previously mailed from the firm when it had first been activated. The trigger would activate the virus in the other company's computers. Tim preferred to do most of his work one system, one company at a time. He would only let his viruses reproduce and mail themselves once, using the addresses from the first firm into which they were implanted. He didn't think the cascade effect, which destroyed many linked systems, was artful. It was more like just a bunch of dominoes you knocked over. The real artistry was getting into each system and wreaking havoc in that particular system. The very last thing someone in a hacked system would see on their monitors was the word "Slayer" written in font that simulated dripping blood. Beyond that the computers would be dead.

All these manipulations of other people's computers would have been discovered long ago had Tim not developed what he called his "magic bullet." He had devised a way to randomly pick a server, and then from that server randomly pick an email address, and from that address access another computer. It was from that location he sent all the viruses. Not a few times the police had detained some unsuspecting citizen on the charge of computer hacking and vandalism. Sometimes it even made the papers! Tim scanned those articles and kept them in a secret file. It was pretty funny when the cops had to release an innocent person after crashing into their house like storm troopers!

Steph Felder had first laid Darby down about eight o'clock. She never went easy anymore. It was crying and screaming usually for at least half an hour. And tonight she was all keyed up from being at the Grayton's. First she wanted a story. Then she wanted a kiss from daddy. Then she wanted daddy to tell another story. Then she had to go to the bathroom. Then she wanted a drink. Then she was hot. Then, then, then. She could "then" you until dawn if given half a chance. At about 8:30 daddy gave her a firm talking to. She snuffled and whined alone in the dark until about 9:00. Finally, exhausted, both parents sat on the couch and looked at one another enjoying the silence.

"She's getting harder and harder each night," said Steph.

"I know," lamented Josh, "and I wish I knew why."

"Marylyn told me her boys were the same way. They just grew out of it when they got a little older."

"How much older?" Josh asked with a whining tone in his voice.

Steph giggled and said in an equally whiney tone, "I don't know!" She feigned feinting and lolled back on her end of the couch.

Josh pretended he had a knife and committed hari kiri. Both laughed and commiserated over their lovely but extremely *wired* daughter.

Josh then sat up and said, "Hey, did you talk to Susan at all about Craig and work? Tonight I mean?"

Steph shook her head and said, "No, I didn't. Did you talk to Craig?"

Josh shook his head too and said, "No. I was just wondering how things were going. He had that huge presentation and all. He was antsy when we played tennis last Saturday thinking about it."

"Yeah, Sue was the same way last I talked about it. I think a lot is riding on this deal for them. They seem to be a little overdrawn, don't you think?"

Josh chuckled lightly, "Yeah? Ya think?" His sarcasm was obvious. "I think they've dug a pretty deep hole. I know they don't have kids, but they sure have a lot for one salary."

"Yeah, I know. That house is beautiful, but I don't see how they make the payments."

"Me either. He can't make much more than I do."

"Hey!" said Steph, "Did I tell you I heard from Esther? She actually emailed me!" Esther was an older woman they had known when they were in college. She had lived in the same apartment complex they had and she'd adopted them as her own grandchildren. It was nice because she would bake for them and sometimes cook. She was just like a grandma. She said she just liked young people. They kept her young.

Josh grinned and said, "No way!" She finally got online, eh?" They hassled her about it incessantly since getting online themselves. "When did she get on?"

Steph answered, "She didn't say, but I don't think it was long ago. She said she was still figuring out her computer. A young couple that lived a few doors down was helping her with it."

Josh nodded and smiled. "She's helping them is more like it. I know how she is.

"Yeah," said Steph. "She's great."

They sat a bit, letting the conversation die. A little later they got up, turned out the lights and went to bed.

Craig lay in bed with his hands behind his head. He stared through the dark at the ceiling above him, listening to his wife's even breathing as she slept next to him. His eyes hurt. He shut them, tried to relax. But found once again that he could not. He looked over at the clock. It blared in red numbers: 1:36 a.m. Craig sighed and leaned back. He turned over and tried to clear his mind, but found it was useless. "A few more nights like this," he thought, "and they'll fire me for my daily work performance. Not just because of a project I blew."

He was referring to the marketing project, of course. Craig worked at a sports equipment company. He had been a great salesman and as the company grew, he was promoted to store manager, then area manager. He made good money, but they'd spent a lot, too much, of it on this house and the ten acres on which it sat. This had forced Craig to do something he regretted. He had taken out a large loan without telling Susan. $50,000 dollars' worth of loan. And technically, it wasn't a loan at all. It was more accurately called *embezzling*.

Craig had figured he could take the money out of a large fund at work that was basically just sitting there, and invest it in a high-return stock. Then he'd not only make the interest from the stock growth, but he could sell the stock and pay back the principle without anyone knowing. He had taken this course because they had bought this house and land before they could really afford it. After the new ad campaign succeeded, Craig counted on a raise and substantially improved finances. But the house would not have been around had they waited. Others were making offers on it, and to get it he had to commit right now. So he had, and had reassured Susan that they could swing it. And since she let him handle the finances completely, she had no idea how deep they were in. If this new ad campaign didn't bring in the clientele they believed it would (he chastised himself for even thinking that), he'd lose his house, and everything else.

Craig's latest project, given to him by the owner himself, was to work with the marketing firm, "Conexshuns," developing an ad campaign that reflected the ideas of the company. Something hip and progressive. Something to grab a bigger market. Conexshuns was supposed to be cutting edge in advertising/marketing, and was supposedly just the ticket to make Craig's company explode. Craig was not so sure. And what was worse, they had sunk a lot of money into the project. A LOT of money. Mr. Alden said it was a gamble, but the only way to make money was to spend money and take some risk. Unfortunately, it was Craig who seemed to be taking the stress and worry over the risk. Sure, Mr. Alden would probably have to close up Exercise One if anything went wrong. But Mr. Alden owned numerous companies. Craig worked at just one and its loss was his loss. *Serious* loss for Craig.

Craig chastised himself again. What could go wrong? That's silly. After all, it was fairly simple. Conexshuns, working with Craig, would come up with a blow-them-away ad campaign. It excites a larger customer base. Sales grow, everyone comes out ahead. And if sales only grow marginally, they still undoubtedly make enough to cover the cost of the ad campaign. And hopefully Craig would still earn a raise by his effort. Or at least that was the plan. Craig thought the cost was pretty exorbitant. But he could not argue. He could only take the assignment and run with it.

Of course, it was easy to say he would just do his job and not worry or stress over it. That's always easier said than done. Hence he had many nights of lying awake, as he was tonight, thinking and re-thinking— what-if-ing himself to an ulcer. Not to mention worrying about the loan (he persisted in using this euphemism), and if Mr. Alden found out how he got it.

Susan didn't like to see him tear himself up over it. But what could she do? She had suggested he might find another job. But except for this one assignment, Craig loved his job, and had no problems with it. And though Sue didn't like the stress on her husband, she did like the perks of his higher salary. And if they did start a family, she'd appreciate even more the raise in pay he would receive. Craig shuddered lightly at the thought of her finding out about the loan. That would make her crazy!

He heaved a sigh, and closed his eyes again. He could only stare at the black ceiling so long before his eyes began to burn. There was nothing to do but get done and see if it works. Tomorrow would end the worry. All the print work had been finished and turned over to Craig today at work. He should have copied them and sent a disk over to Mr. Alden's to safe guard them, but it was late in the day and he had not done it. Still, one night without a backup disk wouldn't matter. He'd print one out in the morning and it would all be done. It would all go out then and within a week or two they would know if it was a bust or a boon.

—

Tim tightened his tie, glanced up and down at himself in the mirror, and headed downstairs to the kitchen. Both he and Molly had slept late this morning. Late for them was 5:15 a.m. or so. Usually, Tim got up early and worked out, lifting weights, or doing treadmill. Molly worked out after she got off work in the afternoon. Their schedules were out of sync with most peoples because Molly worked odd hours at a doctor's office. She had to be at work by six every morning, because they opened early. This was great for those many customers who needed visits outside of regular business hours, but no fun for the staff who worked the early morning shift. The good part was that Molly was off each day at 2:30 in the afternoon.

It was possible to go into the exercise room without seeing the family room. Tim had been downstairs earlier for an abbreviated workout, and had come back up to shower and dress without ever going into the kitchen or family room. Molly had gotten up after Tim dressed, and had just gone down to make coffee a few minutes before Tim. While he was still on the stairs, he heard her shriek from the family room. He hustled the last few steps, wide eyed, and rounded the corner looking for her. He stopped in his tracks at what he saw!

Molly was standing next to one of their easy chairs, holding what looked like most of the innards of the seat cushion in her hands. He had gotten out of his cage in the night, and torn the cushion apart! There were pieces of foam everywhere around the chair, and it looked like Captain Jack had actually begun to shred part of the couch as well.

The look on Molly's face said enough to allay Tim's worries over her safety, but also told him she was just a little angry at her new pet. Tim looked at the cage and saw that the ferret wasn't' there. He said, "Where's the ferret?"

Molly shook her head and said, "I have no idea. But when I get my hands on him!" She didn't finish her thought. They both were scanning the room and froze almost in unison at a faint scratching sound from under the couch. Tim walked over and hefted the front of the couch off the floor, revealing nothing. He said, "I thought I heard something here. Did you?"

Molly nodded and came over. She stopped Tim from putting the couch down again, and got on her hands and knees by him. She looked up under the couch and saw Captain Jack nestled into the insides of the piece of furniture. He'd chewed a hole in the bottom cover. She whispered back to Tim, who was still holding the front of the couch, tipping it back, "I see him. He's inside."

Tim nodded and quietly said, "Can you reach him?"

Molly responded by leaning way down, and slowly sliding her hand up into the couch's guts to where Captain Jack was sitting, eyeing her warily. At least he's not running away, she thought. In fact, she easily snagged him and drew him out, allowing Tim to then let the couch sit back down on all four feet. She cradled the little animal in her hands and then held him up so they were eye to eye. She said in a stern voice, "What the heck were you doing down here?" Again, as earlier, it sounded like she might actually expect an answer. She didn't get one this time either.

Instead, Captain Jack just eyed her with a look Tim thought said, "So, you have any food for me?" He said to Molly, "He looks like he feels he did you a favor by tearing our furniture up!" He was beginning to wonder if his first instincts about not getting the animal were correct.

Molly said, "We are definitely going to have to fix that cage." Then to Captain Jack she said, "You're not doing this again buster! Or you'll be outa here!" Tim noticed she still petted the animal as she put him back in his cage.

Looking at the door of the cage (which was located in the top), Tim thought the ferret had just worried the latch back by hanging on the door. He remembered seeing another ferret hanging from the door of its cage, which was also in the top, and like a slinky, it was banging itself up and down against the thin bars. The door looked like it was taking a beating. Tim couldn't recall hearing that last night. But they slept with their bedroom door closed, and may not have heard it. In any event, Captain Jack got out, and Tim would have to figure out a latch that would hold or they would apparently have no furniture left!

Molly got coffee going while Tim got some wire from the garage. For today he was going to just wire the door closed, and put the cover on the cage. Hopefully not being able to see his surroundings would deter Captain Jack from desiring escape while they were at work. Though right now the animal seemed to be getting ready to nap in his little house. Well, just in case, thought Tim. He wired the door shut.

Molly left as usual much earlier than Tim; it was about 5:40 a.m. Tim left about 8:30 and both hoped they had a house when they returned!

—

Sue was up much earlier than Craig. He had been restless last night again. She always knew when he was restless because now and then throughout the night he'd come over by her and spoon up next to her. She thought he was probably trying to get comfy. It had happened a couple times last night, so she knew he'd not slept well.

She poured a cup of coffee when she heard Craig's footfalls coming down the hall. When he came into the kitchen, he still looked a little bleary eyed. She kissed him and handed him the coffee saying, "Didn't sleep well huh?"

He mumbled, "No," and took as big a swallow as he could without burning himself of the hot liquid. He then shuffled over to the table and sat down. Louise was purring and crisscrossing around between his feet as he sat looking out of sorts, nursing his coffee. Craig was definitely not a morning person.

Susan popped the toast she had been making and put it and two eggs on a plate. She carried them over and set them down in front of her zombie, kissing him on the head and saying, "Here, eat your breakfast and maybe you'll wake up some."

Craig smiled and croaked, "Thanks babe." It was pretty good for him. Usually he was useless for speech until his second cup of Java. Susan smiled back and went to get her own breakfast of cereal. When she returned she brought the paper with her and after taking the local section out, she handed it to Craig. He retrieved the sports section and they sat and ate in silence, reading. It wasn't that they didn't communicate well. They just had an understanding: no talk before breakfast. Craig was just surly before he ate and woke up some. Sue remembered when they were first married. She was a morning person. Or at least didn't mind the morning. She'd talk to Craig, and try to engage him in chit-chat. One day he just said, "Look Sue, we have to talk." He had made it clear, in as loving a way as he could, that he didn't want to talk at all before coffee.

It would have been easy to be angry. But Sue realized people were different. Craig would start to act normal when he got some coffee in him and some food. From then on, until he had some breakfast, she just let him be; let him wake up. She didn't mind. It was a quirk she could live with. They were chatting away about what they were reading within twenty minutes.

—

Darby Felder was up before anyone. As usual. She climbed out of bed and walked down to her folk's room. The door was closed. She tired the knob. It wouldn't turn. She banged on the door. A second later mom came out and scooped her up. "You're up a little early today baby. What's with that?" She kissed Darby on the cheek and hugged her tight.

Darby hugger her back and said, "You have bad breath mommy!"

Steph laughed and said, "Thanks for waking me and telling me that. If you'd get up later like you should I'd have time to brush before I kiss you young lady!" She kissed her again, and set her down, taking her hand and leading her to the kitchen.

A moment later, Josh followed them. He too picked his daughter up and kissed her. "Morning little girl. How'd you sleep?"

Darby bubbled, "Hi daddy. I slept fine but I woke up."

Josh set her down at the table and said, "You did? Why was that?"

She shrugged and said "I don't know."

Steph put some cereal in two bowels for Darby and herself. Josh made some coffee and poured some milk for Darby. Then they all sat and ate breakfast together. Josh read the paper while Darby told Steph about her dream last night.

When they were through, Darby ran off to get dressed. It was hit or miss on whether she'd need help or not. She was pretty smart and had learned many things quite early. Sometimes she ended up dressed just fine. Sometimes mom had to help a bit.

Steph two-handed her coffee mug and said, "How's your day?"

Josh looked up from reading about another overpaid prima donna pro athlete and said, "Nothing special. I think I have a lot of routine things this morning. A cavity or two perhaps." Josh was a dentist.

Steph nodded and said, "I think I'll go over to the mall later with Darby. Get her some shirts."

Josh nodded back and replied, "Sounds good. Meet you back here at five?" He grinned at her. "Shall we synchronize our watches, agent 99?"

Steph giggled, "I'll just take a chance I can get here on time." Later, she kissed him goodbye and sent him off to work. Then she cleaned up the dishes, got some laundry going and read some books to Darby. Mid-morning, when the mall opened, she and Darby went off shopping.

—

Craig had been out to visit one of the stores in the morning, and it was almost 11:00 a.m. when he settled into his desk chair. He could not believe the news. He had talked with the store manager, seen him use the computer, found everything running fine. Sometime between when he left the store and when he arrived at his office at headquarters something had happened in the computer system. As far as they could tell, the entire system was gone. They had called the police, and some computer specialists, but they had no good news as of yet. In fact, they seemed rather pessimistic about the outcome of their work. Craig wondered if Tim could figure something out. He worked with computers and seemed to know a lot.

A lieutenant Tash was just now in Craig's office saying, "We have a specialist who works entirely on computer hacking crimes and he will be here in a moment to fill us in on what we know." Craig mutely nodded his head thinking of the ramifications.

He was still sitting mute when a young man who looked about twelve to Craig knocked on the door frame and came into the office. Lieutenant Tash introduced him as detective Morrison of the CCU—computer crimes unit. He shook Craig's sweaty hand and sat down in one of the chairs opposite the desk. Craig sat down again, having risen when Morrison put his hand out, and said, "So what's the news? What about our system, our files." He restrained himself from screaming at them, "What about my hidden accounts? What about my money!?"

Morrison looked grave. He said, "Well, it's not good. I've seen this rat before and he is very good at his work and very thorough." Craig's heart rose into his throat. Morrison finished, "There is very little chance anything in your system is still functional."

Craig morosely leaned back and asked distractedly, "Why? Why would anyone want to do this to us?" He knew that now there was a good chance his embezzlement would be found out when they re-loaded the accounts onto the system from back-ups. His only consolation was that although he'd dropped the ball and not backed up the files from Conexshuns, at least he could go back to them and get another copy.

Morrison said, "I think we'll find that this is not an isolated occurrence. This guy usually hacks a more difficult system to destroy it. Your system and others were wrecked because you were in the original system's mailing data base. As I said, I've seen this guy's work and he follows the same m.o. routinely. We already think we know the system he originally broke in to. Are you doing work with an ad firm called . . ." at this point he looked at a notebook he was holding, ". . . Conexshuns?"

Craig's shoulders slumped even more. He swallowed and nodded, "Yes, we had quite a bit of money invested in a project with them." He didn't mention that he'd failed to make a copy of the work they'd given him the night before. It was a secondary consideration. His mind was wrapping itself around how to explain the loan when the company tried to rebuild its files.

Morrison made a note in his book and said, "Well, we're pretty sure that's it then. We've had calls from a number of businesses found in their databases. Unfortunately, this hacker is slick and we can't seem to get to him." Morrison didn't detail how they had traced their way back to false email addresses from clues found in the residue of previously hacked systems they had investigated. Each time they thought they had the culprit, they found they had some rube whose computer had been used to send the virus remotely. It was maddening when the criminals were as savvy as the police chasing them. Too much damage could be done before they were caught. And often it ended up being juveniles who couldn't be fully prosecuted anyway.

After long hours of police interviews and what not, it was finally quiet in the office again. Mr. Alden had been out of town and had not been informed as of yet of the trouble. Craig sat at his desk alone and in a deep malaise. He could see no way out of his troubles. He envisioned his life, totally ruined, and a switch flicked over in his head. He'd be found out about the $50,000 and since Conexshuns' data was wiped out, he could not get another copy of their ad files. He had failed to make a copy, and they had no originals.

It was while he was stewing at his desk that Bob Angels knocked on his door. Everyone had gone except Bob. He was a computer tech employed by Exercise One itself. He had been out most of the day and had just come in when everyone else was leaving. It was not uncommon for the computer nerds to work at strange hours when the building was mostly empty. He thought he was bringing Craig good news. He had found a tell-tale in the debris of their database. Somehow, the virus's sender had left his email address in the system. Bob, arriving late, had not talked to the police. He didn't know that the author of this virus routinely supplied a false email address for someone to chase. With a grin of triumph he handed the email address he'd found over to Craig saying,

"I found this. It's the address of the person responsible for this mess. I thought you'd want to see it and then pass it on to the cops."

Craig had taken the slip of paper thinking it was an honest to goodness lead also. Morrison had not mentioned that the hacker whose name appeared on all their monitors, *Slayer*, routinely left a false email address for the police to follow. Craig, broken and filled with rage, wanted to know who had ruined his life. He could not believe what he read: Josh&Steph@Trinet.com. It was his friend! He had gotten his jollies destroying Craig's life. He thought he knew Josh. Craig spent a long while thinking at his desk. Later that night he wandered down to see Bob. He asked if he could get him something at Zips since he was going run over there. They were both working late. Bob said he would do the run since he needed to stop home and get a few things he needed.

—

That night, when Molly got home, she immediately went to the cage to see if Captain Jack had escaped and wreaked more havoc on their house. He had not. He was there, curled up in his house just as she had left him. Though she noticed the water was down and the food slightly depleted. "At least you're not starving as you wait to rip our house apart again," she said. Captain Jack opened one eye and took her in for a moment. He then casually came over to the side of the cage and sniffed at her. She pulled him out, scratched him all over then sat down, letting him crawl around her lap. He found a loose button on her blouse, and began to gnaw at it, tugging and biting it. "Ahhh, back to your old ways, eh?" said Molly, and she quickly pulled him off the button. He couldn't let go of it though, and every time she turned him loose, he'd find his way back to it. Finally, Molly just put him back in the cage until she could go change. "You persist in destroying things don't you?" she reprimanded the ferret. He just sat and looked at her, one eye closed. "I can't leave you alone for one minute." He still stared. With a shrug, Molly went off to get a new shirt.

Tim arrived home from work about six p.m. He worked a little late helping a friend with some problem or other. Molly didn't know exactly what he did. All she knew was that he made microchips. That was why they always had such good computers. He would get a discount on chips. It was the perfect job for Tim. He got his daily fix of computers at work, and though he spent time working at one at home too, Molly didn't lose him to them completely. The first thing Tim said when he came in was, "Well? How's the little vandal?"

Molly kissed him and said, "He's just fine. Though he definitely has a streak of vandal in him. He tried to eat a button off my blouse this afternoon!"

Tim smirked and said, "As long as he doesn't destroy our furniture anymore. Did you call about the chair?"

Molly nodded, "Yeah, we can bring the cushion in this week and they'll fix it up."

"Where at?" asked Tim.

"The place is called 'Shepherds,'" Molly said. "It's over by the mall. They just do furniture repair."

Tim nodded and said, "Ok. You take the cushion in? Tomorrow maybe?"

Molly agreed, saying, "Yeah, I thought I would."

Having settled that, Tim went upstairs to shower. Before he went back down for dinner, after his shower, he booted up his computer and did a quick scan of the news sites he liked. Mostly he was looking for fallout from his games last night. But nothing much was mentioned. No one was arrested. He saw that a hacker caused "serious damage" to some businesses though. He smiled to himself. Slayer strikes again! He left the computer on and went down to dinner.

—

Five forty-five p.m. came and went and Steph picked up the phone and punched the speed dial of Josh's office. She was not angry or anything. She just wanted to know how late Josh would be. It was not uncommon for him to have something come up, an emergency perhaps, or just a procedure that ran long. She listened while the phone rang, watching Darby work in her coloring book. Finally, the answering machine came on. That was a little odd. She said, "Hi hon, I just wondered where you were . . . what came up. You're probably working or on the way right now." She hung up, and said to Darby, "Well young lady, what do you say we have hot dogs for dinner?" Darby grinned and answered, "Yeah!"

At around seven p.m. Steph called Susan and asked if Josh had stopped by and gotten caught up with Craig. Susan said she's seen neither of them. Craig had called and said he needed to work late. Steph then called Molly and asked about Josh. Neither Tim nor Molly had heard from him.

At eight fifty-two p.m. an officer knocked on Steph's door. He came in and wanted Steph to sit down. She was afraid by then and didn't want to, but he insisted. "Ma'am I regret to inform you that we found your husband dead earlier this evening." It was the only line she could clearly remember from their conversation. Steph had already put Darby to bed, and when the officer left, she pulled her knees up on the couch and wept. A little later she called Molly and Sue and told them what happened. They came over along with Craig and Tim and tried to comfort her.

—

It was well after midnight when Craig and Susan pulled into their driveway. Sue felt horrible. What a day. She looked over at Craig and said, "How could all this happen on one day? First your car is stolen, then Josh is killed." She didn't really expect an explanation from Craig.

Craig shrugged his shoulders and said, "Not to mention the fiasco at work." He didn't mention more to her than some computer problems. "It hasn't been much of a day has it?" He didn't expect an answer either.

They got out of the car, went inside and immediately went to bed. They were wrung out emotionally after being with Steph. Susan hurt deeply over her friend's pain. And the thought of some gun wielding crazy car-jacking Craig's car made her feel worse. She fell asleep hoping she could heal a little during the night.

Craig lay down and tried to sleep. He couldn't. Again. So he laid in the dark and stared at the ceiling. He guessed he had maybe a week to figure something out. Maybe he should just leave town tomorrow. Maybe if he came clean at work he'd be ok. He wasn't fired or anything. Not yet. Maybe he could just tell Mr. Alden and be forgiven. Still, it was a huge blunder. The real problem was with Sue. He could lose the house if Mr. Alden didn't play ball. He would lose it. He'd be fired and he'd lose it, and maybe he'd go to jail. And then Susan would leave him. He stared at the ceiling. There were other matters too.

—

Three days later Craig's car was found. It had been beaten up pretty bad, but it clearly matched the description of the hit and run car that had killed Josh Felder earlier in the week. In addition there was some hair and blood that conclusively matched Josh's.

The police stopped by to question Craig again about the car. He had reported it stolen just on the evening Josh Felder had been killed. They didn't really seem interested in him too much, which somewhat surprised him. Apparently Bob Angels had mentioned they both worked late that whole evening. Since the car had been dumped, the police figured the killer had gotten away and left the car. No evidence was found on the vehicle itself. Six months later the case was still open and filed as "unsolved." Craig had bought a new car with the insurance money he received.

—

Craig sat in his new office and stared out the window. It had been nine months since the computer crash. He chewed his pencil with a vengeance. He did that a lot. He worked long hours. He snapped at Susan more and more often. He was wearing down. When the files had been reloaded, Bob Angels had come to him with the anomalies instead of going straight to Alden. Craig had said he'd take care of the matter. He'd quietly made the whole thing go away. He'd even worked it out so his secretary took the fall for the lost Conexshuns files. He beat the whole system. He'd cleared it up. He won. And here he sat, reaping the rewards of a job well done. He snapped his pencil.

—

Tim and Craig were out on the tennis court early Saturday morning. They played early so as to have the place to themselves for an hour or two. It had been over a year since Josh had died, and though Tim and Craig were still friends, Craig had never been the same since then. He seemed to go very quiet when the subject came up. And he tended to withdraw from everyone most of the time.

Tim was trying to casually banter with him as they sat on the bench between sets. "So this ferret is doing the same ol' things. We have been really conscientious about checking his cage door ever since we first got him and he escaped and tore up out house. Do you remember that?" Tim looked at his friend closely, trying to see into him somehow and find out what was wrong with him.

Craig let a small, tight smile cross his lips. "Yeah, I remember." He took a swig of water and toweled his head. He said no more.

Tim went on, "Well, a few days ago Molly thought I had closed his cage and I thought she had. The little guy got out and ransacked the place again. This time he got into the pantry and chewed through just about every box in there." It was a pretty lame story, Tim knew. He just found that it was hard to be with Craig more each time they got together. He was withdrawing more each day and Tim was finding it uncomfortable. He wanted to help, but couldn't' seem to get through. Finally, more for his own sake perhaps than Craig's he said bluntly, "Look Craig, what's up?"

Craig looked at him and said, "Nothing. I guess I'm just tired."

Tim shook his head and answered, "It's not being tired man. Ever since Josh died, you've been circling down. You have to deal with it. You're coming apart. I can't stand watching it anymore." Tim was determined to get into his friends life or just walk away. He couldn't think of anything else. "I've watched you and Sue for a year now. And I have to tell you Craig, you need to figure out what's wrong or your whole life is gonna crumble."

Craig's eyes flickered a little. He regarded his friend with a cool stare. Tim thought it would just continue until they let it drop and went out to play the next set. But suddenly Craig exhaled a large blast of air though his nostrils just like a bull does before it charges. He squared his shoulders to Tim and locked eyes with him. Then he took a breath and said, "Do you want to know what I really think about that piece of crap?"

Tim was shocked and confused. What was Craig talking about?

Craig continued while Tim sat in silence. "I'll tell you what I think. I'm glad he's dead!" He held Tim's eyes with a dark, predatory look. Tim sat still. He had no idea what to say. Craig went on, "You know what else?" He leaned toward Tim closing the distance between them on the bench to a hand's width. All Tim could see were Craig's eyes boring into him. He squinted those eyes a little and whispered, "I took him out myself." He gave a quick jerk of his head as though to signify the finality of his statement.

Tim's mouth dropped open. He searched is friends face for a sign that this was a sick joke. But he knew Craig wasn't lying. He stuttered out, "Why? Why would . . . ?"

But before any more got out Craig said, "You wanna know why? You remember how I almost lost my job over that computer hacking?"

Tim shook his head. He had not heard about that at all. With Josh's death, and all the turmoil, he didn't hear anything about a computer problem at Craig's office. In fact, Craig had never told him.

Craig said, "Well, little Josh was not the nice guy he pretended to be. I know he had access to computers. He talked about being online and all. Well, our system was hacked and it almost destroyed me. But our company analyst found a way to trace the culprit! I still have the name! It was Josh! Josh did it all!"

Tim shook his head and said, "Wait, wait, Josh didn't know enough about computers to hack anything." Tim knew from which he spoke. He had talked with Josh a number of times and could tell he was not very computer literate. Tim would certainly know for he was one of the best hackers around!

Craig said, "No! I know it was him. Bob Angels at work found his email in our system. It was the only scrap of information left except for the hacker's name!"

Tim was pretty savvy about many other hackers. He asked, "How do you know the hacker's name?" He wanted to hear what it was; find out if he knew him. Could it be Josh? It couldn't possibly be! Not unless Josh was a first class con man too. Because Tim would swear Josh didn't have the computer capabilities for any low level hacking let alone something intricate.

Craig raised his voice as he said, "I know his name because he left it scrawled in blood on my monitor! It was Slayer! And Josh Felder's email was where the virus came from! He tried to wipe me out! I'm glad I killed him! I ran him down!" Spittle flew from Craig's lips as he barked out the last few words. He stared at Tim with the eyes of a rabid dog. Tim could see, despite Craig's words, his actions had torn him up inside.

Craig leaned back then, lowered his head and said very quietly, "I faked my car being stolen. Bob covered for me, because the police didn't ask him enough questions. He forgot he'd run out to get burgers and left Craig at the office. The cops figured I was close to Josh and they messed up." Tears were at the corners of Craig's eyes. In the span of a few seconds he had gone from being seemingly berserk, to painfully broken.

Tim looked at his friend and wondered if he was sane. He only thought on it for a second. Then he allowed his mind to address the truth of what he'd heard. Slayer. He'd been Slayer then. He didn't know anyone else who used his type of magic bullet, and no one would dare use his tag. He slumped back into the bench, his breathing became labored. The consequences of his hacking struck his psyche full force as he realized what he'd done. The magic bullet had randomly chosen Josh's Internet provider's server. Then it had gone through Josh's email address to get somewhere, some company that Craig's firm dealt with. It had chewed up that company, then been emailed to Craig's. Then it had chewed up his system and left the false telltale of Josh's email address for someone to find. Tim closed his eyes and began to shake.

Craig broke during Tim's thoughts and started crying. He leaned back and mumbled, "I killed my own friend, I killed him, I killed him...." It was all jumbled through the sobs. Tim opened his eyes and watched him. He felt completely cold inside. Empty. He never realized, no, never wanted to realize the consequences of escaping his life though hacking. He just viewed it as a way to break out of the mundane life which caged him. And now he'd killed one friend, and that was as sure as if he'd driven Craig's car himself, and pushed another one to insanity. Tim looked around bleakly. Craig slipped from the bench and curled up on the ground, crying and muttering to himself.

Tim heaved a sigh. A stone look suddenly passed over his face. He stood up and walked away. It was going to be hard to forget this one.

Chicken

S UE MARTIN DRIFTED AWAKE as her radio came on; it showed 7:00 am. She finally opened her eyes, looked at the ceiling of her bedroom, and stiffened her body into a full stretch. On the radio, KPRB—the public station, a man was droning on in a dry voice, "Animals of all kinds quite often change their environment to improve their chances of survival. . . ." They were replaying an interview she'd heard last week with an animal expert. As a small station, they often played and replayed certain canned show segments. She lay back in her California King, pulled her comforter up and nestled into her pillows letting his voice wash over her. She didn't care for the morning.

—

Barry Sedgwick stepped from bed at 4:30 am with the shrill buzz of his second alarm. He could never get out of bed if he didn't have that annoying buzz blaring at him from the dresser across the room. His first alarm, on the nightstand by the bed, had wakened him with KPRB playing a canned interview with an animal expert: "Almost without fail an animal's nesting site becomes the target of attacks by usurpers, predators and parasites of various types. . . ." He walked over to the second alarm and shut it off. Then he slipped into his workout gear and went to his gym room to begin his morning workout. Today it was chest and triceps. He loved lifting weights, and having a power rack at home made it so much easier. He flipped on the radio in his gym room, KPRB again, and heard the same interview for a moment before tuning in some rock and roll, ". . . defending resources is the heart of territoriality, which is basically about possession, use, and defense of a space for an animal's own needs and desires. . . ."

—

Mari awoke in the cold blackness of the hovel she called home. She lay quietly in the predawn chill for a moment listening to the breathing of her children as they lay around her. The littlest was clearly distinguishable by the rasping wheeze that came with every breath. He had been sick almost since birth, and Mari had no delusions of his chances. He was barely one and would probably not see two.

Mari stared at the roof above her and, as she had to every morning, tried to fight away the hopelessness that crept over her when she woke. Since her husband had died, she had barely made it. She worked her small portion of earth. But the land gave little and she knew that they were slowly starving to death. And with five mouths plus her own to feed, she did not know what her world would be in a year's time.

Knowing that it would do no good to lay and weep, Mari rose and prepared to walk to the well. It had been her job to get water before her husband died, and the children were too small to fetch enough, so it was still her job. She stepped silently over the sleeping forms and stood in the opening of their shack. It was not much, she knew, but at least she could keep some rain off when it came.

—

Sue slammed her phone down and angrily pushed her chair back from her desk. She crossed her arms and tapped her chin with one finger as she thought about the whole situation. She swiveled her chair around from her desk and took in the spectacular view from her 32nd floor, corner office. There were no buildings to obscure her view in any direction.

Over to her right sat a brick building: The main post office. It had the blue and white eagle swooping on the front banner. People bustled in and out, up and down the front stairs. They carried letters, packages, sometimes nothing. The little fat guy was coming to check his box. Sue knew it was almost 9:20. The little fat guy came every day at 9:20 to check his mail. He wore basically the same outfit every day too: Blue canvas coat, tan work pants, black work shoes. The shoes were the kind you saw mail men wearing. Utilitarian. Sue didn't think he was an ex-mail man though. He could have been, but she just never pictured him as that. He was bald, mostly. He had hair on the sides of his head. It was gray. His face was round and indistinguishable from the height of her office.

The little fat guy came to her notice quite a long while ago. Not long after she moved into this office. She was enamored with the view at first, and just looked to see everything there was to see. It probably spoiled her work more than she would like to admit. Those days were gone. Now she took in the view mostly when she needed to think harder. It was a sort of habit that settled her mind. She'd scan the various buildings and streets, people and animals. As she did, she would sector off whatever problem she was working on, as though laying it down on the grid work of the city below. Then she would slowly dissect it into various parts.

The little fat guy became a constant part of the view for her. He was there every day— entering without mail, exiting with mail. Sometimes he would receive packages, but he never brought any. She wondered where the little fat guy lived. He seemed to walk to the post office every time. She had never seen him in a car. Never seen him even hail a cab, or step off a bus. He would round the corner up the street, trundle down to the main entrance, mount the steps, and disappear into the post office. Usually about 10 minutes later, he would emerge, come down the steps, trundle up to the corner, and disappear until the next day. That was the existence of the little fat guy in Sue's mind. Now and then he was just a phantom figure in her eyes. She saw him, but was so engrossed in her thoughts that he registered only because he had cut a swath in her perceptions over and over again. He was not memorable, not even mentionable to Sue. He just was . . . there. Turn, trundle, mount, enter, emerge, descend, trundle, gone.

Sue's eyes quested past the little fat guy to the hot dog stand on the corner across the street and up one. The vender looked Indian, or Paki, or something. Again, you couldn't tell at this distance. But he had the thick rich hair that she associated with a middle easterner and she knew from closer examination that he was. She could tell by the way he moved that he sometimes barked at the people passing by: "Lunch time? Feel hungry yet?" She also knew this because she had walked by now and again and heard him inviting the passersby to eat. She did not know of many vendors who did that. They usually relied on the fact that they were easily accessible, and readily available to promote their business. It was enough for a hungry person to walk by a good smelling hot dog or pretzel. Their mouth would start to water and they would stop for a bite. But this guy would merrily harangue the crowd as they passed, pulling uncertainty into cash for food.

Drifting away from the scene, Sue's mind recounted the phone conversation she had just angrily ended. Idiots! She had spent hundreds of thousands of dollars on surveying and mapping, obtaining core samples, drilling, planning, and preparing. She had had environmental studies done until she and her colleagues were blue in the face! And now IPF and its band of marauding tree huggers were trying to bury the whole thing! If it wasn't because of some bug or animal, it would be because of some endangered culture. Sue was sick of arguing over it, sick of the bureaucratic red tape that could be dredged up by IPF just for the sake of wearing her down until Global Construction Works in general, and she in particular, gave up the whole idea of building a dam in India.

Well, IPF—and especially Barry Sedgwick—would learn that she was not the quitting type. She steepled her fingers in front of her face, and began to plan a way through the court proceedings to come. After a few more minutes she turned in her plush office and began to jot notes into her computer. She loved her job!

—

Barry slammed his phone down and angrily shoved his chair back. If Global Construction Works wanted a fight, he was going to give it to them. Sue Martin could sit in her fat-cat office and look over the world as though she owned it from now until eternity. But that didn't mean she could clutch her fingers around one of the oldest living cultures in the world. The International Protection Foundation was not going to let them destroy a natural resource that the whole world has a right to just because they want to put in a hydroelectric dam and make a zillion dollars.

Barry calmed himself and crossed his legs. He began to tap his fingers on the arms of his leather chair as he looked at the oak and glass display shelf on the other side of his office. There were gifts and treasures from all over the globe, given to him for his help in defending the poor. He looked at a picture of a cricket that lived in Brazil. It would be gone now if not for him and IPF pushing for restraint in the destruction of its natural habitat. It wasn't just the cricket that survived either. It was the entire ecosystem that would have been destroyed. The cricket was just the little bonus he especially loved. Its colors were lovely in the picture— bright, shiny brown with an orange stripe on the side. To think it would have only lived in that picture if they had not stepped in.

Barry stood and walked over to his window. He looked out on the gardens that filled the center of the huge square building IPF called home. There was a Japanese feeling to the garden, though it was not exactly modeled on a Japanese garden of any kind. There were areas that were left untended, and others that were carefully manicured. There were water courses, and bright flowers, stone sculptures and benches. It was a lovely garden that reflected the diversity of mankind; at least that was how Barry saw it. It was a beautiful focal point in the twenty million dollar building surrounding it.

As he stood and watched, Orlen the gardener came out from behind a large bush and went to work weeding a flower bed. He was an older gentleman, probably in his seventies. Barry would sometimes go and eat his lunch in the garden, purposely sitting near where Orlen worked so that he might strike up a conversation. Orlen tended to be reticent about talk. He was not unfriendly, just quiet. But he had a good heart and a feel for nature that Barry admired. Even when he needed to control pests which destroyed the flowers, he always used other insects just as nature would. At the moment he was using some sort of fertilizer it seemed, mixing it into the soil of the flower bed as he worked it. Barry loved to chat with the old man as he worked; he was interesting.

Barry decided he needed to go out and walk a little. He switched off his coffee maker and lights, and strolled out the main entrance. He was a valuable employee of IPF and could pretty much do as he pleased during the work day. He walked out into the sun and headed left down toward the CoffeeShack. He thought he'd get a muffin and then walk down around the park while he thought about his morning's conversation with Sue Martin.

The CoffeeShack was not too busy at 10:00. Earlier, yes. Later, yes. But now, midmorning, it was relatively quiet. He got behind a young lady and within a few minutes was paying for his blueberry muffin. He pocketed the change, and walked out, heading down to the park. The city had built a walking track all around and through the park (supported enthusiastically by IPF). People could enjoy the natural feeling of the area without destroying it. He decided to go up toward the game area where they had put in swing sets and what not for the younger children. He was startled once on the way by a beagle that was running ahead of its master, but other than that he met no one.

At the playground there were a number of moms with their preschool kids. The children ran about while the parents chatted and enjoyed the sun. Barry chose a bench a little off from the area and sat, crossing his legs, and opening his muffin on his lap. He began to nibble bites as he watched a young red-headed boy dangle from the jungle gym. Barry was sure he was going to do a nose dive into the saw dust piled deep beneath him. He looked so small; Barry wondered if his little hands could actually go around the jungle gym bars.

As he watched, Barry again was struck with the necessity of living within the environment. He did not object to growth, but wanted responsible growth in the world. It was corporations like GCW that would pave the world over for a buck if they had half a chance. And it was his job to see that they were stopped. He loved his job!

—

Mari scraped at the rock that stuck in the earth. She had one tool, and it was made of wood. The land around her was dusty and rocky and had not produced much this year. It was difficult work, standing in the heat, bent over, swinging her hoe, pulling weeds away from the crop.

Sweat trickled over Mari's forehead and down her face as she worked. Its salty composition stung as it washed over her dark eyes. She would wipe a hand across her face, but that really did little good and sometimes made matters worse. She resigned herself to the itch of the sweat, the sting of the flies, the heat, and the lack of water on hand to cool her off. She barely noticed her surroundings, working diligently, trying to reap enough to survive.

—

Sue Martin had spent all morning sorting out her defense of the planned hydroelectric plant. She was pleased with her work and with satisfaction turned the light off in her office as she headed out to lunch with Stan Verrington, her office next door neighbor. They got along great, and often ate lunch together, discussing work and their personal lives.

"How 'bout the Mandarin today?" asked Stan as they met at the elevator.

Sue nodded and said, "Sure, I'm famished and could use a big plate. I've been writing up an argument to present for the construction of the hydroelectric plant."

Stan nodded and said, "And what are you arguing about now?"

Sue rolled her eyes and answered, "Let's not spoil lunch with it. I'm happy with my work so far, and don't want to talk my way back into a bad mood with it." She smiled as she said it, but Stan knew she was being serious. Sometimes they both could get pretty worked up over their projects, and it was best just to let it lie at times.

"Works for me," he said. "I'm up to my eyeballs in numbers with the budget on the California bridge project. And I'm about worked out on the whole thing!"

They agreed to stay off work and once seated at the Mandarin they began to discuss office gossip. "I heard she was not going to see him again!" said Sue, unable to contain her amazement at Pam Stenler's foolishness.

"They said they weren't going to see one another," mumbled Stan through a mouthful of pork and rice, "but it's hard to stop a thing overnight. And quite a thing from what I've heard." He grinned, still trying to swallow!

Sue laughed as she piled some more bamboo shoots and chicken cashew on her plate. She caught the waitress's eyes and tapped her tea cup indicating she'd like a little more, and said to Stan, "Well, if I were her, I'd cut my losses and stay clear. Landis is a shark. No matter what pool he is swimming in, whether it be the corporate or the personal pool."

Stan nodded and said, "Yeah, but Pam is not the innocent farm girl she pretends to be either. I've heard she can be pretty wild when she lets go. You saw her last year at the Christmas party. Would you wear a dress like that?"

Sue winked at Stan, then fixed him with a stare and said, "Are you saying I couldn't wear a dress like that?" She pulled her shoulders back and pushed her not inconsiderable bosom forward for Stan's attention.

He laughed and said, "In no way would I EVER suggest such a ridiculous thing Ms. Martin!" Of course, in all honesty, he truly would love to see her in such a dress. Sue was a knockout in his opinion!

Sue smiled and sat back, "That's better. She's younger than me, but I still have the goods both in the boardroom and out of it!"

Stan laughed as he heaped the remaining noodles and pork on their plates. They would only leave about a third of what was brought this time!

—

Barry ate a bit of his muffin, but he was not really that hungry. He wrapped the majority up and tossed it in a nearby trashcan. He'd had a really good breakfast this morning and shouldn't have even gotten the muffin, he decided. But it was sort of a habit to get something midmorning. He was used to eating six times a day. It kept the metabolism up so he could burn more fat. He was working out hard each day trying to cut body fat to about 10%. He loved cranking the iron. Unfortunately, to keep the muscle and burn the fat he also had to eat a LOT of food. More than any normal person would ordinarily consume.

As he sat and watched the children play, he recalled his breakfast with Maura. She was fantastic and he wanted to see more of her. They had met at a mutual friend's party a few months ago and had hit it off terrifically. Since then they had dated a lot, and like this morning, had met for breakfast a number of times.

They had one favorite place for breakfast. Dinners could be anywhere, lunches were usually fast food affairs, but breakfast was one place: The Red Spire. The place was supposed to be chic, as far as he could tell. The menu was not that large, and the seating seemed to be patterned after a French café. They usually had the same thing every time they went in: Bagels and omelets. The bagels were made fresh each day, and since they always arrived at opening time, they were sometimes still warm. And they were great! Chewy, (they never got them toasted), and covered with cream cheese.

Barry sometimes thought he could survive forever on Red Spire bagels and their coffee, which was very good too. A lot of restaurants had good food and average coffee. But the coffee was always great at the Red Spire. Maura had said she thought it was because they had such a limited menu, they must think of the coffee as another item on it. And therefore it couldn't be just average. After all, nothing else was!

And that was definitely the truth. Barry usually ordered a vegetable omelet with his bagel. The cheese was feta, with onions, peppers, spinach, cucumbers, and fresh mushrooms of some kind. It was always tasty and even though it did not fit his diet, he always had one when he went to breakfast there.

Maura liked the wheat pancakes. Wheat pancakes and blueberry syrup. She would get a stack, even though he knew she could never eat the whole thing, and then he would have to eat at least one. But she always said she really felt hungry and didn't want to get a short stack just to be hungry again when she finished it. More often than not neither of them could eat all the food and they would have to leave some of it. Barry always told the waiter how good it was, but that they just couldn't eat it all. He wanted the chef to know he wasn't leaving some because it wasn't good. It was just so much!

In any event, this morning was the same. They had an omelet and pancakes and bagels. And they were stuffed again. But it was fun to be with one another, and the food was just a secondary matter. Barry noticed a little blonde girl swinging with a friend. Her hair was the same color as Maura's and he wondered what their children would look like if they ever had any.

—

Hunching down by the open fire, Mari poked at the little cake-like morsel she had formed from her small portion of rice. The smoke wafted over her for a moment and she coughed slightly and leaned to her left. It was not quite done yet, so she had to endure the unrestrained pleadings of her four older children for a bit longer. They squatted down around her watching the proceedings hungrily. She looked at each in turn, noting the drawn look in their eyes, the unabashed hunger that a child could exhibit. Her oldest saw her looking at him and he grinned saying, "Is it ready?" She shook her head and said, "I'll let you know when it's ready. Now shush!" She figured she could eat a little less today.

—

While Sue walked from the parking lot to the building, she enjoyed the warm sun on her face. It was a nice hot day and she was stuck in her office. Entering the building the air conditioning struck her in the face with refreshing cool air. At least she wouldn't swelter in her leather chair. She absolutely hated it when the power crashed and the air conditioning ceased to run. She could work without her computer, that was no problem, but the heat in her office was unbearable when the air conditioning failed.

—

Barry wandered back to his office in the warm sun. He enjoyed being out in the fresh air, provided it wasn't raining. He would actually have preferred to work outside rather than in his office when it was hot like this. Yes, the air conditioning made his office comfortable; it wasn't the heat that was the problem. He just liked the sun's rays shining on him. It felt good. And besides, he could always be inside. But sunny days should be taken advantage of. At least in Barry's mind.

—

Mari looked at the dark, clear sky above and dreaded the next day as much as she had disliked today. It was going to be hot and horrible working again. She hated the burning heat of the day. It was best to get done all you could in the morning (though it was still hot) and then stay under cover in the afternoon for a bit. Regardless of what she did, she was going to suffer in the heat, for there were no clouds to be seen. And that meant the shack was going to be hot too. The baby would suffer that, but she couldn't leave him out in the sun. That would be worse.

—

Settling down into her chair, Sue spotted her water bottle sitting over by the printer where she left it. She stood once more, retrieved the bottle, and went down the hall to the water cooler. First, she poured out the tepid water that had half-filled the bottle from earlier. She held the bottle under the nozzle of the cooler and filled it with fresh, cold water. Before walking back to her office, she also filled one of the little cups and drank a few mouthfuls. It was nice to have the water cold on a warm day. It was terribly annoying when the water guy was held up and she had to drink from the tap in the break room.

—

Sitting down at his desk, Barry grabbed his water bottle and drank a good half of it. He had begun to drink a lot more water when he increased his protein in order to keep his kidneys well flushed. Water was easy to get. For that matter, his office had a small refrigerator in it which IPF kept stocked with bottled water just for him. They took good care of him.

—

The next day, before she went to the field, Mari picked up her pots, and began again the 1.3 mile journey to the well. She would make the trip three times today, as she did every day. This was the first trip. It was difficult to see in the dark, but she knew the way. She had heard that some villages actually had running water and electricity. She could not imagine that, could not see her small hut with its own light bulb, and a spigot that spewed water that was not filled with dirt.

Reaching the well, Mari dipped her pots into the cloudy water and drew them both full. She steadied them over her shoulders and began to walk back to her children, hoping the little grain she had would be enough for the rest of the week.

When she rounded the corner just before her hut, she saw that her oldest had been tending the fire. He was a good boy, but so young to be trying to handle so much. He had drug the bowel of ground grain out from the hut. She smiled at him tiredly and set the water down. The baby was coughing harshly and her three daughters were trying to soothe him. They were good children. She wondered where they would find enough food to live on. Still, they had survived this far. And she had heard that there may be jobs coming. Jobs other than farming. She hoped so. She wanted lights, clean water, food. She wanted her children to live in a way that was different from the generations before them.

—

On her way back to her office, Sue stopped at the ladies room to use the facilities. When she finished, she straightened her suit, combed her hair, and with a once over in the mirror, she walked on to her office.

—

Finishing his water, Barry decided he'd better use the can before he started working. The only problem with drinking so much water every day was he had to pee all the time too! He laughed as he thought about it, walking down to the men's room. At least his office was close to the bathroom.

—

Mari squatted down in the dark away from anyone. She swatted some flies away from her face as she relieved herself. Then she readjusted her sari and headed off to the fields.

—

When Sue returned to her office she began to order her morning's work into a more concise and clear document. She had written such things before and each time was angered at the necessity to produce it.

Why organizations such as IPF could not see the benefit of a hydroelectric dam was beyond her. The people in the proposed area are all but dirt poor. They have nothing to speak of. They have to walk miles for dirty water, and they have no electricity. They have no irrigation canals, and no jobs. They are undernourished, and have little prospects for the future.

The dam would provide jobs, food, water, electricity, money—all the things that can make life better for a population. Yes, the reservoir behind the dam would flood a good deal of land, and yes some of the villages would definitely have to be uprooted and moved. But that is a small price to pay. How many of those people die from hunger, and sickness, and a host of other problems that such technology would alleviate? Sue shook her head as she outlined such arguments. She was tired of having to make them over and over. She began to type the notes into her computer. This was going to be another long series of discussions and arguments.

—

Barry settled into his chair preparing his arguments concerning the dam. No one argues that the dam provides a lot of technology, but the question is, is it the right technology for the communities involved. He shook his head thinking of all the corporations such as GCW which were trying to build in the third world.

The problem was that the corporations weren't looking at the long range picture of the region. Yes, they would provide electricity, water, more food, and the like. But the sociological issues needed to be considered too. You cannot make the world into one big, concrete, capitalistic society. What about the culture of the villages that are uprooted? There are people there who have lived that way for five-thousand or more years! Is GCW going to come in and wipe that away in the name of growth? If a people group can survive that long, it hardly seems realistic that without the dam they would die out? And it was a clear truth that if the dam is built that culture will be destroyed. He began sorting and typing the arguments into his computer. He envisioned a lot of talk and quarreling taking place over this. In the background KPRB was repeating once again some interview with an animal sociologist: "The hawk versus dove game is sometimes called "Chicken" by the general public. It has been used to model territorial defense and is often associated with political battles, but is used consistently in animal studies as well (from which it gets its name). You see, hawks are aggressive and will fight when the chance presents itself. . . ."

—

Mari headed out to the field to try to coax a little more food from the tired earth. As she walked, she put any thought of electricity, water, and jobs from her tired mind.

The world was a hard taskmaster, and Mari feared for herself and her children. She knew that riches existed, somewhere, but she could not have them. She could hardly envision them. She had a family to keep together, and that's all she could think about.

www.ingramcontent.com/pod-product-compliance
Lightning Source LLC
Chambersburg PA
CBHW051149030726
47504CB00004B/1119